THE THRON

Kelver approached Dava[...] in his stone seat.

"I'm all alone now, D[...] help."

The old man seemed about to speak, but did not.

"Surely you can talk to me. You put me here. When I saw you in the judgment hall, you spoke a single sentence: *The Inquest falls.* How can it fall? It's so great, and I'm the only one, and . . ." But he was speaking to a shell of a man only, to an emptiness.

And then Davaryush said, so quietly that Kelver had to strain to listen: "*Seek out the Throne of Madness. . . .*"

Books by Somtow Sucharitkul

STARSHIP & HAIKU
MALLWORLD
THE AQUILIAD
FIRE FROM THE WINE-DARK SEA
V—THE ALIEN SWORDMASTER
FALLEN COUNTRY

The Inquestor Series:
THE DAWNING SHADOW: LIGHT ON THE SOUND
THE DAWNING SHADOW: THE THRONE
   OF MADNESS
UTOPIA HUNTERS
THE DARKLING WIND

As S. P. Somtow:
VAMPIRE JUNCTION
THE SHATTERED HORSE

THE DAWNING SHADOW

Chronicles of the High Inquest
PART II:
THE THRONE OF MADNESS

•

Somtow Sucharitkul

BANTAM BOOKS
TORONTO • NEW YORK • LONDON • SYDNEY • AUCKLAND

THE DAWNING SHADOW: THE THRONE OF MADNESS
A Bantam Spectra Book / October 1986

ISBN 0-553-26028-6

Published simultaneously in the United States and Canada

Bantam Books are published by Bantam Books, Inc. Its trademark, consisting of the words "Bantam Books" and the portrayal of a rooster, is Registered in U.S. Patent and Trademark Office and in other countries. Marca Registrada. Bantam Books, Inc., 666 Fifth Avenue, New York, New York 10103.

PRINTED IN THE UNITED STATES OF AMERICA

KR   0 9 8 7 6 5 4 3 2 1

This book is dedicated to John Douglas,
who really understands the meaning of the word "spectacle"!

This new version is also dedicated to
Beverly and Tim, in memory of our own planet-destroying
game of *makrúgh*!

Contents

•

BOOK ONE:
THE SHADOW'S SHADOW

hosh sih a kerávishi varungs
zyh vih shtendaín e chítareh
ng' darans dhandandi

He who shall sit on the Throne of Madness
shall see for an instant into the heart
of a dying star.

—from the Inquestral wisdom

ONE: AWAKENING

At first the boy was conscious only of warmth. It seemed that he had been cold for so long; not cold as when the bitter icewind blew in the long winter of his homeworld, but a cold within, a cold of utter aloneness.

The warmth started at the fingertips and the toes. Slowly it worked its way inward. Then came a voice: calm, distant. *Kelver. Kelver.* He thought at first, It must be Ton Davaryush, the Kingling of Gallendys, calling me to see him in the throneroom in the palace in the twin cities of Effelkang and Kallendrang.

He cried out the name "Davaryush, Davaryush."

The voices came again, more urgent now. *Kelver, do not be afraid. Open your eyes.*

He did. He saw the sky first: a seamless soft light filled it. There were no suns, no stars, no clouds. He was lying on a floater that hovered over a lush green field, a field that stretched and stretched . . . there was no horizon. The land went endlessly on, vanishing only at the limits of perception, becoming one with the luminous mist of sky. Here and there were chessboard meadows dotted with flowers.

They are not flowers, Kelver. They are cities. You are on Uran s'Varek now, the Inquestral homeworld, the heart of the Dispersal of Man. Ask anything of me, Inquestor-that-is-to-be. I am bound to answer you.

"Who are you then? Why do you whisper into my mind like this, why can't I see you? And where is Davaryush? He sent me here. He'll tell me what to do."

*I am the greatest thinkhive ever dreamed of by any crea-
ture. I am the soul of Uran s'Varek. I am everywhere.*

Kelver said, "It's really true then. I've been made an
Inquestor. The last thing a boy could want."

*You cannot choose when the Inquest calls you, Ton Keverell
n'Davaren Tath. No one ever wants to be here at first. But
then the magic of Uran s'Varek touches them. Only an
Inquestor can come to this world and leave again with the
memory of it still in his mind, with the music of it sounding
still in his ears. Don't be afraid. After all, you are now one of
the masters of humanity.*

Kelver rose up from his hoverfloat now. With a flick of his
mind he willed it to rise a little. Wind rifled the emerald
crystal grass beneath his feet, and it tinkled, a ravishing
sound that drew a wan smile from him. He couldn't really
take it in yet. It wasn't long ago that he'd been a peasant boy
in a world no one wanted to know about, playing at being a
man, in the shadow of the Dark Country. That he had fallen
in love with the strange girl Darktouch, who might by now
be forever lost to him through time dilation. That he had fled
with her through the desert to the shining cities to tell the
Inquestor of what the girl had seen; that they had faced,
together, the light on the Sunless Sound.

Then, in the throneroom of Davaryush's palace in Effelkang,
he had heard the old Inquestor's words: *I have foreseen the
fall of the Inquest . . . and I know it will come from one who
comes to the Inquestorhood knowing beforehand of the canker at the Inquest's heart . . . who will destroy from within
. . . who will not have known the curse as the others have.*

He had risen from the throne with the yolk of the
shimmeregg still wet on the crown of his head, still caking
against his cheeks as it webbed and stranded itself, drawing
sustenance from his body's wastes and from the dim light in
the throneroom, weaving the shimmercloak onto his bare
skin. He was an Inquestor now: Ton Keverell n'Davaren
Tath. He had taken the patronymic *Davaren* for his surname
because his father was dead. Davaryush was the only man he
could think of as father. He was still just a boy, but Davaryush
had picked him as the agent for the most awesome scheme in
the history of the Dispersal of Man: the fall of the Inquest.

They had not given him time to say farewell to Darktouch.
They had put him into stasis; and stasis was nothing at all: no
passing of time, no dreams. Only the cold. And now he was

on Uran s'Varek, a place beyond the very imaginations of the short-lived.

The floater began to move by itself, guided no doubt by the thinkhive. Kelver was glad of it, for he had no idea where he was, what the geography of this vast world might be. Just beneath his feet, stirred by the floater's motion, the grass chimed. Slowly the craft began to accelerate. Quicker now, quicker, quicker . . . until all Kelver could see was a blur of crystal green shot through with the pearlsoft daylight. "Slow down, slow down!" he said. The swirl of green resolved; the tinkling, döpplered at first by the craft's velocity into a roaring, jangling chord-cluster, and then magically dissolving into silence as the floater quickly overtook the speed of sound, came back in reverse: first the thunder-roar as the barrier was breached again, then, gradually, the quiet music of motionlessness. He was afraid for a moment. "How far have we gone?" he said. "It has been less than an hour, and the scenery hasn't changed at all. We don't seem to have gone anywhere."

Poor child! At last you begin to comprehend the scale of Uran s'Varek. In the period past we have journeyed almost a million klomets.

"But that's impossible." He stared ahead in dismay. The fields still stretched as far as he could see; perhaps here and there a darker patch he hadn't seen before, a circle of jade against the emerald . . . and, at the limits of his vision, what he had thought of as flowers, poppies, perhaps, or rosellas, but which the thinkhive had told him were cities. "A million klomets would take you half a thousand times around any habitable world. It's an illusion. One of your Inquestral tricks. Davaryush told me that on Uran s'Varek anything can be an illusion."

This is no illusion, Kelver. We have come almost a million klomets, but we have barely traversed this single meadow, the edge of the pleasure gardens of Ton Elloran n'Taanyel Tath. There . . . the little red flower in the circle of jade: that is our objective. You were brought here to be alone for a while, so that I could instruct you of the basic nature of this world; I am your first teacher. The solitude is the first stage in the journey to Inquestorhood. It will be some days before we reach the city: bear with me till then. Others will be there, others culled, as you were, from the short-lived, chosen for the great sacrifice.

"You call it a sacrifice then? It is not good to be a ruler of men, one who can break a planet in two with a command and a handclap?"

You yourself know that it is not so. You do not love power, but have accepted it in sorrow, in resignation. Otherwise you would not be here, Ton Keverell n'Davaren Tath.

And Kelver knew that it was true.

For a long time Kelver waited for nightfall; it did not come. No shadows crossed the even lucence of the sky. "How can I sleep?" he said. But he was tired now, and drowsiness was overtaking him even as he spoke.

There is no night here on Uran s'Varek. For we are at the center of the galaxy itself, in a world not built by men, that was here long before the Inquest ever was. In this one cubic parsec shine 1.8 million stars; and at its heart, a hungry black hole; and around the black hole, this artificial globe: 446 million klomets in diameter, opened at the top and bottom to admit the passing of stars into the black hole. And I, the soul of this world, am older even than all your kind.

"That's . . . impossible," Kelver said, "we would be burned alive by the radiation of a million stars, so close to one another."

Look above you. There is an atmosphere of thousands of klomets over your head; it scatters the light from the million stars so they cannot be told apart; it softens it so that you are not blinded in an instant; and so you lie here bathed in perpetual radiance, in the hurricane's-eye-calm at the center of the galactic storm. And there is power here, power for you to play with; power so awesome that even I cannot perceive its ending.

"And the power's source?" said Kelver. The concepts were too huge to comprehend, and he was sleepy, sleepy . . . but the thinkhive's voice went on, droning in his mind.

Slowly, Kelver, slowly, the stars are spiraling into the black hole. But there are banks of thinkhives, each bank covering an area greater than the surface of several planets; I direct them. They are telekinetic amplifiers. They seize the stars from their slow pavane of plummeting, and they ease them into the correct path . . . into one of the abysses that yawn at the poles of this Uran s'Varek; and it is there that they drain away the almost limitless energy of the star's death. It is a grand event, this sunset! The Inquestors call it

Lightfall, *and it happens only every century or so; they all gather here to watch the star's dying and to celebrate with spectacular games of* makrúgh. *Planets fall and planets are created during Lightfall. And so is your power as Inquestors made secure: so are your tachyon bubbles driven, which enable you and no other mortals to break through the barrier of time dilation and to rule by omnipresence your million subject worlds, scattered through the parsecs and the millennia. And you, you Inquestors . . . you have this paradise.*

As the thinkhive told him this it globed the floater with a darkfield, shutting out Uran s'Varek's light. Kelver was almost asleep now; he hardly listened to the thinkhive's catalogue of figures beyond human imagination. Of the rings of thinkhives that circled the poles; of the world's thousand longitudinal segments, each stretching some four hundred hokh'klomets from northern thinkhives to southern thinkhives; and of the few areas inhabited by the Inquestors. Each segment was named for a ranking Inquestor, and the thousand names were redolent with the Inquest's twenty millennia of history: Alkamrin, Ellorin, Varunin, Surellin, Paëlin, Mregát. They were in Varunin now, and were about to cross one of the bridges that linked the sphere's segments together, into Kendrin, the Inquestral commonalty, where the game of *makrúgh* could not be played, and where the young Inquestors learned to prove themselves. Kelver lay in darkness now as the thinkhive's information infiltrated his sleeping mind.

But in his dreams he was fleeing, fleeing once more through the burning wasteland of Gallendys, and he was gazing once more at the light on the Sound, and Davaryush was warning him again of his true mission.

And the desert was folding in on itself, trapping him, burning him alive, then a world of myriad mirrors splintering, the stars stretched into bolts of jagged lightning, and the cold of stasis swooping on him like a pteratyger—

He woke to light and the strains of shimmerviols. The grass had darkened a little; it was not crystalline, but flowed like a woman's long hair. "Are we there?" He knew now of the bridges that spanned the gulfs between the segments of the world, and that they were passing from Varunin to Kendrin, and that Ellorin and Bhimbhesht lay to the east. He wondered where the shimmerviol music was coming from; the floater was crawling now, letting him hear the sounds. It was only the wind playing with the tall jade grass strands, rubbing them together in a faint stridulation.

A day or two more, hokh'Tón.

"Do not call me that," said the boy. "I don't—I mean, it isn't mine, I can't—" For he had remembered himself, crouching, trembling, at the foot of Davaryush's throne. Suddenly, appallingly, he began to cry.

The thinkhive said, *You can weep. There is no one to see you here. You have begun to see the loneliness of the Inquestorhood. You will be feared, worshipped, obeyed; you will seldom be loved, Kelver. When they told you that an Inquestor must not weep, they did not tell you that they all have wept; that they all hide this aloneness inside them. They are like this world, this paradise, this Uran s'Varek: it is the very heart of man, yet underneath its skin of beauty lies an unfathomable emptiness, a black hole.*

And in time Kelver's weeping subsided a little. The music of the grass seemed timeless at first; but at last he perceived the slow majestic movement of it. "Will I see the Lightfall?" he asked. And the thinkhive answered, *In time; after you have learned compassion.*

They were moving northwest across the pleasure gardens of Elloran now; whenever their direction shifted even slightly, the music seemed to change key. In another sleep they had reached lands where the grass was thicker, many-hued, a field shimmering with the colors of olivine and chrysocolla and malachite and turquoise and serpentine and chalcedony; these were hollow grasses and they fluted in the breeze, each shade of green a different tone. And the field was powdered with a fluff of white rosellas, the homely flowers mingling with the exotic.

It was a sweet music, passionless, cloying. When they had sped up again and burst through the thunderjangle into the silence of swiftness, Kelver could make out, at last, in the far distance, a break in the texture of green, a thin black line that stretched across from eyes' end to eyes' end. *It is the ribbon-chasm between Varunin and Kendrin*, the thinkhive said.

As they came nearer Kelver saw a river of intense blackness. Here and there it was spanned by strands of light—bridges into the next realm. And the red poppies that had dotted the grass before . . . they seemed to have opened into crystal structures, crowned by towers that waved like hairs in a breeze. Sometimes, overhead, a fleet of tachyon bubbles, circles of nothingness against the skyglow, hovered for a minute, then fell into a patterned swarm and soared out of sight. "The cities! We're coming to the cities. . . ." For Kelver knew, from his dreamlearning, what the places were. To the right and north began the mountainous structures of the thinkhives. They were colored dull metal; the gray receded into gray-green as the field of thinkhives seemed to climb far into the sky itself, and to meld into the misty light. Behind the cities were more cities, specks of garnet and crimson and blue-white, blooming out of the verdure.

Hold on. We will cross the bridge soon; I will go slowly, so you can see beyond, to the void beneath. It is a bridge of a thousand klomets, one of the thin strips threading the segments of the sphere.

In a few hours Kelver was looking at the edge of a world. The landscape was abruptly sheared off; it resumed a little further on. As they neared Kelver saw the river of darkness widen until it filled his whole field of vision . . . a thousand klomets wide, he thought. The floater took the bridge, which was roofed and bounded by a forceshield so that no one would fall into the endless beyond. For a long time they flew, clinging to that hairbreadth of a human habitat. Kelver did not dare stand in the floater at first, though he knew he was safe enough. When he did, and he finally gazed on the starless emptiness, so featureless that he did not know whether he was time-frozen or speeding, he felt at last the force of the thinkhive's words: *the heart of man, and it shields a hungry emptiness beyond our understanding.* Far below, two hundred hokh'klomets away, was the dark and ravenous star.

Then, without warning, the land rushed into view, first a strip of green then all at once surrounding him in every direction. The floater accelerated again, and all he could see was a slowly shifting kaleidolon of pastel colors. It was as though he were sitting in a bubble of perfect stillness. And then, as the floater slowed, a city resolved out of the swirling.

They were flying over the city now: it opened up like lotuses within lotuses within lotuses, each lotus petal a maze of twisting streets and curved, soaring buildings; from the city's heart rose diamantine towers like stamens, and floaters swarmed over them like snow.

Do not be afraid, Kelver. This world is your world, your homeworld. Nothing will harm you here, though the lessons you learn may give you pain. Come, I will take you to the hall of novices. You will meet your human teachers now; and my task is done, though you can call me at any time, for I am everywhere.

As the thinkhive spoke, the floater's shield dissolved. The sounds of the city burst in on his senses: it was not the music of a city of the short-lived, jarring and jangling, but a solemn, stately blending of sounds. There was order here.

But as the floater drifted downward to the topmost of the stamen-towers, Kelver's thoughts were of a stooped old man with bright eyes, and of a pale-skinned girl with her long dark hair brushing his chest.

TWO: **THE WHITE INQUESTRIX**

. . . and slowly willed the tachyon bubble to dissipate into the pale light; and stepped out onto the dais in the tower-stamen of the central lotus of Rhozellerang, the city where the young Inquestors wait; and stood in the skyshine with her shimmercloak trailing in the *f´áng*-scented breeze, a young white-haired woman with her skin snow-pale and her eyes white as opals.

Turning, she saw a second bubble flicker and dissolve beside her, and she smiled; for it was Arryk. "You followed me." He looked at her blankly with his clear violet eyes; it was for these that she had first loved him, when she found him tending firephoenixes on one of Elloran's worlds, for they were like dawn on a long-dead homeworld.

"There was nowhere else to go," said the peasant-boy-made-Inquestor. "Elloran has vanished. And Uran s'Varek is still new to me. You shouldn't be sulky."

"Perhaps not. But they've just told me something. You know the pilgrimage we're supposed to be going on in a few weeks? The long journey southward?"

"The long aloneness? When we're to think about Inquestor-hood, when we're to decide whether or not to take the irrevocable step, or to remain instead on Uran s'Varek, imprisoned amid luxury?"

"It's just a formality," said the Inquestrix. But something troubled her. "Rikeh, there's another boy coming with us."

"Oh? Who, Sirissheh?"

"I'm not sure. But there's something . . . something, they say, truly remarkable about him. I haven't learned as much as

13

I would like to have, though. The thinkhive is edgy." Arryk's hand brushed Siriss's for a moment; a familiar warmth, a simple *I am here*. For a second it allayed her worry, and yet . . .

"What's the matter?" Arryk said. "Siriss, we've been lovers since you found me in that backworld, since Ton Elloran, in his devious wisdom, elevated me to the Inquestorhood to teach you a lesson in *makrúgh*. But you've spent time on a dozen other worlds, you've followed the Kingling on his overcosmic progress in his flying palace of gold . . . while I, in all my time here, have seen nothing but endless fields and cities and the droning words of old men, telling me about compassion and murder, and compassion and hatred, and compassion and war . . . how can I read what you're feeling?"

"*Makrúgh* is banned from Kendrin," Siriss said lightly.

"You only say that because you can't beat me at it," said Arryk, reminding her of how they had first met. She looked at him seriously then, appraising him: he looked well in his shimmercloak, it drew color from his eyes, but he did not yet have the coldness, the distance, of the experienced Inquestor. He was too vulnerable. Knowing this made her vulnerable to him too.

Side by side, they crossed the vast overlook, skipping from displacement plate to displacement plate. They passed more exalted Inquestors on their hoverthrones, drifting away to the other edge of the platform until they were tiny insects against the carpeting of woven amber-strands. They reached the railings of force that girded the platform, and could see the city beneath them. Some festival was in progress in one of the distant petals of the city; for Ton Siriss saw children gathered into baskets borne aloft by giant kites that mimicked paper pteratygers. They were tossing firestreamers out of their soarbaskets, and she could make out the tendrils of brilliance against the rosy-hued city towers, even though their explosions were drowned out by the music of the city itself: the wind rushing through the crystal flues of the stamens, wuthering through the hollows of twisted towers. She felt Arryk's touch on her shoulder, and she smiled him a secret smile.

"Tell me," Arryk said.

She said, "I'm afraid, Rikeh. I want to see old Elloran. I looked for him for twenty sleeps, all over Ellorin, his kingdom; but you can only find him when he wants to be found."

"And I looked for him too," said Arryk. "And wherever I looked I was told that you had been before. So I came here, to the city where the young Inquestors wait. A summons may come."

"But meanwhile they've told me that we must share our quest-journey with another. It's a boy, Arryk, fresh from initiation."

"Then we've nothing to fear."

"But it was the way the thinkhive told me . . . I'm afraid that the quest-journey will be no formality after all, Ton Arryk," she said, lapsing into a formal mode of the highspeech. She felt him stiffen a little. "I'm afraid that there'll be something demanded of us. Something terrible. Something we don't want to give up."

"But that is in the teaching," Arryk said. "*You will yield up that final thing in your hearts, and you will know from that moment that you are truly an Inquestor.* Aren't you sure anymore?"

She laughed a little. "I should be sure. I've flown the overcosm on the wings of Elloran's golden palace. I've played a game of *makrúgh* that has toppled star systems . . . I, hardly more than a child! I should be sure. I hardly know another life. I keep telling myself I'm ready for the quest-journey, the ceremonial elevation. And now we've become pawns in some Grand Inquestral game of *makrúgh*. I sense it. Do you know who the boy is, who is being sent with us? He has been here only a few sleeps, and they think he's ready to go with us, to challenge the great aloneness of Uran s'Varek itself!"

"Who is he?"

"His name is Ton Keverell n'Davaren Tath." It came musically to her tongue; it was a good name, a name of power.

Arryk seemed puzzled. Of course; he was still new to Uran s'Varek. The patronymics and title suffixes would mean little to him. Idly she turned to watch the ballet of the pteratyger-kites; they were soaring overhead now, and the flametongue streamers crackled as they darted from the children's baskets. She wondered which of the children had grown up on Uran s'Varek, knowing nothing of other worlds . . . and which had been young Inquestors-that-were-to-be, who had turned their backs on the way of greater compassion, had chosen instead to lead lives of little people, powerless, frightened, controlled by *makrúghs* beyond their imaginings. There, for instance, the tall boy, laughing as he cast down a skein of green and yellow fire . . . hadn't he been with her on her first day, when she had first set foot on Uran s'Varek? "No," she whispered to herself. "It can't be. I've left and come back a dozen times, and time dilation has taken its toll, and it must be a son or a grandson or a great-grandson of the boy who turned his face away from greatness . . . I can't remember his name now, even."

Arryk said, gently, "You were telling me of the boy."

"Kelver. Yes. He is younger than either of us. He's probably no more than sixteen years old, and already he has the high ones quaking in their hoverthrones! Can't you tell? It's the *n'Davaren*. He was sent here by Ton Davaryush z'Galléndaran K'Ning."

And Arryk was impressed at last. "The heretic."

"Yes. Who is returning to Uran s'Varek soon, they say, to be stripped of his rank, to be unmade Inquestor."

"But Kelver—"

"His last act from the multimillennial throne was to make this peasant boy of Gallendys an Inquestor. And it is an act the Inquest cannot refute, for to do so would be to say, *An Inquestor has spoken wrong*. And to speak thus would be to shatter the foundations of the Dispersal of Man! And they can't tell what Davaryush was thinking when he created the Inquestor; whether he was sane or mad, whether it was not some monstrous final joke he played on the Inquest."

"How strange, that they could make one yes or no mean so much."

"That is the Inquest's way. And we are to be the boy's companions, understand, his mentors, we're to set him straight when he strays, to take him with *us* on our quest-journey of self-discovery!"

"But we already know how tortuous the mind of the Inquest is," Arryk said. "Why are you so upset at this?"

"Because . . . I'd hoped . . . well, they watch us constantly, the Inquest. This world is paradise, but a paradise of a trillion inquisitive eyes, and I know they're not supposed to spy during the time of aloneness, and I was hoping . . . that we could be together, alone."

They embraced then; and so did their shimmercloaks, the semisentient furstuff sensing the love their owners felt and echoing it with their own. The cloaks swirled as one about them, blushing pink-to-scarlet against the ultramarine. High overhead, the kite-carried children laughed to see their masters so suddenly passionate.

"Let them laugh! Let them laugh!" cried Arryk, and he laughed too; Siriss remembered how he'd been when she first found him, thinking him a pretty peasant, a plaything to be tossed aside. She had thought him all laughter and nothing inside, until he bested her at *makrúgh*.

"How can you laugh?" she said. "How can you, when they're playing such games with our very lives?" But she knew what he would answer. He'd stare at her sadly with his violet eyes wide open and he'd say, *Now you know, Sirissheh, how I felt.*

For the first time Kelver woke not to the subtle chiming of grasses but to a different music: it was as if this city of Rhozellerang had made wind itself captive, that it wailed its prison-chant from walls, from towers, from turrets. There were walls around him and this, after days of the great emptiness, was strange. But when he subvocalized the standard command for deopaquing the walls, he saw out over the many-petaled city and beyond, far beyond, first to a patchwork of fields of clashing colors, jewel-stitched with cities, and then still beyond, to a softer landscape tilting upward to forever.

Compose yourself, the thinkhive whispered in his mind. *I've taught you a lot, Kelver; more than you know, even, for I've whispered secret wisdom into your mind while you slept. But now people will teach you. The High Inquestors themselves, whom even you must call* hokh'Tón, hokh'Tón. *In a while I will lead you to the platform where the young Inquestors wait. You will meet two others whom I will point out to you: the Lady Ton Siriss k'Varad es-K'Ning, who is to inherit one of the many worlds in the domain of the Grand Inquestor Ton Elloran n'Taanyel Tath; and Ton Arryk n'Elloran Tath, a novice like you. They will be your guides in your journey into the great compassion.*

Compassion! thought Kelver, as he shook his shimmercloak into place about his thin shoulders. I've seen that compassion in action.

He remembered then what he'd been trying to forget for so long: the land inside the hollow mountain, a hundred klomets high, a thousand wide, where dwelt Windbringers, called delphinoids by the Inquest, creatures who saw the secret quickpaths through the overcosms, whose living brains, soldered into the hulls of starships, were the only means of navigating the treacherous space between spaces . . . and without whom the Inquest's power would be meaningless. When he was a boy he had tended the farmland in the shadow of the Skywall. The food went into the mountain to feed the unseen people of the Dark Country. He had not known then who they were: a people made blind and deaf by the Inquest so that they could hunt the Windbringers as they soared in the viscous winds over the Sunless Sound, without having to see the songs the Windbringers sang: lightpoems so beautiful they could destroy men's reason . . . so that they would never have to know the anguish they were inflicting on a sentient creature . . . would never know of the deaths of the starsongs. For without the brains the Inquest would lose power, and it wanted power, even if it cost the lives of aliens and the innocence of humans. Kelver might never have known all this. He might have been a child dreaming of starships; then a young man casting those dreams aside; then a middle-aged foreman like his uncle, ordering the food bales shifted from displacement plate to displacement plate; and then an old man who had never even once crossed the badlands of Zhnefftikak.

But the girl Darktouch, a genetic throwback accidentally cursed with sight and hearing, had seen the light on the Sound and had come fleeing from the mountain, and he had found her and taught her speech and together they had flown farther, over the burning desert, until they reached the twin cities where ruled Davaryush, the Kingling, the Inquestor, the Heretic.

And now Darktouch was back on Gallendys, a tool of the Heretic in his single-handed war on the Inquest; and Kelver was here, a spy in the Inquest's heart. How could they not suspect him? He had seen the light on the Sound with his own eyes. He carried the memory inside him. The others that had seen it . . . they had a glow to them, even the madwoman they had seen in the desert, half-eaten by the aboriginal cannibals. How could they not see the light and music of the Sunless Sound clinging to him? They were blind then, these Inquestors. Or the twenty thousand years of the Inquest's power had made them too sure that nothing would ever change.

Come now, Kelver. Your friends are waiting. Kelver sensed

the room moving a little; he knew then that they were climbing within the central stamen of the city. At the summit the room dissolved suddenly. He whirled, gasped; and the thinkhive whispered in his mind, *Illusion, Kelver, illusion.*

And he was standing on the overlook where wait the Inquestors-that-are-to-be: he was standing beside two young Inquestors, who turned to look at him strangely.

One was a young woman whose long white hair trailed down and blended into her shimmercloak. Even her eyes were milky-white; in the pearly light of Uran s'Varek, she seemed only half there, a ghost.

The other was a boy, only a little older than Kelver. He seemed not quite comfortable in his shimmercloak yet. Kelver noticed at first the rough hands, and knew that the boy must come from origins as humble as his own; but the face was well chiseled, the dark hair neat, the violet eyes strangely daunting.

"History there is," said the girl, *"and no history!"*

"What is this? Those are the opening words of the game of *makrúgh!* The Inquestral game of power! But this is Kendrin—" said Kelver.

"Indeed," said the young woman, "it is Kendrin, and I must not play *makrúgh* with you." And then she laughed, a high-pitched, half-taunting laugh. "But I challenge you anyway. Even the ban on *makrúgh* in Kendrin is but part of a grand game of *makrúgh;* and who can gainsay an Inquestor, if one should decide to reject such a ruling? If we are not the masters, who then are?" And she laughed again; but the other one, the purple-eyed one, looked away, almost embarrassed.

Kelver said, "Are you the guides who were promised me, then?"

The other boy said, "Yes. I am Arryk. This is Siriss." For a moment something passed between them; Kelver felt some tension dart between the two other Inquestors, and he sensed, too, that they were lovers who had been playing too many games of power with one another. But as for Siriss's challenging him to *makrúgh*, right there in the open, he knew it for some childish ploy, something born of the need for dominance; and he knew even then that this was something an Inquestor should not feel; for Davaryush had taught him well. How could it be that they considered Davaryush the heretic, and themselves on the side of good?

He froze his face into a mask, as he had been trained to do.

And he said, in answer to Siriss's challenge: "*All things must change, yet all is encompassed in the greater Stasis. We are one; our eyes are illuminated by the one Compassion; we are of the Inquest.*"

Then Arryk burst out laughing. "You see, Sirissheh?" he said. "He doesn't fear you. Why should he? The challenge stands, irregular as it is; and when we reach a land outside Kendrin, you must play your *makrúgh* out, I suppose."

She glared at Kelver, strangely beautiful; for a moment he felt desire for her, though he knew her to be deadly. "You heretic-spawn!" she hissed, abandoning all propriety.

And Kelver and Arryk exchanged another look: Kelver's one of questioning, Arryk's one of resignation. For a while the boy watched the pinpoints that were hoverthrones, weaving in and out of the distant needle-towers.

Then Arryk said, "Let's be friends." Kelver did not know whether he spoke to him alone or to both of them.

At that moment came a whirlwind of tinseldust, circling them, blurring out the landscape. Kelver felt himself falling, falling. . . . "What's happening?" he shouted. And he heard the girl's laughter, joyous now, no longer mocking: "*Elloran! Elloran!*" And the firewind caught the three of them and hurled them onward. Landscapes whipped past, fragmented, starstrewn. Now he was riding a pteratyger that roared as it dived through flame and darkness. Now the fields unreeled and Siriss's laughter reechoed, metal-tinged, over the music of chiming grasses.

"Thinkhive!" he called. "Thinkhive!"

Hokh'Ton the thinkhive's voice responded as though from chasms away.

"What is happening?" The fields were streaked away now, flower-kaleidolons dancing.

This is what happens, Ton Keverell n'Davaren Tath, when a young Inquestor-that-is-to-be stands on the overlook in Rhozellerang! A Grand Inquest has summoned you to his domain.

"Who? Is it Davaryush?" Kelver cried against the roaring, hoping in spite of everything to see the old man's face again.

No. It is Ton Elloran n'Taanyel Tath, newly made Grand Inquestor, the Lord of Varezhdur, Master of Makrúgh. *It is he who commanded that you and Siriss and Arryk be brought together.*

"Elloran . . ."

Suddenly they were bursting from their cocoons of spinning darkness and they were on the backs of pteratygers, great creatures that sprang aloft and glided on pink-feathered wings. The pteratygers roared, a hollow thundering with an aftertinge of mew. They were circling something; an irregular object of gold, half-buried in an endless plain of snow, pearl reflecting pearl.

He turned against the wind. The other two Inquestors were smiling now. They were going to something they knew.

"Where are we?" he shouted to them. But he did not have to shout; as he spoke, the windrush stilled itself; for the wind, as all the other musics of Uran s'Varek were, was an artifact, willed into being to please an Inquestor's ear, and not to drown out his voice.

Over his pteratyger's purring he heard its feline voice, half-screech, half-roar: "Elloran—master—master—Elloran!" Siriss said, serenely, whispering: "It is Elloran. We have crossed over another section of Uran s'Varek, and we have reached Varezhdur, the palace of Elloran. Didn't the thinkhive teach you anything?" But she did not seem to be chiding him.

The palace grew as they neared it: labyrinthine, burnish-glittery, formidable.

Kelver thought about Darktouch, and about Davaryush; and he thought about the vastness of what they had been fighting, a handful of old people and children in a backworld far away. But he dared not show any fear as the pteratygers landed in the snow and the Kingling's palace loomed up to meet the great shining.

THREE: ELLORAN

When the old Inquestor returned to Varezhdur he did not immediately see the three young ones, as he had first intended; instead he found his secret throneroom, in the heart of the tangle of towers at the palace's center. There was a galaxy of fine dust there, swirling slowly in the huge empty chamber; a sculptress, long since dead, had breathed life into it. In the room sat Sajit, an old musician of the clan of Shen, leaning against a recess in the floor of the throneroom; at the other end, a choir of neutered children sang over a dissonance-rich consort of shimmerviols.

He saw the Inquestor approach; but he did not prostrate himself. Instead he smiled broadly as Ton Elloran helped him up. "They play badly now," he mumbled, "since I'm too infirm to shout at them. You've been gone long. I've aged a lot."

"And I. I let it show now, Sajitteh; I've let the furrows dig into my face. Is it becoming?"

"Not much." He could speak this way to the high one because once, in a situation that could never again recur, they had been friends. And they had loved the same woman too: Dei Zhendra, the dust-sculptress.

"Sajitteh, how go the songs of the srinjidas?" For that was all, Sajit knew, that Elloran ever thought of: the music of twenty million voices that the old composer had once dreamed of, and that the Inquestor's whim had now made possible.

"It is finished. But I don't know if even I will hear it . . . I'm very weak, and ill, and irritable."

"Do you remember, Sajit . . ." The Inquestor's eyes seemed

22

to look far away, into the far past, parsecs and centuries beyond reach. "Do you remember how we stood here once, looking at this galaxy of dust, and I said to you, *One day the Inquest will fall?*"

"It was not so long ago. But we were both young men. Now I'm old, but you could be young again, if you chose. You don't take the drugs anymore."

"I have accepted transience." But when Sajit looked at the old man's face, wreathed with wild white hair, he remembered a boy he had once known and loved and to whom he had sworn eternal loyalty. "Today, Sajit, I felt the tremors of that fall. I think it will be sooner than we know. Do you remember Gallendys, Sajitteh? We were there for that grand *makrúgh* of Ton Davaryush's. You played in the clouds, gloriously, while we Inquestors played hard at sentencing innocent planets to oblivion. That Davaryush proved loser after all; that is why I have come back to Uran s'Varek. I am to judge him. But first I must deal with the child he has sent us, the boy Kelver."

"You worry too much, Elloran." And he sang then, in a wheezing ghost of the voice that had once made Kinglings weep. It was some children's song about utopias.

"How long has it been since that game of *makrúgh*, Sajit? A few years, perhaps, in the mind of Davaryush? It seems like a century ago to me. . . . Has the delphinoid shipmind that carries Davaryush only now reached Uran s'Varek then? Will the man even know me, when he comes forth from stasis and sees me thus, aged, stooping, whom he last saw strong and straight? I'm afraid of him. He wanted to destroy us, you know. He, himself, one man, thought he could destroy twenty thousand years, a million worlds of the Dispersal of Man. Is such hubris possible?"

"You should fear the child more," said Sajit. "I remember you well, when you were a child. You took on the great Alkamathdes himself."

"But he was mad!"

"I am only a poor musician, Elloran. It isn't for me to say who is mad. Isn't that what they call the Inquestral Seat—the Throne of Madness?"

"No. The Throne of Madness is a *real* throne, one of the four Thrones of Uran s'Varek. You know the song as well as I do."

"I only speak figuratively, of course."

"Of course."

Sajit let his master help him up; they went over to the throne of gold surmounted by cushions of kyllap leaves and bordered by a frieze of pteratygers. Together they watched the sculpture of dust swirl slowly, glitter in the gloom.

"Perhaps I should greet them here, Sajit? In my private throneroom? Arryk and Siriss have seen it often enough."

"But the other one may play *makrúgh* against you."

"Yes. Yes."

Sajit waved his hand once at the orchestra hidden in the contours of the throneroom floor. All at once came new music: shimmerviols gave way to strident highwoods, and the children's voices colored with the tones of fear.

And Elloran said, "Even if the child plays *makrúgh* with the artistry of a web dancer, I will not be tempted. I have played my last game of *makrúgh*, Shen Sajit."

But the musician did not believe him.

As the three youths set off toward the palace the snow parted for them, piling into drifts on either side; they could make out the displacement plates easily. It was not snow at all, Kelver realized, when he stopped to touch some with his hand; it was a fluff of crushed rosellas. The faint flower fragrance in the air came from them.

The gates opened. They walked through corridors of polished gold with fluted columns from which streamed music; across atria with firefountains and moving frescoes and climbing plants that sprouted and bloomed and wilted and died in a few seconds, so that the walls writhed with the vines' dance of death and rebirth; on hoverdisks they skimmed great pools of fire and vitriol and liquid diamants. And presently, reaching an inner garden walled with waterfalls, they came into the presence of Ton Elloran himself.

The throne he sat on was made of the stuff of waterfall, but time-frozen, bound in a cage of force. When Arryk and Siriss saw him they rushed to embrace him, like favorite children; Kelver lagged, trying to take in the splendor of the room. It was so simple, this garden, yet it must consume tremendous power just to avoid collapsing, drowning them all.

When Kelver saw how the others made much of the old man, he felt resentment, jealousy. When Elloran called him up, the other two looked at Kelver as if to say, *He is ours, how dare you usurp our favored position*, . . . but in old

Elloran's eyes there was nothing but kindness, and so, boldened, he went up to the throne. Through the frozen water, daylight sparkled, and the liquid fire was edged with the colors of the Inquestors' shimmerfur.

"Oh, Arryk, Sirissheh . . ." said Elloran. "You must not look down on this boy because of where he came from. An Inquestor chose him; and he must have chosen him for his compassion. As you were chosen, Sirissheh, Arryk." The two listened to him gravely, drinking in all his words; this man must be to them, thought Kelver, as Davaryush had been to him. "I gave him to you because he needs what you can give him, your love, your compassion."

"You're playing *makrúgh* against Davaryush, aren't you?" Arryk asked. Kelver noted that they used no honorifics with this man, Grand Inquestor that he was.

Elloran laughed; his eyes twinkled. He was an easy man to love, Kelver decided. Then Elloran turned to him. "Kevi," he said, "you must not hate me. I have something terrible to tell you; I have come back to Uran s'Varek, breaking my progress through the dozen worlds of my governance, to sit in judgment over Davaryush. And I have chosen, as you see, as the seat from which to address you, one of the three Inqestral thrones of power: the Throne of Running Water Caged by Force. You know what this throne means. The running water is the universe, time, entropy, that which cannot be reversed. And the force that holds it in place, that molds the running water into a throne, a work of art: that is the Inquest. It is a paradox. We fight time itself; yet our dogma is one of transience. But for a brief second of eternity we imprint our form on the chaos, the forever falling of entropy. Isn't it beautiful?"

"The throne," Kelver said, "is beautiful. But I don't like what you come to do."

"I have no choice, Kelver." The old man reached out to touch the boy; but he flinched. "Davaryush is my friend, Kevi. But he has gone too far now. And for that we will take his name from him. Nothing else: his wealth, his possessions, he can keep. Only the name of Inquestor do we take, for the Inquest is compassionate. In ten sleeps will come the trial, but there is no doubt of the sentence."

"But—"

"His work is all undone in any case. The blind and the deaf in the Dark Country of your Skywall are all dead. They've been dead for almost a century now, Kevi. We've replaced them with servocorpses. Servocorpses have no souls, you know. It is more compassionate this way. The plot is over, quite over. But whatever it was that made Davaryush send you here doesn't matter. You're one of us now. That is why I have sent you Siriss and Arryk, my favorites."

Kelver despaired then. He couldn't even weep; he was too empty. He was truly alone, then. He did not dare ask about Darktouch for fear that, if she were by some miracle alive, he might cause her death. There was no one to turn to, no one else who had seen the light on the Sound, who would fight on his side.

"Do not think, boy, that I'm not on your side! I, too, have heard the rumor that is racing through the Inquest, that is whispered in secret when games of *makrúgh* are done: that *the Inquest falls!*"

Kelver started at this. Did Elloran guess, then, the purpose he'd been entrusted with? But the old man laughed mildly, made light of it. There was much to love in the man, but Kelver knew deep down that they must be enemies, even if he, a boy alone, could never bring about the fulfillment of Davaryush's plan.

"Go now, Kelver. Forget the past. In a few sleeps you will see Davaryush for the last time. You will stay here, go on the quest-journey, grow in compassion. You'll make a very fine Inquestor, I'm sure."

And so Kelver was dismissed, while his companions remained to gossip over little secrets, shutting him out of their tight circle of friendship.

For the midmeal they dined on giant seridons chopped and served up, still wriggling, in their shells. Then Ton Elloran took Arryk aside, to the throneroom where Sajit still sat, directing his music. There were two Rememberers of the clan of Tash there too: it was their duty to remind the Inquest of worlds that, in the course of *makrúgh*, had *fallen beyond*. Elloran half-listened to them for a moment while Arryk waited. It was hard for Arryk not to think of the man as a god, even though he had come to Uran s'Varek almost a year before and had seen many Inquestors and even Grand Inquestors.

"So, tell me truly, Arryk . . . did the boy take it well? Will he do?"

"Siriss is distressed. She challenged him to *makrúgh* almost immediately, in Kendrin."

Elloran laughed mildly. "Let me lean on you, Arryk." They walked up to the galaxy of dust, as they had done so many times before, while the golden palace winged through the light-mad overcosm. "Are you upset, Rikeh, that I repeated the words to the boy? That 'the Inquest falls'?"

"You shouldn't feed him these ideas. You're endangering yourself, Elloran—" He stopped, not wanting to seem disrespectful.

"One day you must stop worshipping me, Ton Arryk n'Elloren Tath," said Elloran. "I am no one special; only a vessel of the High Compassion."

"If *all* the Inquestors were like you, Lord, if only . . ."

"We'd be in paradise, I suppose. You are young, Rikeh, and I have made you a god; but you are learning that the gods are not gods. There are none, you know, except power itself. And the power of Uran s'Varek is the greatest power. Do you think I'll live to see another Lightfall?"

"You could live forever if you chose!" said Arryk, panicking. He could not bear to lose the old man.

"I *should* die, if only to teach you a lesson. Look, the dust-nebula. *Even our hearts will become as dust, as the stars have become. . . .*" It was an old song of Sajit's. "And tell me, Rikeh, do you still love Siriss?"

"Yes, Elloran. But she loves power more."

"Go now, boy. I want you to look out for Kelver. Watch him. Even exiled, Davaryush sends us this gift, perhaps a poisoned one."

"I understand, Elloran. You're still playing *makrúgh* after all. But I'll always fight on your side, Lord, always." Childish, possessive love for the old Inquestor surged in him for a moment; but he had learned well to conceal emotion.

"What you say is so bitter to me. I have forsworn *makrúgh*! I seek only the end of my private griefs; that is why I am retiring from the active rule of my dozen worlds, bequeathing them one by one to others. And now I learn that there is no choice. The short-lived think that we have every choice, but in fact we have none at all. When you herded the firephoenixes in the scarlet snows of Kailasa you were freer than I. Davaryush was my friend, Arryk! But we cannot choose our friends or our enemies. Remember that when you are with Kelver and with Siriss, my boy."

Arryk knew what the old man was thinking. But he didn't want it to be true. "Maybe when I come back from the quest-journey I'll turn in my shimmercloak. Then it won't matter, will it?"

"Ah, but it's only a formality, isn't it, the quest-journey. Isn't that what the others have been telling you?"

Arryk tried to read the Grand Inquisitor's face; but he couldn't tell whether he was joking. "Riddles," he said ruefully.

But the old man only laughed uproariously.

Siriss woke to find Arryk still asleep beside her. They were in a small garden walled in by bushes, through which blew an artificial wind; the ceiling mimicked the night sky on some far world. It had always been one of Arryk's favorite corners of Varezhdur, ever since they had started to explore the palace together.

Lightly she called his name. He did not stir. They had been making love, and he was exhausted. But Siriss could not sleep. Something about that new boy Kelver . . .

She closed her eyes again. She imagined once more the time that she had first met Arryk. It was on Kailasa. She and Elloran and other Inquisitors had gone there for a hunt of firephoenixes . . . she had dared to challenge old Elloran, and he had said simply, "Go, Sirissheh. Pick an illiterate boy from the village and draw him into the game . . . even he will play *makrúgh* better than you!" And she had found him—

The boy: a clanless youth. His village of hovertents followed the great migration across the rift—rich Mountains of Jerrelahf, over the Pallid Ocean and the southlands, watching the birds soar skyward, shrieking, flaming, mating in midflight . . . it had been winter, a season when the birds were fat and turgid and had to be coaxed with effort into making their flight, yet she had demanded that the game be played; she had demanded that the fate of each bird be yoked to the fate of a world in the distant Vauvenizhi starcluster.

"Each Inquisitor," she had told the boy, "who takes part in the hunt has only one phoenix that he may kill, tagged with his personal tag; and almost all the tags are dormant death-crystals that will not link to the living . . . they are a kind of parasite." And she had given one to him. "Quickly! Pouch it! If it clings to your flesh for longer than a single sleep, it will be bound to you until you die!" Hastily he thrust it into his tunic. "I gained this concession," she said. "My crystal will be the only living one. And it will be linked to Kenzh, the most populous system of the Vauvenizhi. And so this gesture in the grand *makrúgh* becomes mine alone, a private metaphor from me to Elloran."

"You're a monster!"

"Surely no; how can you call me that? One world is enough to prove my point, and even that world may not die . . . it would not be compassionate to quicken *all* the crystals, to risk a thousand stars for the sake of a single gesture . . . and it's on your shoulders. Find the sleekest of the firephoenixes! One that will never tire. Then the world's future will be safe from me, the huntress."

And now Siriss remembered the long chase across the sky . . . remembered loosing arrow after arrow into the flock, until the scarlet snow was littered with their flaming corpses . . . and not one of them the corpse of the world she had meant to kill.

She watched Arryk as he lay there in the secret garden in vast Varezhdur. She pulled his shimmercloak open. There was the crystal still, wedded to his neck until death now, gleaming in the half-dark. That was how he had called her bluff. He had taken the world's death upon himself.

And Elloran had raised him to Inquestor.

How she loved him that day. But now Kelver had come, and somehow, in only a few hours, had shattered all her certainties.

He is still beautiful, she thought, looking at the sleeping boy. But somehow he's too . . . simple. He has to have everything in absolutes all the time.

Suddenly she realized that she was still prejudiced against him because of his peasant origins. It was an ugly thought, quickly suppressed. Such a thought had no right to exist, went against every Inquestral precept.

Confused, she stole away, not yet aware of what she was looking for.

Kelver could not sleep; the silence tormented him. He lay in darkness in a chamber of Elloran's Varezhdur. As he moved, the floor contoured to accommodate his restiveness. After a while Kelver sat up and listened to the stillness.

He heard a voice: high, eerie, the voice of a child-but-not-a-child. He could not tell where it came from at first. "Think-hive!" he whispered.

I awaken, came the voice in his mind.

"This alien music . . ."

Why do you not find out for yourself? Or have you not yet learned that there is no place on Uran s'Varek where you may not go? You are a master, and I, the soul of a leviathan world, am but your servant, Ton Keverell n'Davaren Tath.

"You mock me . . . you play *makrúgh* too well, you who are more than a thousand times my age." He was wide awake now. Becoming bolder, he subvocalized to the room for a dim light; it came, apparently sourceless, along the gilt-friezed walls. He tossed aside a pillow stuffed with kyllap leaves and rose, looking for an exit; presently he found the displacement plate and thought at it, *The voice. The voice.*

And he was in a corridor of etchveined marble in which were sculpted in high relief pteratyger after pteratyger, dead stone with living eyes that followed him as he walked on toward the voice.

"Kevi." A girl's whisper. For a second he thought it was Darktouch's voice, when she had barely learned speech. He whirled around: it was Siriss, peering from a pteratyger's wing. The sculpted eyes stared at him, blinking sometimes.

"Unnerving, aren't they?" Siriss said. "I was always frightened of them when I was a girl. Which I still am, I suppose. They are actually quite primitive organisms, those eyes; they are a mollusklike creature from Vanjyvel. Elloran had them sent here for the frieze. They're not really following you, you know. They're just attracted to any blot of darkness that moves down this corridor. Look . . . one of them's dividing." She cupped her hands under a pteratyger's eye; it shivered for a moment, and then an eyeball-thing fell into her hand. Kelver stared at the thing, squirming, its pupil darting to and fro. "They say it's an aphrodisiac," she said, squeezing juice from the eye into the cup of her hands. "Try some?"

Kelver allowed her to brush the fluid against his lips; it was cloyingly sweet. Siriss drank the rest greedily; then she let the rest of the mollusk dribble onto the floor, which devoured it. "Doesn't do anything for me," Kelver said. "But it's a nice story. Why are you stalking me, Siriss?"

"Because I am a huntress."

"Shh. Listen. Listen."

Came the young voice again, shrill in the gloom. It sang no song all the way through: just a phrase here and there, then silence. "What is it?" Kelver said.

"Oh, only old Sajit at work."

"Shen Sajit, the great musician? Here?" Kelver remembered how even on Gallendys they sang the songs of Sajit.

"He's always here. He is Elloran's friend, if we Inquestors can be said to have friends. Do you want to see? Come, follow." She walked on ahead, almost on tiptoe. The childvoice was louder now, haunting. Gathering up his shimmercloak so as not to let its rustle dampen the distant singing, Kelver followed her.

She stopped suddenly and put her hand against the head of a marble pteratyger. "I think it's this one."

"How can you know?"

"It's the hundredth tyger from my room. I know Varezhdur well, since I grew up with Elloran as my mentor."

The pteratyger's mouth hinged open with a wheeze, and she pressed a stud within; the tyger dissolved into emptiness. "It's not like the others, this one; it's a holosculpture to match them, but it's really made of nothing. Come." There was a long staircase that led upward and then twisted out of sight. As they stepped onto it the staircase hummed to life and began to move. Kelver watched as the walls on either side, awakened by the staircase's motion, began to play out colorful scenes: children at *shtézhnat*, the hunt for the now-extinct firephoenixes of Kailasa, worlds where sea serpents battled. At the head of the staircase there was a curious hinged door that would not iris open, but had to be pushed by brute force; it clanged shut behind them, and they were in the sanctum of Shen Sajit.

It was a small chamber with uncontouring floors. At one end Kelver saw a wizened old man and a naked child clutching an instrument to his chest. The child had no genitals at all; its pubis was firm, flat, smooth. It was a neuter then. That was why the voice had sounded so unearthly. For the voices of neuters, lacking as they did the sexual passion that stirred all others, were angel voices. They had stopped when they heard the two come in; now they resumed, Sajit coaxing the thin sound from the boy's lips.

"Easy, child, easy, relax, relax. Don't fear the cold of the whisperlyre. For its resonance the instrument draws the warmth from your body; you must expect the cold, and the more passionate your song the colder *you* will become. It can't be helped."

The neuter sang again. Kelver saw that the child was beautiful, but this was not surprising, for nothing on Uran s'Varek was ugly unless it were by Inquestral design. Its long hair, green as grass, was wound round and round its body; its eyes were a matching green. At a pause in the song, Sajit turned to the two youths and said, "Sirissheh. And this must be the young Ton Keverell n'Davaren Tath. *Hokh'Tón.*"

Kelver was embarrassed that such a distinguished person should defer to him; but Siriss seemed to be used to it. "What are you practicing?" she said.

"A song with which I will greet Elloran next week, when he comes back from the trial; he'll need comfort then."

And Davaryush! thought Kelver. He'll need no comfort, I suppose. He tried not to think about the coming trial, but he couldn't.

"What are the words?" said Siriss.

"Look!" And when Sajit waved his arms, writing appeared for a few moments, as if inscribed in flames, in the air between them:

Den plánzha, den plánzha, hokh'Tón:
den léjeÿ hokt'ÿ.
Dáras den sikláh evéndek.
Zi lávorymas kakoreúr
chom ídora kerávishi zi:
den plánzha, den plánzha, hokh'Tón.

Do not weep, do not weep, High One;
we do not choose what we are.
The stars do not circle forever.
Let your tears be caged
as the water in the throne.
Do not weep, do not weep, High One.

And then the neuterchild began the song. The melody arched up, up, up; it did not seem that a human voice could sustain a phrase so broad, tones so high. To the naked melody the whisperlyre added only a brief note or two, a point of repose. It was music beyond grief and joy.

And Siriss was touching him now, drawing him gently out of his sorrow. "What, here, now?" he whispered, wonderingly. She only smiled at him. "Huntress!" he cried out. They tore at each other's shimmercloaks and fell to the hard floor. The cloaks shifted, hissed as they tussled, came alive as they absorbed the sweat of sexual excitement. In the small room, with the old man absorbed in his teaching and the child singing out his heart, they made love, angrily almost. Kelver couldn't get Darktouch out of his mind even as he devoured the white Inquestrix. And suddenly it was over, and he was as unsatisfied as before.

"Kevi," Siriss whispered. "Why are you so angry? Why do you dance your rage upon my body?" And then they made love a second time, more playfully, more joyously; and as Kelver drifted into sleep he saw her bent over him, caressing his chest, a puzzled look on her face; and she was saying, over and over, "Who is Darktouch?"

FOUR: **THE HERETIC**

. . . and I will be the cankerworm, noticed by no one, gnawing at the Inquest's heart.

. . . through a gauze of warring forceshields, through a spiderforest of metal trees . . .

"Are we there yet? Quicker!" Kelver shouted as the floater, guided by the worldsoul, threaded the tunnels of twisted furwillows. And he thought: They've sentenced him! They've sentenced him! And I have to see him—

They'd all pronounced the anathema together. He and Siriss and thousands of other Inquestors, facing the three thrones of power where sat the Inquestors of Judgment: the Throne of Running Water Caged by Force, the Throne of Crystal Laced with Flame, and the Throne of Black Rock Woven from Starlight. He'd watched them strip Davaryush of his name, and now he was Daavye-without-a-clan, and they had imprisoned him in Kendrin and would soon banish him forever from Uran s'Varek. And for a moment Kelver had gazed, from a distance, into Davaryush's face, and he had known that his master's plan *was* working, after all. He did not know yet how. But now he must find him. It was not difficult to learn where he was, for the thinkhive knew, of course, and it was no secret.

He'd left Siriss, with whom he had been spending all his time, and had taken the hoverfloat, and now he could see, halfway up what should have been the sky but which was merely more of Uran s'Varek's endless surface, Kakobarang, the city of the prison castle. Soon it was rearing up ahead, and what had seemed a small black lotus in a green meadow

34

now grew into a circle of black monoliths guarded by ten mountains carved into sphinxes: the heads of naked basalt crowned with snow, the flanks of brown rock crisscrossed with hardy shrubs, the paws and bellies furred with forest.

Now he glided into the massive portals of the castle. Two childsoldiers on hoverdisks were the only guards; they swooped down upon his floater like hawks.

"The Inquestor-that-was is silent!" they shouted in unison in their piping voices. Their black cloaks flapped and their yellow laser-irises slitted like cat's eyes.

"Take me to him," Kelver said.

"We cannot. He is silenced."

"*Ishá ha!* I command it, I, Ton Keverell n'Davaren Tath!" There, he had spoken as Inquestor to underling for the first time, and almost without realizing it. He felt cold now, trapped, hating the role of master.

"We cannot! He is silenced!"

"I speak as Inquestor, children of the lightning. You are bound to obey. Take me to him."

He saw them hesitate. They were afraid of him, who was hardly older than they, these children who had probably slain thousands and razed a thousand cities. Then one of them, the taller, said, "We obey. But the Grand Inquestors will kill us for it." There was a tear on his cheek, quickly wiped aside with a smart flick of the wrist.

"Follow, *hokh'Tón!*" He raised his arm up, challenging the wind; the hoverdisk followed the curve of his gesture, springing upward. They flew to the farthest monolith, the floater battling the windcurrent, the two children on either side, impassive in the face of death.

They entered the prison monolith through gates in its side; presently the soldiers, jumping clear of their hoverdisks, escorted the young Inquestor to an antechamber where sat Davaryush, alone, on a stone seat. The room was lighted only by torches, and their light was blue, and cold.

The childsoldiers stood a moment, nervous, glancing at each other.

Not yet looking at Davaryush, Kelver said to the taller one: "Childsoldier, how old are you?"

"Ten, Lord. I was impressed four years ago."

"Have you seen much action?"

"Terrible, Lord. Once in the War of Frozen Fireworks; once I even saw . . ."

"A whispershadow," said the other, awed.

"We'll be leaving you now, Lord," said the first one.

It was then that the High Compassion touched Kelver for the first time, and he knew what he must do. "Kneel," he said. Quickly the two genuflected before him. "I release you from your childsoldiery. You will not be killed now, I promise. I name you to clans of your choice."

Hardly looking up, the first said, "Oh, *hokh'Tón* . . . I have always wished to be a ferret, hunting out little secrets . . . and my brother-at-arms here, he's always wanted to build things. Houses. Shrines."

"Very well," said Kelver. "You are so named. I have instructed the thinkhive. You will leave Uran s'Varek on the next delphinoid. You will take no memory of Uran s'Varek with you. You go to a new world." And they scurried away, hardly believing what they had escaped. It is good to show compassion, thought Kelver, and he was tempted by the power of Inquestorhood.

He went up to Davaryush now. He was slumped forward in his stone seat. Behind him, on a dais, were models of the three thrones.

Kelver said, "Davaryush. I'm all alone now. Please help."

The old man said nothing. He stirred a little, and he watched the boy. He seemed about to speak, but did not.

"I know there's an injunction against your directly addressing one of the Inquest . . . but surely you can talk to *me*! You put me here. Oh, Daavye, Daavye, guide me. When I saw you in the judgment hall, you spoke a single sentence: *The Inquest falls*. How can it fall? It's so great, and I'm the only one, and . . . I'm attracted to it. I feel the powerlust tugging at me. Like when I showed mercy to those two childsoldiers; was that so bad, Davaryush?"

But all Davaryush said was, "Seek the Throne of Madness."

"What do you mean? There are only three thrones, aren't there? Besides, they're just symbols, toys."

No reply.

"Daavye . . . I know you're not supposed to speak to me. But listen! I, the Inquestor, command you!" Perhaps it would work; hadn't it worked on the childsoldiers? But the old man did not answer, and the fire was gone from his eyes. "You ruled worlds once." And Kelver tried to weep; but he could not. Not in front of one-without-a-clan. He just could not. And he knew then that the Inquest's talons were already deep in his mind. Then he cried out: "I hate you, all of you, with all your talk of compassion! You take everything from us and give us nothing! You killed Varuneh whom you loved, and Darktouch whom I loved—didn't you? Didn't you? Where is she now, buried in the pulpy mush at the bottom of the Dark Country? I hate all your kind—"

He was speaking to a shell of a man only, to an emptiness. And he was railing only against himself; for he was of their kind. He had only been in Uran s'Varek a few sleeps, but he already hated what he had become.

And then Davaryush said, so quietly that he had to strain to listen: "Seek out the Throne of Madness."

"But what of Darktouch—tell me, tell me—"

Davaryush looked up then. With his eyes he implored the young Inquestor. What did he mean? Did he mean to beg forgiveness? Or had he something to tell, and feared the injunction? But Kelver could feel no compassion for him. He thought of Darktouch; he couldn't conjure up her face. All he could see were Siriss's dancing eyes, her slender hips, her taut breasts, her smile, half-mocking. And he strode from the room, cursing.

Why? thought Davaryush. Why couldn't I have spoken to him? It might not have hurt to show him I still care for him, that the plan is still working.

Darktouch. I should have told him of Darktouch, at least— And he remembered.

Darktouch had been standing on a hoverdisk in the middle of the Dark Country when his floaters streamed down from the roof of Skywall. Darkness everywhere . . . the imagesongs of the delphinoids broken, sharded into the blackness . . . bloodied lumps of brainstuff spurting in the dense air . . . and the whirling of laser-eyed childsoldiers, spinning the discus-death, slicing the airskiffs of the blind men. . . .

Coming up behind Darktouch. Seizing her from behind, crying, "Darktouch, Darktouch. It's over, you must come; the Inquest has sent for me."

And Darktouch holding to her small breasts the shredded corpse of her father. Too proud to weep. Light-echoes of a dead imagesong illuminated her face now and then, and it never changed from flash to flash. She wept for the Wind-bringers, and for her people.

Davaryush whispered, urgent, "We can do nothing. They're

going to kill them all, all your people. They're going to put in
servocorpses to harvest the giant brains of the Windbringers
now. We've unleashed something terrible on this innocent
people. . . ."

He was shaking the girl, but she was numb.

In a while, seeing that she did not listen, he had his loyal
childsoldiers pull her gently into his floater. They left the
Dark Country.

Now she waits, thought Davaryush-without-a-clan, in a
delphinoid ship that circles a distant world, a world I know
she has always longed to see: Shtoma. She is in stasis, and
when I go to her we will begin on our own search for
paradise. The great Ending of the Dispersal of Man is not for
me to create, but for Kelver. . . .

Then thought Davaryush, bitterly: I should have told him!
I should have! It would have made little enough difference.

But it was not in Davaryush's plan to make Kelver love
him. It would be better for him to hate his former master, for
in hating he would be free of wanting to fulfill Davaryush's
hopes and dreams, of being Davaryush's agent. Only then
could he be free of the curse of the Inquestors. Davaryush
would never be free of it. The more he tried to save the
Dispersal of Man, the deeper he drowned in blood of his own
shedding.

But, oh, he thought, I love this child.

And being a man now, no longer Inquestor, he was free to
weep, to show his emotions. But he could not. It had been
too long, and the peace that was his by right continued to lie
beyond his reach.

"You spoke to Davaryush?" said Siriss. "You dared to go to
Kakobarang?"

"No one stopped me." Kelver had returned to Ellorin with
his confusion unsolved; they were standing, the two of them,
by a pool of rainbow water where old women dived for the
roots of the intoxicating madweed. Halfway up where the sky
should have been was the palace Varezhdur, emerging from
the rosella-snow like a sun from a bank of clouds. "I went
right inside and talked to him; but he didn't answer."

"Of course not!" she said scornfully. "You're such a child,
Kelver. The injunction—he wouldn't break the injunction.
And you should know that just because you aren't stopped
doesn't mean you can go where you choose."

"That's not what the thinkhive told me."

"The thinkhive does not rule here. Oh, Kevi, but I love your innocence. You would stand in the mouth of a black hole. You'd sit on the Throne of Madness itself!"

The boy paled. "Why, Kevi, what's the matter? The mere mention of the Throne of Madness terrifies you this much?" Siriss stroked his cheek. "Come, let's see how the weedfishers are doing."

They went to the side of the lake, where the crones sat gossiping. "Hey, woman," Siriss said, "show me your catch." One of them opened a basket full of the madweed. Little pearls clung to the blue-green strands. The woman grinned; her few remaining teeth were blue with the constant chewing. Siriss took a piece, halved it, shared it with Kelver. "It's all right, you silly boy! *We're* not going to rot alive like these women! We're going to live as long as we choose!"

Another woman grinned, too, toothless. "Shall we go swimming?" Siriss tore off her shimmercloak and bound it about her hips; and then she jumped. Kelver hesitated, followed her lead. The water was warm. A school of furry lover fish, sensing the young Inquestors, darted between them, tickling their genitals.

"You didn't tell me!" Kelver spluttered.

Siriss giggled. Cushion fish, aroused from their place on the lakebed, rose to support them as they made love in the wombwarmth. "One of Elloran's playpens," said Siriss. Her eyes sparkled. The cushion fish swam out farther into the lake, and the lover fish wriggled frenziedly between their bodies.

"You'd think the gene-tailors had nothing serious to do," Kelver said as he lay back, letting the scatter-starlight play on his body. The shimmercloaks, gorged on the sweat of love-making, glowed brilliant pink.

The cushion fish took them out to a grotto; in alcoves, nereids, warned in advance by their coming, danced solemnly to the music of stone-pipes through which an artwind rushed.

"But what is the Throne of Madness?" Kelver said.

"It is the fourth throne about which no one speaks," Siriss said, knowing that it was her duty to instruct him. "It is said that only Lightfall can awaken it; and that the Inquestor who sits upon it will be made to see into the consciousness of the dying star, if consciousness there be. But men have searched the perimeter of the pole and found no such throne; though some say that the first Inquestors, knowing its power to drive men mad, hid it somewhere on Uran s'Varek. And if something is hidden on Uran s'Varek, who can ever find it? Who's been filling your head with such thoughts, anyway? Davaryush, I suppose. But you say that he obeyed the injunction."

"Yes." Siriss could hardly hear him, and a terrible sadness seemed to come from him. And Siriss embraced him. For though she liked to feign hardness, she had come to love him a little. Not that she had tired of Arryk, but Arryk was so devoted to Elloran; he could speak of nothing else at times, he worshipped him blindly. An Inquestor shouldn't be that blind, she thought. It's our job to see where others will not look.

Siriss was jealous of Elloran, too, because Arryk was his in a way she could never challenge. And now Kelver had come, and Kelver, in his own way, was beautiful; not daunting-eyed like Arryk, but lithe, shadowslim, feral, the only softness in the haunted green eyes. There was anger always in his lovemaking, and she loved anger, ever since the Inquestors plucked her from a burning homeworld and showed her their terrible compassion.

"Sirissheh," Kelver said, avoiding her eyes, "you're using me to play *makrúgh* with Arryk, aren't you?"

She did not answer him.

"And where is Arryk?" he demanded. "Do you even know? When does our quest-journey begin, anyway?"

"Why are you asking me?" She felt vulnerable suddenly.

"You aren't any huntress," Kelver said. "I love you."

Siriss should have felt triumph; she had schemed to get the boy in her power. But now she felt as though *she* had lost the game. She wondered whether, when they came back from the quest-journey, she would be handing in her shimmercloak after all. . . .

Arryk was in another part of Elloran altogether; it was another of Elloran's pleasure places, a desert of powdered chocolate. Children from a neighboring city had come to play there. They were running about melting the ground with toy lasers into steaming pools of chocolate, and then crouching to lap it up like forest animals. The young Inquestor stood apart from the children, concentrating. He was trying to create illusions.

Here, in the far north of Uran s'Varek as all the Inquestral settlements were, they were near the great bank of thinkhives that hugged the upper doughnut-hole of the world. It was easy to draw on their power, to tug at the physical world, to make castles in the air . . . which was just what he was doing.

A castle was sprouting from the chocolate sand: it seemed of solid stone, with towers studded with jewel windows, with crenellations carved into gargoyles that spat fire. . . . "How am I doing, thinkhive?" he whispered. And the planetary thinkhive answered: *It is beautiful, hokh'Tón.* He shrugged and made the castle turn slowly as it rose into the air, altering a portal here, shifting a window there, making the spires dance like the necks of brontosaurs.

Suddenly he was conscious of low laughter behind him. He whirled around; it was Kelver.

"Don't be embarrassed," said the boy, coming down to him over a dune. "It *is* beautiful." But Arryk had lost control now, and the creation was swirling into a mud-kaleidolon, was dissipating into the clear air. "How did you do it?"

"We can all do it." Arryk shrugged. "You can, too. Just concentrate; tell the thinkhive what you want. Really see it in your head, and then—"

An outline of a huge mountain that seemed to touch the sky . . . for a split second . . . then daylight.

"You didn't do too badly, Kevi." They both laughed. Arryk was conscious of the other boy's closeness now. "I heard that you went to see Davaryush."

He wanted to ask a hundred other questions: what was the heretic like? How could such a man even exist, why weren't they all like Elloran? But Kelver made him too nervous. He was a boy the heretic had touched, had influenced, even as Elloran had influenced Arryk. It was too confusing. And now Siriss was constantly with the other boy too. He didn't need this.

"On my world," Kelver said, "we stared at a great black wall and imagined things. That was the wall I conjured up, the barrier of the Dark Country."

Arryk felt longing then, for the peasant life. "I dreamed about starships too," he said. "And now we own millions of them, more than we can imagine."

"Do you like it here?"

Arryk was startled by Kelver's directness. Didn't he know that you *never* spoke that way? That was what the Inquestral highspeech was designed for: elegance, ambivalence, circumlocution, *makrúgh*.

He said, "I don't know."

Kelver said, "Look at those children. I wish I could bend down and lap up a puddle of chocolate."

"Yes." Why was it so painful to talk to Kelver? Why did he constantly remind Arryk of the past?

And then Kelver asked him a forbidden question: "Rikeh, before you were chosen by Elloran, what were you?"

"I don't have to answer." He stalked off a few paces, avoiding the boy's forceful intimacy.

Kelver did not press him. Instead, he said, "On my homeworld, there was a vast desert like this. We were at one edge; civilization was at the other. Sometimes there'd be mirages that looked like the one you made. They were images of Effelkang and Kallendrang, cities we children dreamed of a lot. And you know what we did?" He knelt down. Arryk watched him, appalled, as he scooped up the chocolate sand with his hands and began to build a sandcastle. Then Arryk laughed aloud.

"Of course," he said. They huddled together in the shade of a high dune and began to build. "Who needs a thinkhive?" He smiled at Kelver.

The boy gave him a perfunctory hug. He smelled of *f'áng* vapor and his skin was strangely dry, and hard. Kelver said, "We have to be friends, Arryk, we have to be, we peasant boys plucked from our villages and given these ludicrous powers! I'm not playing *makrúgh* with you, I swear it!"

"All right," Arryk said kindly. But he wanted to ask: Did Davaryush bend down from his golden throne and raise you up, and when you looked into his eyes did you worship him, did you love and fear him as I do Elloran? Instead he simply said, "Don't be afraid. We don't care who you used to be, before you were chosen. We don't choose what we are, you know. And as we become Inquestors we choose less and less." He was echoing Elloran's words.

Kelver said, "At least we can still choose our friends and our enemies, can't we?"

"Oh, Kevi, I hope so." With those words they embraced, and made love; and so at last the triangle was joined at all its corners.

FIVE: **THE SINGING CITY**

Finally the day came when Elloran called them all to his private throneroom, the place of the galaxy of dust. Kelver and Siriss and Arryk all stood facing him; and Sajit sat at his feet, looking far older than Elloran, though they were of an age. "I thought that this room would never be silent," Kelver said. "They told me you could not bear silence, Elloran." In a few sleeps he had learned to address the Great Inquestor without formality, as the others did; but it still made him uncomfortable.

"Are you ready, then, children, for the long solitude?" he said.

"No!" Kelver said. "How could I be, *hokh'Tón*? Sirissheh has been in Uran s'Varek for years, and even Arryk has had far more instruction than I have. How am I to decide here and now about a life of centuries?"

Elloran said, "Kelver, Kelver. What is there to teach you? The others have been here longer, have absorbed into themselves the music of Uran s'Varek; but are they more Inquestor-like than you? Will the High Compassion touch you just because an old man lectures you for ten years? Some Inquestors do teach their charges that way; *I* don't believe in it. You have all already been chosen; your quest-journey will confirm the choice, I think . . . and if you were to stay here and listen to the chatterings of old men, Kevi, you would make no decisions at all. To be frank, we fear you, we fear him who sent you. We have all heard that the Inquest falls. Perhaps not for another millennium, but it falls . . . we have no time. We need you. Do not think that a few months in the far wild

43

places will be easy. It will seem to you like many lifetimes, Kelver."

There was a distant humming sound; the palace trembled. Kelver gasped; the others laughed at him. "We're in motion!" Arryk said. "Where are we going?"

"A little treat," said Elloran, "before we release you in the wilderness. We shall fly, in my palace, to the edge of my domain, and we will all see for the first time the thing that our Sajitteh has been making these past fifty years: Shentrazjit."

Shentrazjit . . . a name for a city, but it meant simply *Song of Sajit*. What new thing was this?

"A whim," Elloran said, "nothing more. I just want to share with you what my Sajit has done." As the palace shifted in the rosella-snow, Elloran clapped his hands and caused the walls to deopaque, letting in a kaleidoscopic vision of the outside: to the far left, the Dulsivaras, or Candied Kingdoms, where lay the chocolate desert and the forests of marzipan and the palaces of honey-ice; to the far right the Crystallizing Sea, an ocean split into little seas of different saturated solutions where single crystals, growing slowly over the millennia, had reached the size of mountain ranges. Before them lay green meadows such as Elloran's meadow in Varunin; little furrows that were gorges, ridges that were ten-klomet-high mountain peaks; and always the flower-cities nestled in folds of meadow, dotting the hillsides, peppering the green-gray cloud of distance. As the palace rose, the cities shrank to specks, the fields to haze, and still Kelver could see no end to the world. . . .

Excited, he ran to the room's edge to peer over. Arryk was beside him. "What's Shentrazjit?" Kelver asked him, trying not to sound ignorant.

"A city with a choir of twenty million voices," said Arryk.

Kelver only gaped at him.

Then Elloran, drawing him aside, was saying, "Kevi. You asked me why I had commanded silence in the throneroom: it's because I want my ear to perceive utter stillness, to prepare for Shentrazjit. Ah, the gene-tailors have been busy there."

Kelver bowed quickly, acknowledging the Grand Inquestor's attention; but turned to watch the spectacle beneath. But Elloran did not let go. He whispered, "I know you have seen Davaryush, Kevi."

"It wasn't forbidden," Kelver said hotly.

"For your own sake, child, don't seek out the Throne of Madness. Any fool can tell you where it is. And you're just the type who would look for it . . . beware of whispershadows."

"What are whispershadows? The soldiers talk about them, but . . ."

"I know. When in *makrúgh* we create wars, Kelver, they are not against the whispershadows; they are just man against man. Wars are necessary; above all the Inquest must discourage stagnation. But our wars are play wars: in our compassion we let most people survive, we blow up as few planets as we can afford. But there is a real war, too, a war against enemies we have never seen. Uran s'Varek did not always belong to men, you know. Perhaps it still doesn't; for how could we explore it all? There may be a thousand other races here; we'd never meet them."

"But what is a whispershadow? And why is it that I must not find the Throne of Madness?"

"The two questions are linked, you know. Do stars have consciousness? Perhaps they are displeased when we drain them of their energy for our childish games? Perhaps that's what the old poem means. The Inquestors who would know the answers are long dead: it is said that the Throne killed them."

"I don't understand."

"I don't want you to understand. I don't want you to die, Kevi! And—for all the Inquest's terrible evils—I am an Inquestor. I love the Inquest. The Inquest owns me completely; it's eaten me alive and replaced every scrap of my tissue with itself. Can you understand this? Look at what we did to Davaryush. He was my friend. My teacher, too, at times. *I* would not take the Shtoma assignment, but *he* did! He had unending curiosity about the way humans work, inside. But the Inquest doesn't want you to know things. Every time I send a boy or girl out into the wilderness, I hope he'll come back and turn in his shimmercloak. How can I wish on him this anguish, this yearning? We are the utopia hunters . . . because we of all people want utopias the most; we are the murderers of planets because we are the most compassionate." He paused. Kelver watched him, not knowing whether what he spoke was truth or merely a counterstatement of *makrúgh*. But on this matter he could get no more out of Elloran. He would have to ask the thinkhive; but with the thinkhive one had to ask the right questions, and they made no allowances, for they had been playing *makrúgh* since men came to Uran s'Varek.

And so they journeyed for several sleeps. When it grew dark (in Varezhdur it grew dark whenever Elloran needed darkness) the three of them would go to one of the rooms that flanked the corridor of a thousand pteratygers, or they would explore the gardens within gardens within gardens; the labyrinths of hedges where each leaf was a slice of pale jade, each twig wrought from an agate, and the grass green silk; the noisy aviaries; the thronerooms, some glittery, some cobwebbed, some where the palace waifs played furtively, some deserted. There were swimlakes in the palace, too, one of cold blue flame spewed from the mouth of an icedragon as he lay drugged. And Kelver would sometimes wake to find beside him Siriss of the pale breasts and supple hips; or sometimes it would be Arryk's slender arms around him, and he would be staring into the strange violet eyes. Or they would both be there with him, sometimes awake already, alert, watching him. Each had found in Kelver something different to love: Arryk loved their similar pasts, being able to share memories of village life and simple things; Siriss loved him for his alienness and his anger. And Kelver . . . Kelver did not think that he had ever been this happy.

It was only after many sleeps—for in Varezhdur time seemed always to stand still, or to move entirely at Elloran's whim— that Kelver realized he had not thought of Darktouch for all this time, or of Davaryush and his mission to subvert the Inquest; and he had given no thought at all to the mysterious conversation he had had with Elloran. He still did not know what the Throne of Madness meant, or what a whispershadow was: some kind of alien. Were the humans at war with them then? Was this the involuntary war to which Elloran referred? And why had Elloran mentioned the possibility of a star's sentience? They were riddles, problems of *makrúgh* that he was at a loss to solve.

The day came when they were all in the private throneroom together, and he heard one of the neuterchildren cry out: "Masters, quickly, it's Shentrazjit at last—" and the old Inquestor and his musician ran to the viewwall like children, forgetting the three young Inquestors completely; and the palace dropped hawklike from the sky over the city, a plain-enough-looking city hewn from igneous mountains. Kelver couldn't see what was so marvelous.

Then Elloran said, "We must land now, we must ride into your city on pteratygers, Sajit. It shall be beautiful." Turning to the three Inquestors-that-were-to-be, he said, "This is the last boundary of my domain in Ellorin: beyond the city of Shentrazjit I do not rule. Other Inquestors have carved out kingdoms; perhaps their lands stretch southward for as much as one hundred million klomets. Beyond that, only the thinkhive knows. When we have passed Shentrazjit, you will be issued a floater whose maximum speed is fifteen klomets per second. Go as far as you like; come back when you are ready. Go together; go separately. May the powers of powers go with you." He scratched his chin thoughtfully. "And if you need help, ask the thinkhive to contact someone. It extends, of course, into the overcosm as well as the tachyon universe, so it ought to know where *I* am, for instance."

"*Hokh'Tón*—" Kelver said.

"No more. Let's go down to the stables and pick our pteratygers . . . albinos I think, Sajitteh, no?" And he made for the displacement plate at the foot of his throne, while the others hastened to follow.

As the belly of the palace yawned to let forth the four Inquestors and the musician, mounted on silver-white pteratygers whose wings spread wide to catch the high wind over Shentrazjit, Arryk felt the silence even more strongly than in Varezhdur's halls. For it seemed that Elloran's whim had muzzled the very wind; it whipped at his face and his shimmercloak but made no sound, not a whisper. He heard Elloran say, "I've done as you wanted, Sajitteh. I've hushed the world. At your signal we will hear your song, and the city come to life. . . ."

Arryk urged his pteratyger close to Kelver's; Siriss, too, had made straight for the heretic's child, competing with Arryk for power over him. As the winged cat-creature dropped to where Kelver's was treading the air, he heard Sajit's explanation: "Half a century ago, I conceived of this music: a song sung by a city, a nation, perhaps; a song that could not help but be sung. A life-hymn, millions of voices blending in unconscious harmony. And so Elloran built me this city. Today the city wakes. Imagine the creatures that inhabit it, twenty million of them: vendors, soldiers, peasants, landsmen, princes. I have conceived a language that they will speak. The tones of the language, irrelevant to the meanings of the words, are biologically programmed to change from minute to minute according to my score: so that these people, whatever they may chance to say to each other, will without willing it add their sound-mote to the vast harmony . . . individuals they are, living their lives as any unaltered humans; but the sum total of their little utterances becomes a transcendent music, a celebration of the individual and the universal. . . ."

It was a breathtaking concept; Arryk could see that the others were moved. "And the singers of the song, Sajit. Do they know what they're doing? Do they understand why they've been so gene-tailored?"

"In some unconscious way, perhaps. When I dreamed this song I did not know that Elloran would have the city built for me," Sajit said.

Elloran said, "Master musician, perhaps we should begin?" And old Sajit made some gesture to tell the unseen technicians to awaken the city. And at a sign from Elloran, the pteratygers, wings outstretched, glided down to Shentrazjit.

He couldn't hear anything at all at first. And then it began: a single high tone that pierced the wind; Arryk couldn't tell where it came from. Another tone now, leaping from hollow to hollow of the mountain-carved city, rebounding from the desolate peaks. Another hard on its heels; the three tones darting down the once-empty streets that even now began to fill with manlike beings. Then came more tones, each tone given a brief play before diminuendoing into the twitter-texture of accompaniment and being superseded by another tone. "It's the *aláp*," Arryk whispered to Kelver, "the sounding-out of the music's thematic material. The inhabitants of Shentrazjit are all cloned from the same model, you know, and are descended from one of Sajit's favorite neuterchildren . . . their voices are perfect!" But before he could say more, came the first big outburst of the city's song; an alto melody, sinuous, irregular, that snaked down the city's side alleys under a trilling, busy counterpoint, a million fragmentary song-snatches like a war of birds, and beneath it all a collective percussive whispering, and lower still a throb like the slow heartbeat of some vast alien creature, as the footfalls of the city's millions fell unconsciously into step with one another, into the rhythmic cycles of the song. Then came a second alto melody, not quite an echo of the first, solemnly progressing down the city's north-south boulevard to the central square, intertwining with the melody of the alleyways as the sound shifted southward. . . .

The music swelled up to a series of shattering climaxes, each more splendid than the last. Between the climaxes were heartbreakingly poignant returns to the opening *aláp;* each time came the lonely notes, breaking across a soft texture of susurrant murmurings; they were wan, desolate tones that arrowed the avenues of the city. Then, at a climax so powerful that Arryk felt he could bear no more, there burst over the music, from the tops of towers and the peaks of the mountains, a clustered keening, a soundstream like a beam of frozen light; it was as a slow illumination of all that had gone before. For it transformed what had seemed like musical doodling (albeit on an unparalleled scale) into something inevitable. It was as though Sajit had not imposed form on chaos, but had discovered that form concealed within the very nature of chaos itself. And Arryk, Inquestor that he was, wept; for he was thinking of himself and of Kelver and Siriss and of the triangle they had made of their minds and their bodies . . . it had been a game until now, for the three of them. But soon would come illumination, like the light at the climax of Sajit's song; and then, he supposed, all the games we have played with each other will fall into some cosmic pattern not of our making, and from that moment onward we will have no more choices.

"I'm going to give it all up," he said suddenly. Kelver and Siriss turned to stare at him; they'd been listening to the grand music, wrapped in private thoughts, and he'd pulled them rudely away. "Listen to me, powers of powers, Kevi, Sirissheh . . . I want to give it up, do you hear me? You have each other. I don't need all this power!" He tugged at his shimmercloak until it gave at the neck and chest. He ripped the fabric, ripping again and again when the living shimmerfur grew back. Elloran and Sajit seemed to pay him no heed; but the others hovered beside him, unsure of what to do. He managed to strip off the whole cloak now; he held it high, the wind was bittercold, the bristle of the pteratyger's flanks bit hard into his legs and buttocks. He tossed the shimmercloak away.

Then the pteratyger roared: "You—not Inquestor—not ride me—I silver-white of Ton Elloran—I mated to the shimmercloak's scent—" Over and over it hissed the human words. And then it flapped its wings angrily, soaring up into the skyshine, bucking now, somersaulting. Arryk could feel himself slipping, he tried to hold on but the sharp hair stabbed his palms and drew blood from his fingers, the city's voices broke into another clamorous climax as he felt himself tumbling into a huge blackness—

Voices now, immeasurably far away—

Thinkhive . . . thinkhive . . . catch him before he falls . . . save the shimmercloak . . . catch him . . . catch him. . . .

And he was drowning in the angel music.

"You go first," Siriss said.

"No, you, Sirissheh. He's known you longer." And Kelver retreated into a corner of the anteroom hewn from rock. Two of the city-folk were there to see to their needs; they knew instinctively that the shimmercloaked ones were their gods. They were small creatures, looking much like the neuterchildren of Sajit's consort in Varezhdur; on their backs vestigial wings sprouted, for the gene-tailors had wanted them to resemble the angels of ancient myth. These two were identical; their hair was long, silvery, their eyes were gray and with a slight slant to them; they were slender, delicately proportioned, and they moved like dancers. When they spoke their language was a succession of vowel sounds of different lengths and colors, blending instantly with the music of outside. Here, not hearing the music's total effect from above, you could not tell that you were in the middle of a great composer's masterpiece.

Siriss followed the two in; when they spoke to her, the thinkhive translated in her mind. They took her to a tiny room where Arryk sat staring through a window. His shimmercloak lay discarded on the floor; she picked it up and took it to him.

"No," he said, looking away.

"You shouldn't be running, Rikeh. You shouldn't be afraid. Come, we've been lovers a long time. Please come back to us."

"Where is Elloran?"

"Elloran's gone. We're alone here, the three of us. The provisions are all here; our floaters, some weapons and things. We won't need food, the thinkhives will provide or else any cities we pass through will know we're Inquestors and feed us. Come on now, Rikeh."

"Still the huntress, aren't you, circling for the kill?"

"I don't know what you mean." Siriss felt a surge of anger

against him. She hadn't fought to keep him at her side this long just to have him desert her. "Are you playing *makrúgh* with me then?"

Arryk looked her full in the face. His eyes were blazing; she recoiled. She had never known him to be angry with her. "It's not want I want, Sirissheh! You and Kelver, you can have your galaxy-dominating games. While I still have a choice—"

Siriss looked at him blankly.

"You don't understand, do you? Come, kiss me and leave me."

But Siriss ran from the room, too confused to answer.

The srinjid (as Sajit called his created choristers) stood a while, frightened at Siriss's abrupt departure. But Arryk called him to sit by him. "Do you have a name, child, or are you just another of the srinjidas?" he said.

He heard the melodious reply, and the translation in his mind: "I do have a name, high one. It is Aoauei."

"Do you know, child, why it is your words come out differently according to the time of day, sometimes high-pitched, sometimes low?"

"I didn't even know, Lord. I listen sometimes to the music of the streets, but I can't understand its purpose. But you do, don't you, being a god? I am awed even to stand in your shadow."

Arryk laughed. "I won't be a god for long."

"How can that be? They've taught me that a god is for-ever." The child was greatly distressed.

"Poor child," Arryk said, "of course we are forever, of course, of course. Go now; fetch me water."

And the srinjid was running off, chatting to himself in squeaky tones that blended into a shimmering musical tex-ture from the courtyard below.

"Arryk."

"Go away, Kevi. You can't talk me into it. It's not for me. You told me how when you were on the farm you watched the Skywall and dreamed of spaceships . . . well, *I* didn't do that. My dreams were of the phoenixes, and of beautiful girls and boys, and of the scarlet snow thawing and swimming in summer and riding the sea serpents. I suppose you'll go on, now, about my duty, and you'll try to make me feel guilty about not having compassion for the human race . . . but powers of powers, what difference could it possibly make to the rest of the universe if I carve out a little niche of oblivion somewhere for myself?"

"Arryk."

He looked up to see Kelver standing in front of him; his face was half in shadow. The shimmercloak rustled softly; its colors were muted, as if it sensed its owner's shadow. Kelver held Arryk's shimercloak out to him. Arryk said, "I'll live in Elloran's palace and serve him his dinner. Elloran's enlightened, he doesn't have his servants' memories wiped whenever they leave Uran s'Varek, you know. That's why our Sajit is so fortunate to be with him."

"Arryk, do you really have a choice?"

"Of course I do!" cried Arryk, anguished.

"Oh, Rikeh . . . do you remember the chocolate dune in Dulsivaras, when we first had sex? You licked the chocolate from my eyes. Strange."

"*You* licked it from my crotch!" said Arryk, smiling suddenly.

"I love you," Kelver said. Arryk looked at him at last, and he saw in him such need, such loneliness.

And so he did not resist when the shimmercloak was thrown over his shoulders, when the strands began their frantic weaving over his body, feeding on his sweat. They stood, without talking, while the cloak grew brighter, bonding to his body, drawing strength from him.

Finally Arryk whispered, "Either way, Kevi, I'm lost now, lost for good." And he buried his head in Kelver's chest and cried.

[decorative script / constructed language glyphs]

den eyáh dássas kaín;
hokhté es-veún:
Enguéstreh, grávah, greúrekeh.
Hókhtan varégas kíndi
hókhtan y'kíndoten vézash
Mílilas shatreíh hi k'níkai kissóndi
z'hártnai shiklátah, y'shélvolten mezhpénah.
Perpáleis kn'dáras brecháqilei hi.
Eih, dássa adássitah.
Den hókhtan on'z'hártnas shiklátah.
Davéznin ma den plánzha;

den dássaran kízna eyáh,
kal hókhtan varégas kíndi,
kal hókhtan y'kíndoten vézash.

There are no more gods in this universe;
but you have come,
Inquestor, solemn, gray-eyed.
Your eyes are the eyes of a child;
Your face a child's face.
But the childsoldiers will devastate
the landscapes of your childhood;
the deserts of chocolate, the forests of marzipan.
You will juggle the stars in your thousand arms,
you, god of the godless.
Not for you are the chocolate deserts.
Shed no tears for boyhood,
for there is no childhood for the gods,
though you have a child's eyes,
and the face of a child.

—from the *Songs of Sajit:* written, in Sajit's boyhood, for
the boy Inquestor Elloran when he had returned from
hunting his first utopia

SIX: THE ART OF ILLUSION

Davaryush entered the viewroom of the delphinoid shipmind, where the walls had been deopaqued to show the raging of the overcosm. Only the astrogator was there: the other passengers, unable to stand the long loneliness, had opted for stasis, and were lodged in pods in the starship's heart. Davaryush stood a while; he had seen the mad light dance thousands of times, and it held no fear for him, this space between spaces, this pinhole subuniverse through which only a delphinoid's living brain, soldered into a ship's hull and mindlinked to a man's, could navigate.

There sat the astrogator; by her belt of iridescent *zhángeshk* feathers he could see she was of the clan of Harren. Slowly she woke from dreamlike contact with the shipmind and saw Davaryush.

"Inquestor! *Hokh'Tón!*" she exclaimed. "I did not know; forgive me for not greeting you properly . . . they did not even tell me that there was an Inquestor on board my delphinoid." Outside, lances of purple flame darted through chrome-yellow fire-rings.

Davaryush smiled. It had been a long time since he'd smiled at one of the short-lived. And he said mildly, "I am not Ton Davaryush z Galléndaran K'Ning anymore. I am only Daavye-without-a-clan, after all. What can I do? My shimmercloak fades, it is dying."

The woman laughed. "You're making fun of a lowly astrogator, Lord. It pleases you to jest; I will listen."

Davaryush saw the simple worship in the woman's eyes; there was no hypocrisy here. By and large the Inquest was looked upon with awe. He knew that he would not have to do very much to continue to act as Inquestor; to move among the common people, exacting their service and even their love. He had had centuries of practice, after all. "Yes," he said wearily, "I jest, I jest." And so it continues, he thought. I shall never be free. I shall always be practicing the art of illusion.

Davaryush thought, for the first time since his expulsion from Uran s'Varek, of the Lady Varuneh. He had been forced to condemn her to death, this woman he had loved, revealing her to be the Grand Inquestor in hiding, Ton Varushkadan el'Kalar Dath, accusing her of being behind the plot to destroy the Inquest. It was not right! For Davaryush was one of the few who knew that Varuneh had been present at the very founding of the Inquest; had been one of the star travelers who had stumbled upon Uran s'Varek and unlocked its secrets and found the means to rule a million worlds. She had been at the beginning . . . surely she should be at the end!

But if I play my *makrúgh* correctly, he thought, and I have relinquished my right to play *makrúgh*, I have allowed them to strip my very name from me . . . the illusion will be complete.

It is hard to give up being an Inquestor, thought Davaryush as he watched the whirl of lights. But I must, I must! It, too, is part of the plan.

And so is the boy.

It was an awesome plan. When he thought of it it felt very cold. They would be so far away from each other, the boy and the girl and the old woman and the old man; their thoughts could never touch at all.

Davaryush wept.

But the short-lived woman was beside him now, whispering, "Oh, *Hokh'Tón*, the tears of an Inquestor are such precious things; you must not shed them so. Oh, I am so moved to see you weep, Lord. They must be tears of great compassion . . . for a world *fallen beyond*, perhaps, or a people gone astray?"

"For all men," Davaryush said for himself alone. And the lights danced for themselves, too, heeding no man, as the astrogator fell back into her trance of pathfinding.

And now Kelver and Siriss and Arryk stepped out of the cavern-labyrinth and into the streets of Shentrazjit. All at once Kelver heard a jangling war of musics; street vendors screeched the names of their wares, a space opera blared forth from a bank of ampli-jewels set into the façade of a public refectory. The young srinjid came with them; when Aoauei spoke, Kelver could hardly make out the shrill piping sounds. The srinjid led them forward with a light skipping gait, his vestigial wings lifting, windruffled. Soon the noise became unbearable.

"Boy," said Kelver, "how can you stand the cacophony of your city?"

"It's hard, Lord. Often I'm in physical pain from it. You see, my Lord, I am a misfit here; they tell me my ears are overly sensitive. The other boys don't hear as well as I. I don't know what it is that wrenches these sounds from our throats. . . ."

"You don't know, then, about Sajit's masterpiece."

"No, Lord. Who is Sajit—an Inquestor such as yourselves?" It was another paradox of the High Inquest then . . . in Elloran's quest for the ultimately beautiful he had also given birth to anguished dissonance . . . he had casually created a race and doomed some of them to perpetual agony.

"How can Elloran do this?" he cried to Arryk, who was walking behind him, hands over his ears.

They had reached the main avenue now, and the noise had become intolerable. "Thinkhive! Give us silence, or at least an illusion of it!" Kelver cried out. And in a moment they were enveloped in a bubble of stillness. The child cried out in delight.

Arryk said, "Elloran needs his music, Kelver. He needs to drown his pain in it. All the Inquestors need something to let them forget."

They reached a concourse of rocky avenues; everywhere the srinjidas thronged; Kelver could see their mouths open in song as they jostled each other. Many, seeing the Inquestors, crowded around; but the silence-bubble, a force-cage thrown over the four of them by the thinkhive, deflected them: they would rush into a shield of nothing and be sent sprawling onto the pavement.

"Will Sajit's song never end?" Kelver said, to no one in particular.

Arryk replied: "No, Kevi. Not in a thousand years; perhaps it will last longer than the Inquest itself. The song is a spiral, each cycle of it giving birth to an infinitesimally more complex variant. The srinjidas will live and die in the song Sajit wrote; when they are born their first cries for food will be in whatever is the prevailing mode for that moment of the song, and when they die their death rattles will add almost imperceptibly to the song's percussive heartthrob."

"You're moved at this, Rikeh? And you don't see the cruelty of it? Look how this one srinjid suffers, because some gene was mislaid by his maker!"

Siriss said, "How can we stop and think of one soul? The smaller compassion is swallowed in the larger." But Arryk, sullen, didn't answer.

A few displacement plates later they entered a rockhewn hall. Sculptures of the srinjidas, all identical, all with their hands outstretched and their throats swollen with silent song, lined the walls; and at the end of it, shadow-shrouded, carved from the granite of the mountain, was the face of Elloran. Their god. His hair was woven from strands of shimmerfur; his eyes were man-sized crystal cabochons; and from them flowed twin waterfalls. The walls blocked out the sounds of outside a little. Here and there were suppliants clutching the altars that smoked with a redolent incense.

Kelver dissolved the silence-bubble; they did not need it now. Here in this temple Elloran had left the provisions for their journey. There were the three slow floaters, which had a maximum speed of only fifteen klomets per second; it would take months to travel one line of longitude, centuries to explore the whole of Uran s'Varek. The floaters were all they would need.

"Elloran has forsaken us," Siriss said. Kelver felt her alarm; he moved over to comfort her.

"No, Sirissheh, Kevi. This is the way it has to be. He is watching us, I'm sure. And we must make him proud."

Kelver saw how deeply Arryk loved the old man; nothing could touch that love, he thought, not even the fall of the Inquest.

"Let's go then," he said.

Each ascended his own floater; and they drifted toward the temple's entrance.

As they reached it, the clamorous tumult assailed their ears once more. "It's the grand climax," Arryk shouted. "We're standing right against the heartbeat of the song!"

Then Aoauei screamed!

"What's he saying?" Kelver cried out to the thinkhive. And

then he heard the words in his mind: *Oh, oh, I hurt so, I hurt so, I hurt so.*

The srinjid had fallen down on the steps of the temple. Its entrance was perched halfway up the mountainslope. Kelver leaped from the floater as it hovered, ready to fly. "What are you doing?" shouted Siriss. The screaming came from all sides now, deafening. Kelver was lifting the neuterchild up, shielding its ears with his arms; and still he shrieked in anguish and the heartrending cries melded into the music of screaming. The wings felt dry and prickly against Kelver's chest. He lifted the child easily; he weighed no more than forty kilograms.

"I can't stand the noise!" Siriss was saying. "Come away, Kevi, come away!"

"I'm taking the child with us!" Kelver shouted, cradling him in his arms. For he remembered Darktouch, the girl from the Dark Country who had been cursed with too much seeing. And so saying he sprang onto his floater and the three of them rose up as one, slicing the air in an arc from slope to peak of the gray mountain. And as they soared pearlskyward, the twenty million shards of song blurred, blended, united into an awesome ocean of music. Gone was the scintillant hardness of their screaming; instead the mountains resonated as a single instrument.

At a subvocalized command from Kelver, the three floaters came together; when they conjoined, pseudopods reached out to yoke them into one. A single darkfield sprang up to englobe them all; and now the music sounded immeasurably distant, like the sound of the Sea of Tulangdaror, Kelver remembered, from the topmost tower of the city of Kallendrang on Gallendys.

At their feet lay the srinjid; he whimpered, and his cries wove pefect counterpoint to the singing city.

"Why did you save him?" Siriss said. "How can you be an Inquestor, and play *makrúgh* with planets and with star systems, if you must stop to save every child who cannot survive in his world?"

"I don't know," Kelver said. "The High Compassion touched me." He knew, though, that it was because the neuterchild's anguish reminded him of Darktouch's.

"Oh, Sirissheh," said Arryk. "Surely you remember how Elloran plucked me from *my* world. I think Kelver will be a very fine Inquestor."

They flew on for some hours, each cocooned in his private thoughts. Kelver thought mostly of the past, of the Throne of Madness, whatever that was. He tried to puzzle out Davaryush's plan, but he couldn't understand it at all; how could he? Davaryush had been Inquestor for four centuries, and Kelver was a sixteen-year-old boy. Presently the neuterchild stirred a little. When he woke he saw the three Inquestors and gave a small cry of terror. And he listened for the city and could hear nothing. At last he said, "I'm free."

"Yes, child," Kelver said. "Your pain is over."

"And ours is only beginning," Arryk said. And Kelver knew that it was true.

Softly Kelver said to Arryk: "I'm sorry that I talked you into coming with us. But it was true; you were running away, throwing it all away."

Arryk said, "Kevi, your gift is that you can turn to a person and say *I love you* and mean it and wrench them apart with it. Your love's a frightening thing. You'll destroy me, and Siriss, with it."

"How can I help myself?"

"The High Compassion touches you," said Arryk, "not us, even though we've studied the Inquestral wisdoms far longer than you. You're a good Inquestor, Kevi. Too good . . . how could a heretic have picked you?"

Had they found him out? Kelver watched the child stir as the three floaters straddled the big wind. Soon music broke out from Aoauei's lips: he was asking for water. The notes, divorced from the music of the city, sounded random, unmelodious; but their timbre was mellow, haunting. *Our pain is only just beginning*, he thought. A night fell: not a night of the outside, but a night programmed into the floaters' darkfield. In that night the three made love, urgently, as though it were for the last time. And as Kelver fell asleep he saw, through crusted eyes, the srinjid, watching them: wide-eyed, solemn, afraid.

Kelver was ahead, somewhere in the hills, practicing the art of illusion. Sometimes Siriss and Arryk could see castles in the distance, floating on clouds; or sometimes ghostly armies of childsoldiers spinning in the wind. The srinjid had gone with Kelver.

"What is he up to, Arryk? What *is* he, really?"

"I don't know."

Siriss looked southward. Behind three ridge-walls that were mountain ranges she could make out a tangled skein of silver strands that was the Folded River; behind that more mountain ridges; beyond that the land of five hundred nations, arranged in the form of a *shtézhnat* board, fashioned for the whimsy of a Ton Karakaël.

"I don't understand him at all!" said Siriss. "He wants to go southward and southward and southward. Soon we'll be beyond civilization. We'll be so far from the great polar thinkhive that we won't be able to make illusions for our pleasure. Emptiness will surround us, swallow us up . . . I think he means to go as far south as he can. Perhaps we should separate, Arryk; we should go back to Elloran."

"Have you decided then? Is the quest-journey over for you?"

"Powers of powers, Rikeh, it's only a formality, isn't it?" she said, despairing.

"We could split up, I suppose. But Elloran charged us with looking out for Kelver."

"Why? He's such a perfect Inquestor. Better than the likes of us," said Siriss bitterly.

"Too perfect. I suspect *makrúgh*. I suspect illusion. I suspect this love into which we have both fallen so easily. . . ."

"Maybe it's time for us to play *makrúgh* with him," Siriss said.

"I don't think you'll win."

"Nor do I. But Elloran once told me that winning is not the object of *makrúgh*."

"We each play for our own reasons."

"I'm going to him now." Siriss ascended her floater and it took to the air. It flew on southward, sensing Kelver far away, where the Folded River met the domain of Ton Karakaël.

He was standing on a cliff ledge overlooking the Folded River; the neuterchild was at his feet, and when he spoke his words echoed a music ten million klomets distant. When Siriss's floater began spiraling down toward them, she saw that there were wild baby pteratygers circling the pair. A gray-maned mother beast watched them solemnly. Siriss saw Kelver pick up the child, terrified at first, and put him on the mother tyger's back. The creature, old, a little rheumatic perhaps, let out a wheezy roar; then up it sprang, spreading its wings, flying in short spasms. Angrily she settled down beside the boy Inquestor, leaped from her floater, cried out to him, "You're not his friend, you know, Kevi, you're an Inquestor!"

Kelver smiled mildly. "You've come just in time," he said, "to go on with our game of *makrúgh*. Look."

Sullen, Siriss stared at the Folded River below their feet. The naked rock face against which they stood was of pure white marble veined with amethyst and gold; beneath that the river twisted in and out, raveling and unraveling like a woman's silver hair. "What is so remarkable?" she said. "There are a dozen rivers like this in Elloran alone; the mad Ton Alkamathdes made them once. It was a pretty conceit, this braiding of the waterways."

"No. Farther off." He pointed.

Behind the next wall of mountains, almost a quarter of the way up where the horizon should be, were dots of cities. Some twinkled; some were black, dead-looking. The land was checkered like a *shtézhnat* board, each square a little nation; but in a real board the squares would have been alternating colors: green, red, green, red. Now some of the squares were black; and they sparkled like fire-onyxes. "The sparks are burning cities," Kelver said. "The black dots are cities that have been gutted, crisped, everyone killed. The twinkling cities are battlefields. Do you want to play *makrúgh*, Siriss, for a few million square klomets of land, a mere few nations? It would be good practice for the future, wouldn't it?"

"Why do you sound so bitter? It is what we were chosen to do. Besides, it may be an illusion. We ourselves may be pawns in some higher *makrúgh* that the Grand Inquestors play. They may be testing us."

"They may at that." The mother beast swooped overhead, and the neuterchild squealed with delight. "Isn't it beautiful, Sirissheh? The winged boy riding the winged beast."

"I've not time for such folly," she said, not wanting to confess that she was jealous, that she wanted to possess Kelver alone, completely.

"Ready for the game, I suppose."

"I challenged you once."

"For my first gift," Kelver said formally, for *makrúgh* often dealt with strange presents and the interpretation of their meaning, "I give you this kiss." With those words they clung to each other. He really needs me! she thought. He, Kelver, who has been granted the greatest of all Inquestral gifts, the

High Compassion . . . he still needs to love me. And she steeled herself and stiffened and did not yield to his embrace.

"I give no gifts," she said. Calling the thinkhive with her mind, she summoned a ghostly *shtézhnat* board from the thin air. "There are our worlds. Your move."

Kelver laughed. "Do you really suppose they're watching us?"

"Always." ·

"What would you say if I were to tell you that the Inquest has a shadow, and that I am part of it? That one day the shadow will overwhelm the light?"

He's trying to scare me, she thought. To upset my playing of *makrúgh*. "I would say that you were lying, Kevi. Nothing will touch the Inquest."

"You heard what Elloran said. *The Inquest falls*."

"He was speaking hypothetically. About a time millennia from now. What lies has that madman Davaryush been feeding you anyway?"

"I will take the red, and you the green."

"Agreed."

Kelver whistled; the mother beast's shadow fell over them as it swooped down with the neuterchild. It came up to Kelver and purred. Siriss thought the *shtézhnat* pieces onto the board. Kelver closed his eyes for a moment; and the pieces came alive suddenly, they were miniature men hacking at each other with little laserknives. Tiny heads rolled; and the green squares were spattered with rivulets of blood.

"I win," he said lightly. "Your squares have turned to my color."

"Illusion!" Siriss shrieked, angry. "Stupid magic tricks any idiot can do!"

Kelver laughed again. Why was it that she felt so vulnerable to his laughter? Was it that when he laughed at her he did not seem to mock her, but to pity her? In a rage she dissolved the *shtézhnat* board; it melted into the wind. "I hate you!" she screamed. But it was the gift of love in him that she hated, for it mocked the awful emptiness she felt inside.

SEVEN: TOY SOLDIERS

    . . . the smoke! As Arryk burst through the mist-veil that separated two warring kingdoms, two squares of the *shtézhnat* board of Ton Karakaël, the stench came from all around. The grass was blackened all the way to the next kingdom, halfway up the sky. The floater threaded a dead city, half-tumbled buildings interlocked into the charred rib cage of some monster.

So ugly . . .

But he hadn't seen people yet. There seemed to be none; there were no serpent-caravans of refugees coiling through the hills. They seemed to have melted into the blasted earth. Where were the others? He had not seen them for days. As he urged his floater higher he could see a grid of gutted cities linked by avenues of ash. In the next kingdom, the square to the south, were signs of life. Here the highways between the cities were rivers of fire. In this land, the grass was the color of garnet; for to create the perfect illusion of a *shtézhnat* board when viewed from a million klomets' distance, a grass-like alga the color of blood had been imported from the world Kailasa . . . Arryk's own homeworld. The sight was not strange to him then; for all his boyhood he had waited for winter and the coming of the scarlet snow. He commanded the floater to proceed to the capital city, named Yoarah.

"Let the fighting cease!" he commanded the thinkhive of Uran s'Varek. "I come as Inquestor, to heal, to judge."

I shall so inform the leaders of the warring armies, came the purr of the thinkhive within Arryk's mind. The floater came to rest on a charred plain.

Arryk saw, in the middle distance, in the next country, a

perfect cone of a volcano, its base sheathed in mist; around it coiled a serpent of green vegetation, slithering a little against bare igneous rock. "What is that?" Arryk said, wondering. And the thinkhive answered him: *That, Arryk, is a mountain that the people worship; about it winds a dragontree; full twenty thousand years has the tree grown, achieving a dim sentience . . . see how it writhes against the warm rock, drinking the heat and the sunlight for its food.*

As the thinkhive spoke Arryk saw what seemed to be thousands of ants trickling down the crimson plain ahead. "The war!" he cried. "I must go to them!"

Soft! They come to you, Inquestor; for their god has told them of your coming.

At once Arryk heard a whisper as of a far ocean. It grew louder. They were not ants now, as they descended toward him down the endlessly sloping landscape. And now there were other antlike men, their armor gold-glittering as it caught the light. Arryk urged his floater up, and now he could see the battle raging from above. There were thousands of men and women beneath him, but their roaring was like a single creature's. Now walls of fire burst from the ground and phalanxes marched steadfastly into the flames. The weaponry was ancient: no childsoldiers with laser-irises here, but wheeled chariots that spewed out streams of brimstone. Bodies lay in little heaps, blood blending into the blood-colored grass. "It's horrible," said Arryk. "Is this what we Inquestors are here for? To make and unmake such wars as these?"

No! To prevent them. To take the guilt of them upon yourselves. To be the beings of compassion always, Rikeh. And Arryk felt anger smoldering in him for the first time. For even Elloran, Elloran whom he worshipped, had said that wars must be. "I will go down to them godlike, in a blaze, playing on their terror," he said.

As you wish.

Arryk closed his eyes. The noise of the battle grew louder; the smell of blood and burning nearly choked him. "Light," he cried, "clothe me in light. . . ." And he thought the dreamthoughts that Inquestors learned on Uran s'Varek, the thoughts that built illusions; and at once there sprang up around him a corona wreathed with rainbows. From the far mountains came shrill trumpets, drowning the deathroar. At a wave of his hand came thunder and lightning. How can they fight now? he thought. They must fall on their knees and worship me; and I will decree peace.

Slowly he made the floater carry him groundward. As he stepped forth he was in the midst of a sea of human backs; they had fallen prostrate among the corpses. "Your war is ended," he said softly; through an ampli-jewel in the floater the voice carried across the field. And he let his corona dissolve slowly, expanding and thinning until it was one with the sky's unchangeable radiance.

Three old men were coming toward him now; they wore black robes; each had a ruff around his neck, made, Arryk could see, from the fabric of dead shimmercloaks. The man in the center came close and kissed the hem of Arryk's shimmercloak.

"Victory," he said, his voice rasp-dry. "You give us victory, god from the north. You will be our god now, and give us many victories."

Arryk saw that wheeled mechanicals, tall as houses, were sliding through the fields, sucking up the bodies of the fallen through snakelike vacuum-pseudopods. "I didn't come to give you victory," he said gently. He tried to sound like Elloran, so assured, so understanding; but it was not the same. The words came out dry and tangled.

"But of course you did!" said the elder. "Listen. I am High Priest of this country. Our King was dead, and we feared; but then you came, a living star fallen from the sky. The enemy despaired, seeing you approach from the north, which is our country. They are our subjects now."

"You invaded this square of country?"

"Yes, god; it was a dispute over the slaying of King Vazhek the Brave last year. We have vowed vengeance. Look—" Coming up behind the old men was a litter borne by eight man-shaped mechanicals; upon it lay a rotting corpse clothed in finery and wearing a golden crown. The old men turned to the body. A gust of putrescence assailed Arryk's nostrils. "Oh, King Vazhek," they intoned, "see what a conquest we have made for you . . . and now the god has come to live in your house."

"We will fashion another such litter, god of the north; and you and the king whose cause you have blessed will ride together toward the next battle—"

"But I command that you cease! I am of the Inquest!"

"I have heard of this Inquest, god; other gods have spoken

of it. It is far away, is it not? We listen not to them but to you, our god, our god."

Arryk pushed down his burning anger. This might be some test that the Inquest had provided for him. "Tell me more," he said, "of the war's causes."

The old one said: "It became inevitable, god, when the land two squares south of here acquired two gods of its own, a boygod and a girlgod. . . ."

"Kelver and Siriss!" Arryk cried out. He had not meant this to be a game of *makrúgh*. But they had started without him. Suddenly he hated them both. They didn't need him!

"I will be borne into battle with the corpse of your King," he said slowly. And the High Priest turned and mumbled the words to the nearest still-prostrate soldiers; they jumped up, their armor crinkled and blood-edged from hand-to-hand fighting, and gave out the tidings in the local lowspeech; a murmur spread out over the field, an audible ripple of sound that crescendoed into a thunder of cheering. And for a single moment, Arryk felt like a god; but then the silent rage stirred deep within his thoughts, and would not be stilled. Now came a throne of granite from the volcano to the south, dragged forward by a hundred captives; and as he ascended it the roar rose higher, and as he sat down he heard a collective catch of breath, a momentary silence, before the roaring came again and again. . . .

And at his feet they laid the decaying King, upon whose face worms feasted and maggots writhed. His mouth was open in a deathgrin; and Arryk saw that two of his teeth had been carved from rubies.

When I return from my quest-journey, he thought to himself, I will make no deserts of chocolate, no forests of marzipan. I will not build cities that sing. How can I love beautiful things, knowing that . . . it is for people like these that I must feel the High Compassion?

He searched his heart for compassion, but he found it empty. And already, after only a few sleeps' absence, the love that he and Kelver and Sirissheh had shared seemed unreachably far away.

She awoke in Kelver's arms; a scale of the dragontree, bed-sized and covered with gray-green down, had been their resting place. Aoauei was curled up at their feet. Siriss stepped lightly off the dragonscale, thinking Kelver still asleep; the bower-bed bounced a little, as though it were on springs, for it rested on a framework of hooplike tree branches that formed the rib cage of the dragontree. She sprang down to the ground; they were halfway up the volcano's northerly face, and when she looked to the north she could see the mountain mistwall that divided the *shtézhnat*-board kingdoms from the land of the Folded River, and the more distant ridges where the pteratygers played, and beyond them the land where stood Shentrazjit; it was a blur of brown and green and gold, a belt of verdure between two bands of black mountains, each half a hokh'klomet wide, but seen only as strips of darkness. For the land of melting colors sloped upward to infinity.

"Kevi, Kevi . . . they've left food for us." At their feet lay, on a rug, the skin of some peacock-furred animal, pitchers of iced zul, and plates of péftifesht pastry sprinkled with sweet spices. The contents of a central platter were concealed by a cover of woven wicker. Kelver sprang down beside her; he was trying to separate his shimmercloak from hers, for when they made love the shimmercloaks, too, mated, and could not be untangled.

"I can't pry them loose from each other!" He laughed. A breeze sprang up, whipping the locked shimmercloaks over his shoulders; Siriss's fell free, and lay flapping on a granite boulder, blushing pale pink against ultramarine. They lay down on the warm rug now; Kelver reached for the nearest pastry and devoured it hungrily. "Shall we play *shtézhnat* now?" he said, taunting her gently.

Siriss said, "You have won me over, Kevi. We should not play *makrúgh* over a few miserable squares of land, should we?"

"Where is Arryk? We've not heard from him in many sleeps."

"I don't know. I am afraid for him, Kelver. We shouldn't have abandoned him."

"He craved aloneness."

"To be an Inquestor is always to be alone. When we are all together, the three of us, we can sometimes forget that."

"Perhaps he doesn't want to forget."

"Perhaps." She put her hand over the wicker lid. "Come, let's see what the main course is." Daintily she lifted it. It contained two human hearts.

She struggled to control her repugnance; Kelver did not

hide his. "I never asked for this!" he cried. "I never wanted to be a god to barbarians!"

Quickly she replaced the cover. "What's happening?" she said. "It's a test of some kind. A higher *makrúgh* is being played; I sense it in the air. There's something not quite real about all this—"

"Davaryush was right!" Kelver said.

"What do you mean, he was right? What madnesses did the heretic teach you, Kevi?"

"Perhaps, Sirissheh, when I told you that I mean to be the Inquest's shadow, I was not joking. . . ."

"What are you talking about? I thought we had declared a truce in our *makrúgh*, that we would make peace in the name of our love, and bring peace, too, to the natives of this land."

But Kelver seemed not to be listening to her at all. Presently the neuterchild joined them too; he ate quickly, nimbly, twittering as he ate.

Then, from the stirring of leaves, Siriss knew that others were coming. Now she saw the procession: winding up the dirt road that coiled beneath the shade of the dragontree, huge carts pulled by yoked mechanicals; and on the carts small temple-tents of silk.

When the caravan reached the two Inquestors, it halted and curtains were drawn. The mechanicals, their old joints creaking, fell into place, making a rude metal staircase; and the Child-priestess of the Smoking Mountain, who had made them welcome many sleeps before, stepped out. She was a beautiful child, her face unblemished by guilt or time. Her hair, stiffened with strands of iridium, supported a coronet of gold; it must have been hard to bear the weight. Likewise her long robe did not flutter in the wind, for the hems were weighted with pellets of bullion.

"Oh, gods," said the Child-priestess Unyati, "today we have sacrificed to you the hearts of children, for war is coming. And you will ride ahead of our armies to show those of Kethnerat that they shall not step one klomet within the sacred country that guards the Smoking Mountain and the Dragontree."

Siriss said, "Child-priestess, we did not come to lead you in battle, but to make a peace."

"They come with a god that says otherwise. Already they have devastated the kingdom of Yoarazhnat, and the land there is red not from the grass but from blood. They have their own god, Boygod and Girlgod."

"Arryk!" cried Kelver. The neuterchild looked up, startled, a piercing high tone loosed from his lips.

"We didn't ask for *makrúgh*," said Siriss, "but we are getting it anyway." And to the Child-priestess she said, "We will go, and we will parley with their god, and we will cause them to return, without bloodshed."

"But that is not how such things are done!" The Child-priestess's voice had lost none of its ice-edged innocence.

"It is our will as gods," Kelver said. "Lo! We return to you your hearts, uneaten. . . ."

Then the Priestess burst out, sounding like a child at last, "But they'll kill me if they can't have a war!"

"Trust us," said Siriss. But the Child-priestess had already turned her back on them, beckoning them to follow.

They took their places on thrones of sculpted granite within the wheeled temples. At their feet the srinjid played. The caravan began to move, jerkily, down the dirt road. The srinjid made a face, and Kelver smiled.

"What do you see in him?" Siriss asked. There was so much about the boy she could not begin to fathom.

"I see," Kelver said, "a creature much like you and me; a being constrained to sing one song, a song he did not write, just as you and I are forced to follow the path of *makrúgh*, of the High Compassion. We do not choose what we are."

"But there are times when I think you choose. I think you are more than we are."

But again Kelver did not listen; he had turned to play with the srinjid child, an alien like himself.

Unyati's army was in readiness; at its head went the double granite thrones of Siriss and Kelver, drawn by the metal man-mimics. Then behind came the silken temple where sat Unyati. Behind them rode thirty signifers on steeds of metal, whose paws clanked in loud unison against the cobbled high road that led from the Smoking Mountain through the city of Karafkyt, a city of blue domes studded with starlike diamants. Outside the city, and down the high road for many klomets on either side, were vast triangles of metal from which dangled the desiccated heads of wrongdoers; small clumps of people gathered at their bases, staring, jeering, mourning. The army grew even as Kelver watched; every time he looked behind it was as if the monster centipede had grown another joint. Here a company of archers wearing kilts of beaten bark; here slingers, women naked but for the long slings wound about their waists and the stone-pouches that guarded their private parts. Here catapults followed by braziers from which green flame flared.

"If we were not here, drawn into this war against our wills," Siriss said, "I should think this processional most quaint, most primitive. But as it is it frightens me. These are weapons that kill slowly, with great pain."

"Are the childsoldiers that we command any better, because they can slice whole buildings in two if they are careless with their glances?"

"No. But this war is not on a grand scale. Elloran told me that war is necessary, because stagnation is the doom of man; that they limit our population and hone our spirits. But this is personal war, petty war, ugly war."

"It is all like that. Either you have Inquestors sitting at dinner and sipping on their sweet zul as they trade the deaths of planets . . . or you have this. I see no difference," Kelver said. Davaryush had never told *him* that war had to be. As a child he had believed it; he had dreamed of becoming a childsoldier himself. But now he couldn't believe in dreams anymore.

The cart that held their thrones bounced on the rocky pavement. "At least," Siriss said, "this war is not to be. When we see Arryk we'll talk things over; we'll come to some decision that will be for the best."

"Yes. Yes." But Kelver could not believe it. He called out to the neuterchild who sat at their feet, flapping his vestigial wings. Aoauei came and sat beside him. This child is like Darktouch, he thought, who could see too well to belong to her own world. And the srinjid sang to himself, low flutelike tones colored by shrill melismas.

Presently Kelver could see the silver line of the river that bordered the nation of the Smoking Mountain. As they reached the border, Kelver looked back and saw that the volcano was smoking a little: a puffy gray spiral that uncannily echoed the coiling dragontree beneath. He whipped around again, though, hearing Aoauei's cry. And Siriss was trembling too.

Fording the river now was another army. For banners their signifers held up poles from which depended strings of human skulls. Beyond the river, in the red country of Yoarazhnat, were lines of men, metal-garbed, their helmets topped with plumes from the crest of the opal moa. A hush fell over Unyati's army. The Child-priestess approached the two gods; the signifers' standards, upon which were depicted the symbol of the Smoking Mountain, began to belch forth a blue fire that reeked of brimstone.

"The parley!" Kelver cried out. "Let their god come to us!"

Unyati stood proudly, seemingly emotionless; but Kelver saw that she clenched back tears. What had the gods done to these people by suggesting that their war is canceled? Had they unwittingly destroyed something vital to the people's beliefs, something that might crush even their will to live? Kelver began to see for the first time the appalling emptiness within the High Compassion. . . .

But now came trumpeters in chariots drawn by giant birds. From the spokes of their chariot wheels gushed the same sulfurous fire. They halted and sounded a shattering sennet.

The army of Kethnerat did not move, but began to sing a taunting-song; where Kelver stood the lowspeech words were unclear, but the tone was unmistakable. Approaching now were the mounted signifers of the enemy, their skullstrings clattering against the standardpoles like windchimes. And at their head was another granite throne such as Kelver and Siriss sat upon; slowly the mechanicals dragged it forward. In carts behind the throne stood old men in black robes; perhaps they were priests, as Unyati was.

"Look!" said Siriss. "Arryk isn't alone!"

"There's someone beside him. Who is it?"

Then Kelver saw what it was.

There, enthroned beside the beautiful boy, whom they had both held in their arms, was a grisly corpse. And now they were face-to-face, gods addressing gods.

Kelver stared at Arryk for a long time. Was it possible for a boy to look so old? His hair, pressed down by the coronet of gold, was matted; his eyes wild with anger. "Rikeh," he said softly. "Rikeh, come back to us. We are not playing *makrúgh* with you. We are the ones who have loved you, Rikeh."

Arryk said, "I never asked for this." As if in answer the corpse's head lolled to one side, striking Arryk's neck. He did not push it away. "They want me for their god of death, Kelver."

"But we're Inquestors! We can force peace upon them—if

necessary we can summon the childsoldiers to enforce it!"
said Siriss.

"Yes. Of course. I had forgotten." But Arryk made no
move toward them. He seemed strangely drained. Impetu-
ously, Kelver sprang from his throne and went toward Arryk's.
A dozen mechanicals surrounded him, their metal limbs clanking ominously.

"Let him pass," Arryk said: a voice so far away. . . .

Kelver ascended the throne; and now Siriss was with him,
too, and the neuterchild, who followed him always, as a pet
dog might. The smell of decay was everywhere; even over
Arryk's shimmercloak worms crawled here and there. Kelver
said, "Don't be lost, Rikeh. Come back to us. When we are
all three together we are more than just three people. Our
love will sustain you, Rikeh." And the three embraced, their
shimmercloaks rustling and slithering one into another, while
the corpse grinned with its ruby teeth—

Unyati cried out: "Our gods betray us!" The three Inquestors
broke away to see the fire standards and the skull standards
raised up as the metal steeds reared. A crashing sound came
from the north as ten thousand men forded the river at a
dead run. The charioteers sounded an alarm; at once volleys
of fireballs rocketed into the sky. As the army of Kethnerat
reached the southern bank there came a thunder of ten
thousand footfalls, and a wild cacophony of war paeans.

Kelver shouted out, "We've made peace! Unyati, don't you
understand?" But Unyati could not speak; an arrow had pierced
her throat, but she stood there still, like a holosculpture, the
wind not ruffling a strand of her iridium-stiffened hair.

As the two armies collided there came a crunch of metal
against metal amplified ten thousandfold. "They won't touch
us!" Siriss said. "We are inviolate!" It was true enough; the
armies had parted on either side of them. The three gods and
the corpse and the srinjid stood in a puddle of stillness.
Rivers of fire and blood ran through the armies. The ringing
of ten thousand swords resounded like a vast gamelan music.

Kelver said, "When this is over we'll go on, southward,
together."

Arryk did not answer him. Kelver saw that the rage inside
him could never be quieted now. And suddenly it burst
forth, ugly, uncontrollable: "I *will* not have this war, Kelver!
I will stop it in the only way left to me!"

"No!" Kelver shouted.

But Arryk had closed his eyes and seemed to be subvocalizing to the thinkhive of Uran s'Varek. And Kelver could see his lips move suddenly, in the words *Ishá ha, ishá ha; destroy, destroy, destroy*.

Siriss said, "You should not have summoned them—"

But Kelver saw them already. A smudge they were against the distant upward slope of landscape. Then closer, ten silvergleaming pods that had flown southward at Arryk's command, bursting through the displacement fields that ringed the world. The pods hovered over the battle for a moment; then they split open, and Kelver saw what looked like thousands of locusts in a swarm sweeping downward—

Came a war cry from the sky, thousands of trebly children's voices, shrill and pitiless . . . the most terrifying sound in all the Dispersal of Man—

> *Ishá ha, ha, ha!*
> *Ishá ha ha heiy ha!*
> *Ishá ha! Ishá ha!*
> *Ishá ha ha heiy ha!*

—and then the childsoldiers dived in V-shaped waves over the plain; when they neared the fighting armies their laser-irises spewed forth streams of deadly light. Enemies collapsed headless into each other's arms, their necks jetting out fountains of blood. With each dive another line of soldiers fell, sliced by the killing light; and still they came, the childsoldiers, each on his hoverdisk, his eyes his only weapon. . . .

And now a convoy was swooping down toward the throne of the Inquestors. There was fire everywhere; a wall of fire surrounded them, and the air was thick with the stench of brimstone and charred flesh.

"Lord," Aoauei screamed in his songspeech, "they are coming to kill you!" He jumped up to defend Kelver; a killing lightray cut him cleanly in two.

· "Aoauei—" Kelver screamed. He saw the boy's arms turn upward, imploring, his mouth open in an unborn scream; then, a trick of the wind as the lightray sheared through his body cavity, and out of the death-frozen throat, a high-pitched note, crystal-pure; and then the body's lower half thudded onto the bloodied grass. Kelver caught the boy's upper half in his arms. Wind whistled through his dead lungs, and a few more high tones were wrung from his dead lips, heartrendingly beautiful.

The childsoldier responsible came down to hover at their level, his black cape slung smartly over his shoulders.

"*Hokh'Tón*," he said, "we have done as you commanded. The armies are no more."

"But the neuterchild—"

"How could we know he was not dangerous? For what are a million lives compared to yours, whose High Compassion touches us all?" Could the boy be taunting him, with his guileless voice? No; it must be the formula they were all taught to repeat.

"Go!" Arryk cried. "Go, go!"

"*Sheyóh! Sheyóh! Sheyá hoh, hoh!*" the childsoldier called out in his clear voice. The sky echoed him. He whirled once and sprang high into the air; and soon the childsoldiers had gathered into their swarm and disappeared into the gray-green northland.

Silence fell.

Kelver stared at the corpse upon the throne. "This is what we shall all become," he said.

But even as he spoke a curious thing happened: the corpse began to blur, to melt into thin air, and where the odor of putrescence had been came a sweet scent, like crushed kyllap leaves.

"What's happening?" Siriss said.

The firewall fizzled out. They stood in the midst of a plain of corpses; and even as they looked, the bodies began to dissolve. . . .

The earth shook! "The Smoking Mountain!" Kelver cried. It was erupting now. The Dragontree, waked by the warmth, was writhing against the black mountainside. And all around them the bodies were melting dissipating into the air and the granite thrones themselves were softening vanishing and Kelver saw the Smoking Mountain burst asunder and

The light! They stood in a hall of a palace from whose walls emanated a soft radiance. They were walking up to a table at which two figures sat. Each wore a shimmercloak; and they were peering closely at something on the table. All along the far wall, stretching up as far as Kelver could see, were racks of masks: death masks, mummer's masks, opera masks, masks of demons and divinities; a moving ladder ran along this wall, and an aged old man, halfway up it, was wiping away at one of the golden masks.

"Visitors," said a voice.

Another voice . . . a familiar one . . . said, "You see, the childsoldiers *were* summoned. I was not wrong, Karakaël. You see, our *shtézhnat* is at a stalemate." And it was Ton Elloran who looked up from the table, and it was a *shtéznat* board they had been hunched over.

Kelver cried out: "Illusion! All illusion!" And he let the half-corpse of the srinjid slip from his arms at last. Unobtrusively, a mechanical spirited it away. "The srinjid died for the sake of a shadow!"

And Elloran said, "When will you children learn? In the dance of time we are all shadows, Kevi, Rikeh, Sirissheh."

"Ton Elloran," Arryk whispered, "you have truly mastered illusion."

"Karakaël and I have been playing with the thinkhive of Uran s'Varek for many centuries," Elloran said. To his sparring partner he said, "Another round, old friend?"

Karakaël looked up. Kelver saw that he wore a golden mask, with a face like a woman's; living serpents slid in and out of its eye sockets. "Visitors," he repeated. "A different mask, I think. Children, forgive an old man's eccentricity. Sirrah! The seventh one from the top row, the one with the golden eyelids," he cried out to the one who worked at dusting the racks of masks. The slave came down presently and Karakaël turned coyly around to change his mask. When he turned back Kelver saw that his face was now the face of a young hero, ebony in hue, the eyes of gold leaf with lids that snapped open and closed by some mechanical device. "I have not shown my face in five hundred years," said the strange Inquestor.

Kelver looked at the faces: the one concealed, unreadable, the other so open, so wise, so seeming-compassionate. A terrible hatred welled up in him. He knew now what Davaryush had meant by the curse that touches all Inquestors.

For a moment he remembered the light on the Sound: its purity, its absoluteness.

"You High Ones," he said, despairing, "why do you make illusions? Is it to hide the pain of power! To make beautiful that which must by its nature be ugly: death, violence, hatred?"

But Elloran and Karakaël did not answer him: they were

intent upon their game. Raging, Kelver stormed out of the palace, not looking behind to see whether the others followed.

On a bare plain, against the roaring wind—

"His illusions killed the srinjid, the innocent!" Kelver was screaming. Siriss came between the two of them.

"He meant only to teach us responsibility!" Arryk said. "It was my fault, not Elloran's. It was wrong for me to call the childsoldiers! We should not have sought to impose peace upon these people . . . it is utopianism! The ugliest of heresies!"

Siriss said, "Be still . . . it's over now . . . we're still together. . . ."

Their anger subsided a little. Siriss looked from one to the other. She saw in Arryk naked rage; and she knew that if it were not checked this rage would turn inward and feed upon his own heart . . . for Arryk was too compassionate to hate the universe; only himself could he hate. She saw Arryk's beauty contorted by this pain. But in Kelver's eyes she did not see this hatred: she saw only the edge of a terrible sorrow. When Kelver spoke he was calm now, unemotional.

"Siriss, Arryk," he said, "I plan to go southward as far as I can: beyond the lands where the Inquestors dwell, into the older lands of long-dead races . . . my quest is of a different order from yours. The Inquest falls, friends: and I am for the Throne of Madness, to seek it out, whatever it may mean, to find out its secrets. For though the Inquest acknowledges only the three thrones, and dismisses the other as a myth, a symbol . . . I know that its shadow falls always over the other three. Do you know where the Throne of Madness is?"

"Of course, Kevi," said Siriss. "Everyone knows that. It is at the pole, where the stars fall to their deaths."

"Have you ever seen it?"

"No."

"Let's go then. I see my mission more clearly now: for if the Inquest is the shadow that darkens the Dispersal of Man, then I shall be the shadow's shadow . . . it's the High Compassion that speaks through me, don't you understand? The doctrine of transience that the Inquest preaches . . . it implies the Inquest's end!"

As Kelver spoke the wind fell to a whisper. Siriss looked southward: the green never seemed to change at all. She was afraid. She felt a different kind of love for Kelver now: it was not passion, but a firm, hard, knotted thing.

Arryk said: "Kelver, when I first met you I loved you: we were so alike! The way we had grown up, the way we had been snatched up into the arms of the Inquest . . . I don't know you anymore. I must believe Elloran, Kevi, because I owe him everything. I don't want to be a shadow, always hiding, always fearful that my heretical beliefs will slip out, waiting for a chance to stab the likes of Elloran in the back. Elloran has tempted you, Kelver, and you have fallen ignominiously; you have failed the very first test! I am for the light, not the shadow."

"Do you call it light, to rain destruction down upon thousands, to pulverize planets with a single utterance?"

"It is necessary!" Arryk shouted; it was a cry of despair. "I *will* not have you crush everything I've ever believed in!"

"Then it's better that we part now."

"Yes. It is better."

And Arryk turned his back on the two of them, and walked slowly toward the palace of Ton Karakaël, a haze of burnishglitter to the north.

Siriss started to follow.

"Sirissheh? Will you abandon me too?" said Kelver.

She stopped.

Slowly she turned to see Kelver's face. He seemed to be remembering something far away. "Let me tell you," Kelver said, "of the light on the Sound within the Skywall mountain of Gallendys. . . ."

And she found herself answering him, "No, Kelver, no; I will never leave you." For he was beautiful in his grief.

EIGHT THE SEPULCHER

He heard the familiar voices of children . . . surely they were not the same ones as before, though. How long had it been? A century, perhaps? How could he know? But this was the same spot where he had met old Ernad; Davaryush was sure of it. The grass was blood-red, waist-tall, wind-tousled. Then came the children, tugging him forward along the stony path toward the first of the displacement plates.

"Qithe qithembara; udrés a kílima shtoísti!" they called to him: *Soul, renounce suffering; you have danced on the face of the sun.*

At last, through a scarlet thicket of spiderlike trees, Davaryush could see the house where he had rested so long ago . . . when he had come to hunt the utopia of Shtoma. It twisted up from the wood, a structure of transparent domes, open to Udara's light. And now he did not flinch from the embrasure of that joygiving light, the radiance of that sentient sun whose power he had once tried to crush. He bathed in the joy, the joy. . . .

An old woman, fragile but still handsome, came forward to greet him. She smiled; there was something strangely familiar about her . . . like a young girl who had once tended him. . . .

"I knew you would come back one day," she said. "You were the last of the Inquestors to come here, you know. We told you everything. Don't you remember me?"

"Alk," said Davaryush. "The daughter of Ernad." So the old man who had first greeted him on Shtoma was long dead then.

"Grandmother has told us so much!" said a young boy. "You're a legend here, Daavye! Your first coming here, frightened, unable to face the joy. Your dancing on the face of the sun, your liberation."

Davaryush smiled at the child and said, "What are you called, pretty child?"

He said, "*Qithe qithembara*, Lord. My name is Eshly, after my uncle who died in childhood."

"I was there when he died," Davaryush said. The memory surfaced for a moment, troubling him; but then he was touched by Udara again, and it washed away his grief. "I am glad to be here," he said.

"It is our home now, Daavye." Whose voice was this? He looked past old Alk, who had been but a stripling when Davaryush had last come to the land of the cadent lightfall, and he saw a young woman. Her hair was long and dark as space; her skin pale as if it had never known suns' light; and her eyes were daunting-dark. She laughed a little; it was a young girl's laughter. "Do you not know me, Daavye?" she said. It was a low voice; she spoke as if still unsure of human speech. It was this that told Davaryush who it was.

"Darktouch," he said at last.

"Oh, Daavye," said the woman, no longer the girl she had been when she and Kelver had fled to the twin cities of Effelkang and Kallendrang to wring answers from the Inquestors' lips. "You are so old now."

Davaryush said, "I have been to Uran s'Varek and returned without my very name. I am not Ton Davaryush z Galléndaran K'Ning, but simply Daavye-without-a-clan, Darktouch."

"And Kelver? What of Kelver?"

"He's our only hope now! But I have done a terrible thing to him. I stood there like a stone and did not answer him; not a single word of comfort or explanation. I think I have delivered him up to the curse of the Inquestors . . . I was a fool, Darktouch, to think that a stripling could do what I and others could not!"

When Darktouch answered him she sounded strangely calm, as though the conflicts of which he spoke no longer had power over her. She said, "Daavye, you've forgotten how he came with me across the wasteland of Zhnefftikak and braved the ghost people, when he had not even yet seen the light on the Sound. I know he will be true to your vision. You must be at peace now. I have dwelt in Udara's radiance for many years now, waiting for you. Soon we will dance on the sun again, and you will be at one with the great joy. . . ."

They walked on toward the house, and Davaryush talked of utopias, while the children chattered endlessly.

And so there were only the two of them remaining when they left the country of Ton Karakaël. Once, when Karakaël's domain was far behind, they looked northward and saw, hanging halfway up the landscape that had no end, a little *shtézhnat* board, resting as if it were on a table of mist; and they knew that the two old Inquestors had returned to their game. Kelver said: "It's too vast for me, too vast, I can't go on, I can't, I can't." And Siriss saw how the fire in his eyes had dimmed; and she feared for him. For she knew now that Kelver was far more than what he had seemed. And so they flew on; for a hundred sleeps they did not even speak, though they would sometimes make love, swiftly, hungrily, as animals mate. Sometimes they would link their floaters; sometimes he would be flying far ahead, and only the thinkhive could direct Siriss's floater to where he was. But still she followed him; she was in love, she believed.

Another time she said what she had been meaning to ask for many sleeps: "Why are we going southward, Kevi, when everyone knows the Throne of Madness is at the pole?"

Kelver said, not looking at her, "Isn't it the Inquestral way to do everything by opposites? To kill in compassion's name, to destroy utopias in order to maintain peace?"

She didn't know how to answer him. They passed through territories that lesser Inquestors ruled: the land of Orimunden, where the natives were poets of scent, creating sensuous compositions out of perfumes that hung over their cities, shifting from one fragrance to another in stately rhythms; the land of Arrikaeri, where mountains were carved into the likenesses of extinct animals; another land, nameless, where dragontrees ten thousand klomets long coiled around each other in a slow dance of mating. Now many territories had no names; for the Inquest had forgotten them. There were continents empty but for a few souls, hermits, sometimes Inquestors like themselves who had gone on their quest-journeys and after centuries of question still not returned to Rhozellerang to be formally acknowledged Inquestor. There was an abandoned palace of woven shimmerfur stretched out on columns of etchveined porphyry; the walls were painted with words in a language that even the thinkhive could not construe.

Three sleeps they rested there; but Siriss was restless, because she could not break into Kelver's solitude at all. At times she wished for the old carefree days; she and Elloran, the palace of Varezhdur, the trips to pleasure planet after pleasure planet hunting for beautiful things and beautiful bodies. She imagined herself a huntress again, shadowing Kelver in the forest, perhaps. But he did not seem to notice her troubles.

They passed the pteratyger corrals of Ton Ynyoldeh: in the distance they seemed spatters of pink against the sky. As the floaters drew near they seemed like swarms of pink butterflies, and nearer still like exaltations of rose-colored birds; only when they flew straight through the midst of the pteratygers did they hear the yowlings and the mew-tinged roarings as the great beasts circled, crying out sometimes in their blurred purry highspeech. Still Siriss waited for Kelver to say something; but he did not, and as they flew through Ton Ynyoldeh's armory, and saw people bins that had returned from some war, each disgorging its million stasis-frozen refugees into the air like the spores of rosellas, he only frowned a little. In another nameless country, where trees grew tall enough to obscure the sky and the rubbing of their topmost branches issued forth a lugubrious music, as though the stridulations of crickets had been slowed down to the frequency of heartthrobs, they stopped again, and made love; but at the end Siriss heard him cry out the name *Témberash, Témberash*, Darktouch, Darktouch.

She broke away from him. "Who is Darktouch?" she said. It was like that time in the court of Elloran, when they had first made love.

But this time Kelver told her the whole story, omitting nothing. When he was through, Siriss said, "So that is why you never seem to be at peace. These imagesongs you saw have driven you mad, Kevi."

"Perhaps." He leaned back against a tree trunk on which clung a carpet of soft moss.

"And you've thrown yourself into my power, Kevi. Why? You know that I am bound to the Inquest. That I must either tell the Grand Inquestors above me, or clutch this knowledge to myself, to use against you in *makrúgh*?"

"Arryk has guessed already," said Kelver. "Sirissheh, if you love me, you must try to understand; and if you don't, then you will leave me, and they will come for me, and they will strip my name from me as they did to Ton Davaryush."

"The Inquest is bigger than you or I," said Siriss. Surely it was unconscionable hubris for a lone boy to take on the known universe of man. What could be so powerful as to possess him to do this thing? How could a mere interplay of light and song change someone so much? She had heard the phrase *The Inquest falls* a hundred times from the lips of Grand Inquestors; but she thought such a fall would be millennia away . . . and yet the Inquest itself taught that the brightest moment of the day was also the moment where night begins to fall. She had been so sure of herself once.

Kelver said, "Has your love waned so soon, then, Sirissheh? You said you would never leave me." He spoke without anger; she sensed that he thought it inevitable.

"No, it hasn't, Kelver!" she said, because she could not bear his grief.

"The Inquest has killed your love," said Kelver, "as surely as it has stifled its million worlds, and murdered the songs of the Windbringers on Gallendys."

"You're mad, mad, mad!"

"I am for the Throne of Madness." He stood up then and summoned his floater; it broke through the ceiling of treetops and fell softly at his feet. "Arryk has left me already. He'll find only illusions though. We have mastered the art of illusion, we Inquestors, until we ourselves have fallen our illusions' victims. Go back to your emptiness, Sirissheh." Again she marveled, because even as he damned her he spoke with compassion. She couldn't leave him, not even after this dismissal.

She watched as he mounted his floater and closed his eyes, subvocalizing a command to the thinkhive. He did not look back as she called her own floater and bade it follow his. They broke through the country's leafy roof and made for the south, accelerating to a blur.

After another three sleeps the floaters dived down to the surface of the Crystallizing Ocean. It was a band of water one million klomets wide that stretched all the way from the western void-gulf to the eastern. Walls of force separated the little seas from each other; each sea was a saturated solution of some brightly colored substance, and within each sea grew crystals, most as large as palaces, some as large as continents, for they had been growing since before man came to Uran s'Varek. As they looked southward, the water stretched to the very limits of their vision; there were squares of amethyst, of turquoise, of emerald, of topaz-colored water, and every shade between; in the far distance the squares were so small they were mere scintillant dots of clashing hues; the total effect was as a field of ocean sprinkled with jeweldust. In the middistance were continents of glass linked by bridges of force within which was encaptured and time-frozen the stuff of mist.

"Kelver!" she cried. "Look, look!" From the sea beneath there jutted sparkling octahedrons of clear purple.

Kelver said, "Let's go to those crystal continents."

They floated on. Siriss called out to the thinkhive: "How much more land is there to cover, thinkhive?"

And the answer came: *You have covered a mere twenty hokh'klomets, Ton Siriss k'Varad es-K'Ning. It is almost four hundred million more klomets to the southernmost tip of the segment Ellorin, where the southern void begins.*

Siriss despaired of ever making Kelver stop. She, too, had guessed now where he was headed. She said to Kelver, "I'm too tired."

He said, "I didn't ask you to follow me." And he accelerated again, disappearing into misthaze; but she followed him, and soon they were cruising at the maximum speed of fifteen klomets a second, the floaters matching each other speed for speed. Sometimes, when one slowed or the other sped up, he would blur into nothing, and a second later his form would be reconstituted against the rushing patchwork of the many-colored waters.

Presently they reached the isle of glass; they left their floaters by a mist-bridge, and they walked together by a smooth beach cold to their feet. Even the trees were sculpted out of crystal, and in their fronds danced crystal monkeys of clockwork; through their clear skin you could see wheels and cogs. Here and there a penguinoid of glass clattered up and down the shore. Birds fired by catapults arced across the sky.

She held her hand out, closed her eyes, wished: a bird landed in her hand. Its feathers sparkled like ice shavings; and as the wings whirred they produced music as of distant glockenspiels. Startled, she let it drop. It shattered, and a wave bore it away.

"A beautiful world," said Kelver.

"But cold," she said. "And I am hungry. Here we cannot pluck fruit from the trees. . . ."

Then came a voice: a low cackle from the cliffs ahead. It called their names: *Siriss. Kelver. Siriss. Kelver.*

"What are you?" Kelver shouted.

Come!

They found a stairwell carved into the crystal of the cliff. At the top, spread out on a meadow of transparent grass, was a rug: on it lay platters of gold and silver laden with emerald-colored fruit and loaves shaped like ringed planets.

"Who has prepared this repast?" Kelver cried out to the air.

A chuckling sound, issued from fissures in the cliff itself, was all that answered.

Siriss said: "It can't do us any harm. The thinkhive protects us always, doesn't it? Besides, it's probably the natives of this island; perhaps we're in for another stint as gods."

"If so, we'll fight no wars," Kelver said firmly.

They sat down to eat.

After a while a figure approached them: a dwarf, waist-high, with a wizened face, who wore a tunic stitched from leaves.

"Who are you?" said Kelver. They had spoken to no strangers for so many sleeps that Siriss could not speak at all.

"Greetings, masters." The dwarf had a high-pitched, nasal, cheerful voice. At least he had not fallen down to worship them, Siriss thought. "Master Siriss and Master Kelver, is it not? The thinkhive told us of your coming."

"Who are you?" she said.

"I am so sorry, *hokh'Tón,*" he said, bowing low. "The high ones visit us seldom, though we are all taught the high forms of address from childhood . . . not many venture so far south, or care to see what it is that we do. But since you *are* here . . . I perceive that you are on your quest-journey, otherwise you would be far less surprised at my appearing here to greet you . . . it is my humble pleasure to invite you to my land, five hokh'klomets beyond this Crystallizing Ocean. I have journeyed long, seeking you out, masters; I hope you will pardon my abruptness. Please eat your fill before you deign to come with me."

"But what are you?" Siriss said. "And why must we come with you?"

"Lady, it is not for me to coerce you; but when you reach

my land it may well be that you see the end of your journey;
for few have gone beyond it, into the Desert of Twisted
Ruins. As for what I am: my name is Gargeron of the clan of
Saut. Will you follow me now, young master and mistress?"

The dwarf shook his tunic into place and half-skipped,
half-hobbled, to the stair that led back down to the beach.
Moored to a copse of crystal willows was a barge; its prow
was a mechanical woman with her arms outstretched, so
cunningly animated that, did her torso not meld into the
gilt-fringed wood of the bow, she would have seemed alive.
From the mast flew four dragon-shaped sails. Siriss could see,
from the fact that they blew taut in the four directions of the
compass, that they were kept aloft by an artwind and had no
purpose other than the decorative. Upon the deck was a
pavilion of gold so burnished that it seemed to burn; other
dwarfs in leafy costumes ran hither and thither on errands.

"A splendid vehicle," said Gargeron, "for two such beautiful Inquestors. . . ."

Now a flight of steps emerged from the side of the vessel;
it was of force, and thus invisible, save for the carpet of
shimmerfur that rolled down it.

Siriss turned to Kelver. "Should we go with them?" she
said.

Kelver said to the dwarf, "Is your direction south?"

"Yes, Lord. And your floaters have been gathered from
the mist-bridge and placed aboard, ready for your use."

"Tell me, Gargeron," said Kelver, "what exactly *is* the clan
of Saut?"

And Saut Gargeron said, "My Lord, our clan are guardians
of the Sepulcher of Worlds. . . ."

They stepped aboard. At a sign from Saut Gargeron the
ship set off. At first, as it sliced through the purple waves that
surrounded the crystal continents, its pace was stately; later,
as it plowed through seas crimson and ultramarine, cerulean
and mauve, it sped up. The dwarfs scurried about; they spoke
to each other in an incomprehensible lowspeech. Siriss watched
the water as it changed color from second to second like a
grand kaleidolon. "But even at this rate," she whispered to
Kelver, "it will take a year to cross the ocean."

But even as she spoke, they saw the spectral outlines of a
displacement field, a giant halo bursting forth from the water;
and in a moment they had cut across millions of klomets, and
were in another sea altogether. Here there was wind, whis-

tling and wailing through the pavilion; and the tails of the
dragonsails spiraled in the air currents. Ahead were the jagged outlines of a shore, a line of cliffs serrated by fjords.

"Master and mistress," said the dwarf of the clan of Saut,
"the Sepulcher of Worlds lies before you."

Siriss felt dread stir up inside her. "I was born on a world
that is now dead," she said. "Will I find a memory of it
here?"

"Perhaps you will, my Lady," the dwarf said. "And your
former world, Ton Keverell n'Davaren Tath: has it, too,
fallen beyond in the grand *makrúgh*? Or does it yet stand?"

"It stands," said Kelver. But Siriss saw that he was shaking.
Had something moved him at last? She was afraid, though
she knew that Inquestors must show no fear. She wished that
she remembered how to weep.

They led Kelver and Siriss to a quarry of white marble. In
one field the dwarfs, all clansmen of Saut, were working on
great spheres of the marble, perhaps a hundred meters in
diameter, which had been bound with ropes and fastened to
pegs in the ground. There were perhaps a dozen of these
spheres, and on each perhaps a hundred dwarfs clambered,
chiseling and polishing.

"This," said Gargeron, "is where the memorials are mined
and the worldshapes fashioned. There, look"—he pointed to a
row of low huts in the distance—"is where they make the
continents and seas: the continents, the mountains, and the
valleys, are sculpted in a kind of putty, and the oceans from a
gelatinous substance which hardens to an aquiform clarity."

"But for whom do you make these memorials?" Kelver
said. "Surely no Inquestor would have the time to—"

"Ah, we don't know, Lord. But I have never seen it otherwise; and since boyhood I have been trained to guide
Inquestors about the precincts. Perhaps the Inquestors who
brought our race into being have long since died. But . . . I
will show you something a little more artistic than this lathing
operation, which only our apprentices and younglings do.
Come on!" Kelver followed; Siriss came shortly after, hurry-
ing to his side. He did not understand why she still stayed
with him, now that she knew of his purpose. After all, Arryk
had seen the void that lay at the end of Kelver's journey, and
he had fled. Why then not this woman? He thought he knew

her well; she was a hedonist, not a martyr. Her persistence surprised him.

They reached a building of the same white marble; it was built upon tall columns sculpted in the Inquestral highscript, and the wind blew freely through it. There the dwarfs worked on one of the marble spheres. They were painting it. Continents were taking shape on one side; on the other an apprentice with a bucket of blue gel was creating an ocean. "What world are you making?" Kelver said.

"See for yourself," said Gargeron. As he spoke, several dwarfs entered bearing a mountain-shaped block of black rock; and they began to paste it onto the world's central continent. A spiderweb of lines led from the mountain to a miniature sea.

"It's Gallendys!" he cried. "My homeworld . . . killed!"

"No, master, no," said Gargeron. "Not yet. Whenever a world is called for in a game of *makrúgh*, though, we are told of it, and we call forth the maps from the thinkhive's central memory, and we begin to manufacture that world's image. Just in case it is caused to *fall beyond*. Only when a world is destroyed is it placed in the sepulcher."

"But why all this effort?" Siriss said.

"Sometimes there are visitors. And who are we to violate a command of the Inquest, a command which brought us into being and is our only reason to exist?" Gargeron chuckled; the other dwarfs, hearing him, stopped their work and began to exchange jokes in their lowspeech.

Then Gargeron turned and said, "My masters, do you desire to see the Sepulcher itself? It is nearby."

Kelver said, "In a while. I want to see Gallendys first." And he stared, fascinated, as the dwarfs began to touch up the little Skywall mountain.

But Siriss said: "I'll go. There is something I must see."

From the overlook Siriss could see a plain that stretched perhaps a thousand klomets southward. It was thick with the colored spheres that the dwarfs built; in the far distance they seemed like marbles a child had carelessly strewn over the thick green grass. Here and there she could see vehicles hovering; they resembled the nymph-prowed, dragon-sailed ship in which they had come from the crystal islands, and from one or two of them fountains gushed. "What are those?" she said to Gargeron, who had come with her.

"Oh, they are the older dwarfs, their eyes grown too feeble for the fine work of planet-building. They maintain the grounds; they keep the grasses lush and brilliant green; and they dust the planets and hose them down."

Siriss said, knowing that she must ask, but dreading the question all the same: "Is there a world called Keima here?"

"Yes. Beyond the Mounds of Moons," said Gargeron. He pointed to a wall composed of piles of smaller spheres, most a dull-brown and scar-pitted; they were uninhabited satellites that had *fallen beyond* along with their governing-worlds, and had perforce to be re-created in accordance with the completist charter of the clan of Saut; but once built they lay neglected in their piles. Gargeron said, "Why do you seek Keima, my Lady? Is it a world you yourself have caused to *fall beyond* in your *makrúgh*? Or is it your own homeworld, from which they snatched you moments before its death?"

"You should not question an Inquestor about his origins," Siriss said. "What we were before we became of the Inquest can be of no concern to anyone. . . ."

"Except yourself, perhaps, Inquestrix!"

"Impertinence!"

The dwarf laughed openly at her. She considered for a moment decreeing some punishment for him; but it would not be seemly to show such lack of compassion. She realized that it was the thought of Keima that put her so on edge.

"How will I find Keima," she said, "among these thousands of worlds?"

Gargeron said, "You will hear the world cry out its name, Ton Siriss k'Varad es-K'Ning. Your floater awaits you at the foot of the cliffs. And now . . . farewell. I will go and give succor to Ton Keverell." As she stared at him, he whirled round and round until he was a streak of color; and for a moment she thought she could see a halo of shimmerlight as from the raiment of an Inquestor.

She knew that she was once again a pawn in some vast *makrúgh*. Was it Elloran who toyed with her thus, Elloran the wise, the compassionate? Surely it could not be. . . .

But she climbed down the steps carved into the rockface, and she found her floater, and set out into the graveyard of worlds.

As she passed the first of the sculpted planets, she heard its cry on the wind: *Hear, O passerby: I am the world Korreguros that* fell beyond *in the fifteenth millennium of the High*

Inquest, at the makrúgh *of Ton Ymvar and Ton Siembre. Weep for me, for I was a world rich with amber forests and angelbirds of a thousand colors—*

"Quick!" she cried out to the floater. "Go on!"

A memory of Keima touched her: the violet dawn. It was this dawn, whose color she had seen in Arryk's eyes, that had first drawn her to him. As a little girl she would watch the dawn from her bedroom window. They had been merchants, she remembered suddenly, fabric merchants . . . a town named Sheured, by the sea that the dawn had dyed pale mauve. . . .

I don't want to remember this! she thought, trying to drive the memory deeper into herself.

And the painted planets whispered as she floated past: *I am Lothara-Litherion. I am Kennis that was blown up before the people-bins could arrive to scoop up the still-living; weep for me, oh, weep for me. I am Vanjyvarath, the twin world of Vanjyvel that still survives; Ynyoldeh decreed my death. I am Hosh. I am Jandraxa. I am Verulan . . . Tithonilda . . . Karkopharang . . . Erithera . . . Trothbatag . . . Srem . . . Harratarraha. . . .*

Now she remembered the falling fire that had engulfed the citadel of Sheured. She remembered running from her home toward that dawn, and the boiling sea that shot up streaming steamfountains purpled by the dawnlight. . . .

Keima. Keima.

She stood now before a sculpted world much like the others. It had seas and it had continents. The continents were painted brown and green and yellow; and the seas dark blue tinted with violet. She stopped the floater and ran for the world, whose north pole could be reached by a winding stair of marble. In a moment she stood on the roof of the planet that had once been her home.

And the world spoke to her in a plaintive voice, like a young girl's: *I am the world Keima, destroyed in the nineteenth millennium of the High Inquest . . . look upon me, traveler, a land once rich in silks and precious jewels . . . whose violet sunrise was one of the wonders of the Dispersal of Man. . . .*

Siriss remembered how they had dragged her from the shore—

Look on my seas where dwelt rock-eating serpents—

And she was screaming, screaming, as the Inquestor's eyes

probed hers, and the death-bearing wind ripped open her neighbors' house—

"Dead world," she said, "who caused you to die?"

And the planet, brought to a dim sentience by the little thinkhive it carried in its depths, said: *Elloran. Elloran. Elloran.*

"No!" Not Elloran the compassionate, who had reached out to her like a father—

And Siriss sat herself down at the roof of the world, and she found herself weeping like a child. . . .

Presently she looked up and found Kelver standing over her.

Gently, Kelver sang to her the words of Sajit's lament for a dead world; *"O dhándas! O dhándas! T'am-plánzho. T'am-plánzho.* You are dead. You are dead. I weep for you. I weep for you."

"I don't know anymore!" Siriss said, sobbing. "I've remembered how they burned down my world. . . ."

Kelver put his arms around her, but she drew no comfort from them. It was her parents, her neighbors, her old friends that she wanted, and they were all dead. How could Kelver help her? He had a purpose grander than the death of a single world. . . .

"Leave me!" she cried out. "I'm going to stay here until I've cried out all my sorrow. Then I'll know whether I'm truly of the Inquest. This is my quest-journey's end, this is the place of my decision!"

Kelver said, "I'm alone then." He moved off a few paces, and stopped again. She looked up. He was staring at her with such wistfulness, such pain. "I know that you must stay here," he said. "But—"

"I have learned something," Siriss said, "that has broken my heart."

Kelver stepped away, awed by her grief.

How can I tell him, thought Siriss, how much I still love him? I must stay and he must go. And so she said nothing to him at all. And he walked away, over the gelatinous representation of Keima's Northern Sea, to the steps that led downward to the grounds of the sepulcher.

NINE: KELVER ALONE

Kelver waited for Siriss a long time in the country of the Saut; she would not come, and she cried when he came near her. And so, riding his floater alone, he left the Sepulcher of Worlds and continued southward. He didn't know if it was instinct or reason that drove him farther and farther from the lands the Inquestors inhabited; but he *did* remember an old Inquestral text: *arkhéin ishkátas; y'ishkáoten árkha, the Beginning and the Ending are one.*

A country south of the sepulcher was called the Desert of Twisted Ruins; but it was no harsh wasteland such as Kelver had once seen in the desert of Zhnefftikak on Gallendys. It was an expanse of grayish sand, never changing for a thousand klomets at a time. . . .

"Thinkhive! Thinkhive!"

You have not called me for a hundred sleeps, Ton Keverell n'Davaren Tath; I had thought you dead. The Desert of Twisted Ruins invokes a terrible despair in those who travel in it. It is a place of utter stillness.

Kelver stood on the plain beside his floater. His shimmer-cloak, untouched by the slightest breeze, hung heavy against his slim body. Ahead was gray; behind, gray; one gray, a color so dull that it seemed to drain away the pearl-light of Uran s'Vàrek's sky and make it, too, ash-gray. Kelver cried out: "Make me an oasis, thinkhive! A water hole! Even a rat—"

You are far from the northern pole now, Kelver. Illusions will not become real here. Why don't you just abandon your

*quest here? Nobody else comes here. The Twisted Ruins are
not abandoned cities of dead civilizations, but the minds of
those who have wandered too far into this grayness.*

He tried hard, concentrating, trying to will some image
into being, and—

For a split second, flittering against the grayness, the pale
face of Darktouch. "I want—I want—" Kelver gasped.

Did you not want the Throne of Madness?

"I don't play *makrúgh* with you, thinkhive!" Kelver looked
to the south, squinting, desperately trying to force the hazy
distance into an image not gray. Nothing. "I'm hungry," he
said.

You know where there is food, said the thinkhive.

It was true that an Inquestor could not go hungry here.
Kelver knelt down to dig into the ground with his bare hands;
he found a grayish oily nutrient that he lapped up, hungrily,
like an animal, but when he got up he still felt unsatisfied.

"I don't even know what I look like anymore!" he shouted.
"If only I could have a mirror—"

There came a hissing sound in his mind; the thinkhive was
mocking him. *Don't fret, don't fret, hokh'Tón; you're beautiful as always. Your eyes are still as green as the jade grass in
Elloran's pleasure garden, and your hair has grown long and
wild, like amber wheat that they weave into arrases of translucent gold. You have the fragrance of all Inquestors, for
your shimmercloak eats up your sweat and your bodily wastes,
and exudes in their place a soft perfume of godhead.*

Kelver knew that the thinkhive was playing a kind of
makrúgh, making light of his torment so as to force him to
return to the others.

"Why are you always telling me to go back? Are you afraid
of what I'll find?"

*Foolish boy. Before any human ever was I was. I saw the
first ones come, and I shall see them perish. What difference
can it possibly make to me?*

"But you play *makrúgh* with me anyway." He scooped up
sand in his palm, watched it sift through his fingers and blend
into the dullness. Then he rose and went to his floater and
searched for a weapon.

*What are you going to do? Kill yourself in your despair?
Ha, ha!*

Kelver found a little laser knife in the floater's utility pouch.
He sprang down and dug it into the sand, squeezing the

handle for maximum heat. The sand began to run in a rivulet. *What are you doing?* Did the thinkhive feel alarm then? Kelver worked steadily, until he had melted a small square of the sand and fused it together. Then he stood up, triumphant.

"A mirror," he said. "I needn't rely on your description of me, thinkhive."

Oho, the thinkhive said. *I had not heard that one before.*

In the scattered light Kelver peered at his own face.

I remember, he thought, Arryk when he came toward us on that throne, seated beside the corpse . . . *I* look like that now. For Kelver's eyes were lined, a little. How long had he been alone, how far had he come? Too long, his own eyes told him.

Kelver said to the thinkhive, "You see?"

Attá heng, the thinkhive said, conceding victory in the game of *makrúgh*.

"Then you will answer my questions, and answer them straightforwardly! You know who I am, and from whom I come."

You are the heretic's spawn, Ton Keverell.

"Where is the Throne of Madness?"

Any fool can tell you that. It is at the pole.

"Isn't there another pole to the south?"

Of course there is! All things have their mirrors, their shadows. You have just made a shadow of yourself, haven't you?

"Don't the stars fall into the southern void as well as the northern?"

You are wise beyond your years, the thinkhive said.

"But the southern Lightfall is neglected, never watched by the Inquest? Their grand ceremony of *makrúgh* and spectacle is never held in the south."

Why should it be?

Kelver sprang up on his floater and urged it onward into the grayness that seemed to know no ending.

. . . *gray* . . . *gray* . . .
I'm dreaming, dreaming.
In the distance, against the endless wall of gray—
A circle of green, peppered with firedots? . . . *gray* . . .
I'm not dreaming!
The dots were growing now, stipples of eye-burning

brightness. "Where is this place?" he called out to the thinkhive, his voice tiny in the echoless plain.

You have reached an oasis . . . the first in a hundred million klomets of this desert.

Kelver cursed at his floater; it would go no faster. At fifteen klomets per second, the firesparkles grew coronas; the gray of the desert, bare of striations or variant hues, did not blur as other landscapes did when one flew through them at these speeds.

Finally he stood in a garden of firefountains.

They welled up everywhere; some flames were of pure colors, blues, reds, greens, golds; others were braided from a thousand colors as they flared up from pedestals of rock.

His eyes feasted. He did not want to leave, to endure the immutable grayness again. . . .

And at the center of the garden, a marker of plain basalt; and an inscription.

Beyond this bourn I alone have traveled; I, the first, setting the Throne of Madness beyond the thoughts of the Inquest. . . .

Traveler, return!

I, Vara, the One Mother, command you. For this is Vara's world.

Who could this Vara be? Kelver remembered then that old woman who had been with Davaryush, his lover, his mentor. The one he had let die to buy time for his grand plan. Sometimes, in moments of intimacy, he'd heard Davaryush call her *Vara,* but had supposed it a diminutive like *Kevi, Sirissheh.*

Had Lady Varuneh sat on the Throne of Madness then? Was this why Davaryush had sent Kelver to seek it out?

This line is the equator, he told himself. I am halfway there.

He dug for food out of the ground and turned southward again, and . . .

By the fallen mountains beyond the desert he found a lake so mirror-still that he could see himself again; leaning from his floater he gazed at his face. It was harder than before, leaner. The fire had come back into his eyes, but gray had crept into his long hair: a gray like the despairing desert he had passed through. He drank the lake's water; it was fresh and cool; stripping his shimmercloak from him, he dived in, the bracing coldness tingling him.

He wished he were not alone.

And farther to the south, he watched silverdoves darting over the still water; and when he closed his eyes and fiercely imagined the girl Darktouch, he saw her for a moment in the ripple of water, and he knew that the art of illusion was returning to him, that he must be near another source of immeasurable power; he gave a cry of joy, and sped up again, throwing up a frothy wall as the water's stillness was broken for the first time in a million years, and . . .

. . . found a land of blue-iced mountains in whose craters whirlpools spun, churning up mist-clouds, and when he approached the waters they reared up, towered over him, constrained by some inner force to take on the shape of giants, and each giant had Kelver's face and the whirling of water mimicked Kelver's windswept hair, and Kelver shouted out "Who are you?" and heard no reply but the thinkhive's answer: that these were the descendants of sentient oceans that had once, before man's coming, ruled Uran s'Varek; these whirlpools of organic soup had no minds, had lost everything but a blind urge to imitate the shapes of the sentient . . . so Kelver continued southward, and . . .

. . . reached a country where lay the carapaces of huge arachnoids, petrified by time and chiseled by sandwinds into honeycomblike structures where dwelt beings of a hivemind shaped like blue six-legged ferrets . . .

. . . and still another desert, this one of ice now, but now he could force illusions out of the ice, and with his art he lit his way with torches of blue flame, drawing out the lizards from their burrows . . .

. . . and then the statues. Mountains had been leveled to afford a better view of them; descending on his floater he saw first faces through klomet-high windows of rock, faces of a beautiful woman; as he sailed through the rocky openings he saw through broader and broader windows until he could see them all, seated figures many klomets high, completely visible only at a hundred klomets' distance . . . the face seemed so familiar, yet he could not place it. . . .

In the lap of the statue at the center of the group of five, he saw a city; a human city, surely, and not one of long-dead aliens. It was deserted; its streets, built of basalt bricks to last the ages, were untouched. There were pyramids here; their sides were carved into that same face.

At the foot of the tallest pyramid he found a moving stair; as he stepped onto it, it whirred, creaked a little, and bore him upward. In a temple at the summit he found a statue of the same woman. The hair was bunned in an antique style; a half-smile played on her lips.

Something impelled him: he knelt down in front of the statue.

"Rise, rise." A melodious voice, half-familiar. "Don't be afraid. I am no goddess . . . I'm a machine who speaks for Vara."

"Who is Vara?"

"She is long gone to the north, child." He looked up; had the statue's lips moved? It was a trick of holosculpture, surely. "And all her people too. . . ."

"What do you mean?"

"They've gone to play with the million worlds . . . do you seek godhood too, my child, my child?"

. . . the smile . . .

"No, mother," Kelver said, "I've been told to seek out the Throne of Madness—"

"Ah. What Vara found you, too, will find. Welcome to Vara's World: in the old tongue before the highspeech was made, we called it Uran s'Varek, Vara's World."

"But . . ." Kelver was astonished. For now he knew to whom the smile belonged. The old woman whom Davaryush loved, whom Davaryush had killed . . . she had smiled thus at him, in the city of Kallendrang, comforting him. . . . "You are twenty thousand years old," he said in the common counting that is based on the sunpassage of a long-dead planet. "And I am only seventeen. How have I been sent here?"

The voice said: "In a universe without gods, *someone* must be god. I am tired, child, tired. What I have made must pass away. You come to unmake all my making. . . ."

"No! I don't understand any of this! Once, an eternity ago it seems, I saw something in a hollow mountain, in a world parsecs away from here. What can I possibly have to do with you?"

"I am programmed," said the statue's voice, "to know that when you come there will have been many changes in the way men think and are. But I am only a machine. There is a test—"

"I didn't come here to solve riddles!" Kelver shouted. The journey's end seemed more and more unattainable now. "I came only because of what I have seen."

"As you have gained wisdom," said the voice of the goddess, "you have come to understand that there are no choices for those who rule. And especially not for the gods."

"Then give me the test."

"Fie, child! This is not some romantic holoplay, some street opera such as might be performed in the market squares. You have passed the test by your very presence here. You have traversed more than three hundred hokh'klomets to find me. And I cannot send you home. You are my successor. Now I can rest, I can rest—"

Kelver was appalled at this. "I didn't come to relieve you of your duty—whatever *that* may be!" he said.

"Duty? Duty?" the voice whispered. "I am but a machine—a machine—" There came a sterner voice now, and he recognized distinctly the voice of the Lady Varuneh, distorted though it was by time. "You must not pass. I cannot relinquish my godhead. You must not pass. . . ." Then the soft young voice, "I am but a machine . . . but a machine—"

"Let me pass!" Kelver said.

But the voice babbled on, was joined by other voices, all cloned from the voice of Varuneh. With all his strength Kelver willed an illusion of himself into being, and another, and another, pallid self-echoes that knelt in obeisance at the statue's feet; and the voices cried out, "You are not one, you are many, you are illusion, I dismiss you—"

"Let me pass!" he cried again. But even as he spoke he heard the soft laughter of a young girl, an incongruous sound from the statue's lips. A crack opened up in the forehead and snaked slowly down toward the mouth . . . a low rumbling shook the pyramid . . . the crack became a fissure as the statue broke asunder and tumbled into two heaps of rubble, one on his left and one on his right.

"Are there no more words of wisdom, then?" said Kelver. He waited for a long time, and then he tightened his shimmercloak about his shoulders and descended the moving

stairway into the city that rested on the goddess's lap. His
floater awaited him there.

As he rose skyward he saw that each of the five statues of
the beautiful woman now had the same lightning-jag fissure
on its face; and as he sped away he heard the beginning of the
avalanche. But in a few seconds he was already too far south
to hear anything.

. . . *tired* . . .

Kelver stared blankly ahead. Now I know how a servocorpse
feels, he thought. Every klomet of the journey was an agony.
Time had become meaningless; he knew that not a year had
passed since first he left Rhozellerang, but he felt as though
he had been on this quest-journey all his life. Beyond the
mountains of Vara's city there were a thousand more kingdoms; some he passed in a mere hour or two, sensing them
only as a shift in the color or texture of the landscape as it
marbled into that of the next country. Deserts blended into
forests; alien terrain into familiar.

And then, at last, a thin black line at the farthest periphery
of his vision.

The southern void!

He stopped; he was in a sea of fine white sand. Around the
void, he knew, must be the banks of thinkhives that controlled the energy of murdered suns. The power of illusion
flowed in him; he could feel it, he could almost wish—

Darktouch. She was running to him across the sand now.
No! She must be dead now. He murmured her name again
and again. She ran toward him and was always just out of
reach, he could see the black hair flying just like the time
when they had fled the ghost people into the shade of the
Cold River on Gallendys—

. . . *tired* . . .

He had not eaten for a long time. It was not that the
thinkhive could not provide; it was just that he no longer
thought of eating or drinking, only of resting forever. And
then he seemed to hear Darktouch's voice, and Davaryush's
voice too, calling out his name, urging him always southward
to the very void's edge, and he was delirious now, calling
their names as the sand swirled about him, and he was falling
now, falling, falling—

Ahead, in the sand, a plain, wooden chair. Already he
knew what it was . . . he had to reach it . . .

. . . and collapsed, his hand outstretched, almost grasping the leg of old wood.

When he opened his eyes the chair was still there. He rose and staggered toward it. But before he could sit down he heard a distant voice—

"Kelver! I knew you would come here. It was the only logical place."

A handful of sand in his face. His eyes smarted. He started, turned around, saw a figure on a floater hovering just over his head. It was a boy, shimmercloaked, violet-eyed, arrogant. For a second Kelver could not even recognize him, but—

"Arryk!"

"Yes, my friend, my fellow-traveler, one whom I once loved. It's your own Arryk. I don't suppose you're terribly happy to see me!"

"I—"

"You silly boy! Do you really think you're going to sit down on that chair and tap into the wisdom of the universe and topple the Inquest all in a few seconds?"

"Of course not," Kelver said hotly. "There is a plan."

"What plan?" Arryk brought his floater down now. He pulled Kelver away from the throne and stared him full in the face. "Don't think I don't understand you, Kevi. Even *I've* had my grand notions about the way things must be, in the course of this quest-journey. But I've remembered who I am. Elloran chose me, in his compassion; I can't betray him. I'm not going to see you destroy what twenty thousand years have created. Not that I believe you can do it anyway. It's absurd. Do you want to know why you can't, Kevi?" Arryk clenched Kelver's arms tightly, hurting them. For a moment Kelver felt a surge of the old love; then he felt nothing but pity.

"It's you who are foolish," he said softly. "Even Elloran said that the end must come."

"Listen, Kevi. Siriss has returned to Elloran's palace; and she brought with her your story. I listened, but I told no one, for the sake of our old love. You have seen something of such power that it has driven you here. Let *me* show you something, Kelver, if you dare to see it! I, too, have seen a thing of power. A dark and hungry thing. No, don't try to climb up on that decaying old chair! The founders of the Inquest did well to hide it here, and to make of it only a myth. It's no good, Kelver. Don't!" He pulled Kelver away again, toward his own floater.

Kelver did not argue; he was too drained. "The quest-journey has broken me," he said. "I won't fight you, Arryk. Not you, not Siriss. Once the Inquest was a faceless force to me, an evil that stifled the Dispersal of Man. But now it has a face: the face of those that I most love! Powers of powers, how can this be?"

Arryk's voice did not soften. He merely said, brusquely, "Come, Kevi. All ways lead to darkness."

"I don't know what you mean."

"Nothing will ever change. Come, I will show you." He drew Kelver onto his floater and commanded it into motion.

Kelver watched the Throne of Madness shrink into a speck. Ahead loomed the void, the window into the all-devouring black hole, the canker in the heart of paradise.

den om verék en-tinjet
in dárein shirenzheh,
zenz kel skevúh varúng
e varande.

aivermatsá falláh setalikas!
tekiánveras yvrens ká!

o-tinjet
in dárein shirenzheh!
sarnáng, varunger shentraor!
eih! min zhalá, zhalá,
hokhté Enquester, min zhalá, min zhalá,
sarnáng,
varunger shentraor, varunger shentraor. . . .

No man alive has touched
the silence between the stars,
without being driven mad,
or reaching enlightenment.

For now the delphinoids fall through the overcosm;
the tachyon bubbles breach the cosmos;

but I have touched
the silence between the stars! I,
the mad singer!
Ei! Envy me, thou High Inquestor,
Envy me,
the mad singer, the mad singer. . . .

—from the *Songs of Sajit*

TEN: THE VOID

At the edge of Uran s'Varek there was a forcewall thousands of klomets high; its function was to prevent the atmosphere from leaking, for the atmosphere was all that shielded the Inquestors from the deadly radiation of a million suns packed tight within the galactic core. There, half-buried in the sand that ran from the great band of thinkhives that circumscribed the southern void, was a silvery ovoid shape. "It's a space cocoon," Arryk said, "for going short distances between planets; a children's toy, really. Get in, Kevi."

"Where are you taking me? I'm so tired. . . ."

"There. Out there. Into the big nothing."

"Why? Why?"

"So you'll see how useless you are, so you'll turn back, so you'll accept what has to be. Come on, Kelver, come on."

They climbed into the cocoon; noiselessly it began to move; the forcewall that held in the pearly sky parted and closed up, though Kelver did not sense it. The two were hunched together; the walls pressed in on them. In the cold blue luminescence Kelver could see his friend: some inner anger had honed his features; there was no softness in his eyes anymore.

After a long while Arryk commanded the cocoon to deopaque its walls; it seemed that they rested on emptiness, in a darkness of overwhelming immensity. Quietly he said to Kelver: "This is where it all ends. Below us: the dark heart of the Dispersal of Man."

Kelver looked out at it. There was no starlight; no illumination save for the blush of their shimmercloaks. "The silence

103

between the stars," he whispered. They were words from an old song of Sajit's; he had heard them long ago, on another world.

"It will drive you mad if you stare at it long enough!" Arryk said harshly.

The monotony of the gray desert had been nothing compared to this featureless expanse. There were no perspectives here: only the all-devouring blackness.

"Do you see now that you cannot win?" Arryk said. "You must come home, Kevi. We're waiting for you, Siriss and I; waiting in the light. Don't abandon us."

Kelver said, "There are no choices, Rikeh."

"Look at you. Care has been eating away at you. Your eyes are lusterless. I did not come here to scorn you, but to save you from the prison of the heretic's injunctions. It's not for you, this battle! We are for beautiful things: for palaces, for frozen fireworks and star hunts, for the worship of trillions, for symbols of the High Compassion. Don't let the words of Davaryush turn you into less than you are."

"Arryk—"

Their lips touched briefly in the big darkness. But when the kiss was over, Kelver knew he was truly alone, for ever and ever. He could not bear to look at the boy that he had once loved, or at the blackness that engulfed them. But he could not close his ears to Arryk's words.

"When next we meet, Kevi, it will be as enemies. We will play the deadliest *makrúgh* the Inquest has ever seen: the Dispersal of Man itself will be the stake . . . why don't you answer me? It's not too late to turn back. . . ."

"Arryk, it's no longer a game. And I'm not a child anymore." As he spoke he realized that it was true. He had left his innocence behind long since, somewhere in the four hundred hokh'klomets that lay between Rhozellerang and the southern void. "The big darkness has drained away our very love from us."

"Yes."

"I pity you, Arryk. You should have turned back at Shentrazjit. I blame myself for forcing you onward. It is true that you are for the beautiful things; for when you saw the ugly you couldn't bear it, you reached out with blind anger. It's not you who have stifled the life from the galaxy: it's the Inquest itself, because it won't let you be a human, it forces you to be a god!"

"But don't you see? When you begin to preach the Inquest's end, people will come flocking to your side: not because of what you say, but because of *you!* Your gift is to wring love even from the heartless. And when they follow *you* and not your message, you will become a god yourself; and the trap will close around you too!" said Arryk, anguished.

"I have no choice," said Kelver.

He looked out at the darkness: it no longer seemed chill and comfortless. He longed to be one with the darkness, to relinquish all feeling. When Davaryush had charged him with destroying the Inquest from within, he had not thought he would have to give up so much, even love.

On the way back they said nothing to each other. There was no more to be said. Arryk left Kelver behind in the sand, in sight of the Throne of Madness; and he flew northward in his silver cocoon, soon vanishing into the featureless glow of sky. His quest-journey was over; he had found himself.

There was the old wooden chair, still planted in the sand, its legs almost buried in a low dune. Kelver saw a wind in the distance, stirring the sand into a churning cloud of white.

He sat down on the Throne.

. . . music: high sweet srinjid voices stretched straining to sheer heaven, surround-engulfing the echo-cho-cho-cho-thedral of the height and limitless sky—

Who are you that wakes me from millennial slumber? Let me sleep, child, sleep, sleep, sleep.

Sand swept over him: the sky's radiance was blacked out. A storm, and Kelver at the still point of it.

"Give me answers, Throne of Madness, answers!"

I will tell you, then, what I am, creature of dust. Once there came another like you; I gave her power unlimited, until she betrayed compassion. . . .

"Lady Varuneh?"

She had many names. It was long ago. I no longer remember. I am the soul of the southern thinkhives. My might is greater than that of the north: for you I can build tachyon bubbles that will shatter the overcosm in a second, for you I can build castles of wind and citadels of gold and silver. That's all you want, isn't it? Four thrones the humans found when they first came to Uran s'Varek, and with their power they overcame all the Dispersal of Man. But only one dared to tap my powers. Now never again. I will drive you mad, dust-child. Not for nothing have they fled the southlands and built their habitations by the northern pole. The thinkhive of the north is but a slave; I am the true world-soul . . . before ever man was, I am!

"Then Uran s'Varek itself is mad, for the other thinkhive told me that *it* was the world-soul," said Kelver, his voice almost drowned by the interweaving strands of warring dissonance.

It is a conflict that existed long before the coming of you dust-children; and it will last an eon after the last of you perishes.

"I will strike a bargain with you."

Are you prepared to pay the price?

"I come in the name of the High Compassion; to strike down the Inquest; to unmake the making of the Lady Varuneh."

Lofty goals, dust-child. The voice thundered against the whistling sandstorm, against the intertwisting music. *But if I give you power, it will sear you, it will make you mad. How will you undertake such an enterprise? Are you not but a single dust-child, a single sandmote that withstands in vain the sandstorm?*

And Kelver, seeing the plan of Davaryush at last fall into place, said: "Everything has its shadow, Throne of Madness. Here in the southland I will create a Shadow Inquest. I will call for all Inquestors who have doubted the ways of twenty millennia; I know that they exist. We will restore utopias. We will turn *makrúgh* against itself."

You will make war in heaven, pit god against god!

"I am no god! If I ever forget that—"

I will tempt you. I am very wily, dust-child, and older than your race. Other races have tried to use me. I was not built to fuel the petty wars of gnats, but for a higher purpose that you may one day learn . . . if it does not drive you over the brink of insanity. And one day will come Lightfall . . . the next star to fall southward comes in a mere century from now. And when it falls, I will tempt you even more, for it is said that he who sits upon me during Lightfall will see into the heart of the dying star. And it will kill you, Kelver.

"I'm not afraid anymore."

Good, child of dust. To you I extend my compassion, dustling that dares to stare in the face of the sun.

"Why have you not killed me, Throne of Madness, or driven me mad?"

Because once . . . twenty thousand years ago . . . I made a bargain with your Lady Varuneh. And she has sent you to me. You are the true agent of ending. I have looked into your soul, and I have seen the remembrance of the songs of Windbringers. That, too, has a connection with my purpose, although mankind itself will not live to see that purpose fulfilled. You are free of the curse of the Inquestors. Only you shall tame me, child of dust.

It seemed that Kelver slept for a very long time, years perhaps; he dreamed of great wars and exploding suns. Perhaps they were prescient dreams. At long last he awoke.

The chair he sat in was a throne of kyllap leaves; around him the desert was shimmering, melting into meadow. A baby dragontree, coiled at his feet, reared up to spread shade over his head. Birds sang. From somewhere far away he could hear the sound of a waterfall.

"An illusion!"

No, child of dust. My power, coming as it does from the deaths of stars as they fall into the black hole, is not one of illusion. Through me, you can fashion shapes of whimsy that endure for a moment or two, then fade: but my own power is to transmute, transform, repattern the very particles of matter.

"Then you can transport me home too? You can grant me a tachyon bubble?"

More than that!

And so he rose, and cried: "Rhozellerang!"

And he was back on the overlook of the many-petaled city, where the young Inquestors paced back and forth, worried about their forthcoming tests. They seemed like children to him now. In a voice of authority he summoned a floater to him, and commanded it to take him to a house of rest.

I have relinquished everything, he told himself, for the power to crush the greatest of powers. But they shan't take my soul from me! I will never give it up.

And for the first time since he began his quest-journey he felt a sense of release, of joy. He knew who he was now. The path was chosen; and in impelling himself to take the dark road he had made himself free.

And he thought of Davaryush and Darktouch and the Lady Varuneh; he felt their shadows over him now. They would haunt him always: Darktouch, his first love, who had first given him the dream; Davaryush, who had lent him wisdom;

Varuneh, who had somehow set it all in motion and had not lived to see its ending.

I will never betray them, he thought fiercely.

And in that moment, because Kelver had known the imagesongs and had come face-to-face with an absolute beauty, and because he had known love and grief, and because he had placed these things higher than the might that held the human galaxy in its grasp . . . imperceptibly, inexorably, the Inquest's fall had already begun.

Siriss walked down the corridor of pteratygers in the palace of Varezhdur. She let her hand trail along the cold ridged marble wingfeathers of each sculpted beast; she had done it often as a child, but now she had to stoop to play the game.

Once more, as on that day when Kelver had first come to Elloran's domain, she heard a neuterchild's sweet voice, a broken melisma from a far corner of the palace. She stopped her ears, but she could not stop the pain. She had chosen Inquestorhood, after all. Inquestors must not turn away from pain, least of all their own.

She found the displacement plate, glinting at the end of the dark corridor; and then she was in the presence of Ton Elloran n'Taanyel Tath, in the golden throneroom with the galaxy of dust. He looked up at her for a moment, beckoning her forward; and then he turned to some business with a messenger. A Rememberer stood nearby too; Elloran had been listening to a tale of some long-dead world, no doubt, feeding melancholy with more melancholy.

"*Hokh'Tón,*" she said humbly. "Father Elloran . . ." She knew now that it was her duty to tell Elloran the truth about Kelver. That he would command that Kelver be devived, as was compassionate, for the sake of the salvation of the Dispersal of Man. But as she was about to speak, Elloran hushed her with a gesture. She sat at his feet, and he smiled at her, not quite looking up from the message disk he held in his hand.

"Not a word, Sirissheh. I am glad you are back. I know what is on your mind, but you must first listen to this. . . .

"*To Ton Elloran n'Taanyel Tath, Grand Inquestor of the High Inquest, Lord of Varezhdur and its subject Principalities: I, Ton Keverell n'Davaren Tath, bring word that I will host a grand Lightfall one century hence.* Makrúgh *will be played as always. And I name, too, the Lightfall's location:*

the southernmost tip of Ellorin, in the continent beyond the city I have named Pendevarang, the city of the five statues of Mother Vara. I, of the High Inquest, challenge you and welcome you; history there is, and no history."

"Father Elloran—you know, then, that Kelver has betrayed us all!"

"It is well, Sirissheh. Accept the invitation," he commanded the messenger. "When he has had his century to prepare, I shall play *makrúgh* with him. It is inevitable."

"Aren't you going to stop him?"

"Child, oh, child: should I stop the wind and the sea, the dawn and the twilight? I am only a man . . . but there is something else on your mind, I think."

"No."

"I think you are hiding something from yourself." Siriss looked up, gasped: for a moment she thought she'd seen a much shorter figure in a leafy tunic. . . .

"You . . . Gargeron . . ."

"I am a master of illusion, am I not? Let's just say that I took his place for a moment. I care deeply about you, you know. I cannot help but interfere. You had to know that it was I who burned down your world. Because of the decision you must make."

"What decision, Lord? You are like a father to me. I would follow you always."

"I am the destroyer of your home, the despoiler of your planet's treasures. What I did I did long ago, when I was a mere boy. I burn no more worlds now, Sirissheh. But you must know what I am: he who killed your parents and made you alien from all you ever knew."

"You are my father, Elloran. I love you like my own father." But she could not meet his eyes.

"Did you know that Keima was also the birthplace of Davaryush, the heretic?"

"You're playing *makrúgh*, *hokh'Tón!*" Siriss protested. "Can't this wait a little, until I've rested from this awesome quest-journey?"

"No, child of my heart, this is no game. Soon I will bequeath you Kailasa, one of my own worlds, and you will attain the rank of Princeling. You will know many beautiful things, but always you will yearn for another—for *him!*"

"It's not true!" But already Siriss was thinking of Kelver. How she'd first stalked him like a huntress; how he'd poured out his heart to her in the southlands; and how she had said to him: *I will never leave you*. She could not bear the thought of him alone against the hugeness of the Inquest's injustice.

"If you must go to him," Elloran said, "you must. I will not betray you. Believe me when I tell you that *makrúgh* has gone from my heart."

Siriss stared at Elloran in wonder; he only beamed at her in response. She said, "Whose side *are* you on, Ton Elloran? The Inquest's side? Or the side of shadow?"

"I am on no one's side, dear child. There will come a great conflict; it will come upon us sooner than we would like, we who have ruled in splendor for so many centuries, and watched worlds tumble to their places in the sepulcher. I no longer yearn for power. Let the children play *makrúgh*; let Arryk and Kelver, who have loved and now must hate, divide the Inquest and so hasten the long-awaited fall. And you, Sirissheh: who will you follow?"

She shook her white hair from her opalmilk eyes. "I can't—"

"You don't have to say it. I know who you belong to. I know you will seek him out, that you have already become his disciple; that you have already decided to flee to this shadow Inquest that Kelver must now form."

"I love him."

She uttered the words as if they had been wrenched from her; but only by speaking them aloud did she know at last that they were true. She had been hunter and quarry: now she transcended both.

She felt Elloran's hand on her cheek, soothing her. "It is difficult to change, to grow; more difficult still to change the entire Dispersal of Man. If I were still young, I might have joined you; for there was a time when I, too, dreamed of change. But I have laid *makrúgh* by. . . ."

"Oh, Elloran," Siriss said as her tears welled up, "I love this palace. Light is everywhere in it: in the burnish-glitter of the thronerooms, in the soft organic shining of its hallways, in the arc-soaring voices of Sajit's neuterchildren. I am for the dark now, and I don't want to leave it behind!"

"Hush, child," Elloran said. He took her by the arm and led her to the galaxy of dust. "An Inquestor does not weep." They watched the dustmotes slowly swirl from light to shadow, light to shadow. "We are all shadows; we all wrest but a lightmote from the big darkness, and then we are no more. It has been said that the Inquest itself is a shadow, a cormorant darkness hovering over man's soul. If Kelver seeks to stand as shadow over the High Inquest, it is well; it is well, child! Be comforted! You are not for the darkness. For light, Sirissheh, is the shadow's shadow."

BOOK TWO:
THE WOMAN IN THE SERPENT

Eih! asheveraín
am-planzhet ka dhand-eruden,
eih! eskrendaí
pu eyáh chítarans hyemadh?

Shenom na chítarans hyemadhá
u áthera tinjéh erudeh,
z'irsai yver tembáraxein kreshpáh,
z'purreh y'Enguestren tinjéh.

Ai! When man dispersed
we wept for the dead earth.
Ai! We cried out:
"Where is the homeworld of the heart?"

We yearn for the heart's homeworld,
Where the sun touches the earth;
and rainbows gird the mountains of darkness;
and the Inquestor touches the beggar child.

—ancient folk song;
adapted into the highspeech by
Shen Sajit, among others

ELEVEN: SERVOCORPSES

     . . . red sunlight streaming, tall reeds in the mud, moat beside the sandstone fortress . . .

"When I grow up, I'll have my own world! And I'll be Queen of it, and rule forever, and be wise and compassionate, and live happily ever after. . . ."

"Yes, Vara dear. But it's suppertime now. Watch out for the pinkskinned fishes. There, one of them's stuck in the reeds. Shall we have it for supper tonight? Yes, yes?"

> *. . . tall reeds, red sunlight, little girl by the sandstone fortress . . .*

"*Lulla, was the sun always this red?*"

"*No, dear. But you needn't worry, Vara, Varusha, my sweet child. Oh, your smile's sugary.*"

. . . little girl a handsbreadth too short to touch the tallest reeds in the red sunlight by the moat shadowed by the fortress of sandstone . . .

"*When I grow up I'm going to have my own world. Vara's world. And I won't allow any fighting.*"

. . . running now, the silvery shivery fish wriggling in her tiny fists . . .

My memory! the old woman was thinking. She lay in a faint putrescence, her eyes crusted over. Memory . . . darting away like a fish from the reeds.

She rubbed her eyes. "Why aren't I dead?" she said aloud. It was dark; the walls against which she leaned were fleshy, throbbing a little. Suddenly she felt a contraction, a spasm, racking the room itself. It was so dark . . . she groped for an object, any object . . . there was nothing but the walls of living-seeming tissue.

She closed her eyes, remembering—

. . . *red sunlight, the little girl* . . .

So long ago. More than twenty millennia ago. "I thought I was dead!" she cried out, yearning for release. She remembered that Davaryush had commanded her death. Davaryush who had loved her. To buy time. He had told the Convocation of Grand Inquestors that Ton Varushkadan, the Grand Inquestrix whose name all dreaded, of whom a thousand songs were sung . . . had led the plot to destroy Gallendys and the Inquest's only source of the delphinoid shipminds, without which they could not rule the Dispersal. But the execution *had* taken place! She had witnessed it herself! As she sat down to drink the wine of oblivion from the death-lecythus, carved from a single flawless sapphire, she had seen her face in the pale blue liquid, the only antidote to the life-prolonging drugs that only the Inquestors used. She had seen the life drain from her face; had seen the veins of fungoid blackness crawling up her neck, into the cavities of nose and mouth; had heard her own death rattle—

Dark. Dark. But presently came a cold blue luminescence. She could not tell where it was coming from at first; but then, crawling carefully across the effluvid floor of her prison room, she found a shimmercloak. Her own. It had fed well. This *was* a living place then. Davaryush had sent her away, hidden her somewhere safe from the Inquest. Where, she could not tell.

She called out in the highspeech: "Let me out, let me out." There was no reply save an oozing echo, liquidescent, cavernous. She gathered her shimmercloak about herself; quickly it bonded to her, drawing nourishment from the wastes she had lain in, licking the slime from her face, her wrinkled arms. She called out again, resolving to follow the echo. A fleshy fissure became a passageway; a passageway became a honeycomb of caves, their walls pulsating as one. She thought: I could almost be in the entrails of a living creature.

Now came scaffolds of steel and forcefields; tanks, walled in some glassy substance, containing some bluish liquid. There was more light now; globes of pseudofire hung at regular intervals from recesses in the tank walls. A figure moved in the water: a technician? A tank-cleansman? She walked boldly toward him, making sure her shimmercloak was clearly visible; for she had never been unmade Inquestor, and her person remained inviolate.

The figure walked on the tank floor, mechanically, not seeing her. She pressed her face against the cold glass, peering at him. It strode by, wavery in the water. It was naked, a man. She saw its face. Dead, dead. It continued its measured pace. Varuneh smiled a little, realizing what Davaryush's ruse was.

"A servocorpse . . . this is a factory for servocorpses . . . the one place where it would seem natural to send the cadaver of a devived Inquestrix! Oh, that demon of a man. . . ."

But why did the walls ooze rheum and undulate like a slow trampoline? Here and there she saw pipes; nutrients, perhaps, to feed the tanks of deadmen; but why did they twist and branch and meander so, like . . . tiny blood vessels? . . . Lady Varuneh walked on now, as the labyrinth widened and she could see vats packed with human carcasses; grisly merry-go-rounds of corpses perched on steel rods, being bathed from a central sprinkler, their mouths stiffened into grimaces, their bodily orifices dribbling yellow slime. All had been doused in a heavy perfume, one such as might have been found in the whorehouses of Airang; yet it could not mask the putrid smell of death. Varuneh walked quickly now. She had never become used to death, not even after twenty millennia as her long-dead homeworld measured time.

In another chamber the corpses marched to and fro, their feet thudding in perfect unison. In another they were piled in heaps, perhaps awaiting the cosmeticians' art. In one hallway stood necrophilids, servocorpses whose beauty had singled them out for those brothels that specialized in the bizarre; there were boys and girls there, their faces rouged and their eyes kohled and each hairstrand lovingly electronetted so that it would stream enticingly even in the windless lovebooth of the coupling-house. Varuneh shuddered and walked on. There must be humans somewhere. The pathways forked and forked again. She walked on, not knowing whether she had doubled back on herself. She called out in the highspeech for a human or a thinkhive.

In another room the bodies were headless and in racks; attendants were trying different heads on the various bodies, essaying a more perfect match than nature might have provided. A balding man in the yellow tunic and human-scalp sash of the clan of Dhan was directing them. . . . "No, no," he said in a degenerate variety of highspeech, "that won't do, you see the hair shades of armpit and crown don't . . . of course it's important, it's an art, you fool, not some infantile jigsaw puzzle. . . ."

Varuneh said, trying to ape the inflections of the man's lowspeech, "Excuse me, Clansman of Dhan, but what is this place? I am—"

The man whipped around and gaped. "What is this thing?" he cried.

An attendant rushed to seize her by the arms. "Came out of the unwoken cadaver rooms, Dhan Aropash. Locomotive mechanism must be out of adjustment; I'll just open her up and . . . wait, there's no—"

"Let me be!" Varuneh said in the highspeech.

"A shimmercloak!" said Aropash the corpse-waker. "This woman is not dead . . . and she is of the Inquest besides!" Trembling, the attendants fell at her feet, clamoring for mercy.

"My Lady . . ." Dhan Aropash said, genuflecting before her, "we could not have known . . . your body was one of thousands that come here every sleep. The serpent rises daily to greet the sun; and in his mouth he catches the shuttles from the delphinoid ships as they land to disgorge their cargo, and at sunset, when the serpent rises again to sing his lament for lightsdeath, the ships issue from his mouth and return to whatever distant worlds they came from . . . we are only a poor factory of servocorpses, Lady. How could we know you had not been fully devived? Do you bring a message from the High Inquest? Let me bring you to someone in authority."

"Be silent," Lady Varuneh said, in the commanding tone that Inquestors learned to use for exacting instant obedience. "I am not a messenger. I ask for sanctuary here, and secrecy."

"You know, Lady, that when the Inquest speaks the universe listens."

Oh, I am tired of these formalities of expression, Varuneh thought. "What is this place?" she asked.

"The planet Idoresht, Lady, in the system of the star Telissarat. It is a world completely covered with water; near the surface float serpents huge as cities, and it is in their dismal innards that we colonists eke out our lives. We are here in the serpent's Kepharang, its city of the head; a spongy tissue with many passageways forms our capital and is where our main factories are; deeper down are the dwellings of the poor and the slaves and the miners of the serpent's flesh, for we are parasites and nibble at our host's flesh and use his nutrient fluids for our hydroponic farms."

Varuneh looked up, around. The walls rippled. "Is this not dangerous?"

"The Inquest commanded centuries ago that we make our home here; a people-bin, a million stasis-frozen colonists, was emptied here. We had to make the best of it. It is well; our serpent, Kalivorm, breathes for us, rising daily from the sea and incidentally providing us with our spaceport."

"But doesn't the sea snake ever . . . move, migrate?"

"Sometimes. But Kalivorm stays near the surface. One day, however, he will find a mate; and then, in the frenzy of his lovemaking, our homes will all be destroyed . . . do not fear, Inquestor. It happens but once or twice in a serpent's lifetime, and then we, too, have our fertility ritual, making love with wild abandon, so that all our women will be ready to bring forth new lives to replace those that must be lost in the cityquake of the serpent's amorous thrashings."

This, then, was the safe place to which Davaryush had sent her! Varuneh laughed, a quick, bitter laugh. She wondered why he had not killed her. That would have been the only safe course, after all. They had both agreed on it. To live in the body of a monstrous sea serpent, waiting . . . for what? The Inquest's end? And would the boy come here in person to inform her of it, when he had seen Davaryush's mission through to its end?

A memory surfaced for a moment . . . the sand. The Throne of Madness. *When I grow up I'm going to have my own world. . . .*

The corpse-waker was saying to her, ". . . and your arrival is a most blessed one, my Lady. We had thought that the Inquest had forgotten us completely, that we labored in the slime among the dead, and all for nothing . . . we are a poor people, but we welcome you and give you honor. . . ." Now he was dispatching an attendant to broadcast the news. She heard a cry of astonishment far away, the sound muddied by the odd acoustics of the cranium of an underwater creature.

"No!" she cried to him. "I am here in secret!" The man turned around as if slapped; and knelt to beg her forgiveness. "No, Master Corpse-waker. Give me only shelter and seclusion. Do not let me enter your city in triumph, like a Kingling, for I am only a silent observer from the Inquest." The lies came easily to her; so often had she lied, when hunting utopias, when manipulating minds devious as her own in the game of *makrúgh*. "But let your leaders come to me in private," she added, her mind racing ahead, wondering how long she could keep up this pretense of authority. "I will give them words of wisdom and compassion, and seek to know more about your serpent Kalivorm."

Presently they fetched attendants for her, trembling girls, daughters of high lords no doubt, unused to the presence of one so far exalted above them; and they took her by the hand and led her down a ledge of bone, away from the halls of corpses, toward a city hollowed from a protuberance in the serpent's skull. . . .

Once there had been a world here; but the Shendering system had *fallen beyond* two centuries before, and now there was only the hollowed-out moon Kilimindi, palace of Ton Karakaël, the Lord of a Million Masks. As Elloran's palace Varezhdur burst free of the light-mad overcosm into realspace, Elloran and Sajit were standing in the great throneroom, whose walls had been blanked to show the starstream and the darkness. "I see Kilimindi already," Elloran said. And old Sajit, seated at the foot of the throne of gilt-friezed pteratygers, saw it too: a glowing sphere artfully checkered with ice-fields, so that it seemed to be wrapped in a *shtézhnat* board.

"You never did like Karakaël, did you, Sajitteh?" Elloran asked the old musician.

"He plays too many games."

"That's only to be expected of an Inquestor. Come, give me music. You've done a music of appropriate grandeur, I hope, for the docking of the two palaces?"

"Yes . . . but you're many sleeps early for this round of *makrúgh*, aren't you?" said Sajit.

"I don't intend to play, but to observe. Something very exciting is about to happen."

"The mythical plan of Davaryush again?" Sajit could speak freely now; they were alone. "I never believed in it, Master Elloran. If the Inquest falls it'll be through apathy, through the toll of time, not by some violent act." Sajit did not know what to believe; but he was too old to long for change now.

He had composed the Symphony of the Srinjidas; his life's work was done. "When are we going on our great journey, Elloran? The one you keep promising. Years ago, when we found young Arryk and you elevated him to the Inquestorhood, I thought you had a successor in mind. But still you're clinging to—"

"To what I know, Sajitteh. I am afraid. I have lived a long time: centuries, Sajit, centuries. The longer you live the less familiar becomes the long oblivion, and the more frightening it seems. I thought I'd accept it by now, the Ending, I mean; but now I want to see it, almost to grasp a piece of the Ending in my own hands, to—"

"Meddle, my Lord?"

"Meddle. Meddle. Powers of powers, how I love to meddle!" Elloran turned to see Kilimindi, its icy squares like facets of an insect's eye. "We're approaching. Call for the docking-master." The walls, picking up a subvocalized command, bore it to waiting servants.

His own palace, a tangle of corkscrew towers and twisty passageways painted in gold, of balustrades that buttressed burnished domes, and lightsails of tissue-thin gold that gauzed the stars' soft light, caught silver fire from Kilimindi's brilliance. Through the deopaqued throneroom walls, the two saw the two palaces spit forth docking platforms like tongues of liquid silver; tiny men in pressure skins, harnessed by thin lifelines to the platforms, were darting back and forth in their graviboots. In the lightstream that passed from palace to palace the workmen swam like a school of silverminnows. "Always a wonderful sight," Elloran said, "two Inquestral palaces meeting thus in the ocean of space, becoming one."

Sajit smiled in answer; his own thoughts occupied him.

"Metal mating with metal," Elloran rhapsodized.

"Yes, Elloran." Sajit noticed a convoy of shuttlecraft being ejected from a square of the palace. "Look. I think you'd best assume your official demeanor now, my Lord. Shall I get hold of some music?"

"Yes, something impressive, not subtle at all, I think. Karakaël's forte has never been subtlety."

"Loud, then. Brash. Overwhelming." Sajit's mind raced; he must consider what resources could be marshaled, what musicians were on call at this unusual hour; for it was the hour just before Ton Elloran liked to retire, and usually only the shimmerviols and a few favorite neuterchildren were kept up so late in case Elloran's whim should demand one of the seventeen Somnolescent Nocturnes Sajit had composed long ago, when they had both been young. "The megaconch-consort," he said. "Those can be rousted, I think. And five of the bucineers are still awake; we can arrange them at the four corners and center of the throneroom, in the classical style of a quincuncial lozenge . . . the niceties of style will not impress him, but I rather think the noise might."

Elloran's eyes sparkled. "Come, let's not make too much of a joke at his expense," he said; but Sajit saw that his master thought little of this Lord of a Million Masks. "Go, Sajitteh! This man may be ludicrous; but he's powerful. And he is, in a manner of speaking, my friend." And Elloran turned to watch the shuttles approaching. They looked a little like those ancient electrical vehicles; but they bore Karakaël's personal stamp. Over each of the portwindows hung a larger-than-life reproduction of an item or another from his collection of a million masks.

The order for music had been given. Sajit suggested as his piece one of his own juvenilia; its was a brash, brassy piece within which the five bucineers interwove in a sinuous, wailing concertante. They gathered around the displacement plate at the center of the throneroom, on either side of Elloran's galaxy of dust; at a signal from Sajit they began. Sound echoed and reechoed as it was fed into and out of the marble ampli-caverns at the far end of the palace. Sajit winced a little at the music's facile ingenuousness; he'd grown a lot older since he dashed off those notes, he thought ruefully. But it would do.

As the music swelled, Karakaël materialized in front of the dust-galaxy. This time he wore a black mask with its severely angular features highlighted with strings of tiny rubies. The canine teeth, exaggeratedly long, glistened with a crust of diamants. The mask had a wig attached, a blend of red, orange, and gold that streamed like fire.

Stiffly he came up to Elloran. "*History there is*," he said, "*and no history.*"

Elloran did not take up the challenge. "Not *makrúgh* already, my friend, at this hour! None of the combatants are here yet; and I plan only to watch this time. *Shtezhnat* I will play, but not a killing game, Kaarye."

"You will come, though. It will happen amidst the most lavish splendor that Inquestral artifice can devise."

"Of course I'll come. Have you ever known me to miss one of your spectacles?"

Watching, Sajit signed to shimmerviolists on hoverdisks above to underpin each of Elloran's statements with an eloquent soft harmony, while Karakaël's he accompanied with resounding brass.

"But I wanted to discuss other matters with you, Elloran," Karakaël said, his voice strident as the booming bucineers that played along with him. "For instance, those three boys . . . or is one of them a girl? . . . that you once sent out on their quest-journeys. How have they been doing?"

Elloran said, "The boys and the girl . . . but you know very well what they've been doing, Kaarye, else you would not ask about them."

"Powers of powers! Isn't it true that one of them has seized the Throne of Madness, turned heretic? I myself have received one of his ludicrous . . . invitations to Lightfall."

"To take that Throne," Elloran said, "is not in itself heretical. To seek change is not a heresy, but an inherent purpose of the Inquest."

"But change for *ourselves*—!"

"We will see. We have all the time in the universe to prepare for the deviving of whatever he plans to send against us. Personally, though, I no longer care."

"Your compassion is the envy of all of us, Ton Elloran n'Taanyel Tath," Karakaël said softly, menacingly. "But the girl?"

"She is with him. She has told me that they go to hunt utopias."

"What utopias? Under whose authorization?"

"An Inquestor needs no authorization, Kaarye, to hunt utopias," Elloran said mildly.

"And the other boy—Ton Arryk n'Elloren Tath—"

"I see that you have done more research than you care to tell me, Kaarye," Elloran said. "You know their names and their titles by heart."

"None of this petty parrying!" Karakaël said, almost forgetting the proper Inquestral reserve. "I have seen the boy Arryk: his mind has been seared as by a sun's fire! He has become a fanatic, Loreh. That he is a fanatic on our side is all very well, but fanatics, in their inability to bend, will snap like twigs . . . I propose to send him on some errand; for that

I seek your counsel, for it is you who gave him to the Inquest."

"Let him, too, hunt a utopia."

"Which one? Karrandis? Ophryjivarn? Laramendesht? Or Shtoma, which no Inquestor has ever brought down?"

"Why not? It is far from most of the worlds of the Dispersal of Man, Ton Karakaël. A commendable idea. And if he has become as fanatical as you say, perhaps he will break Shtoma. . . ."

"Perhaps. Although frankly I have written that world off; it hardly matters that it is not within the Dispersal's fold."

"But you wish, for some reason, to torment poor Arryk, or to teach him something. You toy with fire, you know that."

"I know that!" At those words, Sajit commanded the music to a crescendo of great violence, a sound-maelstrom; a strange juxtaposition to the serenity of mien that the two Inquestors showed, yet reflecting well their inner thoughts.

"Very well," Elloran said, very softly. Sajit had to strain. "You have my endorsement, which as a Grand Inquestor yourself you hardly need, unless it be to lure me into your forthcoming grand *makrúgh*, as a beast-fighter maddens his quarry with his quirt. I don't think I've misjudged your motives there, Ton Karakaël."

"Perhaps not," Karakaël said as he stepped back onto the displacement plate and flicked out onto his shuttlecraft. Unceremoniously, Sajit allowed the music to gurgle to a stop, leaving only the radiant shimmerviol music from above.

"He would be funny, Elloran, if he weren't so powerful." Sajit moved toward the foot of the throne, so that none of the musicians, attendants, scribes, Rememberers, and kallogynes, who had come out to provide the kind of pomp with which Karakaël loved to be greeted, could eavesdrop on them. "And what did that mask mean, the black face, the knifelike eyebrows, the bloodred hair?"

"It is one of his masks of war," Elloran said, sighing. "That's why I feel so heartsick."

"But you let him destroy Arryk, whom you love."

"There is a plan, Sajit, greater than any of us. I don't see it all yet, but . . . once there was one who did, and we have taken from him his name."

"You support Davaryush?"

"I am only a watcher," Elloran said wryly.

*   *   *

The tachyon bubble broke into realspace just over the city of Zaq of the world Bellares, where there was a training center for childsoldiers.

"Look!" Siriss cried. "The war fields where they practice the skill of laser-irising." Kelver looked down as the bubble descended through a gray cloud layer, over open scrub-grass plains mottled by patches of mud-brown. Here and there were tall gray blocks that imitated buildings; as they watched, one here and there would topple, cleanly sliced in two. They were not close enough to the ground yet to see the child-soldiers, though.

"I don't see how this will work," Siriss said.

"Why not?" said Kelver. "It's our privilege to call child-soldiers to our service as suits our needs, isn't it? We're merely using the weaknesses of the Inquest against it."

They were swooping down now over the plain. A laserlight-swath crossed their path; but since the tachyon bubble did not even, by the laws of realspace, truly exist, the two Inquestors were not touched. They saw several dozen of the childsoldiers now, each riding his hoverdisk; they formed and re-formed in midair, and their eyes wove webs of killing light. The tachyon bubble passed through the laser-skein. As they caught sight of it the soldiers desisted one by one; they fell into a V-formation and streamed groundward, where they waited for the Inquestors to reveal themselves.

Kelver and Siriss touched ground; Kelver dissolved the bubble with a flick of his mind.

He looked at the children; they were scarcely shoulder high to him. Their slitty eyes, topaz-yellow, were turned on him; their black cloaks were thrown over their shoulders; their graviboots gleamed. At a sign from their leader, they began to trill out their cry of greeting: *"Yahey hokh'Tón! Yahey hokh'Tón millílaran!"*

Kelver held out his hand for silence. "Which is the troop leader?"

A girl stepped forward. "I am Tya-without-a-clan, *hokh'Tón*. Your visit here is welcome."

Together, a score of treble voices, a shout: *"Ishá ha, hokh' Tón!* Your visit here is welcome."

Together, a score of treble voices, a shout: *"Ishá ha, hokh'Tón!* We fight. We die. We storm like locusts over the deadworlds. *Haheha!* Let us be your will, your baleful gaze, your insect plague, your purging fire, your deadly thunderclap!"

To Siriss, Kelver said softly, "The Inquest created this?"

"The childsoldiers know no compassion," Siriss said. "But we, who claim to be the vessels of the High Compassion, must lay claim to these too. I saw them burn my homeworld, Keima, once, long ago."

"They're the creatures of our own hypocrisy!" said Kelver, not caring that the childsoldiers heard. "They only do the things *we* dare not admit to ourselves we do. . . ." He looked at their faces, each one hard, ruthless. But there was somehow an innocence in them too. They had not been taught guilt. No; the Inquest carried all the guilt of the human race upon its own shoulders; it had lifted man's burden, and in doing so had rendered itself no longer human. Kelver called Tya-without-a-clan to him.

"Have you fought wars before?" he asked her gently.

"Yes, Inquestor, seven. I've survived every one of them. I hope to win a clan name before I turn thirteen."

"Suppose I were to release all of you now?"

"That is your privilege, *hokh'Tón*, for our very lives are in your hands."

"Listen, then, children. There is a new Inquest. A Shadow Inquest, and I am a part of it. I would release you from childsoldiery and enlist you in another kind of war, a war against suffering . . . do you understand me?"

"We follow you always! What matter your motives to us, who are illumined only by your High Compassion?"

Kelver turned to Siriss, despairing. "They won't understand! The Inquest has bled them of their souls; they'll follow us blindly, as though we were gods."

But Siriss only repeated the words that he had first heard on the quest-journey: "In a universe without gods, *someone* must be god."

"Come then," he said to Tya. "There is a new war for you. You will be loyal to me alone, you and your troop. I shall so give notice to the thinkhive of this world, so that you will not be missed. And I promise that each of you will win a clan name before war's end."

Tya-without-a-clan turned smartly around and shrieked out a command to the others. They roared in bloodthirsty unison; then they burst into a war song: "*Ishá ha! Ishá ha! Destroy, destroy! Burn, burn! Kill, kill! In the name of the High Inquest! Ishá ha!*"

"No! Not those words!" Kelver screamed. Abruptly they

ceased. "Arryk was right. How can I fight the void itself?" he said to Siriss. "Our cause is lost before we've begun! How can these monsters be our weapons of peace?" For a long while the children stood in sullen silence, not understanding their new master's unwarlike qualms.

Siriss took Kelver's arm and stroked it, calming him. "They're not monsters. They are only children, Kevi, children who have lost their way in a galactic labyrinth of the Inquest's making." To Tya, the young leader, she said, "Hush, girl. We will teach you a new song, and your weapons will heal, not hurt."

It was strange to see Siriss take control like this. She had come to him weeping and confused from Elloran's palace, after all; and Kelver had not been sure of her sincerity in wanting to join him. Already he was afraid of spies, of Inquestral traps, of falling victim to *makrúgh*. When they had first met she had been belligerent, always the challenger; it hid, he knew, a fear of weakness. But in her newfound gentleness there was strength. Kelver needed her strength. For above all he feared the void, the final aloneness of his calling.

"Thank you," he said. They kissed, and the childsoldiers tittered a little, but he did not scold them. He meant them to be free.

It's a poor excuse for a world, Kail Jannif was thinking as she sat in a *fáng*-induced torpor in a drughouse in the only spaceport of the planet Charra. There's been a famine; all you see are those bony children with their dull staring eyes. A servocorpse looks livelier; at least the thing's got a smile sewn onto its face. . . .

Suddenly she noticed a dark blue glimmering through the *fáng* mist. A touch of pink too. "Inquestors," she said aloud. She was not keen on Inquestors.

She made out a face. It was a boyish face; they were haunting, those violet eyes. They were beautiful, those Inquestors, no doubt about it, even if it could hardly be said that nature made them that way. She groaned, searching her mind for the right forms of address, the long-forgotten lessons in the highspeech. "*Hokh'Tón*," she said at last. "Do you seek me out?"

"Perhaps." The shimmercloaked figure came nearer. Jannif had never seen an Inquestor this close; his look held her.

"You're the first stranger to set foot here in a while, aren't you?"

"The same might be said of you, Lord."

"Do not mock me! I asked a question. You came from Bellares, didn't you? I am looking for . . . friends of mine."

"Inquestors?"

"Yes."

"Unlikely, my Lord, that I'd keep such exalted company! And why would they come to this hellhole? I was on my way to Idoresht with a cargo of dead bodies; servocorpse factory there. Strange world . . . their spaceports are the mouths of giant serpents, you know." Why am I babbling like this? she thought. It was the *f´áng* . . . the Inquestor was likely as not to have her executed on a nod or a handclap . . . but the *f´áng* had only fueled her already considerable recklessness.

"I don't know either," said the Inquestor. "Something a thinkhive in Bellares told me, though, led me here."

"You seem lost," said Jannif, suddenly concerned.

"More lost than you can imagine," the Inquestor said. There was more pain in his voice than the words warranted, and Jannif was fearful suddenly, even through the artificial cheerfulness of the *f´áng* vapor.

"What do you mean, Lord?"

"I mean," he said, "that I am waging war against those I most love, and that one day I will have to kill them."

"Well, it's the way of the universe," Jannif said, trying to make light of the pain; that had always been her way. If only she could be back on the ship, communing with her delphinoid shipmind, pinholing through the overcosm! But her delphinoid was not well; she had left it in orbit to heal, and had come down to this pit to pass the time. No company on the ship, after all, except the dead. They weren't pretty, either; she'd gotten them cut-rate, off a petty war between a couple of backworlds.

The Inquestor had turned away, his thoughts no doubt preoccupied with some galaxy-shaking issue beyond Jannif's interest. She relaxed in the wombwarmth of the chamber, feeling the *f´áng* soak into her pores—

A cry from outside. Screams from all directions. And, from a far height, a thin wailing that she had heard before, too many times. "Childsoldiers!" She was alert now, grabbing her tunic from the drying-stone, running for the entrance. It wouldn't do to have a building collapse on you at a childsoldier's stray glance!

She jostled her way into the crowd now. Beggars were everywhere, their hands still outstretched, tugging at her legs. "Childsoldiers!" came the cry from all sides; people had fled into houses and were fighting off those who tried to crowd inside. The streets were full of the homeless, the maimed, the diseased now. They were running into each other, stumbling, moaning, tripping, crawling, weeping. There was no sense in running now. Jannif looked up at the sky, where a single dull-red sun shone over this town of gray brick and no windows. The childsoldiers were raining down now on their hoverdisks. Everywhere the luckless poor had buried their faces in the filth of the streets, sobbing as they waited for certain death. "Curse the Inquest and their wars!" Jannif shouted. Somewhere in front of her a shimmercloak rustled. I'll bet *he* had a hand in this, that violet-eyed boy, she thought bitterly.

The convoy swerved now, streaming downward—

Something hit Jannif in the head, knocking her over. She grasped at it. It was soft, spongy. She struggled to her feet and saw—

They weren't blowing up the town at all! They were throwing down . . . she gasped at what was in her hand. The beggars had scrambled to their feet now and were clutching them under their arms, their chins, between their legs . . . loaves of fresh peftifesht bread . . . then came a hail of arjents, each bearing the Inquestral stamp, each worth a month's food for one of these people. . . .

All were looking skyward now, waiting. Some had timidly crept from under the awnings of their doorways. Others had climbed up on roofs and balconies.

It started as a circle of dazzling light, no larger than one of the arjents. It grew into a sundisk that eclipsed the red sun, around which shone corona upon corona, layer upon layer of light. It played over the gray buildings, and something in the stone, some tiny crystals, perhaps, that the red sun had never awakened to light, began to glitter. For the first time the town had become beautiful.

And at the center of the circle of radiance, a floater that descended slowly earthward; in it stood two Inquestors. One was a woman completely white, even to the color of her hair and eyes; the other a man, or man-boy, with eyes of clear green. It was this boy who spoke, his voice picked up by ampli-jewels and resounding through the town.

Do not be afraid, the voice said. *The Inquest's shadow has lain too long upon the Dispersal of Man. But now a shadow falls over that shadow. You need not live in terror. You need not be hungry, or be forgotten by those who rule. The Inquest is dying, dying. Remember me. Follow me, Kelver, the shadow's shadow.*

The crowd parted as the floater drifted down onto the street. Slowly the radiance faded; the fire in the brick walls died down. The childsoldiers hovered above, still throwing down their loaves and arjents. Jannif was so close that she could almost touch the two Inquestors. They were like gods, she thought. This was how the Inquest should be, not a community of bickering old fools whose every utterance spelled the destruction of star systems!

Just as the one called Kelver was about to speak again, there came another voice from behind, and the other one approached them, the one with the violet eyes.

"Heresy," he said hoarsely. "Utopianism . . . is this the kind of power the Throne of Madness has given you, Kelver?"

"Oh, Arryk," said Kelver, and Jannif could see that he loved the other and was hurt by him, "you followed our trail, and now you have come as an enemy . . . is it heresy to feed the hungry, Rikeh? Believe me, I am as fettered as these poor, though I am called Inquestor and can command more power even than most Inquestors. I am tethered to the Throne of Madness, Arryk, by a chain that threads the tachyon universe and makes my mind its slave. Why should I not do good, while I can, before I must pay this knowledge's price?"

"What will you do? Rush from backworld to backworld with your ridiculous circus of largesse? Remember the void, Ton Keverell n'Davaren Tath! The void cannot be sated."

"This is only the beginning."

"Of what?" said Arryk angrily. "Already they're worshipping you. You can't prevent it. And their worship damns you forever to be that which you despise the most! I warned you that your gift for wringing love from people's hearts would turn against you."

"Rikeh—" Kelver stood with his arms outstretched, imploring. And Jannif understood that this man of compassion was a renegade, that he might one day be hunted down by the Inquest and destroyed; and she could not let that happen. Such a man she could follow, could worship.

Timorously she reached out and caught the hem of his shimmercloak. "My Lord Inquestor," she said.

He turned to her.

"My Lord . . . could I serve you? I am Kail Jannif of the clan of Astrogators, and my delphinoid shipmind waits in orbit for me. . . ."

There was a fire in his eyes. He was possessed by some awesome vision, Jannif saw. He reached out to touch her; she flinched as though from a flame. "Don't be afraid," he said. He, an Inquestor, showed concern for the short-lived, she thought, wondering. Then Kelver cried out: "Here is one who will follow the shadow's shadow! How many others are there?"

And there was a thunderous clamor that seemed to ring from the very rooftops of the town. A strange wild joy took hold of Jannif; she was one with the crowd's surging ecstasy. But beside her stood the other Inquestor, the violet-eyed one; he did not smile at all.

TWELVE: THE MASKING

"No, to the left. The gold one with the turquoise tassels and the eyeholes rimmed with polished azurite."

Ton Karakaël sat on his hoverthrone, in the masking room of his palace, now docked with Elloran's Varezhdur. Masks lined the wombwalls, tier after tier of them, the last rows vanishing into a layer of mist, slow-swirling, artificial. Though it was tall as a hollowed-out tower, the room was dark, the walls oppressive; it was Karakaël's favorite room, into which only his most trusted servants were ever permitted. Orin, his maskslave, was one such. Half-blind now, stooping, he had tended the masks since childhood, like his father and grandfather. Orin had found the mask Karakaël asked for now, and he hobbled to his master, holding it high in the prescribed ritual of presentation.

Karakaël took the proffered mask and stared into its sightless eyes. A pile of other masks lay at his feet; masks hung from the armrests of his hoverthrone; a torn mask lay, facedown, on his lap. Today he was wearing a mask whose every detail mimicked his own face; only in this room would he wear this mask, and it was the closest he had come in five hundred years to revealing his true self to another.

"Orin!" he cried.

"*Hokh'Tón.*"

"The game of *makrúgh* that I am hosting this time is a very special one. I will want twelve masks, Orin. Twelve maskstands set out in the reception hall. They will all be masked, Orin; they won't be able to tell who they've bargained with or whom they've betrayed!"

"An elegant conceit," the old man wheezed, but Karakaël knew that he agreed only through habit, for the inner workings of *makrúgh* must surely be incomprehensible to a bondsman. But it was a grand plan. Already he had spoken to the palace cooks. A stunning banquet would be the background for this game of *makrúgh*, and the very arrangement of the different courses on the platters would represent, to the more observant Inquestor, clues as to Karakaël's true intentions, as to which mask he was hiding behind. "The twelve masks must be perfect," he said. "Look at this one!" He held it up: it was a woman's face, hair knitted from clingfire strands. "The face is torn in a dozen places, and will need to be restitched."

"If your Highness would not mind . . . I think we have another like it. . . ."

"No! You will repair this one." Its face, he reminded himself, had been lifted from a woman he had loved once, a short-lived one of course, a courtesan from Airang, no one of importance. He had visited her masked as a beggar; she had told him she loved him, as all of them were trained to do, and he had felt curiously wounded at that. For those words he had ordered her devived, and had torn her face from her and encased it in pliable plastiforce. Each of the masks for the grand *makrúgh* would be like this one. Each would have a personal meaning to him alone. And thus, as they played the great game, they would unwittingly be playing a more intimate game too; they would replay the most private moments of his life. Out of little sordid secrets he would manufacture universal statements, gestures that smashed whole worlds to dust. "Am I not cunning?" he mused aloud.

"Of course," said the bondsman, smiling innocuously, "of course, *hokh'Tón*."

"This gold mask, now." He had found it in a dead king's tomb, on a planet whose name no one remembered. "Polish. Polish until it shines like sunlight."

"Yes, *hokh'Tón*."

"And I want their voicemakers in perfect working order too. Each one is to have its own distinctive voice, no matter whose voice sounds beneath it. I don't want the guests to be guessing each other's identities from the sound of their voices, you understand."

"No, *hokh'Tón*."

"That is all."

And Ton Karakaël was alone at last, and free to slip off the mask that was exactly like his own face.

He looked into its empty eyes. Perhaps I should give it up, he thought. It is, after all, a mere eccentricity.

As he sat, a whisper in his ear: the throne's voice, receiving news from outside the palace of Kilimindi. Another palace was docking at the southern port: it was Ton Satymyrys, asking for permission to call on Elloran and on Karakaël. "I'll go," he said, but he did not move. The throne would take him there; already it was rising from the floor and moving toward the displacement field in the center of the room.

He would wear the same mask, he decided, taking a last look at it before he put it on. The mask: the face of a child, an anguished child.

Arryk's tachyon bubble touched down once more on the backworld Charra. He dissolved it and stood in what had once been the square of the spaceport town, where he had last seen Kelver. It was a ruin now. Blackened streets radiated from where he was standing. A single firefountain played in the square, guttering, discolored. In the sky, a string of childsoldiers threaded the clouds; he had just dismissed them. Their work was done, the city dead, its few survivors herded into pens to await the coming of the people-bins that would transport them, stasis-frozen, to new worlds.

A stone column, its votive inscription smudged by burndust, tottered, tumbled. A figure stirred; it moved toward him, mechanically, in a manner not quite human. "Who are you?" Arryk cried, startled. Then he noticed with relief that it was a servocorpse. "Go back. You were not summoned."

The corpse did not move. Arryk stared at it. There was something not quite right about it, for its eyes moved rhythmically from side to side, and its mouth twitched in time. A loose connection in the neuron paths, perhaps. Arryk did not want to look at corpses, even animated ones. When he subvocalized a command of dismissal, though, the corpse paid no heed; and when Arryk stepped back the servocorpse stepped forward, not letting him be distanced from it. It was unnerving, and at first Arryk wanted to call down a childsoldier to have it removed. But what could a corpse do? He was ashamed to seem cowardly, he who had just ordered the burning of a world.

"Listen," he said to the servocorpse. It raised its head and seemed to look at him from its blind, unblinking eyes. "You can't make me feel guilty, you know. Who had sent you, you poor flawed artifact? Is this Kelver's doing? Are you the opening move of his *makrúgh* against me?" The servocorpse did not move. It was an old man, grizzled, white-haired; for a moment it reminded him incongruously of Elloran. "I had to destroy Charra!" Arryk protested, vulnerable suddenly. "It would have fallen prey to the heresy of utopianism." For he could not yet admit to himself his bitterness over the love of Kelver and Siriss. They had each other now, they were complete without him. And as Kelver had come clothed in light, so must he be the darkness. "Powers of powers," he said at last. "I stand here, trying to justify myself to a thing without a soul, a man-mimic. What am I doing?"

Forget, forget, he thought. I must forget.

With a subvoked command he reached out, linked with the thinkhive on his delphinoid shipmind, and captured a bubble out of the whirlpool of the tachyon universe. The tachyon bubble materialized beside him, a circle of utter nothing that cast an inkblot over a smoldering public building. As he moved toward it, the servocorpse fell in step beside him. He made for the man-thing, started to push it away, but it backed off, maintaining its exact distance.

They were yoked, then, by some kind of forcelink. Only an Inquestor could wield such a device over another Inquestor. "It *is* Kelver, isn't it, who sent you!" Arryk said. "To follow me wherever I go, to be the specter of my guilt, never to let me forget that I killed the world you might have made beautiful . . . a visible token of my inner torment . . . can't you speak? Have you no voicebox to project the thoughts of the man controlling you?"

The eyes that could not flinch stared on, reproachful somehow. Carefully, Arryk said, mindful that the corpse's hearing might reach the machinery of Kelver himself, "You are only a thing without a soul. I cannot fear you; what I fear is in myself, and I will conquer it. We'll wait this out, Kevi! I know you'll soon be severing the forceknot that tethers me to this corpse."

He stormed into the tachyon bubble, and the dead man slid in beside him. He thought he heard a sound escape its lips, a remarkable human sigh; but he dismissed it and thought only of forgetfulness, of drowning out the pain.

*　　*　　*

"Where is your master, Orin?" Elloran asked the maskslave of Karakaël. A whim had drawn him to Kilimindi, for though he thought he had long lost his desire to play *makrúgh*, its processes fascinated him still, more than he liked admitting to himself. And Karakaël's strategy of masks was an unusual one. As Elloran looked around the antechamber into which the displacement plate had sent him, he counted twelve maskstands in a line in front of him, at the gauze-curtained entrance to another hall. The floors were carpeted with shimmerfur that had been fed only sporadically, for patches of it had died, and made pools of stubborn dullness as the periodic blush of pink on ultramarine swept across the floor.

Some of the maskstands were already occupied; directly in front of him, set at eye level on the polelike stand, was a reptilian mask whose eyes were compounded of thousands of minute black crystals, and from whose fanged mouth a forked tongue slithered and darted. Orin the slave went up to it and started to dust it with a little suction mop. "There, there," he was whispering to the mask, "he won't do anything to you. . . ." The tongue lolled, a dark sputum frothed against the fangs, and the mask hissed. "It's all right," said Orin, soothing it. After a while he remembered that he was in Elloran's presence, and he looked up apologetically from his work.

"Do you always talk to them?" said Elloran, amused.

"They are more real than we are," said Orin. The mask's tongue flicked at the air.

"What is it called?"

"The Mask of the Snake."

"I should have guessed," Elloran said.

"It is an old mask, *hokh'Tón*, older even than my master himself. My grandfather described it to me, and only on my thirteenth birthday did he let me touch it. It came, he said, from old Earth itself."

"The mythic homeworld of the heart, of which Sajit sings so eloquently?" Elloran smiled. Ever since Karakaël had challenged him to a game of *shtézhnat*, when they were young together on Uran s'Varek, he had been forced to listen to old Orin prattle about the history of the masks. Oh, they were valuable enough, and gaudy enough too, many of them. But Karakaël had always gone in for quantity, not quality, and there was much junk among the masterworks. "There, for instance," he said, advancing to the next maskstand, "what is *this* thing?"

Orin said, "Master, Ton Karakaël calls this the Mask of Making."

"An extravagant title for so unprepossessing an object!" Elloran said, laughing. For it was a plain, roughly carved face made of coarse wood and daubed here and there with orange paint.

"You should not laugh in their presence," said the slave, almost sternly. Then, to the mask, he crooned, "Lie there now, my pretty, don't be angry." He touched a stud in the mask's forehead, and it burst into flame; the eyes seemed to come alive. Its cheeks twisted spasmodically. "It burns, *hokh'Tón*, yet never is consumed."

"Oh." Elloran reached out to touch the fire; it was ice-cold, an illusion. "There's so much pain in it," he said, "though it's not even living." And he knew then that Karakaël had chosen the masks for his *makrúgh* very carefully. This was to be no frivolous game, whose consequences were but a few dead, a planet displaced here and there. Not for nothing had Karakaël mentioned Shtoma, that perpetual thorn in the Inquest's side, when he had paid his courtesy call on Elloran! Nothing good had ever come of sending an Inquestor to Shtoma. Surely Karakaël must understand that, vast as the Dispersal was, it must encompass *some* anomalies. Only in the mind of a thinkhive could an unblemished paradigm exist . . . poor Daavye now, destroyed by Shtoma, plotting his impotent plans somewhere, no doubt . . . Elloran was sure that the fall was coming, though he had heard it spoken about only in whispers. But before it came it would bring about the downfall of those like Davaryush: good men, men of compassion. Who would be next? Arryk, whom he himself had raised up from phoenix herder to demigod, who was capable of so much love and so much hate? Or Kelver, who wrung love from others and yet seemed untouched himself, as though he had once set eyes upon an absolute beauty, and could no longer be tormented by the world's passions? Or Siriss, always too eager, the first to shoot the arrow, the first to seek martyrdom?

As these thoughts drifted through his mind, he noticed that the old slave was still talking, explaining the finer points of the various masks.

"How stupid we are," Elloran said suddenly, "to be playing

these games amid trappings of such splendor. We think that we rule, when in reality we are deader than the very servocorpses."

The old man stared at him, uneasy. Elloran said bitterly, "Does it surprise you, sirrah, that I should dismiss your master's work so lightly? You who have been bred to worship us?"

The maskslave looked at the shimmerfloor, avoiding his eyes. "Your compassion touches us all."

I must remember, Elloran thought, that this man is younger than I, although age has furrowed his face and misted his eyes. And so he listened to the catalogue of masks, their meanings, their attributes, letting the man have his say. Finally he interrupted: "But where is your master, Orin? He was due for a game of *shtézhnat*, you know."

"He's left the palace, Inquestor, wearing his Deathmask."

"What does that mean?"

"I saw him at the tachyon bubble sending station. He could be on any planet of the Dispersal of Man by now."

"And the Deathmask?"

"A whim, *hokh'Tón*, nothing more. He told me to ready the masks. The grand *makrúgh* begins later today, at the twenty-ninth hour."

"I see." Elloran turned away from the doorway into the main chamber, away from the row of masks, the Mask of Making still aflame. Then he said, "And the other guests? Their palaces have docked with ours?"

At a gesture from the old man, the far wall deopaqued, and afforded a view of the starstream; Elloran saw his own palace burning against the blackness. "Aft," the old man cried out, and the view changed: there was no palace of Varezhdur, but an edifice shaped like a hawk, from whose eyes shone twin swaths of cold blue light, and whose wings shivered with the iridescence of mated mirror metals. "Ton Ynoldeh is here then," he whispered. "The Queen of Daggers."

"She has been named arbiter," said Orin.

"Does he realize how dangerous a *makrúgh* he plays?" said Elloran. "Quick! Show me the other palaces that have docked with Kilimindi."

The viewscreen changed again. This time Elloran saw another palace, vaguely phallic, its sides embedded with a mosaic of erotic scenes, lovers moving back and forth in slow motion; it was extruding its interconnective airtubes like spiderlegs. "Ton Satymyrys," Elloran said. "I haven't seen *him* since we were young together, and hunters of utopias. I see that he hasn't changed."

Again the view changed, and Elloran saw a palace shaped like a flurry of snowflakes that constantly dissolved and re-solved into faces against the stars, iceflake-faces that grew old and dissipated and re-formed into the faces of children; and each flake was a room of that palace that shifted position constantly along an invisible forcegrid governed by a capricious thinkhive. "It is beautiful," Elloran said. "Whose is it?"

"My master does not tell me whom he has invited," said Orin. "And besides, word of this game of *makrúgh* has by now spread throughout the Dispersal, and my master spurns no challenges, as you know, *hokh'Tón.*"

"Indeed." Old memories tugged at Elloran. He had loved the game once; had loved the trappings of power, the cruel beauty of it. He was excited despite himself. Who was that strange Inquestor? He could not recognize that palace, and yet it seemed familiar. He would have to search the memories of thinkhives for this. Every scrap of knowledge about my opponents is important, he thought. And then: opponents? he thought. Why do I think of opponents, I who have forsworn the game forever, who live only to await the end?

Abruptly he turned his back on the view-wall. He watched the masks and the old maskslave pottering around, wiping, dusting, braiding hair. The Mask of Making still burned; and he imagined himself as that mask, aflame forever, trapped in a torment by which he could never be consumed. And always the game drew him, as the songs of the boy Sajit once had, so long ago . . . Sajit will die, he thought, and I will go on until the fall itself . . . death drew him too, like the game, like music, like love.

In a chamber of Jannif's delphinoid ship, Kelver felt a moment of intense pain. It was the thinkhive of Uran s'Varek, reminding him that no distance could ever loosen its hold on him, for they were linked, beyond spacetime, by chains forged into the tachyon universe . . . Jannif looked up, startled.

"It's nothing," Kelver said. Siriss was beside him now, putting her arms around him. Around them burned the overcosm, light gone mad in the spacetime between spacetimes.

"Oh, Kevi, it's Uran s'Varek again, I know it. The thinkhive touches you even here?"

"It's past. Don't grieve for me, Sirissheh. I chose this."
Kelver rose from the contoured floor; it flattened itself to
support him as he stood. Around them, through the deopaqued
wall of the room, he could see incandescent whirlpools of
light, twisting, funneling, sending out jagged spraysparks of
color. He reached out in his mind for the thinkhive again; but
the connection was more tenuous now. He did not know
whether Uran s'Varek had lost contact with him, or whether it
was taunting him, tempting him with a moment of false freedom.

Others had gathered in the room now. He saw their faces,
eager, lined with worry. There were those who had been
childsoldiers, who had now become children of the shadow,
in their black tunics sashed in flameburst colors. Kelver allowed them to see him always, to break unannounced into his
chambers as if they were as exalted as he. Others were
astrogators of the clans of Kail and Harren, like Jannif, who
had heard his call and followed. He had never commanded
them as other Inquestors would have. There were pleasure
girls and boys, there were artists; and here and there stood
those Inquestors who had come to the shadow's side. And
these did not stand aloof from the others, but mingled with
them, as though circumstance had never made them lords of
life and death. Kelver saw their concern, and it distressed
him.

"Don't be afraid," Siriss said. "Things are going as planned.
Ten worlds from the Dispersal's periphery have joined us.
And look—" She pointed into the swirling overcosm.

Threading the whirlpools were other delphinoid ships,
silverflashy, like segments of a cosmic centipede.

Another voice said, "A group of runaway slaves from the
world Endreas persuaded an Inquestor to bring them to you.
Look." Kelver saw the ship the childsoldier indicated, a
distant link in the metalsnake.

Another voice, strong, resolute: "Four Inquestors have
sought permission to come into shadow with us, hokh'Tón."

Another, raspy with age, "An old Inquestor, weary of
makrúgh, seeks to die in your service."

"It is not my service!" Kelver shouted. Then came the pain
again, cresting, ebbing, pounding at his skull, his spine, his
hands.

Quickly, Siriss said, "Leave him. Please."

The crowd cleared, bottlenecking out through the displacement plate at the center of the room.

They were alone together now, the lovers. They fell into a hungry embrace. But Kelver could not be satisfied. "I'm thinking of Arryk," he said, "poor Arryk. Do you remember when the three of us were together? It seems so far away." Kelver reached out with his mind, across the tachyon neurons that joined him to the Inquestral homeworld. "Where is Rikeh now?" he cried.

Before their eyes there formed a holosculpted image: a burning city, a young man with despair in his violet eyes . . . and, shadowing him, a servocorpse, hollow-eyed, gaunt-cheeked, lips forced into a permanent cold smile. Arryk seemed so real. Kelver saw that Siriss was moved at this. He knew how gladly he would have welcomed him back, forgotten their parting anger.

Siriss stared at the image of the boy and the servocorpse, wondering. "What world is it? Why is it burning?"

"Answer, Throne of Madness," Kelver whispered.

As the voice, made spectral by distance and by the crossing between universes, sounded in the chamber, Kelver already knew what its answer would be: *Arryk is on Charra. He has destroyed all that you made. Save for those you rescued, and who follow you now, the world is lain waste.*

"Why?" said Kelver.

His report to the Inquestral Convocation: a necessary and cautionary act of destruction, occasioned by the presence of elements of the utopian heresy.

"But no one would ever go that far," Siriss said. "Has he lost his compassion, this man who as a boy-without-a-clan shamed me into losing a game of *makrúgh*?"

"No one will stop him. He is within his rights. He is an Inquestor. He doesn't lack compassion, Sirissheh. In undoing our work he thinks he works for the greater compassion. The shadow's shadow, Sirissheh, has found a shadow itself. Where we go he will follow."

"What about Elloran? Elloran won't let this happen! Elloran loves us."

"Where is Elloran now?" Kelver cried.

The holosculpture dissolved and was replaced by another image: a palace like a jewel of a million facets, around which, like insects on a web, hung other palaces on tiny silkstrands that were docking tubes: Kelver saw Varezhdur in miniature among them, a mass of interwoven spires and spirals of glitterburnished gold. There were other palaces too: one like a hawk, another like a phallus, yet another like a haze of snowflakes.

Siriss said, "Elloran has gone to Karakaël's *makrúgh* game. Even though he has sworn never to play again."

"Whose palaces are those?"

The thinkhive's voice: *Of Satymyrys, Seeker of Pleasures; of Ynyoldeh, Queen of Daggers; of Ton Varushkadan el'Kalar Dath, Mother of the High Inquest.*

"Lady Varuneh is not yet dead?"

Dead and not dead, said the thinkhive. *She is between life and death. But I have called up this image of a palace she once ruled, ten thousand years ago; a palace from which she once exploded suns to watch the pretty lights, and swayed the hearts of Princelings. I have prepared this palace in case of her return. It is yours too,* hokh'Tón, *and you are its lord. I think you will want to play a role in this game, Ton Keverell.*

"I am ruled," Kelver whispered. "I'm not a ruler. Come, show me Arryk again."

And the web of linked palaces disappeared; and there came the image of Arryk again; this time he was walking the streets of a towering and garish city. A few steps behind him followed the servocorpse.

"What is that dead man doing?" said Siriss. "It's not like Arryk to rely on the services of the dead."

It is dead and not dead, said the ghostly voice, and Kelver fancied that it laughed. *Arryk believes that you,* hokh'Tón, *have sent the dead one, to be your eyes and ears, to watch him. But it is someone else who has done it.*

"Who?" said Kelver.

Suffice it, said the thinkhive of Uran s'Varek, *that your plans are bearing fruit. I will watch over you, Ton Keverell n'Davaren Tath, and when the time comes you will pay the price.*

"If it's death," Siriss said, "I'll die for him."

It is not death, and you cannot take his place.

"It's time for us to go to Shtoma," Kelver said at last.

"Shtoma? The notorious utopia that has crushed so many of the Inquest?"

"Yes. There's someone there I want you to meet, Sirissheh."

Arryk dissolved his tachyon bubble with a flick of his mind. He was in Airang, the city of love, of the pleasure planet Alykh, where men go to forget their pain. Ahead stood the

towers of the varigrav coasters, black needles against the
artificial rose of Alykh's twilight; behind him a masked street
opera screeched and vendors tugged at his shimmercloak.
The air, stale, jangle-rich, blew hotly in his face, with mingled fragrances of perfumes and putrescence, of sweetmeats
and sour wine. He turned a corner and saw the servocorpse,
waiting . . . he ducked into another alleyway, where a dirty
boy played with a feather-tasseled stick. He looked up, wide-
eyed: "Guide, *hokh'Tón?*"

"No." The servocorpse slipped into a shadow striped by a
harsh glare from a barred window opposite. Arryk pulled his
shimmercloak about his shoulders and faced the servocorpse
uncertainly.

"Who sent you?" he said. For a servocorpse, even if mute,
must know at least its master.

The corpse stepped from the shadow; Arryk saw its blank
eyes flare for a moment, and heard a strangled cry issue from
its lips. But it said no more. Kelver had done this for sure.
Kelver, who seemed good beyond good, reduced to torturing
one who had loved him with the very image of his guilt.

Then the corpse laughed.

"Why are you laughing?" Arryk turned his back on it. The
alley forked and forked again. The child, tired of his game,
followed, prattling: "I can show you the varigrav coasters,
master, show you how to ride them. Forget your pain. Just
throw me a couple of gipfers and I'll be your slave for the
day. My mother's dying of the wasting heart and we don't
have money for somatic renewal." He talked on in a high-
pitched monotone, the words rehearsed by rote, no doubt,
but his heart not in them. Arryk tried to ignore him as the
alleyway branched again and the damp walls, reddened now
in the dusklight, pressed in on him. There was the corpse
again, black-cloaked, smiling the smile of the dead.

"Who are you? Are you Death?" Arryk screamed at it. For
the Inquestors occasionally, when in their compassion they
were forced to command a deviving, used the dead as their
executioners. Arryk ran now, bursting through a wrought-
iron gate topped with cold fire, into—

People everywhere! Above, floaters were caught in a jam,
and lordlings in their gaudy clothes were cursing at their
drivers. One floater was wedged in between the eaves of two
squat buildings, souvenir shops, and a crowd had gathered,
streaming endlessly from the two displacement plates on

either side of the square. The servocorpse was behind him now, would have been breathing down his neck if only it could breathe—

"This way, master, if you'll only throw me a gipfer—" said the street urchin. Arryk tossed the small credit disk at him and the boy skillfully and callously elbowed a path through the throng. "Make way for the Inquestor," he piped. Seeing the shimmercloak, the crowd parted; some prostrated themselves, backing into each other and falling over themselves in panic, and a murmur-wave of *hokh'Tón's* rippled through the tangle of conversations. The boy pulled Arryk by the hand and yanked him toward the plate, and as they stepped on it they reappeared—

Stillness! The awed crowd staring skyward from the square, as pteratygers soared and their riders pierced a levitating sunsphere with bright laserlances. . . . "Quick," the boy shouted. Arryk looked up: a trick of the light? Or was the servocorpse itself riding the wind among the tygerriders? They plated again—

—chessboards of light and darkness, with the varigrav towers growing, growing against a sky exploding with false fire, crisscrossed with searchbeams, dotted with birdflock shuttlecraft—

They stood outside the entrance to a varigrav coaster, a klomet-high pillar studded with amethysts, from whose summit you were meant to cast yourself down, and be borne aloft on the varigrav fields, soaring, plummeting, flying, diving, until you had washed away all your pain. . . .

The servocorpse loomed up behind him—

"Quick! Up the airchute!" the boy yelled. Arryk ran to the entrance to the airtube that would carry him to the top. Gleefully the child jumped in beside him, holding out his hands for another gipfer. "Did I do well, *hokh'Tón?* Is the servocorpse gone?"

Soon the two of them had reached the summit. The city spread out beneath them, a blazing light-grid at the confluence of two mountain ranges. Arryk jumped, feeling the gravicurrent buoy him up. He soared, nestling in a pocket of the wind. The tops of minarets careened close, then vanished into pinpoints. He cried out, but the great wind drowned out his voice. He screamed his pain to the great roaring. Again he veered skyward, toward the stars that echoed the dazzling city beneath. Then the coaster current jackknifed, his stomach flopped, he was dizzy from the free-fall, and the streets widened, widened, and he cried out like a child, remembering the cities burned at his command, the fire-rivers riving the narrow streets of Charra—

And the coaster dropped him, featherlike, on the ground. The boy was already walking away, toward the market square whose bustle he could hear from behind the curve of a decaying cloud-maker.

"Boy," he called out.

The urchin turned: Arryk noticed the rags now, the hunger-haunted eyes.

The boy smiled a little, hoping for another coin.

"Boy, what is it you want? Why have you been following me all this while?"

"Because, my lord, you are an Inquestor. You have the keys to all the universe."

"You are so naïve, boy." Arryk pitied him. "What door shall I unlock for you, then?"

"I want to run from here, to be a childsoldier. The part about my sick mother, now, that was true."

"You do not know what you ask." Arryk pulled a coinbag from his shimmercloak; it contained a few arjents, a hemior, a handful of gipfers, and one irydion. "This will buy her a somatic renewal. I think we've lost that servocorpse that was following me around. I owe you something."

He tossed it at the boy, who dashed into the crowd. Then he turned away sadly and walked south, toward the prostitutes' quarter. For the pain gnawed at him still, and he longed for his old homeworld Kailasa, where he had herded phoenixes and worshipped the Inquestors from afar. But he could not turn back time itself. He could only find little oblivions here and there, brief respites only from what he knew now to be inevitable. . . .

The pimp led Arryk into a small bedchamber. A fountain of blue fire mingled with blue water played against a cracked wall; the fountain was a fine work of art, the rest of the room decaying. He waited, bowing.

"The girl," Arryk said, "I thought you were going to show me a girl!"

The pimp looked at him. He seemed to have grown strangely tall suddenly. His withered features, plastered as they were with cosmetics, began to shift . . . suddenly his face began peeling slowly from the top downward . . . Arryk stared, fascinated. It was a woman's face now, and the pimp's mask, paper-thin, like the molted skin of an insect, had fallen onto the furfloor of the room . . . he knew the face, though it was already shifting again, subtly shifting. . . .

"Siriss!" he whispered. "I knew that you and Kelver were behind this, taunting me, when all I was trying to do was follow the teachings of Elloran, to find my own way to the great compassion. . . ."

The face melted away into a syrupy liquid that frothed as it ran down to the floor. Now it was Kelver who looked at him, Kelver of the green eyes. "I can't bear it," Arryk said. He reached out to touch the boy's face; his hand burned, he snatched it back with a cry of pain. The figure, still in its pimp's robe, reached up a hand to rip away yet another mask . . . and Arryk saw that it was the servocorpse that had been following him since Charra.

"You're right," he said, bitter. "Our love is dead, Kelver, Sirissheh. I don't feel anything. You're utopians, heretics, and I'm going to destroy you, for the sake of the greater compassion, for the sake of the Dispersal of Man—"

The corpse laughed: a rattling sound, emotionless.

Arryk could not control his anger. He shook the corpse, he smashed his fist into its face. Its laughter did not stop. He seized its hair; hanks of it came loose in his hand, but he did not stop. Flesh tore from the corpse's cheeks, fresh blood ran down its empty eyes, the whole face came apart in his hands, and then—

The laughter stopped abruptly.

A voice, cynical, familiar, said, "Illusion, Rikeh, all is illusion."

"Karakaël!"

Arryk could not know for sure; for beneath the four masks was another mask, of course, a mask of gold in whose cheeks were incised scars of iridium, and whose eyebrows were set with hair-thin crystals of diamant.

"Quite the hysterical performance you gave, lad, for your friends' benefit! I'm sorry you got my identity wrong. It's been known to happen before."

Arryk looked at the floor. Plastiflesh was seething as it dissolved into the floor. The hair was writhing as though it were alive. "Why have you come?" he said. "Why did you try to trick me?"

"I want to know where you stand, Arryk, in a game of *makrúgh* that I am preparing. You're invited, of course; any Inquestor who dares to brave *my* vicious endgame is welcomed at Kilimindi. But first, the Convocation has a mission for you: a utopia hunt."

"I have a different game to play now, Ton Karakaël. I am on their trail."

"The utopia which you are to hunt, lad, *is* their trail. It is called Shtoma, and is at the far periphery of the Dispersal of Man. A dozen Inquestors have failed to crack its secrets; I trust you will succeed."

"Shtoma . . . where Davaryush . . ."

"Exactly. If Shtoma is the source of this terrible heresy, son, you will probably also find there the way to destroy your enemies, Kelver and Siriss."

"They are not my—"

"Yes. You loved them once. Now you no longer love them. Don't you remember the void?"

"I remember," said Arryk, feeling once more the talons of that terrible pain. "I no longer love them." But as he spoke he realized that he had obeyed without thinking, without feeling, as a servocorpse obeys.

THIRTEEN: THE ORACLE

Elloran's throneroom: the dust-galaxy swirling: the walls deopaqued: against the starfield, the hawk palace in the middistance, the pleasure palace half-hidden by Kilimindi, and, peering from the burnished moonlet's glittering horizon, the ice palace of an unknown Inquestor.

In the throneroom, seated, immersed in the suffocating sweetness of a hidden choir of neuterchildren, alone: Elloran.

"Sajit!" he called out. The music wilted, became a mere murmur.

A girl came, bearing a message: "He cannot come." She stepped onto the plate and disappeared. And abruptly, Ton Elloran n'Taanyel Tath, Lord of Varezhdur, Kingling of Kailasa and its tributaries, rose from his seat of power. He did not feel like all those things anymore.

He went to the displacement plate, subvocalized a command; he wandered down half-remembered corridors now, dark places lined with pteratygers. But he could not be alone for long. For the palace had a million eyes, and knew always where he was; and soon there came attendants, shuffling out of the shadows: here a pleasure-girl, always standing just out of sight with a demure smile just waiting to alight upon her lips; here one of the newly created harpmutants, ready to pluck on the gutstrands that grew across the hollowed cavity between its breasts, a creature deformed and bestial, from whose cavernous breast issued exquisite music; here a clothier, here a brace of childsoldiers, armed against the negligible possibility of a traitor in the palace; here an old Rememberer muttering about dead planets . . . the dark passageway was

150

alive with the whispergibbering of these invisible companions. Elloran thought: I shall never be alone, never, never.

He found the entryway to Sajit's quarters. He rode the turning stairwell to the small chamber with its wooden floor, cold to his fursoles. He found Sajit squatting, alone, toying with a whisperlyre. He heard noises behind him; he turned quickly, knowing that the unseen attendants would draw back. "Let me breathe," he said quietly, and their whisperings died away. Sajit looked up and saw his master, and smiled weakly.

"Sajitteh, I sent for you."

"I'm thinking," said the old musician, and Elloran saw how the wrinkles had cross-stitched his face, and how his eyes had misted, "about dying, Elloran."

"Are you ill? I won't let you die, old friend. If necessary, you shall have the life-prolonging drugs that only the Inquestors can have."

"You know you can't do that."

"I know. But I am Inquestor here! Should I not break the rules as I see fit?"

"No, Elloran; to do so you would cease to be an Inquestor . . . and you are a fine one, the noblest we have ever known. If you did not let me die, you would be untrue to yourself. Man is a transient thing. You have removed yourselves, you Inquestors, for a time, from that transience, and therefore taken men's griefs upon yourselves. I don't want to be like you, friend."

Elloran knew then that even as he walked down the corridors of his vast palace, watched by a million eyes, attended by a thousand followers, he was alone, terribly alone.

"Stay, Sajitteh. At least until we see the end together."

"Perhaps, my Lord." His voice wavered. He touched the whisperlyre, a tiny tinny sound, for it drew no resonance from a living body.

"Do you remember, Sajitteh, when we were boys thrown together by an accident, on the planet Ymvyrsh, and you first sang to me the song of the homeworld of the heart, and you killed the Grand Inquestor Alkamathdes who had gone power-mad?"

Sajit smiled. "When we both loved Dei Zhendra, the dust sculptress, but learned that she loved the dust more," he said, remembering too.

"Do you remember Kerrin, my sister, whom we found

after a fifty-year search, preserved by time dilation as a little girl, in a planet I was about to have destroyed?"

Sajit said, "You remember these things? It has been a century, more perhaps. I have already lived too long. You have your Rememberers, Elloran, and you will lose these memories, even these that seem most precious to you, and when your Rememberers come whispering them to you, you will wonder why it was they were so precious: We short-lived ones are like the snow and the rain, Elloran, and you Inquestors are like the mountains on whom the rain falls."

"But, Sajit . . . the rain weathers down the mountains, and eventually carries them to the sea."

"That is what I meant. Men will die and men will come again; but when the Inquest is gone it will be forever."

They looked at each other, these two men who were of an age: the one near the end of his life, the other perhaps not even halfway through his. And Elloran knew that, if he lived long enough, he might forget even Sajit, even the strained friendship they had shared, that crossed the abyss that lay between man and the Inquest. "I swear," he said, "I will not forget." But he knew better. The memory just could not contain all an Inquestor's life; that was why there were thinkhives who stored memories in minute detail, and Rememberers who could recite the histories of forgotten worlds.

"You have compassion, Elloran."

Strangely, the words stung him. He said, "I can't deny, Sajitteh, that there are Inquestors in whom compassion does not run true."

"But you are not one of those, Elloran. Be comforted. You will always be of the light. I will love you until I die, and when I have been taken to the servocorpse factories my songs will still love you."

"You mean to die then."

"Yes, *hokh'Tón.*"

"Do not call me by that hateful honorific!"

"No, Elloran. But before I die, take me to Shentrazjit and put me at its center. You will know when that is. In the moment of my passing you will hear a new music in Shentrazjit. It is all part of my own plan. It may seem nothing to you, Elloran, you who toy with whole star systems; but it was made for you, and it is beautiful, I think."

Elloran turned away, sunk in his own thoughts. Sternly, like a parent rebuking a wayward child, he told himself: *I am an Inquestor, I am an Inquestor.* He tried to remember a time when he had not had Sajit: but all he could see was a burning city, a father's corpse crushed by the weight of its funerary vestments, a sister who was dead now, buried somewhere at the heart of this very palace. He composed his mind, lulling himself over and over with the words of the Inquestral texts, words that now seemed hopelessly inadequate and inapplicable. And he left his friend, knowing that persuasion would be useless, although a simple command would have sufficed to make Sajit go on living as long as Elloran needed him. Even as Inquestor, Elloran would not command those who loved him.

So he left the chamber of Sajit, and went down to the corridors of concealed attendants, and back to the throneroom, to the seat stuffed with kyllap leaves over the throne of sculpted pteratygers, and he prepared to receive the Queen of Daggers, the deadly Lady Ynyoldeh, in audience. Already the musicians were in place and had readied themselves to play one of Sajit's most eerie compositions, *The Kiss of the Serpent Death*.

The first thing Siriss noticed when she and Kelver stepped from the tachyon bubble was Shtoma's strange light: a pale light streaking through gaps in the canopy of bloodred forest. They walked into the light. And suddenly she felt an overwhelming heartache, a homelonging, such as she had not felt since renouncing her baser passions to become an Inquestor. "What is it I feel?" she cried out.

Kelver said, "It is joy, Sirissheh. Davaryush told me of this world, where a sentient white dwarf sun has embraced all its inhabitants in a dance of joy, and their words of greeting are: *Qithe qithembara; udres a kilima shoisti. Soul, renounce suffering; you have danced on the face of the sun.* It was here that Davaryush lost his faith, for he learned that utopias can exist after all."

Siriss looked wonderingly at the forest. Crimson ferns sprouted spiderlike from the burnt-red ground; in the patch of sunlight they grew in such profusion that they mingled, intertwined, their very leaves braiding one to another. The yearning in her grew ever more intense; she was afraid at first to recognize it for what it was. Then, as the sunlight bathed her once more, she cried out with a joy fierce as pain. "It feels like—" she said.

Then she looked at Kelver, knowing how he must feel the same thing. Kelver said, "Like none of the bad things have ever happened. As if I'd never been touched by the light on the Sound, as if I'd never been chosen to be an Inquestor."

"Like being a child again," Siriss said, and she saw that Kelver seemed changed, that for the first time since his meeting with the intelligence within the Throne of Madness the great grief seemed to have left him. "As if the dark Inquestor had never come to fetch me from my burning homeworld."

For a long time they looked at each other; seeming to discover anew what they had first felt for each other. And then they made love, with the innocence of two children who have just begun to explore each other's bodies, among the bloodred ferns; around them the forest chirped, buzzed, twittered, for alien creatures lived in it. At last Siriss closed her eyes, afraid to be overwhelmed in the white sun's joyous warmth. . . .

Suddenly, as she climaxed, she heard high-pitched laughter, children's laughter. "Someone is watching us," she whispered, gathering her shimmercloak to her breasts. She listened. There was nothing except the chitterings of the forest animals. Perhaps it had simply been another such creature. She turned to Kelver again, kissing him.

The laughter came again, now from behind. In a second, it came from somewhere in the trees. Kelver started and shouted out, "Who is it?"

Then came another laugh: warm, watery, a woman's laugh. And Siriss saw a snow-pale face peering from the shadows; Kelver was gaping. The woman stepped out: long midnight hair swirled, and she smiled. She was older than the two Inquestors, and startlingly beautiful.

"Why, Kevi," she said, "after all these years . . . another woman too!" But her tone did not rebuke him.

"Darktouch," Kelver said. "But you're so much older than me now. We were just children when we ran down the Cold River together."

"Time dilation," said Darktouch. "We've traveled our separate ways. It's a miracle, really, that you even find me still living; a century or more has passed, in realtime, since the days of our youthful love on Gallendys, and all my people, the deafblind ones that the Inquest fashioned to hunt the Windbringers, are dead, their carvings sheared from the rockwalls of their hidden country, their dwellings gutted to make way for shelves of servocorpses . . . I am the last of the Dark Country, Kelver. And I see you still a boy, almost like the boy I loved, but a boy weighed down by the trappings of terrible power."

Kelver said, "Just now, in the sunlight, I thought I was a child again. But now that I see you I know that I'll never retrieve the past."

And Siriss saw that there passed between the two of them memories that she could never touch, sacred memories that even a trained Rememberer could never bring to life. She was sad, then, because she loved Kelver, and she wanted selfishly to be everything to him. And Darktouch was so beautiful . . . I am not important, she thought. The great plan of Kelver and Davaryush—*that's* important. It was dreamed up long before I even knew these people, before I was even born. How can I compete with the grandeur of their visions?

She walked away from them, into the patch of sunlight, trying to shut out the joy. There were children now, leaping from the branches, prattling incessantly, running underfoot; one stopped and sang out to her: "*Qíthe qíthembara!*" and she clutched her grief to herself, hating the sunjoy. But she found the woman Darktouch beside her and felt her arms around her waist and smelled her clean scent; and Kelver, too, was by her side, kissing the nape of her neck; the children stopped to stare rudely, curiously, but Darktouch dismissed them with a smile, saying in their language, "Off with you, go and find your other mothers, go ride the coasters!" And then Siriss felt the embrace of sunlight and four arms, and the voice of Darktouch whispering, "Don't be sad, Sirissheh. Give up your sorrow. Udara, the sun, watches you. You are in love with grief, but now grief has fallen from you as a garment drops from the shoulders of a girl who is about to make love." And they did make love, though at first Kelver was violent, like a chained pteratyger, and Darktouch so gentle that Siriss hardly knew that she touched her; but then, as the sun touched them, it severed the jesses of Kelver's passion, and he skimmed her arclike as a hawk the sky, while Darktouch was the earthy one, striving, clawing. And Siriss began to weep. She did not know if it was grief or joy, for they were so mingled as to know no name.

As she lay exhausted, she heard once more the children

tittering. She was drifting into sleep. But she could hear Kelver and Darktouch talking softly, seriously:

"You will not know him. He is so old now."

Kelver's voice: "I am afraid."

"Here you can forget fear."

"But even here I am tethered to the Throne. When I want I can see so many things: visions, nightmares. That's why I came. I need him, Darktouch."

"You're his successor. From what you tell me the plan is working."

"Oh, it's working. There's dissension from within. Many worlds are ready to break away. The Inquest is falling apart because it cannot bring itself to believe that it *could* fall apart. . . ."

"It is good that you're here. They're sending another investigator."

"Another? After what happened to Davaryush?"

"It's a young man. A tachyon bubble came bearing the message. The same old nonsense; they've heard the claim that we are a utopia, and wish to examine everything so that if it meets the right criteria Shtoma will be accorded some signal honor. It won't wash here; we've seen too many of them. When the time comes Udara will touch him, and he will be healed. Already it is happening to you and Siriss. He'll be on our side soon. I'm sure of it."

"Who could it be?"

Siriss heard another voice now, an ancient voice, dry-raspy. But there was so much compassion in it. She wondered who it could be.

"His name is Arryk, Kevi."

Kelver did not reply. Was it his weeping that she heard now? Was the old man Davaryush, the heretic, who had spawned all this madness?

The old man's voice—so loving, so gentle: "We cannot send him back, Kelver. Some higher power must want to crush him, to play him in a game of *makrúgh* and destroy him in the process."

"Not Elloran," Kelver said.

"No. Not Elloran. Elloran would not do this thing. He is truer to the Inquestral ideal than the others; and so, in the end, I suppose he stands against us, and this grieves me. No, I don't know who would want to break young Arryk. But perhaps he won't be broken. Perhaps he, too, will dance on the face of the sun, and have the hate washed out of him. You've arrived in time to go with us into the arms of Udara."

Kelver said, "I do so want Arryk to come back to us." He sounded like a lost child suddenly.

They went on for a while, discussing less pressing issues; gradually the sounds faded from Siriss's consciousness, and she fell into a strange sleep: luminous, dreamless, childlike.

A vague motion like the docking of a delphinoid ship . . . she started awake and cried out. One of the attendant girls came into the sanctum, cradling a fireglobe in her hands; she let it go, and Varuneh watched it floating up to the ceiling, a fold of flesh held in place by a splinter of Kalivorm's bone. "What is wrong?" Varuneh said. "Leave me alone."

Again came the motion: the flesh-floor undulating, the phosphorescence flickering on the walls.

The girl prostrated herself. "Prophetess . . . the governors of the city need you."

Another oracle, Varuneh thought. She had adjusted to her new role well, keeping apart in this sanctum, enforcing secrecy among the city's rulers, playing the part of Inquestral observer who must not be questioned, occasionally coming up with mysterious sybilline utterances for them to ponder. In the past months their awe of her had increased rather than declined, for she had allowed them no familiarity with her person. No, she did not want them to come close, to see her frailty.

Let them worship, she had thought ruefully, since that is what they seem to need and want. . . .

They were coming now, the high officials of the city. There were half a dozen of them, old men and women clothed in scales from the sloughed-off skins of Kalivorm. Varuneh surveyed them, her face masklike. "Welcome," she said, "Lords of Kepharang."

The eldest came forward. "Inquestrix," he said, "you have felt the tremors?"

"Yes. What do they mean?"

"I am afraid, *hokh'Tón*. I think that Kalivorm has found a mate. It is thousands of klomets distant, but its pheromones, dissolving in the sea water and borne hither by slow currents, have already reached us."

"I disagree," another said, her voice raspy, unpleasant. "It's merely an upset stomach, Elder Hakra. I've studied the serpent's habits all my life; everything I know I learned from Knower Jithora, who was actually conceived during the last mating. Which among you has actually been present during serpentmating, that you dare to assume that it is upon us?"

Varuneh said, "Quiet, Lady Knower. Have *you* experienced this serpentmating?" Reproved, the woman was silent. Varuneh thought for a while. "You know that all I can do is advise. But surely you have thinkhives that can answer a question like this."

"There have been no thinkhives, Lady, since we settled this waterworld. How can there be? We lost everything in the water. We've built this civilization from nothing," said the Elder.

"There must be a place. The Inquest is compassionate. We have never abandoned a people. Somewhere there is a thinkhive that will know your answers. Where did the people-bins land, which brought your people here so long ago?" As she spoke the whole room shuddered again, and she was afraid, although she concealed her terror well.

"The waters drift, Inquestrix," said the Knower. "How can we know such a thing?"

"But you have legends, perhaps."

"We never leave the serpent's mouth, Inquestrix," said the Elder. "Starships come and go in the dawn, and we load them with servocorpses, but we remain. Our oldest records show that the people-bins were unloaded at Dragonstooth, the only bit of land to rise above this ocean. It is a thousand klomets from here."

"Then the hulls of the people-bins will remain; and within them, thinkhives capable of understanding the life forms of this planet. We should go there."

The old ones looked at each other, fearful. "What cowards you are!" Varuneh said. "Once your ancestors crossed parsecs to reach this waterworld. But now you will not stir to know whether your homes will be destroyed. You parasites, you vultures . . . you live off the dead."

Elder Hakra said sadly, "That is true. What can we do? We are helpless."

"No, Hakra! Come with me. The traders in the spaceport will have floaters. I will go out to this Dragonstooth. Give me servocorpses to help me, to carry me when I grow weak."

The old woman, the Knower, laughed. "This is not how things are done in Kepharang, nor thoroughout Idoresht."

Varuneh said, "I do not command as Inquestor; my presence here is a secret. But I will go and find out your truth for you, because I am touched by the High Compassion." She turned her back on the Elders and left the pulsing chamber. Only Hakra followed her.

They went down corridors where the only light came from the shimmercloak; drawing its sustenance from organic wastes, the cloak glowed dazzlingly. They reached an elevator, a basket woven of old snakeskin and pulleyed up a taut sinew in the serpent's laryngeal cavity. It was dawn; soon they would reach the mouth, the spaceport, and Kalivorm would yawn wide to receive the shuttlecraft from the delphinoids in orbit.

They walked across the wide avenue that was the central ditch in the serpent's tongue. The spaceport, a dingy collection of bone buildings, lay ahead, a few dim lights in the cavernous darkness. Then the serpent's mouth opened wide, and sunlight streamed into the immense cavern, and a seawind sprang up, howling, moist. The great fangs were dagger-silhouettes against the brightness, and cast vast shadows over the serpent's tongue.

In a bar of the port they traded the use of a floater for ten servocorpse certificates; and when they were ready, Varuneh and Hakra set forth, bursting from shadow into a bright white sunlight. Servocorpses tended the floater, guarding its precarious railings. The Elder of Kepharang sat huddled in a corner, his snakeskin cloak thrown over his eyes. But Varuneh did not flinch. Below, in the mirror water, echoes of gold-edged clouds. Ahead, water to the horizon's end. And behind them, the serpent's head, thrown back, with the spaceport in its jaws. Its eyes were closed, as though ensorcelled by the sun's warmth; water, full of the food creatures that sustained its life, flooded into its jaws and under the stilts of the port. Quickly, Varuneh subvocalized a command to the thinkhive of the floater, and it skimmed the water, seeking out land, as the seawind rose and made her graystreaked hair stream and her lips taste salt. . . .

There it was now, a pointed pillar looming from the water. At its base the water thrashed. And soon Varuneh saw what she had been seeking. In a crevice between two rocky jags a hulk lodged. It was metallic, cylindrical, most of it was submerged. It was hard to believe that such a flimsy artifact once held half a million people, stasis-frozen, fleeing a dying planet, that, towed by a convoy of delphinoids, it had sailed the overcosm until the Inquest declared a new world ready for settling.

"Uncover your face, Elder Hakra," Varuneh said gently. "We are here."

The old man peered from the cloak, gaped at the column of black rock that held the people-bin at its base.

"Inside," Varuneh said to the servocorpses. They stared blankly at her, and then set to work gracelessly. In a few moments they were sailing into the metal husk itself; Varuneh saw the metal glinting as it haunched above them, and the ripple of the outside light in the water, on the silvergleaming walls. The floater moved slowly. There was no sound save the quiet lapping of water against metal.

"Watch, old man," Varuneh said. But she knew that she was much older than the man could ever be. Will I die here? she thought. The thought of death was a strange one, unfamiliar. She thought of Davaryush, the last man she had loved. Where were they now, the children who had dreamed of bringing down the Inquest? Varuneh felt a savage bitterness. She wanted to abandon these people who lived like maggots, who fashioned servile simulacra from human corpses.

But how can I die now? she thought. And she thought back to the time when there was no Inquest, when the Dispersal was young. As long as she was alive, that memory still lived.

"Inquestrix—" the old man said.

She paused, listened for a moment to the murmur of waters. Then she cried out in her aged, thin voice: "Thinkhive! Thinkhive!"

There was no response at first; only her own words, shifting from panel to panel of the people-bin. "Thinkhive!" she cried. "It is I, a Grand Inquestor, who summon you! I override your previous programming, I, Ton Varushkadan el'Kalar Dath, Grand Inquestor, Hunter of Utopias, Kingling, command that you speak to me!"

She turned to Elder Hakra. There was fear in his eyes, as she knew there would be. For she had never before spoken with such authority, as though it were to be expected that even the oldest of machines, older than any of the commonfolk, must obey her.

"Answer me, thinkhive!" she cried again, her voice almost lost in the resonance of mingled echoes.

Then came a quiet voice, a metallic voice: *I hear you, Ton Varushkadan. Demand of me, for I am your servant.*

"I release you from your servitude to this people-bin. No longer must you steer this craft through the overcosm, for the people have found their home. Instead you will answer to the people of this world. You will send your eyes and ears out over the world, and you will tell them all they need to know."

A thousand years have passed, Inquestrix . . . I wake to the sound of water. I see an ocean dotted with huge serpents. One, a thousand klomets distant, is stirring, fired with the lust to mate.

"You have your answer, Elder Hakra," Varuneh said to the old man. "Your doomtime has come. What do you choose to do about it?"

"We will do what we have always done, prophetess. We'll spend the last days of the city with mass rites of fertility, praying that all our womenfolk will be impregnated, so that the city may be rebuilt when the serpent's lust is satiated."

Varuneh thought of it. The bony structures crumbling as Kalivorm thrashed in the throes of love; the people making love in a desperate passion as their homes tumbled around them. "There must be a better way. Why don't you set out to sea and wait? You could build boats of bone fragments. You could wait until the time is over and return when Kalivorm is sated. Couldn't you?"

At her words Hakra began to weep. Varuneh could not understand this. The short-lived were so much like children. "Why are you weeping?" she said. "I have shown you a way you might save more lives."

"All my life I've dreamed of leaving the serpent; of establishing floating cities, perhaps, and becoming independent. But the Knowers who study the ways of Kalivorm don't want change. If only you, Inquestrix, could command it . . . those lives might be saved. But I can't do it! More than anything, our people grow up with the fear of light, of wide watery spaces!"

"So be it then." Varuneh saw the trap of compassion open up as it so often had before in her long life. She no longer loved the burden of responsibility, the godlike power of Inquestorhood. But once more she had to exercise it. Because of the compassion, the terrible compassion. If only the Inquest had been made in some other's image, not in hers! If

only it had lacked compassion! Then it would never have
been weak. It would have been a machine. As it lacked
compassion, it might also lack that terrible cruelty with which
the Inquest had ruled; for cruelty, she thought, is compassion's dark shadow, and the two are forever intertwined. And
so she said, "Go. I command it: the making of boats, the
putting to sea. In my compassion I command it. The oracle
has spoken."

And she gave the subvocalized command that drove the
floater away from Dragonstooth, back toward the serpent's
jaw. Their journey had lasted only an hour, and there would
be plenty of time before Kalivorm closed his mouth and
submerged himself once more, and the people of Kepharang
were shielded again from the light they feared so much.

FOURTEEN: A CADENT LIGHTFALL

To a dozen worlds came the childarmies of shadow. They swooped down like the deathbringers, screeching their childish warcries. But instead of laying waste to the cities, slicing the mountains, and burning the fields, they scattered loaves and arjents. Instead of ordering the populace into peoplebins, to be frozen and packed and let loose into the overcosm, they broadcast a new message: *The Inquest falls*. People were moved; they embraced the new doctrine, not really understanding its meaning, for they lived for their families and their countries, occasionally for their planet or their clan, and had no real notion of Inquestral mysteries, of Dispersalspanning philosophies.

And though a few worlds saw the shadow armies, the Inquest ruled a million planets. On many worlds it was but a name, a bogeyman. In others, the heartworlds, the Inquest's power was complete and unassailable; these were worlds easily reached through the pinhole paths of the overcosm. Kelver was not yet concerned with these. But he had learned from Davaryush that the Inquest's hold was far more precarious than it thought. In twenty thousand years many links had grown tenuous, and there had always been many worlds like Shtoma, too distant, too much of a bother for the Inquest. It was to these worlds that he sent the shadow armies. Sometimes Inquestors went with them. The Inquest had many heretics now.

Alone in a room on Shtoma, shut away from the joygiving sunwarmth, Kelver sat and communed with the southern thinkhive of Uran s'Varek.

And parsecs away, the shadow armies swooped down on forgotten worlds, and the heretic Inquestors talked of hope, of rebellion, of utopias; and they denied that man was a fallen being. And this was a heresy that struck at the Inquest's very heart, for not even Davaryush had ever denied that man had fallen from grace . . .

In the little room, Kelver summoned up holoimages of the shadow armies. He saw old men grinning. He saw a childsoldier embracing a beggar in the street of a decaying city. He saw bread rain down on a hungry crowd, a single tear glistening on a mother's cheek; and the line of childsoldiers on their hoverdisks like a jeweled bracelet thrown into the air. And he saw the faces of his soldiers, and they were no longer hard, innocent of pity; they were children's faces, laughing, weeping, unafraid of their emotions.

Kelver reached out across the parsecs with his mind, reached out to the Throne of Madness.

How is your plan proceeding? said the thinkhive. *Have you saved your little Dispersal of Man from all that ails it? Or has my power driven you mad already?*

"I am not mad," Kelver said.

He watched the shifting holoimages. He saw a huge throng in a city square, and they were all chanting his name like a prayer, a word of power.

Godhead becomes you, said the thinkhive.

"I am not a god," said Kelver.

The images flickered. And then he saw one image that disturbed him. With a flick of his mind he stopped the flow, broke into the holostream. There it was again. The mauve eyes slitty with anger. There it was. Against the russet man-tall grass, the blushing of a shimmercloak. "He's here," he whispered.

He watched as the holoimage of Arryk looked around, turned, sent his tachyon bubble back into the sky. He subvoked to the thinkhive, bringing the image closer into focus. Now he saw Arryk's face more clearly. The softness he had loved was gone from it. For a moment Kelver wanted everything back the way it had once been, in the deserts of chocolate and the forests of marzipan.

"Do you think," he said, "I could bring him back on our side? In a few days they will have the ritual of the dance on the face of the sun. Arryk will have to participate, if he truly means to hunt this utopia, and perhaps—"

Perhaps, the thinkhive said, *compassion has blinded you, Kelver. I thought I had cleared your vision, not clouded it.*

Kelver did not listen to the distant thinkhive's words. He gazed on Arryk's face: defiant, beautiful. Who had forced him to come here, knowing full well that this utopia had broken so many wiser, more experienced Inquestors? He blinked away the images and let the sunlight into the chamber. He saw Davaryush and Siriss outside, deep in conversation; Darktouch, too, was there, and many from the village.

I must go to join them, he thought, pulling his shimmercloak tighter about his shoulders, so that we can meet Arryk together.

He was afraid of the encounter, terribly afraid. Of all the others, only Arryk had ever understood him. Arryk had been a peasant boy too. Arryk had shown him the void and tempted him. He knew that Arryk would tempt him again, and that only Arryk had the power to destroy him.

The guests had gathered. Karakaël wandered among them, wearing the black mask of a servant. This was not playing fair in the game of *makrúgh*, but Karakaël had never been one to play fair. That was why he never showed his face.

There were a dozen masked Inquestors in the banquet hall. Above their identical shimmercloaks were the bizarre visages Karakaël had selected: the hissing Snake Mask, the flaming Mask of Making, the Mask of the Whore. As the Inquestors conversed, vocal distorters within the masks acted to change their voices beyond recognition, for the illusion must be complete.

The first course was being served; it was a dish of miniature phosphorescent jellyfish swimming in a hovertank of dark blue water; braided seaweed sprouted from an ocean floor simulated with powdered onionwort. In the tank, small girls dived, spearing the twinkling jellyfish with their glowskewers and garlanding a garnish from the strands of kelp. As the divers emerged, each bearing aloft her tidbit, leaping in one graceful motion out of the water to kneel at the feet of each Inquestor with their wands of food upraised, the Inquestors applauded languidly. Karakaël was pleased; this had been one of the chief cook's most diverting ideas. As the Inquestors bit into the still-squirming jellyfish, they began to moan with delight as they discovered that the skewers themselves were not only edible, but released, when crunched, an intoxicating juice that rendered more piquant the gelatinous texture of the coelenterates.

Karakaël moved swiftly and silently among the Inquestors. They did not see him; in his disguise he was beneath their notice. Once he paused to pour zul for whomever it was who wore the Serpent Mask; the mask flicked out its tongue to lap from the goblet of chased rainbow metal. Karakaël stood for a moment, eavesdropping.

The Serpent Mask was saying, "I saw the most exquisite creature today, a real flower of the streets. I shall return to Airang, I think, and seek her out, and elevate her to some ludicrously lofty position. . . ."

The reply: "You'll never find her in the sewer labyrinth, and she'll be dead by the next time you go back to Airang anyway. . . ."

Karakaël smiled. The first speaker was surely Ton Satymyrys, whose thoughts never strayed far from pleasure. Unless, of course, some other Inquestor was imitating his mode of speech in order to fool another into giving up some advantage of *makrúgh:* a planet, perhaps, or the right to deal the death-blow to a star system.

The Inquestor of a Million Masks moved on, blending into the throng of servants that flitted about the chamber on their errands. Everything had been perfect. The first course—the phosphorescent jellyfish representing, naturally, the star systems being bartered in the game's first round—had been a masterpiece of symbolism; it had even tasted good. The latter was not of primary importance, since in the *shénjesh* or expository sequence of *makrúgh* the elegant gesture, the exquisite conceit, was all that mattered, and, since the banquet was to consist of one hundred twenty-seven courses, each inextricably linked to a stage in the planned *makrúgh,* one would hardly expect the guests actually to eat every course. It was a waste, Karakaël decided suddenly. And a bore. Never had a game of *makrúgh* seemed so dull. The fun was all in the planning, not in the fate of a few miserable insignificant planets, whose inhabitants (in our compassion, he remembered to interject into his thought, in our compassion) would all be relocated anyway.

Karakaël wrung his hands nervously. He left the reception hall and paced the hallway outside, where several masks still hung on poles, and where the deopaqued walls still provided a view of the many docked palaces and the starstream.

He saw the snowflake palace now, and wondered once more whose it might be. There was a memory, far back, in his childhood, on the verge of surfacing, of a day before he assumed his first mask . . . he did not want to think of it.

He summoned Orin his maskslave with a handclap. The man was there immediately.

"Bring me one of the Masks of Worldweariness," he said. "I'm leaving the banquet. Tell me . . . did Ton Elloran come today?"

"No, *hokh'Tón.*"

"Get me a shuttlecraft. I'll pay him a call, I think. Anything, rather than another deadly round of this game! The ennui is quite unbearable."

"Yes, master."

"Elloran will cheer me up. He always did. Even though he was always a trifle holier-than-thou about the duties of the Inquest. Is the craft at hand?"

"Of course."

Orin had already vanished and returned with a selection of masks; he averted his eyes while his master selected one, a clown mask that wept continual rose-scented tears. Karakaël made for the displacement plate.

As he began to subvoke the command that would take him to the shuttlecraft, he turned around and saw once more the ice palace.

"Whose is that?" he cried. It was the one thing that made his intricately staged *makrúgh* game less than perfect. He wondered, suddenly, whether the mysterious Inquestor the palace must contain had already appeared at the banquet and was even now in the process of bluffing his way to victory. It made him uneasy, like all surprises.

It only took a few minutes for him to arrive in Varezhdur. The Princeling, they told him, was in a private garden. Ignoring the lackeys' attempts to detain him, Karrakaël had sought out the very garden—it was one where Elloran had once entertained him with his somewhat archaic expoundings of Inquestral philosophy—and he found his old friend there.

"Ah, Kaarye. Tired of your own game, I see."

Karakaël said, "I am tired, Loreh, tired."

"So were several of our friends," Elloran said, his eyes twinkling. He gestured; from behind a bush Ton Satymyrys emerged, leading by the hand a ravishingly androgynous kallogyne whose eyes and hair were the color of fine rose quartz. Karakaël was confused; he did not speak at first. Then he heard laughter from a treetop, and saw a young Inquestrix juggling with gold and crystal balls.

"But the banquet—" he said at last.

"You're not the only one," Elloran said, laughing mildly, "to be overcome by the oppressive game of strategy and control—"

At this, Karakaël had to laugh, though he did it gracelessly, for he was brooding about the palace of snowflakes, worrying at some forgotten secret.

Already I hate this world, Arryk thought, as he dissolved his tachyon bubble and stepped out onto the crimson plain of the main settlement of Shtoma. There was terror in the very sunlight. It seemed as though waves of joy swept through his mind, and he had to fight back to maintain the composure proper to an Inquestor.

An old man in a shapeless cloak met him on the path. He was hooded; all Arryk could make out were the piercing eyes. This was a representative of a so-called utopia? He would find out all its flaws at once and report back to Karakaël. He was far more interested in pursuing Kelver and Siriss and wiping out their trail of heresy. He looked at the old man without interest.

The man said, "*Qíthe qíthembara*, Ton Arryk n'Elloren Tath. Renounce suffering, soul; you have danced on the face of the sun."

What was the meaning of this? Arryk knew the questions he must now ask. Why Shtoma was said to know no crime, no madhouses, no places of punishment. Why its people seemed so guilelessly content. Whether they had been drugged into this false state of happiness. Joy is not good, he thought. You can get drunk on it, and then you no longer understand anything.

The old man said, smiling suddenly, "I know what all your questions will be. There is only one answer . . . feel the sunlight. The love of Udara. And then . . . dance on the sun."

"What do you mean?" Once more came the joy, engulfing him, battering at his defenses. With a supreme effort of will he controlled himself. He couldn't lose control! He must be faithful to the Inquest's precepts, faithful to the High Compassion, and above all faithful to Elloran who had raised him

up to the Inquest, who had believed he could be more than a
phoenix herder on a backworld. If Karakaël had chosen to
send him there, it must be some kind of test. And Ton
Karakaël always played *shtezhnat* with Elloran, didn't he?
This must have something to do with one of those games,
Arryk thought. And I must never let Elloran down, never,
never. He thought of Elloran's compassion, and he drew
strength from it. They would not have sent him to Shtoma if
it were not indeed flawed, if its claim to be a utopia did not
hide some dark secret. That was what the hunting of utopias
was all about, after all.

"What do you mean, dance on the sun?" he said again, but
the old man did not answer him.

Children ran by laughing. In the real world they should
already be warriors, or at least working at some useful task.
He watched them sternly as they vanished into the woods,
red, spidery, menacing.

In the distance he saw varigrav coasters. These were not
like the coasters of Airang, though. They were far taller. The
columns were more than a klomet high, and purest white,
not gilded and studded with gemstones like the ones of the
pleasure cities. There was something almost religious about
them. Some dark cult, perhaps. He remembered now that the
varigrav coasters, and the black boxes that controlled them,
had originated on this world. They were harmless enough
toys; a trivial use indeed for something so important as gravity control.

And beyond them, where russet hillocks overlooked the
plain, he saw clusters of glass houses. Open to the sun Udara,
he noted. Open to that insidious outpouring of joy. What
could it mean?

"I am your host," the old man said, and Arryk noticed that
he spoke without honorifics, as though they were equals. "I
will guide you to your place of rest; and tomorrow I will show
you my world."

A breeze sprang up; the old man's cloak rustled a little.
Suddenly Arryk caught a glimpse of something under it.
Something blue and pink and shimmering—

"It's a trap," he said. "You're an Inquestor." Who could it
be? "Karakaël, of course! Spying on me, ready to win some
bet with Elloran!"

The old man laughed, without malice. He seemed so kind,
so unlike Karakaël. And then he cast down his robe and

Arryk saw that the shimmercloak was frayed, bald in spots, as though it had not been properly fed. He had never seen such a shimmercloak except—

He studied the face now. Why was it so familiar? And then he knew the old man. "You're the heretic," he said.

Davaryush laughed again. "So it was Karakaël who sent you. I knew Elloran would never be so dastardly."

"I serve the Inquest," Arryk said stiffly.

There was a trap here. He knew he was walking into it. But he had to play along for a while. At least until he solved the mystery of Shtoma. After Davaryush led him to the answer . . . then would be the time to flee, back to beautiful Varezhdur, to forget. . . .

Davaryush pointed behind Arryk. Arryk whipped around and saw Kelver and Siriss, arm in arm, walking down the path. He was confused. There was a woman with them, a pale woman with jetstranded hair. He turned again, looking from one to the other.

"*Attá heng*," he said, using the ritual formula for conceding a game of *makrúgh*. "You have surrounded me."

Kelver said—his voice seemed so strained, so thin—"Arryk, you have come to Shtoma in the cadent lightfall. In a few sleeps we will dance on the sun together, and you'll understand everything . . . we'll be together again, Rikeh, like the old days."

Arryk saw him: the face emaciated, the green eyes lined. He sensed Kelver's need, but he said nothing. For a long time they stared at one another, quenching their emotions. Finally Kelver said, "Come with us. You showed me the void once, Arryk. You burned a void into my heart. Now I'll show you the joy that can fill that void. You owe it to me."

"I owe you nothing!" Arryk said angrily. "The breaking of joy is the beginning of wisdom." As he repeated these, the first words of the Inquestral writings about utopias, he threw his shimmercloak over his face, trying to shut out the sun; but the shimmercloak entrapped the light within its fibers, and once more the euphoria welled up inside him. "Go on, show me the secrets of your utopia. I'll hunt down its flaws and I'll destroy it!"

"In your compassion, of course." It was Siriss who had spoken.

"In my compassion!" Arryk said. But all he could feel was hate.

* * *

Ton Elloran took his old friend Karakaël by the arm and walked with him farther into the wood that grew within the inner gardens of the palace of Varezhdur, enclosed within a vast metallic globe upon whose surface were projected constant holoimages of a night sky. They left Satymyrys still sporting with his kallogyne behind a leafy curtain. Now they seemed to be alone, though Elloran knew they were not; hidden in the trees were shimmerviol consorts, and now they played one of Sajit's nocturnes, the soft sounds following the Inquestors as they walked deeper into the wood. Elloran saw that Karakaël had assumed his clown's mask, a thing of whiteface and exaggerated features; but tears streamed from the onyx-inlaid eyes and carved out canyons in the thick paint of the mask.

"You come here, Kaarye, then, seeking out me and a dying man's music, when you could be making and unmaking the lives and deaths of billions? What is this, my friend?" said Elloran. "You don't usually pick *shtezhnat*, when *makrúgh* is available. What's the matter with you then?"

"There's no life in the game, Elloran."

"That is not too surprising, Kaarye. Shall I show you why?"

With a wave of his hand he summoned a viewglobe from the tree under which they stood; it fell like a crystal apple that his command had ripened. Elloran caught it easily, and the two Inquestors peered into it. "Show me the vestibule of the banqueting hall in Karakaël's palace Kilimindi," said Elloran.

A tiny voice, like a child in a storm: *I obey—but an Inquestor's palace—is sealed—I cannot send out—the farseeing—without the ruling Inquestor's—permission—* .

"I override!" Karakaël said, and Elloran saw the ghost of an interest in his eyes.

"There is a break in the proceedings right now, is there not?" Elloran said. "Between the . . . fourth and fifth courses of your meal. Are they not about to enter the vestibule and unmask themselves?"

"Let me see!" Karakaël said, excited as a child.

Within the crystal apple was a distorted image of the hall of the twelve masks. Now the figure with the Mask of the Metawolverine emerged from the banquet hall and Orin helped him with his mask.

"Just as I thought," Karakaël said. "It is Ton Charadan, a harmless enough woman, hopelessly outclassed. I spotted her mannerisms right away. She was playing against the Snake, I think. Her worlds will *fall beyond*."

"The Snake emerges," said Elloran. Knowing what was to come, he could not suppress a little smile. The Inquestor of the Serpent Mask came out and unmasked.

"I don't know that face," Karakaël said.

"Closer, viewglobe!" said Elloran.

The viewglobe, reacting to sensors deep within the thinkhives of the palace, and linking electromagnetically with the thinkhives of Kilimindi, focused more closely on the unknown Inquestor's face.

Elloran turned the viewglobe to give Karakaël a better look.

"It's a servocorpse!" he blurted out, unbecoming in his lack of the Inquestral composure.

"Not a few servocorpses were at your dinner party, old friend, while their masters graced *my* somewhat humbler dinner table. Do you understand now why your *makrúgh* lacked life? The dead have no souls, and cannot be programmed to play imaginatively; they can only repeat what their masters have told them."

Stunned, Karakaël looked away, into the dark recesses of the artificial wood. "Always you beat me at *makrúgh*," he said, "even when you are not even playing . . . *attá heng, hokh'Tón*. You have vanquished me."

Elloran said, "Come, come. Vanquishing is not my purpose." But he was disturbed, because he had not planned to get caught in another spiderweb of *makrúgh*. It had not been his idea for some of the Inquestors to slip away from Karakaël's grand *makrúgh*, leaving servocorpses in their stead, and to come to Varezhdur to walk in Elloran's gardens. But for the past sleep he had heard nothing but gossip about Karakaël: his relentless vulgarity, his heavy-handed symbolism in *makrúgh*, and there was constant speculation on why he wore his masks. The masking had gone on too long—five hundred years was surely long enough for almost any obsession—and Satymyrys had wanted to challenge Karakaël to take off his mask.

But Elloran, above all compassionate, said nothing of this to Karakaël. They walked a little farther into the wood; here the trees themselves were shimmerviols, genetically tailored to play Sajit's music by the abrasure of their boughs, which oozed a constant rosin to sweeten their sounds. Here and there were winged children and fauns, and ornithentomids that darted from branch to branch, six-legged and with phosphorescent feathers. The wood was made with consummate artifice, and it was cool and fragrant with *f'áng*.

"Something else troubles you too, Kaarye."

"Yes."

"What is it? Have you, too, grown weary of *makrúgh*? You wish to join me, perhaps, in laying the great game aside?"

"No, Loreh, never that. But I have been watching the snowflake palace that has docked with my own, and wondering. Once, long ago, I think I saw this palace . . . a dream, perhaps. Surely before I was made Inquestor."

It was not seemly to talk of what an Inquestor had once been, before his elevation. So Elloran did not probe further. Instead he asked him how the game was going.

"Not well. I had thought that Ynyoldeh, whom I have named arbiter, would come, but her hawk palace has detached itself from its moorings, and it circles Kilimindi as though my moonlet were its prey. And the unmasking does not reveal her presence. What do you think it means?"

"Inviting Ynyoldeh is always ill-omened, Kaarye. Surely you knew that. She is wily and cruel. That is why she was made Queen of Daggers, isn't it? I hate to say this about a Grand Inquestor of her standing, but I believe her to lack a certain compassion. . . ."

"That is not true, Loreh. Once, in the hunt of firephoenixes, she pursued my bird to the very poles of the world Kailasa; but having killed it, spared the planet."

"But that was centuries ago, Karakaël, and now she has grown twisted and vicious. I have heard that she has an allergy to the drugs that keep us from aging; that she cannot die, and yet rots alive."

"Stories, Elloran. I will not hear her name discredited." And Elloran wondered that Karakaël should show such emotion over a woman so widely disliked among the Inquestors.

"Nevertheless," he said, "you can't finish the game without her, if you've made her arbiter. When the sides are finally chosen, it will be up to the players to woo her with gifts and witty words, if their attack plans are not to remain empty bluffs."

"True." Karakaël, who had been gazing into the viewglobe, now tossed it up into the air; it flew into the treetops and was consumed by the overhanging foliage. "Shall we return?" He seemed now suddenly to be full of resolve. Elloran wondered what he had said to make Karakaël lose his melancholy. Perhaps it was the wood itself that had worked its magic on him.

In a moment they stepped out into the complex of gardens. Elloran's gardens overlay each other, terrace upon terrace. Some were planted with the exotic shizmenaras, tiny colony-animals that mimicked flowers to perfection; others with common flowers; one in particular was peppered with wild rosellas. Elloran saw that the Inquestors who had sought refuge in his palace were all gathered there. He drew a circle with his finger on the ground around Karakaël and himself; subvoked a command to the thinkhives that controlled the garden; and they rose up on a hoverdisk of grass and earth and floated down, past seven waterfalls of increasing height and magnificence, to where the others were.

"Loreh," Karakaël said as they landed, "you should join us. Your *makrúgh* is so masterful, so tinged with compassion. I am so crude a player by comparison." A moment of rare self-awareness, Elloran thought.

But he replied, "No, my friend." He watched them walk one by one to the displacement plate that glinted at the center of the rosella garden; and one by one they dematerialized. Finally Elloran was alone. Alone, that is, except for the hidden attendants.

Perhaps, he thought, I *should* go and play the game. I should restrain them from their excesses. We should not forget the true purpose of *makrúgh*, after all, which is to take upon ourselves the guilt of the Dispersal of Man.

As he made for the displacement plate, though, another plan struck him. He thought of Lady Ynyoldeh the Cruel, and the stories he had heard of her wasting away in an innermost sanctum of her hawk-shaped palace. Why had she not emerged? One does not come to a game of *makrúgh*, he thought, and allow oneself to be named arbiter, without even intending to play. He had not seen her since the game they'd played on Gallendys, when they had all baited Davaryush the heretic. She had not shown herself then either, but had spoken through the corpse of a beautiful young girl that was borne in the quadribracchic embrace of a burly mechanical.

Why had she not shown herself?

He decided then. He would send her a message disk, asking for an audience; then he would go out to the hawk palace and ask her why she had not yet deigned to join the game. She might tell Elloran, after all, if he disclaimed all participation in this game of *makrúgh*.

He was *not*, he told himself sternly, playing *makrúgh*; he was not! Only calling on another Inquestor. Surely it was possible for one Inquestor to visit another without having to play *makrúgh*!

He cast his mind back over the centuries, slowly coming to the realization that this was something he had never truly done before. But then, he thought, the Inquest falls; and one day new games will be played, and *makrúgh* will be no more.

Resolved now, he made for the displacement plate. . . .

He had tried to explain this new thing to Arryk, but Arryk would not listen. Now, as the small ship left the scarlet plain of Shtoma, bound for the sun, he tried to explain once more.

"The sun," Kelver said, "is sentient."

"What has that to do with utopias?" said Arryk. He sat cross-legged on a hoverdisk, watching the others prepare themselves, but never joining in. Outside, the white dwarf sun Udara grew; already a many-layered darkfield shielded the viewwalls from its glare.

Kelver himself had not yet danced on the sun, but he had heard of it from Davaryush and Darktouch. He knew it must be wonderful. Even on the surface of Shtoma the sun's light bathed him with joy; how much more here, close to its heart? He could not explain the essence of the experience, though. He looked for one of the Shtomans, or for Davaryush himself, to come and tell Arryk the truth; but Davaryush had unaccountably decided to remain on Shtoma, telling him only that he did not want to infect Kelver with the Inquestral curse by involving himself too much in their cause.

"A sentient sun, Rikeh, born of some fearful cataclysm, with which the people of Shtoma have acquired a symbiotic relationship. And once every five years, all the world's inhabitants dance on the sun's face, and purge themselves of their fear, their hate. Udara is alive, Arryk! For us he has made a spot of coolness on his surface; for us he drives the graviton fields and controls our flight, catching us in the arms of his love—"

"It's just a very big varigrav coaster, then, Kevi! You can't believe all the mystical nonsense that goes with it. You're an

Inquestor. Have you experienced this thing yourself? Or do you take it all on hearsay, on the words of heretics?"

"I believe it. Because once, on Gallendys, I saw an absolute beauty. It was when the delphinoids sang their songs of light. I do not believe that one whom these imagesongs have touched would try to delude me. It's something we've shared, Daavye and Darktouch and I, and it is truth."

"You've gone mad already!" Arryk could not meet his eyes, and Kelver felt, beneath the animosity, a ghost of concern. "I warned you of the void. The power in the Throne of Madness is too much for a man. That's why we abandoned it twenty thousand years ago."

"It's not too much," Kelver said calmly, "when you've seen what I've seen."

"It has turned your head. Oh, Kevi, I never expected that of you."

"Dance with us. Then you'll understand." He had put on his wings now, and Udara filled half the viewscreen ahead. On the star's face there was a black spot, perfectly round; Kelver knew that it was cool and dark only by the fierce light of what surrounded it, and that when they arrived it would appear incandescent, blinding.

Kelver was afraid now. For though Davaryush and Darktouch had shared this thing, it was his first time. This was something that till now excluded him. Just as he'd taunted Arryk with not having seen the lightsongs on Gallendys. How could he have? They were so alike, so alone.

Kelver allowed a child to help him with his wings. They were splendid ones, rainbow-colored, gossamer. A woman, passing quickly through the viewroom, gave Kelver the pills that would release oxygen into the bloodstream during his fall into the sun. She handed them to Arryk, too, who absently swallowed them. Then she strapped a pair of wings to his shoulders, and Arryk let her do this, doing nothing to help, like a servocorpse that has not yet been awakened.

Then Siriss and Darktouch were beside him. Weakly he tried to smile at them. "Follow us," said Darktouch.

Onto the displacement plate . . . past the black boxes that contained captured pieces of the sun . . . already they were beside an airlock. And then it opened—

Blinding light, featureless, cool. And a strange roaring. In the great distance, prominences soared; he knew they were tall enough to swallow all Shtoma, but he was not afraid.

When his eyes grew used to the brightness, he knew that it welcomed him; its touch was warm as a lover's.

Darktouch laughed, as though greeting an old friend; Kelver felt a twinge of irrational jealousy, but the warmthlight soon dispelled it. Siriss and Darktouch leaped now. They seemed to fall so slowly, so gracefully.

"Hold my hand," he said to Arryk. "We'll go together. It'll be like the old days, in the desert of chocolate."

Arryk said, "No."

"Come, Rikeh!"

"I feel what you feel, Kevi. It's tempting, this joyflood that threatens to engulf me. But the breaking of joy is the beginning of wisdom. Elloran taught me that. I have to resist it—"

And Udara called to Kelver, a music he could not resist; and he seized Arryk by the hand and tried to drag him to the edge of the airlock; he struggled. "No!" Arryk cried. "I will fight the fall, fight the drunken oblivion of this joy!"

—*whiteness*—

"You're losing control—" Arryk shouted, wresting his hand free, and in that moment Kelver fell—

A graviton tide caught him, flipped him up high, he saw the others tossing like specks of dust, saw Arryk's anger and hopelessness as his face receded, saw the jagged ships concatenated over the huge whiteness—

And fell—

The voice, he told himself. There will come a voice, dispelling my terror. The sunwind roared in his ears, more overwhelming than any ocean. There will come a voice, he thought, giving in to the stomachwrenching gravity fields as they dragged him sunward and then thrust him spaceward . . . he cried out with pleasure like a little boy. And still he waited for the voice Davaryush had told him of, the voice that said, *Trust me, trust me.*

He heard nothing.

He fell, a split second stretched to forever. At last Udara's love embraced him; but there was a coldness too. He sensed he was not being touched as the others were touched.

In his mind he cried out: *Where are you, Udara? Why can't you reach me?*

He heard a low watery laughter now. *Kevi, Kevi.* He knew the voice in his mind. "The Throne of Madness!" he cried. "Can you touch me even here, in Udara?"

We are linked forever, Kelver. You cannot escape me, nor I you. You will never feel Udara's love as ordinary mortals do. You are different. Look at the others! They have surrendered themselves, and the sunlight has washed away all their pain. But your pain is greater than theirs. It encompasses even the deaths of suns, for it comes from the void at the heart of Uran s'Varek. . . .

Kelver closed his eyes, trying to shut out the brightness, but still it burned him. He tried to abandon himself to Udara. He saw the others, dancing dustmotes that had caught fire from the light.

"Why?" he screamed.

You have acquired a whispershadow, Kelver. Do you know what that is?

"They're myths. Bogeymen. Invented alien enemies that the Inquest uses as a pretext for wars. They don't exist."

They do exist, Kelver. And our destinies are all linked in more ways than you can possibly imagine. After your little Galactic Empire has fallen, its power crushed, there is still a greater war to be fought. It is then that you will pay the price of your power. For a while the whispershadows will serve you. Your power comes from them . . . but Udara will not love you, for he sees the source of your strength. . . .

"I don't understand any of this! Davaryush never told me—"

Davaryush has never sat upon the Throne of Madness.

Angry, Kelver struggled against the grip of the gravity wave, but it held him fast. Now it hurled him upward, now he swerved and somersaulted and plummeted and soared screaming. At first it was exhilarating, this battle of sensations; later he felt nothing at all, but flew insensible in the suntides . . . at last a wild sleep overcame him. As he rode the sunwind he dreamed of the lightsongs, and of the Windbringers sliced by the laser-irises of the childsoldiers, and it seemed that the sunlight that touched him was tainted with blood.

Kelver awoke: they had taken him out into the windtousled meadow outside the bubbledome house where Davaryush lived. As he opened his eyes he felt Udara; he saw the scarlet grass that stretched out to the forest of spidertrees. He was lying on a soft pallet; when he sat up, it quickly contoured to his posture.

A tachyon bubble was coming from the sky, bursting through the pale clouds lined with gilt. There were people about.

Kelver mumbled; he did not know what he said; but others, waiting, no doubt, for the first signs, came clustering around him. Children (they were everywhere on this world, and no one ever scolded them) surrounded him, pointing, chattering their concern.

And then he saw Arryk. "You're leaving." He groaned.

Arryk came toward him. His shimmercloak was pulled tight, against the sunlight. The breeze toyed with his hair, and Kelver looked into the clear eyes of mauve that he had once loved, and found no response. Even in coldness they were beautiful though, like the eyes of a sculpture, or cloudless amethysts.

"You'll go back to Karakaël?"

Arryk nodded.

"You'll tell him . . . what? That Shtoma in no true utopia? That this island of peace in a galaxy of hate and hostility is seditious, dangerous, heretical?"

Arryk didn't answer him.

"You wouldn't try it. You wouldn't jump into the sun. Why were you so afraid?" But he spoke without conviction. *He* had not felt it after all. *He* could never be cleansed of all his pain.

Arryk said, "I couldn't do it. I would have lost, you see. I knew I would succumb to it. I felt it even here, in the sun, in the laughter of the children, in the unseemly smiles of the commonfolk. This is a world that cannot exist."

"But it does. And by its existence it negates all your Inquestor philosophy, all your cold, harsh dogmas."

"It will not exist much longer. I am going to Kilimindi now. Karakaël is there, and Elloran. They are playing *makrúgh*. I will join them, and I will play this world."

"You know that's unethical! Shtoma's a backworld, minimally populated, not under the direct rule of a Kingling. It should escape the notice of *makrúgh*."

"It will not escape, Kelver." For a moment, Kelver thought that Arryk was on the verge of tears, that the gem-clear eyes betrayed emotion. But in that moment Arryk turned his back on him, and entered the tachyon bubble which had landed beside him, and took off into the incandescent sky.

Kelver moaned. How long had he lain unconscious? He slept again, fitfully; another time he awoke to find Darktouch beside him, stroking his head; another time Siriss, who was murmuring, excited, "Wasn't it beautiful, Kevi? Wasn't it wonderful?" And he was forced into some quick, ambiguous response, because he did not want her disappointed.

Later, when he was feeling better, Davaryush himself came. They were alone together, the two heretics, ancient and adolescent.

Kelver said, "You never told me it would be like this. I would never have accepted the responsibility. You trapped me."

"I had to!" the old man said. "You were free, but I was bound by my centuries, by my own cowardice, and by the curse that comes to all Inquestors, compassionate though they may think themselves. But you were pure of all these things, boy. You were our only chance."

"Udara would not touch me."

"I—that is terrible! How can you endure—"

"Daavye, Daavye: they are all linked. The delphinoids that fly the overcosm. The suns that stand at the junctions of the quickpaths. The whispershadows, whatever they may be. And the void at the galaxy's heart. The Inquest's power is just a momentary dissonance in the vast pattern. The Throne of Madness is showing me . . . things I don't even have words for."

"Are you abandoning the rebellion against the Inquest, then?" Davaryush said. And Kelver realized that Davaryush understood nothing of what his former disciple had said; that even Davaryush's vision, encompassing as it did all humanity, was not enough.

"No, Daavye," he said. "The Inquest will fall, and men will be free again, as they were always meant to be." It was strange. When he said those words, he had the distinct feeling that it was he who was thousands of years old, and that Davaryush was a mere child . . . but the moment of unease passed. There was much love between them, after all; for they had stood in the Dark Country together and seen the light on the Sound.

"And now, Davaryush," Kelver said, "you must tell me one more thing. Arryk means to play Shtoma in *makrúgh*. The one who can stop this is the Lady Varuneh, and you must tell me where you've hidden her."

"I had hoped," Davaryush said, "to keep her forever hidden."

"She will have no choice. She is an Inquestor."

Kelver saw the old man weeping. Compasison touched him, but he could not heed it now.

FIFTEEN: BROKEN CIRCLES

At first Elloran wandered among the Inquestors in Karakaël's palace unmasked, for he had no wish to play. Thirty courses had been served: pastries carved into planets were flambéed in the tears of chichangas, night creatures of the planet Taor that wept when they made love; drinking horns that muttered the names of dying worlds had been passed around. After a dull start, the Inquestors were getting into the swing of things. Already they were taking sides, the masked Inquestors, though they could not know whose visage the masks hid.

A man in an obscene mask stopped him. "Elloran, join us! We're having such fun. Twice I've made a wise guess, and if the arbiter smiles on me I'll have my way: a necklace of people-bins strung across the overcosm from here to Laaresht!" Elloran smiled, not liking to talk to someone whose identity he could not ascertain.

"Come, Loreh, it's Kaarye who begs you."

"You bluff well," Elloran temporized. In his hand he clutched a message disk from Lady Ynyoldeh. It contained a single word:

Come.

"What's your message?" said the bothersome Inquestor, who might or might not be Karakaël: Elloran was sure it was not.

"Den shénjo makrúxeh," Elloran said in the highspeech, unambiguously. "I'm not playing *makrúgh!*" He turned and left the room, entered the vestibule where old Orin was dusting masks not yet claimed. He looked through the view

181

wall, at the hawk palace of Ynyoldeh. Parts of it were deep in shadow; it was as if the hawk's face, its poised wings, erupted out of the darkness. It was a fine palace.

With a flick of his mind, Elloran communicated with the thinkhives within Varezhdur, telling them to respond to Ynyoldeh's message. It was done instantly. As he looked at the hawk palace, its wings flapped once; its mouth yawned wide to disgorge a tiny hawk, a shuttlecraft, a perfect miniature of its parent, which arced upward, across the starstream, searching for Kilimindi.

When Elloran knew that it had come and was awaiting him in the shuttleport of Karakaël's palace, he walked slowly toward the displacement plate. He wondered whether he could avoid playing *makrúgh* with old Ynyoldeh. If he could not, he would undoubtedly lose. He was not used to losing.

Three tachyon bubbles had fallen over Dragonstooth.

"Tachyon bubbles," said Varuneh, certain now, to the shivering young girl who had been sent by the Elder Hakra to summon the oracle; for the thinkhive had spoken to her.

"Tachyon bubbles?" The girl did not understand. How could she? There was only one thing a tachyon bubble could portend, coming as it did to a world so undesirable, so remote. It must be *makrúgh*. Only *makrúgh* could reach its tentacles this far, to make this loveless world, whose only living came from the exploitation of corpses, *fall beyond*. It was death, then, and she meant to be ready.

A tremor shook the cavern. Only a few sleeps remained before Kalivorm, convulsed with lust, would begin swimming toward its destined mate, its tail lashing the ocean into half-klomet-high waves, its jaws slavering, pungent pheromones spraying from the crevasses between its scales. . . .

"Bring the Elder Hakra to me here," she said. "And divulge nothing, girl, do you hear! Nothing!"

"I hear the oracle," the girl said, even more frightened now.

Another tremor. There was no time to lose. I have come, Varuneh thought, surprising even herself, to love this world.

Hakra had been the first surprise. After the day of terror, when they took the floater out to Dragonstooth and heard the words of the thinkhive, Hakra had actually acquired a taste for the outside world. Varuneh had appointed him master of the survival plan, and he reveled in it. He supervised the prying loose of Kalivorm's half-sloughed scales; part of the serpent's crown was desquamate now, each metal-hard scale floating on the still-calm sea like a lotus pad. He dragged the most powerful families of Kepharang to the spaceport, forcing them to look outside at the ocean. He put them to work, installing the floater boxes in the scales; each would suffice as a boathouse until Kalivorm had sated his lust. Varuneh had become proud of him; she had toyed with his mind, opening his eyes to many of the commonplaces of her world. Sometimes she had toyed with the old man's body, too, finding in its embrace a somehow refreshing naïveté. It had, after all, been many centuries since she had loved a creature more powerful than herself; and for that creature's sake she had almost destoyed the known universe. . . .

Enough, she thought. To one who knew, Hakra's report had no ambiguity at all. *Two circles of darkness, so smooth, so delicate, as they figure-eighted around a smaller third.*

Perhaps all her efforts were doomed, then. If the world was destined to *fall beyond*, what did it matter that in its final moments she had opened the eyes of a few of its hapless denizens? But there would be people-bins orbiting above, waiting, once more, to take the survivors to a new life. *We are not a cruel race,* she thought, quoting from the Inquestral texts that once she had written herself, as a guide to her successors, who had immediately proceeded to disobey everything but the strictest letter of those texts. . . .

Who will remember a world of water and corpses? she thought. She recalled the day she had first opened her eyes, in a foul-smelling chamber of the serpent's head; of the tanks full of corpses, marching in measured steps through the nutrient fluids, their eyes unwavering, unblinking. It had seemed a nightmare.

And now she saw the Elder Hakra; he entered through an aperture in the snakeflesh that dilated and closed up behind him. "Do you know what has happened?" she cried. "Can you understand what the Inquest has done?"

Hakra said, "Vara, the snakescale city is finished! The floater mechanisms are all in place; we can be off within two sleeps, within two hours, if you command it." He stopped. In the silence, Varuneh heard the distant thunder of the serpent's heartbeat, and she felt the floor beneath her throb, heave, twist, ripple. It would be soon now.

"Hayeh, Hayeh," she whispered. They almost touched now;

the old man was diffident, knowing how deep was the chasm between their two stations in life, knowing he could only come near when commanded. He waited for her to complete her thought. In that moment, Varuneh knew that their relationship was over. There was no way they could ever communicate again. She should not have pretended, have toyed with the old man so. How could he ever understand what was at stake?

"Hayeh," she said, "we have done a wonderful thing together, haven't we?"

"Of course." The old man was surprised. "You have made my people see that they no longer need to fear. You've given them the courage to face the open sea."

"There are some who haven't listened to my oracular pronouncements, Hakra."

"Yes," he said ruefully, "and even now they're beating the orgy drum outside the bone temples and the burrows of the rich. The final orgy is about to begin. . . ."

"And they laugh at you and me and our silly dreams."

"But we know better. A few of the faithful, a few doubters, they are slipping away to the snakescale city, and are getting ready to float away to safety—"

"And if I told you it was all for nothing?"

"How can that be? The heroism of these people will be immortal! Their names will be known from snake to snake, from sea to sea! And it was you who taught us not to fear."

"Foolish shortlivers! You always bandy about words like *immortality* . . . I have lived only a few millennia, a blink of an eye in eternity, yet even I see things you cannot dream of—" Varuneh stopped, ashamed of her outbrust. Let them have their illusions, she thought. Let them think, as the firedeath scorches their world, that they have made themselves immortal. . . .

No time to lose then. She wanted them to have their illusions for as long as possible. They would have to move out immediately, to set forth, leave the thrashing serpent far behind . . . and if they could, she meant to follow the trail of the tachyon bubbles. If she could somehow make contact with them, exercise her Grand Inquestral rank—for no one had yet stripped her of that office—force them to leave Idoresht be, to pick on some other world!

It was no longer a question of the greater compassion and the smaller, the lesser of evils. Varuneh no longer cared to play *makrúgh* with anyone. She would simply command, and by commanding save those she loved.

"Come!" she shouted. The two slipped out of the chamber into a moist narrow corridor. Already there were naked couples making love, seeking warmth under folds of flesh and in crevasses of the serpent's pulsating tissue. They passed broad hallways where the drummers pounded; oily fluids flowed from burst vessels overhead, and the ground shook constantly, and everywhere they were coupling, moaning, shrieking, hysterically wailing . . . children too young for sex capered and ran rampant among the writhing bodies. Old men blew screechy tunes on the raucous ceremonial highwoods, built specially for the occasion and never played until now. The two old ones, Elder and Inquestrix, turned down an alleyway, sliding along the path in the viscous ooze. A troupe of celebrants, waving torches, filled the corridor; Hakra and Varuneh pressed themselves against a gelatinous wall. In the ceiling, the torchlight and the shadow played with the phosphorescence, stars, and clouds. More music now, as in the distance resounded the Gongs of Sensual Abandonment, and cheers and screams of passion made watery echoes from the hallway behind.

"The surface!" Varuneh said, "How can we reach the surface?"

Hakra pulled her arm roughly. They ducked into a tubelike pasageway that pulsed in time with the blare of highwoods. "Here," he said. "When I was young, I played here, and we knew these paths well. . . ."

A sickly odor. The walls were of some spongy substance. Shakily Varuneh followed Hakra into a tunnel. It twisted back and forth like passages in coral. The stench was overpowering. But the music died to a whisper. Oily tears oozed from the walls. "What is this?" she said.

"Some gland," Hakra said. "I don't know what. But it's a shortcut to the surface." They popped out beside the basket and pulley which Varuneh remembered from her previous journey. She ran now, feeling immeasurably old. Hakra was pulling the basket, attached to the sinew ropes. It would not come. She went to stand beside him. There were lovers in the basket. Giggling, they tugged at the two old ones. They would not have dared approach the oracle and a city elder in normal circumstances, but their world was ending.

"Forget decorum," Varuneh said. She got into the basket,

squatting down on the faces of two lovemakers. They murmured drunkenly. She pulled old Hakra up.

"Give us more room, oldsters!" one of the young men said, his voice muffled by a fold of Varuneh's shimmercloak. Hakra, succumbing to terror at last, shivered against a corner of the basket. What could be done? Varuneh saw that the sinew rope had caught on a wedge of serpentbone on the far wall.

She stretched out her arm but could not reach it. "Quickly," she said. "Throw all your weight against this side of the basket!" She pulled at Hakra, who was stone-cold with fear, and shoved him against her own corner; then, with all her might, she pushed against the basketwalls. The sinew stirred a little. "No use!" Now the walls vibrated as the serpent's passions grew further inflamed. The basket began swinging violently. The lovers stirred, shrieking their pleasure. One, a girl hardly past puberty, stood up, swaying, laughing. The walls shook, a million liquid stars of phosphorescence twinkled in them . . . Varuneh watched with horror as the girl walked obliviously toward the far side of the basket. They would never be safe now. They would die, and the Inquestors would come, and after the Inquestors the childsoldiers to boil the seas and cook the monster serpents alive—

"Get away!" she tried to scream, but the floors and walls began to shake in a violent convulsive rhythm, drowning her cry. Fragments of bone began to fall from above, dislodged by the heat of the serpent's lust. Through it all the girl stood unsteadily, singing a love song, wrapped up in her own thoughts. She hardly screamed when a piece of bone struck her squarely in the crown of the head, when she fell, clawing at the sinew rope, wresting it free from the bony outcropping . . . they were rising now, and Varuneh could see the girl falling to her doom, and she forced herself still to look, knowing that it was her Inquestral duty. . . .

Now they had reached the entrance of the gullet. They stood in the avenue of the serpent's tongue. Suddenly would come blinding light flashes as Kalivorm opened and closed its mouth. Ahead, the ruins of the spaceport; it had lain abandoned for some weeks, as the outworlders sought accommodations elsewhere, within the jaws of some safer snake. The other occupants of the basket, still locked in the throes of sexual excitement, had been left behind. Varuneh had thought of urging them to follow, to save themselves; but she knew it was too late.

They ran now, two old people . . . though Hakra was immeasurably the younger, yet Varuneh could see that he suffered from old age far more than she. She did not think he would make it. Once again the serpent opened its mouth. The entire tongue lurched forward a little, throwing them a little closer to the jaws. Ahead, the teeth glistened like metallic architectural columns. Suddenly, through the cage of teeth, Varuneh could see another serpent, its head above the water, in the middle distance. Its tail was held high, and the sunlight poured from its golden scales. It was a sight of startling beauty, and Varuneh was moved in spite of her terrible weariness, in spite of the heartache she felt. . . . Yes! We must snatch a few more moments of beauty before the Inquest forever darkens this world, Varuneh thought, angry.

Suddenly the jaws gaped wide. The tongue flicked. Hakra and Varuneh were flung out into the dazzling sunlight. For a second they arced up toward the sun; then Varuneh felt the smash of the wombwarm water. She struggled against the waves created by the serpent's tail. Then there were arms about her. She was being pulled upward. She opened her eyes. There was light everywhere. She was on one of the snakescale boats; she was bathed in reflected sunlight. Next to her was the Elder Hakra, unconscious; they were trying to revive him even now. But Varuneh's shimmercloak, enveloping her in its protective warmth, had kept her from passing out. Varuneh stood up. She saw the serpent's head rear up from the water like an ugly mountain. Tall waves lashed threateningly. The serpent's head was bald, for its scales lay like petals on the water, and each petal contained a family that might escape the holocaust. She saw them now, tens of them, gold-glittery specks that freckled the ocean. And in the distance, the other sea snake, undulating, its tongue flicking in and out of its glittering jaws.

Varuneh stood tall.

A voice rang out: "Hail, our oracle, *K'Ninga Talázmaran*, Queen to the people of the sea!" The shout was taken up. From across the water it echoed. Pride, Varuneh thought, I must beware of pride. The shouts came once more, tinny in the roar of the waves. She waved for silence. She looked long at the sky, wondering if there would be an omen.

Presently she saw them. They streamed out of the sun itself, tiny circles of topaz, like a flock of jeweled silverdoves. Why had I hoped otherwise? she thought. The tachyon bubbles could only mean one thing . . . childsoldiers would soon be on their way. There was only one reason why Idoresht would have been picked in the game of *makrúgh* for destruction. They must have found out that she was here. It must all be over then, the grand revolution for which she had been willing to destroy the Windbringers of the Dark Country. She tried hard to remember those days. She pictured them clearly, but she could feel nothing at all. Only the outrage, and a moment or two of searing beauty.

There were the childsoldiers then, swooping on Idoresht out of the sun itself. Soon they would spew forth the laserdeath from their citrine eyes. But now they merely danced on their wings of light, intagliating the sky with intricate patterns of yellow light. Already some of her subjects had seen it, too, and they were pointing at it, staring at its beauty, not knowing it meant the death of all their dreams.

Presently the young man she had appointed admiral of the snakescale city came to her. "Where shall we set our course, *hokh'Tón?* For Dragonstooth, or for the open sea?"

"Bring me," Varuneh said, "four poles of fine bone. Set them up, here, like supports for a canopy." She stripped off her shimmercloak and threw it at him. The others gaped; one quickly threw her a robe of dried skin. "Stretch out my shimmercloak over the four poles. Make sure that it catches the sunlight. Then set a course toward the dancing lights."

When the man hesitated, she shouted at him. "Obey, child! Don't you know that once, a thousand years ago, a Princeling blew up a planet for love of me, so I could watch the pretty fireworks?"

It was useless. All feeling was gone from her as she watched them raise up the standard of her shimmercloak, and as the floater mechanisms began to whirr softly into action. A salt wind battered her face, her withered arms. Already, in the wind, she could hear a whisper of the words of death:

Ishá ha, ha, ha!
Ishá ha ha heíy ha!

But none of her newfound subjects heard the childsoldiers' war cry; they could not know to listen for it behind the windroar, and they were too flushed with their new life to think of imminent death.

Ton Elloran stepped into the reception chamber of the hawk palace. He looked around; it was a dank, confined hallway carpeted with dying shimmerfur. He called out Ton Ynyoldeh's name. A feather fell, drawing a curlicue in the musty air.

"Ynyoldeh!"

He heard a child's laughter.

He took another step forward; beyond the displacement plate there hung an arras of interwoven kestrel wings.

"Ynyoldeh!"

Another feather fell, and the child laughed again. The sound was coming from behind the curtain.

"I do not come to play *makrúgh*," he shouted. "Let me through, Queen of Daggers." Again the shrill and silvery laughter. He yanked the arras aside. Four metal arms shot out in warning . . . a mechanical.

"Stand aside, robot. I've a message from your mistress." The mechanical did not move from its place, but shuffled two steps forward and two steps backward, over and over again, its arms swaying, like a disconsolate ape. "Come, man of metal. You know you must obey an Inquestral command, even if it means your life. . . ." Elloran pushed at the mechanical; it collapsed suddenly into a pile of metal parts and rust. He watched the dead thing at his feet. The head moved slowly around; he heard a sound from inside, like the snapping of a spring; and then it was still. And, somewhere deep inside the palace, the young girl laughed again.

"Ynyeh," Elloran repeated. The voice was muffled by the room's closeness, by the layers upon layers of feathers that lined the walls. He stepped past the useless mechanical and into the next chamber. It was furnished just like the first; if anything the shimmerfur of the floors was even more luster-less, and even more dust filled the folds of the feathery walls.

Elloran remembered the last time he had seen her. He had been much younger then. It was that ill-fated game of *makrúgh* they'd played on Gallendys, at Sajit's cloud-concert; that was the first time he had become convinced of Davaryush's irre-versible heresy. A four-armed mechanical had carried her image everywhere, a servocorpse fashioned from the body of a startlingly beautiful young girl, devised just before puberty; Ynyoldeh had never condescended to join their game of *makrúgh* in person at all, but had spoken exclusively through the mouth of her grisly surrogate. It was this that had con-vinced him that the story that she might be herself a living corpse, rotting away yet unable to die, was true. The servocorpse was indeed one of the most elegant design; it had even been observed to eat and drink, and rumor had it that it responded directly to implants in Ynyoldeh's nervous system, so that its smiles were her smiles, its grimaces her grimaces.

There was another arras at the end of this chamber; and Elloran half expected that servocorpse, beautiful and dead, to emerge in the cradling arms of another mechanical. But nothing happened. The room was utterly still.

Was it a trap?

If so he had come too far to turn back. The taking of risks was an Inquestral commonplace. He had to know why Ynyoldeh would not come to Karakaël's lavish game, would not send even the corpse as surrogate.

A noise, muted . . . clanking of metal feet. . . .

He strode forward, listened at the arras, ripped it wide—

Nothing! The gloom gathered; dust settled on his hair, his face, his shimmercloak. He passed more chambers, each mustier than the last. In one, feathers flew wildly, as if someone else had just been in the room. He drew reassurance from this, and pressed on.

Again, the clanking. An ambush? The room he was in now was dark, the air so thick he could breathe the dust. Feathers grazed his head. Why is there no light here? he thought. Why has the Inquestrix wrapped herself in such gloom? Perhaps . . . perhaps he could command the light himself, override the presence of the mistress of the hawk palace.

LIGHT! he subvocalized abruptly.

A bright beam of light materialized in one corner of the room. More feathers fluttered. The light grew, running swath by swath along the walls. At the far end of the chamber sat four mechanicals, their eyes blinking rubies, their arms moving up and down, up and down, their heads turning endlessly from side to side. *AWAKE!* Elloran subocalized. But they did not come to life. Was Ynyoldeh there at all, or was it all some ruse, some ambush? If the walls were willing to hearken to the subvocalized commands of an Inquestor not their master, surely it meant that the Inquestrix was gone from there; yet the mechanicals made no such response.

The light brightened once more, hurting his eyes. At his feet was the corpse of a beautiful young girl, twisted like a *drezhgo*-twig into an impossible angle.

The corpse laughed: a lilting, liquid laugh.

"Do you dare face me, Ton Elloran n'Taanyel Tath, Lord of

Varezhdur, who has been so cowardly as to abjure this grandest of *makrúghs*?" the voice said. And the voice was at once
like a sea breeze and a kitten's miaow, but the corpse's breath
was fetid, foul, nauseating. Elloran stepped over the body.

"I will only speak to you, Ynyeh, you alone!"

Came another voice like the first, but from farther within
the palace: "Then come to where I am, you silly Inquestor. I
refuse to make a spectacle of myself in front of all these nasty
dead things. That would be vulgar, wouldn't it, Loreh?"

He reached over to tug at the curtain. But it parted by
itself, and the next room was as brightly lit as the one he had
left. More of the girl corpses now: one hung by a thread from
the ceiling, grinning inanely. Another, chained to the wall,
showed signs of having been savagely beaten. It giggled now,
like a child caught in some shameful act, shamming innocence. "Curses on you, Ynyoldeh!" Elloran cried. "Is this
how you pass your free moments, by flagellating corpses? Is
this how you exercise the High Compassion?"

"Corpses," said the sweet young voice from a room even
farther within, "have no feelings; one can force them into a
semblance of suffering for one's edification, but one need feel
no compassion for them, poor Elloran. Do not mistake the
appearance for the reality!"

"We are both too old for games," Elloran said sadly.

At this the giggling became a wild cackling. The taunting
was taken up by the other corpses; one by one they shook
themselves free of their chains and advanced toward him,
pointing, shrieking maniacally. He pushed one aside and
advanced to the next chamber.

The stench of it hit him at once. He gasped as he looked
around him. The light was dimmer here; the curtain at the far
end had already been drawn, and the doorway was a rectan-
gle of bright light that shone over grisly mounds of arms and
legs, all dripping half-jellied blood. Here and there among
them were heads of the same beautiful young girl: the eyes
wide and grass-green, the hair silk-fine and luxuriant, the
small mouth painted red and parted in a voluptuous pout.

"You're testing me," Elloran said. "I don't know what for. I
told you already I did not come to play games."

"Honesty itself is a game," said the heads of the young girl.

Elloran picked his way gingerly among the piles of putrefy-
ing body parts until he reached the doorway of light. For a

moment, something held him back. "If I ask you what I came to ask," he said, "will you tell me?"

"Stuffy to the last, Tom Elloran! Of course I'll tell you. You'll say that all you want is to know why I'm not down there playing with your friends. But I know better. You're here because you are driven by a desire to strip me of my veil, to see me as I am, to know whether or not the tales you've heard are true!"

Elloran struggled to control his startlement. He should have known better than to enter the Dagger Queen's lair, conscious as he was of the temptation that *makrúgh* well played held for him. How should he answer this woman? With the truth? Surely he would receive no answers at all with the truth . . . but what lie should he give her? What she wanted to hear, or what she wanted not to hear? How well Ynyoldeh understood the finest points of *makrúgh*, and how well she had arranged this spectacle of simulated gore to pique his curiosity, to goad him on, to make him forget his lines!

Nothing for it now, he told himself, but to tell the truth, and try to back out of the charade as quickly as I can. "You are right, Ton Ynyoldeh. You've seen the deepest truths of my heart." He waited for a withering reply.

"I was hoping you'd be honest," said the little-girl voice, shorn now of its sharpness. "But look around you . . . it *is* me that you see. Once I was as beautiful as these servocorpses— for every one of them was cloned from my own tissue. I could have melted stone with such beauty, could I not? I could have lived out my brief life, like a flower that in winter becomes nothing more than memory . . . but you made me Inquestor. You gave me a life of centuries . . . centuries of hell and horror, since I was allergic to the life-prolonging drugs we all use! I waste away. I cannot die. It is not true that my heart has grown warped with the years of pain, Elloran. It is only that I hurt so much, that I have come to hate myself so completely—"

The heads were silent for a moment. Here and there a limb wriggled, the pseudolife not yet quite gone from it.

"And the game of *makrúgh*?"

"I renounce the game forever! They can bluff each other's brains out. I don't care. I'll not be arbiter at all; I'll leave *every* Inquestor the keys to my armory. Let them have their toys, and let them ravage the Dispersal. I no longer care."

"But that may mean . . . a *real* war."

"Was it not a real war, Loreh, when you destroyed the Shendering system in search of your sister, thus breaking one of our most precious precepts, that one's former life, the time before one attains the Inquestorhood, must be forgotten, must never again be referred to?"

"It was." Ynyoldeh knew many secrets. How well she had researched his every weakness. He had been young when he scoured the Shendering system for his childhood memories; centuries later, she would not let him forget.

"It is nothing, Loreh," said the sweet voice. "I do not hold it against you, for I have tens of crimes more heinous to plague my conscience, and you at least did what you did for love, a true emotion. . . ."

"You're tempting me, speaking like a heretic."

"Powers of powers, Ton Elloran! Haven't you learned yet that we are humans after all, that we've no business setting ourselves above the human race, stealing their very guilt from them? Can you deny the pain inside you, the pain that is the human condition? Of course you cannot. I will show myself to you, Ton Elloran n'Taanyel Tath. As for my decision to arbitrate for none and for all, it is yours to do with as you please. You may play it in a game of *makrúgh*, or you may clutch this knowledge to yourself. It is nothing to me, nothing, nothing. And now you will step through the beam of light that hides my presence from you. That is what you really came for, isn't it? I always give more than people bargain for."

Elloran hesitated; he had never expected to learn so much. It was not bloodlust but compassion that had driven Ynyoldeh to this strange extremity.

"Suddenly afraid, world-burner?"

"No."

"Then what must I do to make you step across? Must I entreat you by opposites, must I perhaps plead"—and here her voice became tiny as a mouse's— "oh, Loreh, Loreh, don't come in just yet, dear, I must finish my toilette?"

"It's a trick!"

"All is illusion! How well you remember your schooling on Uran s'Varek, so many centuries ago—"

Elloran stepped over the threshold of light.

First he saw nothing but a pool of seething liquid, bound by walls of force. He recognized the motif as taken from the

Throne of Running Water Caged by Force; it was a common enough decorative idea in Inquestral palaces. Around the hallway, mechanicals stood to attention.

"Are you looking for me?" A croak of a voice, coming from somewhere above. He looked up.

A figure draped in a shapeless shimmercloak was drifting downward toward the pool of fireliquid. The eyes were sunken, buried under layers of withered skin. The arms were skeletal and covered with open sores. The head was bald, its only ornament a centipedelike wound that oozed blood and pus. A black rheum trickled from the creature's eyes.

"Look," said the voice, "Ynyoldeh the beautiful."

He stared, horrified and fascinated. There was a kind of grace in the way she fell, her descent slowed to a stately drifting by a columnar artwind. He knew now what was in the pool. It was some deadly acid that would burn her alive.

"I can't countenance this!" he gasped. "I can't stand here and watch an Inquestor fall to her death!"

"You caused the fall, my dear, when you stepped past the beam of light. It was a trigger, you see. Now you will know that Ton Ynyoldeh, Queen of Daggers, plays *makrúgh* even with her own life!"

"But you denied you were playing—"

A hideous cackling rent the air. "Oh, Elloran, do not deny my last request. Before I hit the burning water, take away my Inquestorhood. I would die human, Elloran, not a god—"

Now she was only a few meters from the acid. She ripped off her shimmercloak and tossed it beyond the aircolumn, into the far side of the pool. Elloran heard it hissing. . . .

He looked away.

"Unmake me Inquestor!" that croaking voice insisted.

And so he began to utter the words of unmaking, covering his face with his shimmercloak: *"Den eis Enguester! Din rilacho st'Enguéstaran! Evendek eká eis! Enguesti tembres! Enguesti dhandas!"* In the middle of the ritual he thought he heard a splash, an effervescent explosion. He did not take off the shimmercloak that veiled his face. She must not see my tears, he thought, irrelevantly. I must not show grief for her, a heretic. . . .

Slowly he turned his back on the bubbling pool. Only then did he lower his shimmercloak. As he entered the room he had just left, he saw that the shattered limbs were still, that the bloody heads had ceased to purse their lips and pout becomingly, that their eyes were dead.

And in the next doorway, and in each subsequent doorway, there appeared a message in letters of light:

o-lúvet kykýlleh
I have broken the circle.

As Elloran stepped on the displacement plate and rematerialized within the hawk-shaped shuttlecraft that Ton Ynyoldeh had sent for him, he determined to reveal nothing of what he had seen. It would not do for the likes of Karakaël and Satymyrys to know the extent of their freedom.

For, though Elloran could feel the Inquest's end looming up, its very shadow chilling on his heart, he wanted no wars, he could no longer stomach the prospect.

No, no one must know that Ynyoldeh had relinquished control over the armory, had in effect declared an open season in the game of *makrúgh*, for the deathtoys were now available to any who would demand them.

He would keep silent!

And so, by his very abstinence, he found himself drawn against his will into Karakaël's game . . . his silence was Ynyoldeh's trump . . . he had been challenged by the death of a sick old woman, compelled by the taunting of severed heads.

SIXTEEN: THE COUPLING OF SERPENTS

Ton Karakaël looked up. The servants were bearing away snow-piled platters on which had been displayed the land-eels of Therudash, obtained from the cones of ice-volcanoes, at tremendous risk, by four-armed boys so trained from infancy . . . the eels were not dead, merely drugged; an Inquestor, picking one up to take a bite, had been bitten himself, and had to be taken away for somatic renewal. "My apologies, friends," Karakaël had said, "a natural mistake for one who has never partaken of this costly dish; I trust all the rest of you realize that it is customary, before the eels are sliced into the stew, for the host to display the fine quality of his catch on platters of sculpted snow that simulate the creatures' former environment. . . ."

Upon reflection, he decided not to add the truth that all now knew: that it was Ton Satymyrys, who was well-known for his culinary ignorance, who must have perpetrated this particular solecism. How tasteless a man. But he had given himself away completely, and the dish of land-eels had been revealed as another masterstroke of *makrúgh*. Every deal that the Mask of the Whore had made since the beginning of the current session had now fallen suspect, because they all knew the face behind the mask.

Brilliantly done, he thought; sometimes I surprise even myself.

A hand tugged at his shimmercloak. "Pssst. Ton Karakaël."

"I am not he!" Karakaël said stiffly, hoping that his Mask of Making concealed all.

But the other figure, who wore the Mask of the Rabbit, made a secret handsign that Karakaël alone could know.

"Very well. Come." Together they left the chamber.

In the vestibule of masks, under the dome of starlight, Karakaël watched Arryk take off his mask. He did not remove his own; under it, after all, was yet another mask, and he had a mind to leave a tiny shred of doubt in the boy's mind, so that later, if need be, he could deny that this conversation had ever taken place.

"Shtoma?" he said, studying the young Inquestor's face. There was pain in it. Good. You could feed on pain. Karakaël understood pain well, beneath his many masks.

"They are all there. Kelver. Sirissheh. Davaryush."

"I sent you to investigate a utopia, boy."

"I know why you sent me. It's part of your game with Elloran, isn't it? And you want to crush me in the process. But it'll never happen."

"You poor child . . . so innocent, so direct . . . what compassion I am forced to feel for you!" Karakaël adjusted his mask. He was thinking of other things. His thinkhives had informed him that Elloran had been invited to the hawk palace, had ridden there in Ynyoldeh's own shuttlecraft. That was outrageous. He *must* have some dark ploy hidden in his shimmercloak somewhere! he thought.

Perhaps Ynyoldeh had even told him the unthinkable . . . the secret that only a few of the oldest living Inquestors knew . . . the reason he must wear the masks. Karakaël shuddered.

"Ton Karakaël . . ." Arryk was saying.

"What?"

"I say we should play Shtoma in the game. It's a useless world. It's poisoning the minds of our best people."

"But the black boxes they send us, the gravity-control devices—"

"Toys, Ton Karakaël. Varigrav coasters. There's nothing useful about them. We have other means of achieving the same things."

"Is it not cowardly, to destroy that which we fear, merely because it does not fit into the niceties of our doctrines?"

"You know as well as I do that you want to play Shtoma."

Trapped! The boy's directness was not at all ingenuous, but calculated to challenge him to action! He should have known better, he told himself, than to underestimate a pupil of the wily Ton Elloran.

A better day, and he would never have fallen victim so
easily. But today he was uneasy. Because of Elloran's visit to
Ynyoldeh. Only Elloran would know whom the Queen of
Daggers would favor for the final disposition of weapons;
without her decision, their games were all empty bluffs.

Ynyoldeh had been kind to him once, had shielded him.
There had been another Inquestrix, too, the Inquestrix with
no name; he had thought her inconceivably old, the day he
first saw her, in a place best forgotten.

Surely she must see him now, he told himself. Surely!

Arryk waited for the older Inquestor's response. "Ah, yes.
Shtoma," Karakaël murmured, making sure that it seemed as
though the matter was of little consequence. "Shtoma, that
backworld, that false utopia, that place that builds pleasure
toys for pleasure cities. By all means, dear Arryk, you must
play it. For me it is too tiny a gesture, but for you it will be a
first challenge; magnificent! A splendid notion!"

Having firmly thrust the responsibility onto Arryk's shoulders, he turned away, thinking only of Ynyoldeh and of how
he might win her favor.

"Where is the place of the people-bin? We should begin
there." The tachyon bubble was spinning, spiraling seaward
through the luminous blue sky of Idoresht. Kelver lost sight
of the other bubbles, with which he had been communicating. One contained Siriss; the other, Kail Jannif, the astrogator
who had been with him almost from the beginning, and who
now piloted his personal delphinoid.

As the bubble steadied itself he saw the others now, black
circles of nothing punched out of the gem-blue air, and he
called out through his ampli-jewel: "Come, join forces, dissolve the bubbles!" And the three bubbles were suddenly
one. Siriss, jolted, landed in his arms, laughing.

Each bubble had carried a piece of a floater; now, respond-
ing to Jannif's subvocalized command, the jigsaw sections
knitted together. "Is the bubble dissolved?" said Kelver. For
within a bubble one could not tell of a bubble's existence; it
was, after all, woven out of nothing at all. Only an outside
observer would see a sphere of utter blackness, a little moving hole in the fabric of the universe. Jannif nodded; Kelver
leaned against the railing of the floater. The sea beneath . . .
no sign of land at all. The ocean placid, almost mirrorlike.

Only in the distance, a thin line of wave crests, a sparkling filament of sea spray.

"We are ahead of the childsoldiers by about half an hour," said Jannif, and Kelver was pleased that this time she had remembered not to use that opprobrious title *hokh'Tón*.

"Good. Perhaps there'll be no need to use them. Come, Jannif, you're the one who's been here before."

"Only to pick up a cargo of stiffs, sir! And I'd hoped never to come back. These people live in the heads of giant snakes."

"Unnerving," said Siriss, with a smile. Her experience on Shtoma had softened her, stolen her old edginess from her. Kelver watched her with love and envy, too, because he had been denied the fullness of Udara's love.

Jannif continued: "There's but a dozen or two of the . . . ah . . . inhabited snakes; they've to be millennia old, and a bit infirm, if humans are to live in them without them wanting to swim off every few minutes . . . but they still mate, once every few centuries, and *that's* a sight. Hearsay, that is, my Lord, and I hope never to see such a thing."

The floater had now reached the surface of the sea, and Kelver called for a forceshield to fend off the spray.

"You have the locations of all the serpents?" he said.

"Yes, Ton Keverell. There are, as I say, only a few. They're scattered in an area perhaps a thousand klomets in radius, with Dragonstooth at the center; it's the warmest part of the world. Shall I summon up a holosculpture?"

"Let me. I can probably do a little better than you." Indeed he could. He reached across the parsecs to snatch power from the Throne of Madness itself. Presently an image of the water formed in the floater, at their waists' height; they seemed to be wading in water they could not feel. Here and there were wiggly worms of light, schematic serpents. They did not move. Elsewhere, as Kelver's finger skimmed the illusory waves, were others that dived and swam and burst from the water. "Where are we now?" he asked, feeling the Throne probing his thoughts. "I don't have too much time, and we need Lady Varuneh."

Oh, Vara, Vara, Vara, the Throne mused, *how well I remember.* "Our location!"

A blinking light over the pictured waters. It appeared just above one of the most frenzied serpents. . . .

How well I know both your thoughts and my own, said the distant Throne. *We both seek the same woman, though for*

*different aims. Follow the thrashing snake, boy, and you will
find Mother Vara.*

"Does this mean—"

*Yes. The snake beneath you is about to have an amorous
tryst with the residence of our beloved.*

Before Kelver could reply, a monstrous tail came thrusting
from the sea, and waves pounded relentlessly at the forceshield.
He saw the tail again, its scales metallic, gleaming, lashing
the water and breaking the rhythmic cycles of the floater
mechanism, so that now they swooped beneath the water and
now they were flung up high over the wavecrests—

"But where is the head?" Siriss said.

Jannif pointed, far into the distance.

Kelver saw it all now: the snake's body, a river of gold
beneath the rushing water. Far off, erect and fierce, the
flame-eyed head with its gaping maw and its slavering, flickering tongue, wide as the broadest avenue of the city of
Kallendrang. When the head plunged into the water, the
waves soared two hundred meters or more. When the snake
writhed, the whole sea seethed.

"Follow it," Kelver cried, "wherever it may lead us!"

The floater swooped down on the serpent's head, circling
it like an insect. Far in the distance the tail was lashing the
water. From the serpent's crown rose a crest of rainbow-
edged scales and bony spires, minarets of gilded ivory. Kelver
saw the eyes now, each eye a lake of blackness; from each
there dripped a viscous waterfall. The floater moved closer,
secure in its bubble of force, feeling nothing of the raging of
wind and sea. It parted the spiny forest of the serpent's crest,
glistening through the spray. Crisscross rainbows darted over
the scales. Across the top of the head were breathing mem-
branes, like the wrinkled craters of volcanoes. Now the whole
head jerked back in a spasm, and the jaws gaped wide; and
Kelver saw within them an abyss of profound blackness ringed
with fangs. A building fell from the snake's mouth as he
watched. He saw specks that were people now, clinging to
splinters of bone or to each other. Some were locked in
lovemaking as they spewed from the cataract of the serpent's
jaws. One group, trapped inside a room that had broken off
the building, seemed to be carousing. Others were already
dead.

When Kelver saw the bodies, he despaired. Surely Varuneh
would be trapped within the body of that other snake, unseen

still, but coming inexorably nearer. . . . "My mission is doomed," he said.

"No, Kevi, never doomed," Siriss said.

"I'll have to go to Kilimindi alone." Though the sea and the wind must have been roaring deafeningly, there was within the forcebubble a strange echoless silence; and though Kelver could see countless snakedwellers screaming their deathcries, and could see buildings toppling and being dashed against the fangs of the serpent, he felt strangely distanced. "Am I losing my compassion?" he said suddenly.

"Surely no, Ton Keverell," said Jannif. "I remember when I first saw you, how you lit up the beggars' eyes and taught them hope."

"Perhaps it was better without hope."

And in his mind, across the parsecs, laughter came. The throne! "I will have to play in their *makrúgh*," he said, "in Kilimindi, and bring them all to their senses somehow."

The silence again, unbearable.

Siriss said then: "I have seen how Arryk plays *makrúgh*. I couldn't beat him even when I was already an Inquestor and he was only a peasant. And Karakaël is far more terrible than Arryk. But Elloran, at least, will be neutral."

Kelver was grateful to her for talking at least, for filling up the void. "How far is the other snake?" he said, knowing that it was almost certainly too late.

Even as he spoke they saw it cross the horizon and appear. And Kelver's heart sank when he saw it, undulating, coiling, a dancing rope of silver-gold.

Siriss talked on; he could not hear her, for the silence was filled with the laughter of the distant throne.

They were all looking at him now, waiting for a command. Even Siriss, herself Inquestor. I can't, he thought. He felt as impotent as when he had fallen into the sun of Shtoma and the throne's voice had come, not leaving him alone, depriving him of the sun's catharsis.

But Jannif, seeing his indecision, had already sent the floater spinning skyward. Below them was the golden snake. Fountains of water gushed from its jaws, and the sea was threaded with human blood. Ahead was the serpent of Varuneh; he learned from the holomap that its name was Kalivorm. It was paler than the other sea snake, its scales the color of silver seen through amber. As its head rose below them, parting the water into a circular wavewall, Kelver saw that

Kalivorm was bald. The scales at the top of its head had been stripped off, revealing scabby, whitish tissue. Its crest was stunted.

Somewhere inside the snake was the woman from the time before the Inquest.

The laughter came again, pounding at his skull. "Can you fly this thing straight into the serpent's mouth?" he said.

"Nothing easier, Lord. And with the forceshield, you can't be harmed anyway." Jannif brought the floater to rest a few meters from the chasm of the jaws. As the serpent yawned, in pain perhaps, Jannif subvocalized a quick command, and the floater flew straight into a sudden darkness.

"Is there no light?" Kelver cried out. He had not felt such an oppressive darkness since . . . since Arryk showed him the great void itself. . . .

But now, at Jannif's command, the floater gave off its own light, cold, bluish. They were in a cave with walls of living tissue, glistening, pulsing. Behind them were the stalactites and stalagmites of teeth. Water was everywhere, and beneath them an abandoned spaceport lay, water pouring into its inns, its souvenir stands, its brothels; here and there were advertising signs, some still flashing. As the jaws opened and snapped shut, there would be sudden flashes of blinding brightness. In those moments Kelver could see humans clawing the stilts of the spaceport. Every day, he thought, the Inquest condemns people to such lives, in the name of the High Compassion.

"We should save them," he said. "All of them!"

"We can't," Siriss said.

"We must," he said. And ahead, the snake's gullet: blacker than the blackness that surrounded them. He urged Jannif forward; she obeyed, and the floater in its cushion of force sped up and entered the pitch-dark passage. For a long time they flew in the corridor of the snake's esophagus, a vaulting tunnel ridged with fleshy protuberances and veined with slimy blood vessels, which pulsed constantly with fresh blood. It was flooded; half-digested sea creatures bobbed up and down in the pulpy liquid. No humans could live here, he thought. "Higher . . . perhaps beyond the nasal cavity. . . ."

Reversing the floater, Jannif brought it up once more to the entrance of the gullet. Here and there they glimpsed other passages. Some were lined with spongy material; others were bonier, like limestone caves. They threaded through one of them, still bubbled in silence. Now they found houses hollowed from the bone, but empty, abandoned. Now they passed a servocorpse factory, tank upon tank of lifeless bodies that marched rhythmically through the fluid that both fed and embalmed them.

Kelver said, "Lower the forceshield."

"Kevi—" Siriss said.

"We're Inquestors. We cannot hide behind barriers of silence. . . ."

At once, the foul liquid that had been pelting the forceshield began to ooze into the floater. Quickly Kelver spread his shimmercloak over the three of them, hoping to protect Jannif; the cloak hissed as it fed on the organic matter and gusted forth a counteractive fragrance. They turned into a spiraling passageway lined with caves. In the distance Kelver heard drums. The people must have gone mad. They burst out of the tunnel into a city whose sky was palpitating flesh starred with specks of phosphorescence. Steps of bone led upward to a citadel, from whose marmoreal columns hung huge drums of serpent membrane; six men pounded on each, wielding a drumstick like the oar of an ancient ship. The sound echoed and reechoed in the vast cavern. Beside them, other celebrants waved torches and beat gongs, and old men puffed out screechy tunes on bony highwoods. And around them, between them, running this way and that, playing tag among the pillars of bone, there were children, some waving snakeskin garlands, some throwing firebrands into the sky, some hurling pitchers of blood and gall on the celebrants— and all of them shrieking out the melody of the city's deathsong, a yell of joy and terror over the relentless pounding:

> Death has come to Kepharang,
> Death masked as Love,
> Love masked as Death;
> Embrace the fall! Embrace the flame!
> Jump! Jump! The sky falls down,
> and Love has come to Kepharang,
> Love masked as Death,
> Death masked as Love.

Every step of the hillock that led to the citadel was covered with naked bodies, writhing, moaning, as they coupled in frenzy. Now the children ran among them, up and down the steps, kicking, taunting, laughing. As Kelver watched, one of the bone columns tottered and tumbled, crashing down the steps. He could hear the crack of bone against bone and the splattering of swatted bodies. The lovers on the steps did not move out of the way, but ignored the corpses as they bounced and clattered down the steps. They were all tangled now, the dead and the living. In the purple sky, blood vessels burst and spattered them with a thick rain. Kelver's shimmercloak glowed, glutted. Rose and ultramarine rippled across it in brilliant waves. Kelver saw that Siriss's, too, shone. A sweet vapor emanated from their cloaks. They stood in a pocket of fresh air; yet even through the protection of the shimmercloaks Kelver could scent a stale putrescence. He could not bear to watch. "Land the floater," he said.

"It's not safe, Inquestor!" Jannif shouted above the din.

"We must find her," Kelver said. The other two had to strain to hear him.

—*Love masked as Death,*
Death masked as Love—

Now they circled the citadel, coming ever lower. Here the drumbeat was deafening, the shrill highwoods maddening. As Jannif brought them down, another tremor wracked the mountain, and another column fell, rolling down the side of the citadel and making bodies fly in its wake. Kelver sprang from the floater. The ground shook. He tried to call out Varuneh's name. Surely she would not be here, participating in this final madness. Children ran by, knocking the wind from him and making him gasp.

—*Death masked as Love,*
Love masked as Death—

He reached out to seize hold of a child. The girl struggled, wriggled free; he grabbed again. She turned and caught sight of his shimmercloak. She screamed.

"Do you know the shimmercloak?" he shouted. "Do you know what it means?"

The girl whimpered, afraid. More children had come; some had stopped their chanting and were staring, curious; others, still shrieking their eerie song, were tugging at her arm, trying to make her follow.

"Let me go!" she squealed. "I'm breaking the circle—"

"Don't you know what my cloak means?" Kelver clutched hard at the child's arm, drawing blood.

"The oracle! The oracle!"

"What oracle?"

"To leave the serpent—on boats made from the scales of the serpent's head—let me go, let me go!"

She slipped from his hands. He watched her as she picked up her torch and rejoined the dance. They had circled the floater now and were throwing up their torches and catching them; now and then one would break away to set fire to a column.

To leave the serpent—on boats made from the scales of the serpent's head—

Of course! How could he have been so foolish as to imagine that the Lady Varuneh, who had survived for twenty thousand years, and was man's only link with a time before the Inquest, would not engineer a means of survival? He was elated now. She was at sea somewhere. It only remained to seek her out, to tell her that Arryk intended to play Shtoma in *makrúgh* . . . she would know what to do.

He turned around to go back to the floater. But all at once the fleshy ground started to shake. He could see the floater slipping . . . Jannif had been thrown against the side and was unconscious. . . . "Jump!" he screamed at Siriss. Could she even hear him? Drums thundered, children wailed, and the moans of a thousand lovers blended into a windroar He pushed aside some old men who were playing their highwoods, and ran toward the floater as the ground trembled ever more violently. "No!" The floater was being dislodged now, it was sliding in the viscous mush of organic liquids, it was going over the steps . . . there it was now, rolling over the bloody torsos of celebrants, sending arms and heads catapulting into the air: and he could see Siriss, her mouth wide open, shrinking, shrinking—

Quickly Kelver made up his mind. He would save them all. One did not do anything to save a dying city, according to the High Inquestral precepts; to do such a thing was to substitute the lesser compassion for the greater; for man was a fallen being, and suffering a necessary evil. This was the very root of the High Compassion. The pages of Inquestral teachings flashed through his mind as he made his way to the highest point of the city Kepharang, as he began to subvocalize quick instructions to the army of childsoldiers who hovered, waiting, in the sky outside. Once only he turned to see the floater still skidding down the immense staircase. He had brought Siriss into this, and he had loved her, and he would save her. It was then that he realized that it was not because the Inquest remembered compassion that it must fall; rather, it was because it had renounced love.

And even as he thought these thoughts, there came a tremendous cracking, sizzling sound from high above. For a moment the tumult subsided; then the singing went on as before, and the men lashed the skindrums ever more fiercely. A smell of burned flesh tendriled downward. And suddenly, through the roof of quivering flesh, Kelver could see the jagged lines of brilliant blue that meant—

Childsoldiers! They had sawed an opening in the snake's head. The revelers screamed anew at the unwonted bright-ness. The light burst over the piles of corpses and of lovers wriggling like maggots over Kalivorm's flesh. Startled, lovers disengaged themselves, staring at the zigzag brilliance. And then, through the opening to the sky, the childsoldiers came, their deathpaean drowning out the screams and the raucous music. One after another they dived down on their hoverdisks, somersaulting in midflight, leaping from disk to disk with stunning precision. As they cried out their *Ishá ha!* they pierced the air with golden laserlances that streamed from their eyes, weaving a smoke-grid over the citadel. . . .

Kelver raised his shimmercloak high so he could be seen. He beckoned to the floater, still slipping into the mass of lovers and pulped corpses far beneath.

Quickly the swarm of childsoldiers divided; one group streamed downward to the foot of the citadel. In a moment they had dislodged Siriss and Jannif from the debris, and they were soaring once more, arcing toward the crack in the sky. And now the inhabitants of Kalivorm, afraid at last, were running to take shelter beneath the columns of bones; and the beaters of the orgy drums had abandoned their posts and were cowering, gazing at Kelver in dismay.

The leader of the childsoldiers—it was the girl Tya, the first one Kelver had sought out for his shadow army, on Bellares—landed in front of Kelver.

"They've made contact, Inquestor!" she said urgently. "You have to come now. We've saved Ton Siriss and Kail Jannif. If we don't leave now, the snakes will—"

The last few columns toppled now, crushing those who had sought to hide behind them. The ground shook. As Kelver gazed down from the citadel he saw that the people of Kepharang had panicked now; their rituals forgotten, they

were scrambling hysterically, crushing each other, trampling
over the dead and the living—

At his feet, an old man wept soundlessly.

Another one, dropping his gong, which rolled clanging
dwon the steps, fell at his feet and tried to touch the hem of
his shimmercloak. "Inquestor—" he said, groaning.

"Come, Lord!" the girl cried.

But Kelver said, over the rumbling, "We must save them."

"We can hardly save you, Lord, if you don't come!"

Kelver looked down from the high point of the citadel. The
celebrants had lost all pretense of joy; in the light from the
broken sky, their world seemed sordid, somehow ludicrous.
They were weeping now, sobbing in each other's arms, waiting for death. The light played on their bloodied faces, and
the corpses among which they lay.

"We will save them," he said quietly. "Then, when they
are safe, we will go and seek Varuneh. I can't ask her to show
me compassion if I go to her fresh from the deaths of these
people."

"But come first," said Tya.

Kelver sprang onto the childsoldier's hoverdisk. Tya-without-
a-clan uttered a shrill screech of command; immediately, the
swarm of deadly children gathered around her. With a jerk of
the head Tya made the disk swing upward. All together the
children shrieked their war cry and tossed their ceremonial
slicers in the air, releasing ribbons of flame over the suppliants' heads. Fearful, the people moaned. "Come away, come
away," the young girl shouted. The hoverdisks swept into
formation, forming an arc of yellow light. The crack in the
serpent's head grew now; and as Kelver burst through he was
blinded by the sunlight.

The two serpents had come face-to-face now; their fins
were fanning the water, churning it into frothy wavewalls.
The heads clashed like metal mountains, a harsh and cavernous sound. Now they swam side by side, their intertwined
bodies making a crescent-shaped chain of islands for many
klomets. Below, Kelver could see the bald serpent, the zigzag gash the childsoldiers had sawed in its head extruding a
river of blood and pus. "They'll die," shouted Tya. "Look, the
head's going under, it'll submerge, the city will be flooded—"

And already the head was sinking below the waves, while
far away, the braided tails rose sunward from the water, their

metal glitter-burnish burning his eyes. "Boil the water," Kelver said. "Let him find no comfort for his pain—"

At his command the childsoldiers spread out around the head of Kalivorm, their eyes projecting stream after stream of laserheat into the water, which slowly began to seethe and steam. He detached another group, ordering them to form a grid and weave a net of forcelines in the air. The sea around the head began to bubble, and Kalivorm's head, half-sunken, began to roll about in torment. A strangled roar escaped his throat, and wind whistled through the cavity they had carved in his head. Again and again the soldiers activated their laser-irises, until it seemed that the head was encased in a cage of topaz light. Clouds of steam rose from the sea, and Kelver began to sweat, though his shimmercloak absorbed the liquid and cooled him . . . at last, Kalivorm could bear it no more. The monstrous head began slowly to rear up; always the eerie wind howled through the hole they had made. Through the gash Kelver could see the fallen citadel and the people scurrying like ants. The head rose like a sea volcano. Now they could see the neck with its even rows of gold and silver scales.

"Now!" Kelver waved to a third contingent of the soldiers, who ringed the neck and began to saw at it with spurts of laserlight. The body, still coiled around that of the other snake, began to thrash wildly. The childsoldiers went on, each one working over a small spot of the neck.

All at once it snapped! Boneshards flew into the air. The tongue flicked out for the last time, flinging the remains of the spaceport over the back of Kalivorm's lover. Enraged, the second serpent thrust herself loose, and Kalivorm's head tore free and Kelver was drenched in blood and pulp; and then came the weavers of the forcenets, flying in their precise pattern, catching the head in their grid of forcelines. Brainless now, the body of Kalivorm still twisted and coiled, blood gushing from its neck and mixing with the still-boiling water, so that the very steam was red. A film of oily purple was spreading over the water.

And ahead, carried aloft on a forceplane woven by a hundred evenly spaced childsoldiers, sailing in the sky like some whimsical Inquestor's pleasure palace, was the lifeless head of the serpent Kalivorm, from whose still-open eyes still dripped twin streams of rheum over the sea beneath.

And all the soldiers sang, triumphant:

Yahé hokh'Tón!
Yahahé, hé, hé!

The traditional words of victory, to be sung after a world has *fallen beyond*. . . .

Another floater was on its way to pick him up now; it carried Siriss and Jannif, still not quite revived from their fall. He had Tya land the hoverdisk on the floater, and together they went to the serpent's head, landing beside its broken crest. Other childsoldiers landed beside him, ready to protect their master.

He climbed down. The wind was strong, salty; it toyed with the tower-tall wattles of the serpent's crest. He saw the wound, a yawning chasm ahead of him. He started to climb toward it along a narrow ledge over the eyes, steadying himself now and then against the sharp edges of the scales. The ocean was calm now; for the second serpent, no longer sensing Kalivorm's sexual pheromones, had swum away to seek another mate. In a while Kelver reached the edge of the pit and eased himself down for a look. The people below were still huddled together, afraid.

They should not be afraid of light, he thought.

He summoned the childsoldiers and set them to work widening the wound. Light flooded the citadel of Kepharang for the first time. Below there were cries of terror at first; but they turned to pleasure. The children ran mad, their arms outstretched as if to touch the sun, the light source. And presently the boldest ones were climbing up, using the jutting bone tissue as leverage, and soon, too, one or two of the older ones were following their lead. One by one, blood-stained, drenched in the stench of the serpent's body fluids, they emerged, standing unsteadily, feeling the wind. When they saw Kelver they began to kneel, prostrating themselves against the burning metal of the scales. More came out now, chattering in their lilting lowspeech.

"Don't kneel," said Kelver, "don't be afraid. You should have listened to your oracle, you should have left while you could. All things change, even the things to which you cling for comfort, hoping that they'll never change."

Those who had prostrated themselves did not move.

"Understand!" he cried, grieved. "You're free now, free of the serpent that governed your lives. You're not tied to Kalivorm anymore."

But he heard them continuing to mutter among themselves, worrying over such things as the next shipment of corpses, or how best to reconstruct the old factories. Kelver turned away. Why couldn't they understand that he was not their master? Now and then they would stare at him, when they thought his gaze was turned elsewhere, and he saw that fatal worship in their eyes.

Presently one of the childsoldiers came to him, pointing excitedly at the horizon. At first he could make nothing out; and then he saw them, specks of gold at the juncture of sea and sky—

"Ships?" he said, uncomprehending at first. "I thought this planet had no ships. . . ."

"They're ships of a sort all right," said Tya, who had come up behind. "And look, leading them . . . can't you see? That radiance. I thought for sure you'd spot it before anybody."

It was true. The frontmost of the specks of gold was different. A tiny circle of bright blue billowed above it, a blue that blushed pink—

"A shimmercloak! A shimmercloak!" Kelver cried, delighted. His despair fell from him; it seemed to have dissipated into the wind, the sun. Tya gave a shout and a smart gesture of command; at once the hundred childsoldiers below, maintaining the forcegrid that kept the snake's head airborne, turned in sharp unison, and the head shifted. With a crash, Kalivorm's left eye fell shut, spraying them with dark tears.

Now the people of Kepharang saw the boats and the shimmercloak standard for the first time, and Kelver heard them whisper among themselves: "The oracle was right. There *is* a snakescale city of the sea. We have not been abandoned." And he knew what Varuneh had done; she had not only saved herself but she had given them a new dream, had traded their dark dreamworld for a new vision of air and sunlight. And as they flew to greet Varuneh on the floating mountain that had once been a serpent's head, he understood for the first time the greatness of this ancient woman. For people like Elloran, like Davaryush, wise though they were, had never lived a single moment without the strangling hold of the Inquest. Only Varuneh could remember a time of real freedom. Even the people of the snake, degraded as they were, must have felt something of this power.

But Kelver had seen the myriad statues carved from mountains of Mother Vara in her youth; and he had heard the lost cities of Uran s'Varek's south cry out her name, though not a soul had lived in them for twenty thousand years. And the Throne of Madness had known her too. She had been at the beginning, and she would see the end.

"It should be Vara, not me!" he whispered. Only the Throne would hear. "What she cannot do, how can I possibly achieve?" But only the wind replied, keening through Kalivorm's cavernous wounds.

Under the canopy of shimmerfur sat the old woman, watching the still sea. Where were the dancing lights, the phosphorflies of gold that she had seen as they left the dying city? There was nothing. At first there had been storms and high waves, caused no doubt by the distant coupling of the serpents; and Varuneh had feared for her people's lives. But now there was an unearthly calm; the waters hardly rippled, but shone like a single sheet of mirror metal. There was no wind. A hundred snakescale boats lay motionless on the water. Where could the childsoldiers be? By now they should have set the very sea on fire. . . .

"Hakra," she called.

The old man came to her. "We're safe now," he said. "There are fish in the sea, and already an edible vegetation has attached itself to the sides of our boats."

From behind, wails of mourning. "Why are they weeping then?"

"Because they have lost their friends, their loved ones." Hakra sat down at Lady Varuneh's feet. "It will take a long time for them to forget, and to grow used to this constant searing brightness."

"There will be night too," Varuneh said, remembering that these people knew little of the realm of sunlight.

Suddenly, a smudge of gold against the cloudless sky—

"What was that?" Varuneh cried out.

The people of the snakescales turned to look. At first there was nothing to be made out . . . then she saw what seemed to be a flying mountain of gold, supported by a grid of tiny yellow dots . . . and then the crest, its spines truncated . . . the closed eye like a hump of silver, the open one like a lake of obsidian . . . her people cried out in amazement.

"Who are they?" Hakra said. "Why do they bring the serpent's head?"

It came ever nearer now. What a fool she had been to think that it was worthwhile to buy for these people a few more hours of their dream! As the head approached she saw that it drizzled blood onto the sea beneath, freckling the blue with purple. And now she could make out swarms of childsoldiers, hovering and darting around the monstrous head like scavenging flies.

"What shall we do? Where shall we flee?" Hakra said, his aged voice cracking.

"Nothing, Hakra, nothing. We are becalmed. It is up to me now." She stood up and walked to the boat's edge, and she peered hard at the approaching head. Was that not a shimmercloak, that spot of blue and pink between the two eyes? Why would an Inquestor condescend to come himself to direct the killing of a world? That was not the Inquest's way. Others should do the killing, that the Inquestors might feel the more compassionate.

Concentrating hard, she directed an intense subvocalized command at the thinkhive of Dragonstooth. It *must* hear her!

Lady Varushkadan, came the whispermurmur in her mind.

"Send these words to the Inquestor that stands on the head of vanquished Kalivorm," she commanded, and then she gave out, in full, the first challenge of *makrúgh* players, though she had once sworn never to play the game again: *There is history, and there is no history!* For no Inquestor would dare reject a challenge to *makrúgh*, yet while the game was in progress the destruction must be halted. She knew that she would soon hear the answering formula: *All things must change, yet all is encompassed in the greater Stasis. We are one, our eyes are illuminated by the one Compassion; we are of the Inquest.* And the game would begin, and the fate of Idoresht be allayed for at least a brief while. . . .

Instead, there came no answer. Enraged, Varuneh cried out: "Vultures!" and turned her back on the serpent's head.

But in a moment there came a hubbub from the assembled people of the snakescale city, and Varuneh turned to face the serpent once more; and she saw that childsoldiers had broken from their formation, and were soaring overhead, their laser-irises throwing out spurts of flame . . . they were drawing laser letters in the air itself. . . .

Hokh'Tón, said the fiery message, *I am the boy Kelver, with whom you once watched the light on the Sound.*

Kelver! The light! There was so much to remember . . . the flight of Windbringers over the Sunless Sound . . . the two children trapped in the Cold River, who had taught

Davaryush to remember the meaning of love . . . that ill-fated revolution. It was all so long ago. . . .

The head was not far away now, looming up like a volcanic island that had torn loose from the sea. She saw an enormous wound in its side; around it were clustered some townspeople of Kepharang. The people of the boats had seen them, too, and were leaning eagerly forward, trying to spot old friends.

The message of fire dissolved, and the childsoldiers who had delivered it swarmed together and flew back to Kalivorm. Then, two by two, they formed a diagonal line down to the sea, each pair weaving, from one to the other, a step in an invisible staircase of force. When Varuneh saw what they were doing she urged the boatmen: "Forward, toward the lowest ranks of childsoldiers! Use oars, bones, clubs, and hands!" And the fleet of golden petals began to move toward the head.

The ramp of force was finished. All at once the people of Kepharang came pouring from the wound, running down the sky between the two lines of childsoldiers. They came carrying their maimed, they came crying in each other's arms. And when the boats had reached the foot of the steps of nothingness, the sea people, too, ran, diving into the water and running up the solid air; and there, halfway between the flying head and the floating kingdom, they met, embraced, and welcomed those they had left to die, weeping and ululating for joy.

I must rejoice, Varuneh told herself sternly. It was I who dreamed this dream for them, and the dream has come true.

But she had already divined the reason for Kelver's coming.

Now he was coming down the forceramp to her. Still there was no wind, for his shimmercloak hung stiffly on his shoulders. At first he seemed to have changed very little; that he was taller was to be expected, for she had last seen him a child. His eyes were clear green as ever, and his body still compact, taut, hard; his hair, longer now, was still unkempt. But when he came nearer she saw that it was streaked with gray, and that those eyes were lined. Behind him walked a young Inquestrix with milkwhite hair and opalescent eyes; where, then, was Darktouch? It had been so long ago. Perhaps a century or more would have passed, as the Dispersal reckoned time, and only through flying the overcosm had they contrived to stay so young. Now he had descended onto the boat; quickly Varuneh called for the shimmercloak to be stripped from the posts of bone, for she meant to greet him in her full rank, as his superior. She did not trust him yet; perhaps Uran s'Varek had changed him.

Behind him was an honor guard of childsoldiers. There was something subtly different about them; perhaps it was their faces. When had a childsoldier ever smiled? They had all the surly pride of childsoldiery, their sable cloaks were thrust precisely back, their graviboots gleamed spotlessly . . . yet their eyes did not hold the expression of utter pitilessness, of sharp-honed anger, that always seemed to come with the uniform. She knew then that the revolution had begun.

He stood before her now. At last the old memories surfaced, suddenly clear, the two children fleeing in their innocence to seek the answers that they knew the Inquest must have.

They embraced; but it seemed to Varuneh that she clutched a holoimage, an emptiness. "You poor child," she said softly, "Davaryush laid too much on your shoulders."

"It is well, Mother Vara."

"You've been south then."

"I've been to the Throne of Madness, and I've drawn power from it."

"Is that what Davaryush told you to do? Oh, Kevi, Kevi, he did not know what he did, he could not know what you would go through. Only I know."

"Udara withheld his love from me, because I am followed everywhere by a whispershadow. Oh, Varuneh, it is terrible to be the focus of such power!"

"Why have you come? Where is Davaryush, and where is the girl Darktouch?"

"They are on Shtoma. They have found utopia. I have not."

"Do you think, then, to call me from this world, to make me take your place upon the Throne of Madness? Once, Kevi, I possessed that Throne; and, dreaming upon it, brought the Inquest into being. I had a fierce love of beauty then, and of freedom. But later I loved power more. And only much later, after a terrible madness which the Throne visited upon me, did I learn of compassion. After twenty thousand years I sought to undo what I had made, but it had its own life and would not be undone. It is you, the innocent, who must break all asunder, Kevi. Leave me be; let me be leader of this little people of the sea with their simple dreams. I am tired, Kelver, tired."

She saw despair flicker in the boy's eyes. She could not look at him. She could not speak.

At last Kelver said, "By Kilimindi, Ton Karakaël is staging a grand *makrúgh*. Arryk, whom once I loved, has left to join the game. He means to play Shtoma, Varuneh, and destroy it if he can."

Varuneh looked around her at the people of the snakescale city; they were hushed, waiting. Even the sounds of rejoicing, of reunited lovers, were stilled. "How can I leave? I have just been midwife to this city, and I want to see it grow strong and happy." But even as she spoke she knew she would go.

"Outside Kilimindi," said Kelver, "a palace has been seen. No one knows who it belongs to. It is a palace built from snowflakes and platelets of ice."

And Varuneh remembered that same palace; centuries ago, she had commanded that it be built. She, too, felt the tugging of the Throne of Madness, though she thought she had wrested herself free from its web of power long before. *Be still, be still!* she cried out with her mind. And then, "I will go."

For the first time the boy smiled. There was beauty in him still, she thought. And she summoned Hakra to her. He came, still quaking from the day's many traumas.

She said, "When I came to you, you knew it would not be forever."

"But we are your children! You cannot desert us."

"Even children must grow up," said Varuneh, smiling wanly. "And one day, when my part in this grand scheme is accomplished, I will come back."

I haven't said enough, she thought suddenly. She wanted to tell old Hakra so much, to try to justify herself, to make him understand that all would be well, that they did not truly need her, that she was not really deserting them. But she knew that all they would see would be the glittering panoply of the Inquest, the clouds of childsoldiers darkening the sun, the dazzling displays of deathlight. They could not know of the struggle within the Inquest. They would see only that she had joined her own kind, had ascended into that inconceivable skyworld where the gods dwelt. She would not burden him with her cosmic anguish. Impulsively she turned from

him and took Kelver's hand; and she began to mount the
invisible steps. She saw that tachyon bubbles had begun to
rain down, holes in the sky. They climbed. The people of
Kepharang had come down to the boats now, and the serpent's head was empty save for the old city's shell, and the
dead, and the living dead in which its citizens had trafficked.
They had climbed up high now; as they ascended each step,
the childsoldiers turned off the forcefield of the step below
and flew up to join their fellows, somersaulting from hoverdisk
to hoverdisk, their childish shouts bell-like in the unstirring
air. I will not turn my back, Varuneh thought.

They reached the summit of the forceramp; each stepped
into his tachyon bubble and disappeared from view, slipping
smoothly into circles of nothingness.

The leader of the childsoldiers gave a shout; another took it
up; the clamor resounded like the echoing of many flutechoirs.
Suddenly Varuneh was reminded of the music of Sajit; she
had not heard it for so long . . . could it have been a century,
even? For a few moments the paean sounded; then it fell
abruptly still. With a single gesture the hundred childsoldiers
whose forceweb had been holding Kalivorm's head aloft cut
loose their interconnected forcestrands and scattered skyward. The head fell; forever it seemed to fall, in a single
moment stretched taut to eternity. As it hit the water, she
could hear the people of the sea cry out in awe and glee and
perhaps a little grief; for their old life was irrevocably ended.
At last Varuneh willed herself to look back.

She saw the snakescales thronged with people; the fall of
the head had given them a push toward the horizon, and it
seemed, too, that a breeze had sprung up to start them on
their journey. She could not make out Hakra or any of the
others whose names she had known. Then she turned to
watch the head of Kalivorm sink slowly, until all that remained was the one unbroken spine of its crest, a white
needle striped with blood. She closed her eyes.

When she opened them again, she was standing in a vast
vaulted throneroom, and the water world of Idoresht was a
thousand parsecs away.

BOOK THREE:
THE UNMASKING

Dhelyá sarnáng z tóraka z níshis
  hokhtin verapo pa'jítaren mi
    pa'zérveras, pan qériah dídeas mi

Hokhté, hox váshis hokh'keliassá
  'ktes chítara lúktuu luktárashi zi
    hókhtai vidérai kesei min yrshílteryh
      z kárakit kes min essondaréh;
        hokhté, amúdar, anáemat—

Eih auraín aiunaín,
  min yverprendéis práxein
    suvítek, chom níkans ebrénden:

Yrshíltraor, Urázbedar,
  eih eih hokh'kelassiaísti mun,
    dhelyáin z tóraken z níshien.

I, a slave, a chattel, a nothing
  throw before you all my heart,
    my thoughts, the works of my hands;

O you who bask in the High Compassion
  whose heart is illumined by its radiance.
Yours are the wings that shelter me
    and the milk that sustains me,
High One, immutable and unattainable.

At the final hour
  you will take me up into your arms
    suddenly, as in a planet's destruction.

O protector, skyfather:
  have compassion on me,
    a slave, a chattel, a nothing.

—a hymn, taught to the children all through the Dispersal of Man; to be sung by an army of childsoldiers
on the eve of a world's annihilation

SEVENTEEN: ENDGAME

Nervously, Ton Karakaël stepped from his shuttlecraft's displacement plate into the first of Lady Ynyoldeh's receiving chambers. There had been no objection to his subvocalized demand for ingress; and he had seen, as he was leaving his ship, from the corner of his eye . . . another shuttlecraft, rounding the outstretched wing of the hawk palace, apparently making its way toward one of the many palaces docked with his own. He had not come a moment too soon. This was a new ploy of Ynyoldeh's, then, forcing the Inquestors to leave their game and woo her privately. It was unorthodox, but chillingly like the Queen of Daggers.

It had been many years—over a century, indeed—since the last time he had come into Ynyoldeh's presence. But nothing seemed to have changed.

There were the feathered walls, shivery with shifting shades of crimson, amethyst, rose, cerulean, bronze. There was the floor of unkempt shimmerfur. There were the kestrelwing arrases, the chromegilt pillars studded with ruby tears and crowned with frozen fire.

"Ynyeh," he whispered. An overpowering fragrance flooded the chamber, like that of a young girl rising from a perfumed bath. She must have known he was coming, to have set this hallway up in an exact replica of their last meeting.

They had been lovers then. He had made love to her from behind a bodymask of silk threaded with green copper; and she had concealed her true self behind the corpse of a prepubescent girl, chillingly beautiful; still, it had been love, as Inquestors understood it. And she had told him of her

221

terrible affliction, and he had dared to tell her of his past. Once, though, it seemed, there had been another Inquestor present, a crone, a quick flash of shimmerfur, curl of a withered lip behind the hawkwing arras . . . she had dismissed him then. He had not understood why, but had returned to rule over a world of lepers and degenerates; in only a decade he had parlayed his way up to a high *makrúgh* between Grand Inquestors, and had won the Shendering system for a prize, though only its moon, his palace, was left to him. That did not matter. There was the game, and there were the million masks.

"Ynyeh—"

The silvery laughter. . . .

Faint, so faint. . . .

"Ynyeh. . . ."

Was the laughter in his mind alone then? He waited for a few moments, and then called out her name again, saying, "It is I, Kaarye, who once loved you in a mask of silk." But there came no response.

At last he heard the metal footfall of one of Ynyoldeh's mechanicals. The curtain parted; the robot stood before him, its four arms bending and twisting into gestures of esoteric grace, like the posturings of a symbol dancer. But it cradled no lovely servocorpse in its arms.

"Where is your mistress?"

The mechanical spoke, in a strained parody of a young girl's voice: "She cannot see you, Ton Karakaël. But she bids me give you this, and to say these words to you: *Of seven armories am I Queen, of Kendrys, Jandrys, Sárapys, and Aung; of Theradamá and Zumgézanweh and of blood-drenched Ath-Keránthwei. Take, Master of Makrúgh, the seven keys; and may compassion bless your killing hands and mercy temper the blazing of your million eyes.* And furthermore she bids me reproach you for disturbing her peace, and asks that you never more set foot in the palace of the hawk." And it threw into his hand the clear disk that was imprinted with the names and the commands to be subvocalized for opening up the seven worlds where the weaponry was stored.

He caught the disk, gazing in wonder at the smooth round thing. "This is unprecedented," he whispered. And, addressing the mechanical: "Where is your mistress? Has she fallen ill? Has she lost her senses? Why won't she let me see her? We were lovers once, metalman."

The mechanical stood: tall, silent, gleaming.

It must be a trick, a master stroke of *makrúgh* whose meaning he was expected to fathom. Or even a ruse; perhaps the disk was no key at all. How could an Inquestor named arbiter dare give so much power to a single player?

The fragrance filled his nostrils, maddeningly sensuous. Only this scent could bring those dormant memories to the surface . . . and now he remembered all of it: the frantic press of silk against cold flesh; the bloodgrid from the abrasure of copper wire on the dead skin; the artificial whimpering of the young girl's corpse, fluting from a crystal syrinx embedded in her throat; the semen spurting down the hard inner surface of the bodymask, flooding the phallus of silk and ivory, warm and sticky on his hidden flesh. . . .

No. Ynyoldeh would not have betrayed him. He had understood her, hadn't he? He alone had gladly loved the corpse and not asked after the true Inquestrix's condition. She had been grateful to him; she had lived, if vicariously, for those moments. And they had exchanged their hidden secrets. Betrayal was unthinkable. No, Ynyoldeh had entrusted the keys to him out of love. . . .

It was not necessary even to return to the game of *makrúgh*, now nearing its final round. For the sake of appearance he must, but he knew he had already won. The others could do nothing but bluff; he held all seven armories.

And his secret was safe. That was what he had feared the most; that in a vicious move of *makrúgh* Ynyoldeh might have betrayed his past to Elloran.

A thought nagged at him: there *had* been one more Inquestor once, who had known; the Inquestor who had found him, pitied him, raised him to the shimmercloak.

But that one was long dead.

The heretic Davaryush had killed her in a feeble attempt to cover his own treason.

I'm safe, he thought at last. I have walked the tightrope to the end; I need only await the applause.

And elated, he stormed from the room.

He did not see the feathered walls dissolve, grow moldy, catch a sudden dust. He did not see the shimmerfur grow suddenly dim, or the chromegilt columns lose their fiery coronets, or the oily dullness creep across the once-coruscatory curtains. For when they no longer sensed his presence, the thinkhives of the palace ceased to generate their holoscupted images, plucked from their library of remembrances; they had only obeyed some last instructions of their dead mistress. As she had died, so they, too, would begin to die; the hawk would soar the overcosm on wings of starlight, blind and unhearing, until all its energy had dissipated into the space between spaces.

This, then, was Karakaël's great failing: that so concerned was he with practicing illusion on others, he could not see himself illusion's victim. And he had a great need for love.

Three figures floated down the tunnel of force that linked the snowflake palace with Kilimindi. They had pulled their shimmercloaks over their faces and tucked them under their fursoles, so that it seemed they were three glowing shrouds of deep blue and rose. Ahead loomed the orphaned satellite, its icy surface carved into a monster *shtézhnat* board. The three drifted in an air current scented with *f'áng* and peppered with the petals of rosellas.

They came to a doorway shaped like an immense eye; its iris was a gelatin of powdered semiprecious stones, and its eyelashes branches of polished ebony. The doorway blinked, admitting them, for Karakaël had commanded that none with shimmercloaks should be turned away.

Attendants carrying ceremonial laserlances and wearing kilts of dark purple, upon whose chests were hung cuirasses of bronze on which were sculpted masks from the masklord's collection, ushered them from displacement plate to displacement plate, always deferential, always soft-spoken. They passed magnificent hallways; though Siriss, walking ahead, thought them too showy, too gaudy, their monumental splendor cold compared to the warm gold of Varezhdur.

Another hallway, and then a marble throneroom, sunken, its mosaic floor depicting a sun's death; across the floor leaped the littlest of childsoldiers, exercising, playing tag, their short black cloaks thrown in a heap over a prominence of the pictured sun, their yelling tiny in the marmoreal vastness. "It is meant to daunt you," Varuneh said. "I know Karakaël too well, my children."

And Siriss, who had indeed been daunted, drew comfort from the old woman, understanding the emptiness of Karakaël's posturing. She had known Varuneh for less than a single sleep, but already she loved her; she was wiser even than Elloran. "I can't help but be afraid."

"Don't lose your fear, Sirissheh. It is a gift."

Siriss turned to embrace Kelver; though still hooding them, their shimmercloaks melded together, hissing with desire. "After," she said, scolding the cloaks, "after, after."

Another room was of cement in which had been embedded the skeletons of monstrous saurians, each spread-eagled in an attitude of crucifixion. A tragic mask had been constructed for each of the dead creatures from leather and cloth and papier-mâché, painted in grotesque colors.

Another displayed a tapestry on which was pictured a hero of the ancients, chained to a rock, his innards being gnawed out by a pteratyger; from his eyes flowed circular tears, and each tear was a planet: some were pitted with craters, some lush, some ringed, some shrouded in mist. And always the attendants urged them on, beckoning politely at the next displacement plate or pointing to it with their laserlances.

Finally they came to an antechamber; they could hear laughter and conversations from beyond a doorway of gauze. Above and around them shone the stars, and they could see many palaces docked with Kilimindi, and tiny craft flitting from palace to palace; servants on errands, officials bearing gifts.

To one side stood the maskstands; most were empty. And in the doorway stood Karakaël himself, as yet not masked for the game, for his face was covered with a simple king's chryselephantine mask, with a wig and beard of shaved lapis lazuli; and when he spoke it was not in the artificial voice of the *makrúgh*-mask's voice-disguiser, but in the voice she recognized from their last meeting, the day she and Kelver had played god for the people of illusion.

"Welcome," Karakaël said. "You are just in time. It is the final session of the game; I see that there are three of you, and three masks left. How lucky I am, to have rightly gauged the game! Welcome, welcome. I see you have taken the wise precaution of shielding your faces; that is good, for to see you now choose masks would give me an undue advantage in the game. Orin, my maskslave, will explain the choices that are left to you."

The aged slave stepped forward; he had been dusting the nearer mask, a mask so lifelike it must be made of human skin. It showed a child, a childsoldier perhaps, for its eyes had been replaced by twin topazes. Its features were highlighted with a pigment of powdered gold and gypsum. "The

Mask of the Child," the old man wheezed, "an innocent, not yet given a clan name, perhaps a killer; he has not yet learned guilt or pity."

It was Siriss who stepped forward to take it from Orin's hands; they were dry on hers. Had Karakaël seen those hands, and could he guess from that alone? Trembling, she assumed the mask; its lining contoured to her face, and when next she spoke, it was in a stranger's voice.

"Thank you," she said to the mask attendant, who bowed deeply and turned to the two remaining.

"The reptilian one," he said, "is the Mask of the Snake." As he spoke, the mask extruded a forked tongue, and fire flashed in its beady eyes.

"Most appropriate," Varuneh said, stepping forward.

Karakaël was nowhere to be seen; as the rules required, he had stepped discreetly aside so that masks could be selected in private.

Only one mask remained. And as Siriss watched it, it burst into flame. "It is the Mask of Making," the old man said, lifting it from its stand—it did not burn him—and handing it to Kelver.

He put it on. A stranger's voice cried out: "Again I have no choice, it seems." Cold fire played on the mask's anguished features.

As if by magic, Karakaël reappeared. "Come now, friends. The game is dull, your presence will no doubt replenish our enervated appetites. The object of the game is a most unexciting one—the fate of a world called Shtoma. Have any of you heard of it?"

Shtoma! The dazzling white . . . it hurt Arryk, that remembrance. Today he had chosen a war mask, the Mask of the Wolf; destruction was his goal. The mask was cunningly crafted from asbestos shreds, bleached to resemble snow-white fur; in its jaws, a coal brazier glowed and let fly sparks of vermilion heat.

Arryk was standing in the center of Karakaël's reception hall as the hundred and twenty-seventh course of the banquet was brought in. Fourteen symphoniae, all different and all loud, blared from the various corners, balconies, and alcoves of the polygonal chamber. With a flick of his mind he commanded the mask to filter out the warring musics. He must concentrate. He must find his prey. His prey was Kelver.

Ever since the game began, Arryk had been seeking him out. He could not refuse to come when the stake was Shtoma. Arryk had led many of the participants on, speaking in veiled language of things only Kelver might know. But he had baited no one.

Sifting the throng with his gaze, Arryk saw that three new Inquestors had entered the arena. Attendants had offered them bowls of zul, and they were making their way in his direction. Perhaps one of those was Kelver . . . they came in the Masks of Serpent, Child, and Making. He watched them. The Child was particularly suspicious. He could not penetrate the blank expression of its lemur eyes, but the wearer walked cautiously, as though he were new to the game. Arryk approached—

"*History*," he said: the short form of the ritual.

"*History*," replied the artificial voice of the mask.

What to say now? "And have you seen the cadent lightfall?" he probed. "Have you danced the dance of chocolate and marzipan?"

"Oh, Arryk," said the Child, "you give yourself away so easily."

"Kelver!"

The Child laughed. "But the firephoenix soars over the desert."

"Siriss!"

"I cannot tell." The Child took his hand. He was still not sure whether it was Kelver or Siriss. He had been steeling himself for this confrontation, but now he was unnerved.

He said, "I do what I must. I have the power. Yesterday I had an audience with Ton Ynyoldeh, and he has granted me the keys of seven armories. . . ."

"Arryk, Arryk, come away! You don't want to do this, to destroy your friends. Forget this anger, Arryk."

"Oh, Sirissheh . . . are you Sirissheh? . . . do you want me to betray what Elloran has taught me?"

But the Child said, "My mother told me to beware of wolves," returning to the make-believe of masking. And then he (she?) broke free of him and disappeared into the crowd. Who then was Kelver? The Serpent, surely the Serpent!

Just then, a blaze of trumpets; it was Ton Karakaël who entered, for he wore the Mask of Unmasking, which was no mask at all, but a clear sheet of lucentine. Through it, Arryk could see Karakaël's personal mask, the one of gold and ivory.

Karakaël motioned imperiously for silence.

"My beloved friends, most august and select Inquestors—comes now the final moment, the grand revelation, when we all find out whose side we have all been on! You will all have gorged yourselves a dozenfold, and availed yourselves many times of my chambers of purgation, my acropoline vomitoria. Hah! There are many who call me vulgar . . . I have heard your insidious gossipings myself often enough, when one of you mistook me for an accomplice . . . I am no mean player." He continued, his voice dripping with irony: "But you will not care what the final result of our little games is. What is important is the High Compassion, is it not? The greater compassion must swallow the lesser. So we should take a moment to consider who we are, we of the High Inquest, and to understand that in playing this game we have taken upon ourselves the universe's guilt . . . that, though undoubtedly lots of fun, my friends, war is still evil. So let us now think in silence on these things, and remember in our hearts the world we are about to *send beyond*." Perfunctorily he crossed his arms over his heart and bowed his head. Quickly the others all did the same; Arryk also, though he longed for them to know the ache that he knew, the true pain behind the ritual. Perhaps, when he grew in Inquestral status, he, too, could be this jaded.

"Are you ready now for the casting of the final views? Are you quite, quite ready?" Karakaël continued.

And all responded, in the highspeech formula: "*Vereidóm! We are ready!*"

"Well then, well then. But first, one minor matter, a tiny thing which yet is of the utmost importance—" The crowd sighed, a great collective wuthering. "Dessert"

Applause broke out, deafening, apparently sincere. Karakaël was a master of the *narijésh*, the self-parodying, satirical speech that was traditional at this point in a game of *makrúgh*. Things were still going as planned then, Arryk thought, caressing the warm snout of his Wolf Mask.

Contemptuously Karakaël surveyed the scene. By assuming the Mask of Unmasking himself, he showed that he had nothing to hide, and disdained to bluff about his position. He was confident now, more worried about the perfect texture of his dessert than about the death of a useless world.

The applause had become rhythmic now, as the dessert was wheeled in on a winged chariot drawn by thirteen yoked pteratygers, a new breed with wings of downy white and fleecy pelts. Floating above the chariot, controlled by one of those very black gravity boxes from Shtoma that would soon cease to exist—a massive sorbet of white candy-ice, spherical, from whose glistening surface spurted a million snowy prominences. Around it, circling in a groove of force, was a cherry-red sphere of sauce. Udara and Shtoma. What a conceit! It was both ludicrous and magnificent; just the right tone for this particular *makrúgh*.

"Is there anyone here who does not recognize in this exquisite artifact," said Karakaël, "which we are about to devour, the very world in question?"

More applause, brief now, for naked slavechildren, each painted in bizarre geometric designs, had flung themselves upon the simulated white star and were scooping up the cold sorbet in their hands; now they were running from Inquestor to Inquestor, proffering, teasingly lifting the candy-ice to their masters' lips. Once more they gorged, the masks' mouths moving up and down as their ingesting-motors whirred into action.

After a few moments, Karakaël asked whether the Inquestors were indeed all in agreement.

"I protest!" said one. It was the Mask of the Rabbit. Karakaël had already divined who might be wearing it.

"Come out, Satymyrys," he said. "You can't hide from me long."

The mask fell to the floor; a slave whisked it away. The Inquestors laughed mockingly; for Satymyrus had been the fool today, and had not been able to hide from anyone.

He stood now, staring at Karakaël. What an impoverished face, he thought, what sunken cheeks, unbrightened by those circles of vivid rouge . . . Karakaël waited for him to say *attá heng*, the ritual formula for conceding victory.

Instead, Satymyrys said: "You think you've caught me, Kaarye, but not this time. You think I've been playing the fool, but it is you who have been fooled. Behold!" And he threw a silvery disk at Karakaël. It sailed over the chariot of the silver sun where the snow-white pteratygers pawed the

air, and landed in Karakaël's hand, its homing device trig-
gered by Satymyrys's subvoked command.

"What is the meaning of this?" Karakaël peered at the
chiseled letters; then he began to read aloud. "*Of seven
armories am I Queen, of Kendrys, Jandrys, Sárapys*—what is
this nonsense, man?—*Take, Master of Makrúgh, the seven
keys*—" Karakaël stopped, stunned at the man's duplicity. He
had not thought Satymyrys capable of such a subtle bluff. Ah,
but if he only knew. . . . "I call your bluff," he said, carefully
selecting, from his repertoire of vocal inflections, his most
jaded voice, for he wished to give Satymyrys short shrift.

"This is no bluff, and I demand, as possessor of all arms,
the right to preside myself over the termination of Shtoma."

Angry now, Karakaël drew his own disk, gift of Ynyoldeh,
and threw it at his adversary. "Ynyoldeh does not give the
same gift twice," he said scornfully.

From another corner of the hall came a third disk, slicing
through the sorbet sun and landing at his feet. It came from
the wearer of the Mask of the Wolf. But that was Arryk, who
he thought was his collaborator! He reached down to snatch it
up. Its message was identical.

"Karakaël," said the Wolf, its eyes glowing crimson, "*I*
demand the right; you have stolen my thunder; you have sent
me to Shtoma, but you deny me the privilege of the act of
compassionate devivement—" He threw off his mask.

Karakaël felt a cold rage seep into his mind. Mustn't lose
control . . . Ynyoldeh *has* betrayed me after all! he thought.
Ynyoldeh, the one person who—

"Ynyoldeh!" he blustered, forgetting for an instant his
Inquestral composure. "I know you have come here, I know
you're watching me, taunting me—" Silence fell; the onlookers were outraged at his display, and shocked, for he had
comported himself with proper control all through the last
few sleeps of the game. Now he stormed into the throng,
seizing the first Inquestor in his path, and rudely yanking his
mask from him.

"Heresy!" that Inquestor shouted; the first syllable of his
utterance was in the characterless tones of the mask, the last
in his own voice, tenory, squeaky with fury. Karakaël, angry
that this was not Ynyoldeh, cast the mask aside; it flew onto
the face of a pteratyger.

"I will expose you," he said, evenly, compressing his anger
into every syllable.

Suddenly, from the throng, behind a gaggle of slaves, behind the wall of stiff attendants, the shrill laughter of a girl, the fresh fragrance—

"You!" Instantly the slaves parted ranks. A shimmercloak rustled. A mask—the Mask of the Whore. "It is as I expected." The figure came toward him, its childish laughter incongruous in its overpainted face. Karakaël stripped off the mask—all propriety had vanished now—and flung it at the sorbet star.

The shimmercloak fluttered to the ground, and—

A gasp from the onlookers. Then, in the appalling silence, Karakaël saw—

A corpse. No, less: a cinder that had once been human. Pus had hardened around the empty eyesockets; the extremities were like black twigs, and an acidic smoke curled upward from the yellow skull, on which still hung some brittle wisps of hair.

As they watched, the body dissolved. Blood sizzled and bones imploded, turned to ash. And the fragments settled on the old shimmercloak. And then came maggotlike creatures, greedily sucking up the dust of death.

The little girlvoice spoke for the last time: "Once, Karakaël, you made love to me."

He could not speak.

Then he heard Arryk's voice: "I do not understand what we have seen, friends. But this is a game of *makrúgh*, and not a street opera in Airang. If you will all agree to cry *attá heng*, I would be honored and saddened to accept the duty of the devivement of Shtoma. . . ."

This was not the plan! But Karakaël heard others cry *attá heng*, *attá heng*. He stared at the pile of dust, not yet comprehending that this was Ynyoldeh, who had killed herself as a gesture of *makrúgh*. He only knew that he had reached that moment in the grand scheme of *makrúgh* when his star was no longer rising, and he must watch another overtake him in cunning. This was to be expected; transience was in the nature of things. This fact was the heart of the Inquestral philosophy. For we, too, he thought, are like those worlds we rush out to destroy; we are not immutable.

These thoughts gave way to others: Elloran! It was Elloran who had first been admitted to Ynyoldeh's presence. He must have known all along, while always denying that he

even played in Karakaël's game. Elloran and Ynyoldeh, hi
two most trusted friends, had plotted to destroy him!

It's good that I am forever masked, he thought, knowin;
that his face would instantly have betrayed him.

The chorus of affirmation continued; and Arryk steppec
forward to begin his mission.

But suddenly there was a dissenting voice. And Karakaë
turned to see that the wearer of the Mask of Making had
challenged Arryk. It was against all propriety! One should
concede gracefully. Arryk was young, certainly, but in his
actions he was assuredly governed by the best Inquestral
principles. Surely no one would have the heart to snatch a
small victory from the boy. . . .

But the Mask of Making said: "No, Ton Arryk n'Elloren
Tath. I have a counterproposal. I have traveled far to deliver
it to this assembly; and I will, if I may, insist on delivering
my challenge."

There were murmurs; it was irregular. But no one ob-
jected; *makrúgh* was in essence a game of compassion, and it
would be unseemly not at least to hear out an argument in a
planet's favor.

As he spoke, Kelver was forced to look at Arryk, who could
not yet know who he was under the flaming mask. He saw an
older boy than the one whom once he had loved; his eyes no
longer betrayed his vulnerability, but burned cold, like polished amethysts; his cheeks were hollow; he had lost his
smile. I, too, he thought, must seem that way to him. How
far away the chocolate desert seemed now. For within those
violet eyes now lived the shadow of the void beneath Uran
s'Varek. This is not Arryk, thought Kelver, but a man possessed by that unforgiving darkness. And his old love welled
up inside him, but he pushed it away, buried it deep within
himself.

"I do not will," he said, "the destruction of Shtoma. When
a thing is an affront to our philosophy, we must not seek to
spirit it away; we must rather question that philosophy itself."
The mask's voice spoke his words to the assembly; its tones
were measured and crystalline, not at all those of a revolu-
tionary. But already he could hear cries of *heresy, heresy;* he
turned up the volume of his mask with a mental flick, trying
to drown out the shouts. "Behold, Ton Arryk!" he said. "I

myself will stand in the way of your destruction, and as my intention's pledge I throw you this!"

From his shimmercloak he plucked a message disk. It was another copy of Ynyoldeh's keys. For he, too, had visited the palace of the hawk, and taken the disk from the dead Queen's mechanical. . . .

He held it high, so all could see. And then he threw it in Arryk's face.

Arryk caught it, his face paling.

Oh, Arryk! Kelver cried out with his mind. Why couldn't you have seen what I saw? Why must we be each other's shadow, we who are so alike?

He was glad now that he had come masked; for tears had come unbidden, and he dared not lose his advantage.

Karakaël came forward now. "Sir," he said, "in attempting to interpose yourself, your armory, your forces of warfare, between an Inquestor on a mission of the High Compassion and the object of that sacred mission, you have broken the principles of *makrúgh*. We are not planet-bound barbarians that squabble over a cave or a river. We are the rulers of the galaxy! Or have you forgotten your place?"

Kelver said quietly, menacingly: "I have not forgotten your place, Ton Karakaël. You have just called blowing up a planet a mission of the High Compassion. I have broken no precepts and no rules. I do not even play, Inquestor. But I tell you this. In the name of compassion, in the name of the greater stasis and the lesser change—you have renounced love; and in rejecting it you have cast out its ugly sister hate, and a myriad other emotions of humanity. How can we feel what the short-lived feel, sitting in our palaces of vacuous grandeur? Why should we not lead the fight ourselves?"

"You're talking about a war," Karakaël said at last, "an ancient plague that men have long forgotten. You are saying that we, the High Inquest, should pick up clubs and staves, and have at each other like animals. Is this a marketplace? You have abused your high office, Inquestor. You should not do that even in a game."

"Do you say that wars are forgotten? Go! Call your Rememberers, and let them remind you of the worlds you have heedlessly brought down."

"Only a child would say such things. This is reality, Inquestor; how shall we wish the cosmos other than it is? But I do not think you are a child, *hokh'Tón*. I think that only an

Inquestor of the greatest subtlety would dare voice such heresies without fear of being cast out. An Inquestor who has docked his palace with mine, but who claims to have forsworn *makrúgh*, to have dedicated the remainder of his life to some nebulous meditative philosophizing? Do not think that you can hide from me."

"I am not who you think I am. And I do not bluff. My threat is nothing more or less than the truth."

Karakaël's face contorted in maniacal laughter. "Behold! I expose you"—he marched over to Kelver and ripped off his mask—"Ton Elloran n'Taanyel Tath!"

Kelver smiled. "It is hard to believe the truth," he said, "when the truth is obvious, and when it hurts so much."

Karakaël looked away, stunned. Kelver saw that the others did not speak, and that some were already casting off their masks, seeking relief from the long charade. And some were even crossing over to where Kelver stood, praising his boldness; for he had spoken aloud words that had needed to be spoken for a thousand years. And Kelver knew from this that he had many more allies than he had hoped for; that among those of the High Inquest there must be hundreds who had nourished the canker of outrage in their hearts, but who had feared to be ostracized.

"You are a foolish child," Karakaël hissed. "Before the day is out you will have been stripped of your name."

But Kelver did not hear him. He had eyes only for Arryk, who gazed at him in longing and terror.

As the tumult subsided, another Inquestor stepped forward. It was the wearer of the Mask of the Snake. Varuneh, Kelver's trump card in this game of *makrúgh*.

"I ask to speak, Inquestors," she said, and the mask's tongue flicked in and out, in and out, and its voice was that same toneless voice that all the masks had spoken with. "If you will not condescend to play *makrúgh* with a mere boy, perhaps you can battle me."

"Elloran!"

The Snake laughed. Kelver cast his gaze about the chamber, wondering if Elloran were indeed there; for only a few Inquestors remained masked, and none was Elloran. Of those remaining, there was Siriss in the Mask of the Child; another wore the Mask of the Fool, a thing of whiteface and rouged cheeks; a few wore animal masks. Why couldn't Karakaël believe that Elloran was not playing? Perhaps it was because his whole life was the game, and life without the game was meaningless to him.

There can be no doubt now, thought Karakaël, of the speaker's identity. It must be Elloran; he will now go on to explain that all was an elaborate conceit, a show of brilliant words, and that now we will return to normal, and rescind this absurd talk of warring amongst ourselves.

"I will listen," he said, freezing his face, beneath its chryselephantine covering, into a second mask of stoic composure.

The Snake—he must not, by the rules, yet think of it as Elloran—spoke.

"I will tell you a parable." At this Karakaël relaxed; the telling of cautionary tales was a standard gambit of *makrúgh*, and he knew from this that the Snake was forcing the game back onto its original track. He was grateful to Elloran for this. The younger Inquestors were certainly becoming excessive, endangering the entire status quo with a few ill-chosen words. It took an Elloran to restore wisdom and order. He settled down to hear the parable, which would no doubt be comfortably familiar.

"Once upon a time," said the Mask of the Snake, "there lived, in the sewer labyrinth of Airang the City of Love, a very poor family; the mother and father were beggars, and they had a single child, a boy of considerable beauty. They lived by the great sewer of Thrath, above which, in the suburb of Orenzang, were the consulates and embassies of a hundred outworlds, so that they never lacked for food; for every day rich viands and elaborate confections were emptied into the sewer."

Karakaël became uneasy; the tale was familiar indeed, perhaps *too* familiar. I must not be paranoid, he thought. If I interrupt, someone else may guess—

"The boy grew; but the day came when, by Inquestral command, the suburb of Orenzang was razed to make way for an amphitheater that would show, for the edification of all, the fighting of giant saurians from the planet Páraÿs. In the year it took to build the great circus, no food fell into the sewer, and its denizens became bitter, quarreling and killing each other. The family starved. Finally the father said in desperation to the mother: 'We need money, but there is nothing we can do. But the boy is beautiful. Let us sell him to one of the palaces of pleasure in the center of Airang; at least, then, the three of us will eat.' The mother pleaded with the boy; but the boy had other dreams. Dreams of starships and of conquest, and of winning a clan name for himself. Driven by terrible hunger, the parents decided on an ugly plan; for there were in the city those palaces that catered to darker pleasures, and whose customers preferred the company of the dead. They persuaded themselves that the plan was one of mercy; for here was this child who dreamed of the impossible, and would never find happiness in his lot, but the parents dreamed only of food, and could find happiness by a simple act of murder. And so they struck him on the head with a rock, being careful not to mar his good looks, and he fell senseless on the dirty ground of the sewer; and thinking him dead, they put him in a sack and brought him to the nearest palace of necrophiles."

Suspicion gnawed at Karakaël. He wanted to speak—

"Let me tell my tale, Ton Karakaël z'Karakit Kerún! You prize your composure, do you not? Very well. The necrophiles. But the boy was not dead, though unconscious. And they threw him naked on the floor of a cold room; everywhere, on shelves, were the bodies of others who had been sold and had already been turned into servocorpses, but had, for the moment, been switched off and put in the storeroom for repair, for the customers of the palace had little need to respect those already dead, and often mistreated them. Five guards had been set to watch the place, for the goods were valuable. There were two men, two women, and a hermaphrodite; rough people, mercenaries. They were used to wars and were new to this kind of duty, finding it demeaning. On a whim, they decided to molest the merchandise; and seeing that the boy had just been delivered, and would still be fresh and unputrescent, and that he was reasonably attractive, they began to beat him savagely and to violate him in every orifice—"

"Enough!" Karakaël screamed. For it was his own secret, the secret he had guarded for five hundred years, the secret that Ynyoldeh alone had known—

But the others, both horrified and strangely entranced by the tale the Serpent told, turned on him and told him to be quiet. And so the Snake continued in its inflectionless voice. "The boy," it said, "awake to horror; he cried out. But the guards were maddened now, and gleefully continued their assault, reviving the boy with vinegar and brine whenever he passed out; then, their lust glutted, they decided to activate the dormant servocorpses stacked on shelves around them. They rose now, these dead ones, scores of them, disheveled, scarred, festering, mutilated. The guards were unskilled in the commanding of servocorpses; so as they surrounded the boy they twitched and shambled; as they raped him they stumbled and groped and drew blood, and the guards fell to snoring, not bothering to rescind their commands. At last, gathering up all his little strength, the boy wrenched free. He shook with shame and rage. He seized an old sack from the floor and covered his face with it, poking out eyeholes with his fingers. He never wanted anyone to see his face again. And he ran from the storeroom, ran through the labyrinthine corridors of the palace of pleasure, pursued by gibbering zombies with branded breasts or gouged eyes or festering erections of stone-dead flesh. He ran to the sewer labyrinth to find his parents. But when he found them he could not reveal himself to them. Anger had glued the sackcloth to his face. He tried to lift his mask; but it seemed to be made of the stuff of dwarf stars. And so he ran away again; and an Inquestrix found him, weeping, in an abandoned courtyard; and because she was visited with compassion, the Inquest's plague, she took him in, thinking that this hideous trauma might yet generate some good, that a seedling of compassion might be made to bloom within this garden of pain. And so she gave the command; and since she was of the High Inquest, lo! that command was law. One night he spent, still barely conscious, in a palace built of snowflakes; and when he awoke she sent him to Uran s'Varek, the rough cloth still clinging to his face."

Rage seized Karakaël as he relived a horror five centuries dead. Ynyoldeh had told Elloran—he had wormed this buried trauma from her—they meant to shame him utterly, to destroy him! "You slime, Elloran, you despicable creature!" he cried, seizing the Serpent by the throat. The shame, the pain, burned in him as freshly as it had five hundred years before. "You know as well as I do that after one's elevation one's personal life is meaningless, that an Inquestor rejects his former self completely, that we never speak of our pasts! But in order to destroy me, you've overturned *makrúgh* itself!"

Wildly he looked about him. They could see him . . . they could see his face . . . he could cover it with gold and lead and ivory and stone and still they could see, they could see. . . . "No! I will not be vulnerable!" he shouted. And he pulled the Serpent Mask by the tongue and ripped it free—

But it was not Elloran.

Karakaël recoiled. The hubbub crescendoed.

"Be still! I am Ton Varushkadan el Kalar Dath."

And now there were shouts of incredulity from every side. Karakaël saw an ancient woman, white-haired. It was indeed the Inquestrix who, that day, had led him to safety; but how could that have been the famed Varushkadan, the legendary Vara who, some said, had been present at the Inquest's very inception, who was rumored to have exploded stars to watch the pretty fireworks, whom the heretic Davaryush claimed to have had executed? Karakaël was distraught with the chaos of new events and the anguish of ancient ones. . . .

"Oh, Kaarye, Kaarye," said Lady Varuneh, "be comforted. I did not tell this story to destroy you, but for another purpose altogether. But my telling it is good for you too; for to heal, you must first accept that you are hurt, Karakaël."

And Karakaël bowed his head, and the ridges and hollows within his chryselephantine mask were filled with tears.

It's like a dance of many veils, Siriss thought. And now we're stripped naked, and defenseless. Varuneh had not told her or Kelver how they would play, and it had been terrible to see Karakaël crumple before the onslaught of so much truth.

Now it was Kelver and Arryk that she watched. Since Lady Varuneh had begun to speak, they had seemed transfixed, staring at each other, not daring to express their mixed emotions. She looked from one to the other, pitying them both. It's been my fate, she thought, to love both the light and the shadow, and never to have learned to distinguish between them. . . .

And now Varuneh spoke again, after the commotion had died down a little: "Listen, all of you. There will be war; brutal war, a war of lover against lover. The story of the Inquest is the story of that brutalized boy who will not show his face." She pointed at Karakaël, who, sunken, mute, had collapsed against the chariot of the sun of sorbet, rousing the restive pteratygers to bite their bits and roar. "For we have turned away from our private pains; we have masked ourselves as gods, thinking that we do good by confining our hatred and our anger into an elaborate game. I, too, thought as you do once. It was I who invented the game of *makrúgh*, Inquestors. But now I, its creator, turn my back on it. We never banished our dark selves. We only chained them deep within us, and they fed well, and grew strong. We are no longer of the light. But now the boy has come. And as we once sought to be saviors of the universe, he will be our savior. Now we will all shed our masks. When we can hate again, we will be able to love again. That is why *we* will have this war; not nameless soldiers, not peasants on a distant planet, but we, the gods. Some will fight for the control of this pocket universe of ours; others will fight for the right to relinquish that control. And it is this war in heaven that will free our myriad earths, and bring back the homeworld of the heart."

Whispered conversations now, rippling through the room. Siriss caught a word here and there: *Utopianism. Heresy. Commitment. War. The invitation to Kelver's southern Lightfall.* Still she watched the two men that she loved, knowing that they three were linked forever in a chain that stretched from the loving warmth of Udara down to the hungry void at the heart of Uran s'Varek.

One by one the last Inquestors unmasked themselves. They had taken sides now, mostly; those on Arryk's side of the chamber, beyond the chariot of the sun, were about equal in number to those who stood behind Kelver. Then the one who had been wearing the Mask of the Fool spoke: "Oh, Kaarye. You should know who your true friends are. I could never have been so treacherous as you imagined." He took off his mask; it was Elloran. "I came today only out of deference to our old friendship, and from simple curiosity. . . ." He walked over to Karakaël and touched him tenderly on the shoulder.

And Karakaël whispered—it was inaudible, but Siriss could lip-read the words—"*Attá heng, hokh'Tón*; you have vanquished me."

"Never, Kaarye, never," said Elloran. And Siriss herself wanted to say some little word of comfort; but she was moved beyond words, beyond tears.

She stood between Arryk and Kelver now. She reached out to touch them both, to clasp their hands, willing herself to bridge the void between them. Amid the tumult the three seemed suddenly alone. She squeezed the two hands tight.

All she was conscious of now was their two pulses, a half-beat apart, pounding, pounding.

At last Arryk spoke: "Kevi, in the end the whole war will come down to just you and me."

Kelver nodded. For the tiniest moment, Siriss felt some spark, some twinge of their old love, flow into her hands. Then it was gone, suddenly, completely, as though it had never been there, like a tachyon bubble.

Arryk said to her, "Sirissheh, you must choose."

"I have chosen," she said.

"I know." He twisted free from her then; she could not bear to look at him, but heard the patter of his fursoles across the carpet of Inquestral shimmerfur.

The lights were dim now; only Varuneh and Karakaël were left in the cavernous hall.

"The time for masks is over, Kaarye," she said softly.

"Yes." But he did not move.

"You fool! You foolish child! Here you stand in the ruins of your own vulgarity. Come to your senses!"

Slowly, Varuneh saw the mask of gold and ivory fall to the floor. It rested on the shimmercloak where the ashes of Ynyoldeh lay, still smoking a little. Poor Ynyoldeh, Varuneh thought. In her own twisted way she was the most compassionate.

And wonderingly she looked into the face of Karakaël, whom she had once found weeping in an alleyway five hundred years before.

It was still much the same face, though much older, of course. "Not much to see, is there, Vara?" Karakaël said, and he smiled a little.

"You will heal." She could not be cruel to him. She had used up her last reserves of cruelty. She put her hand to his face, then flinched involuntarily. For she had touched some rough fabric. Yes, it was still there, the mask of sackcloth; skin had grown over it where it had clung too long, and the mask and the face were meshed together, inextricable.

"Poor Kaarye. What will you do now?"

A small voice: *"The breaking of joy is the beginning of wisdom."*

Varuneh wept.

EIGHTEEN: **SHENTRAZJIT**

Once more Varezhdur came to Shentrazjit the Singing City. Once more they rode forth from the belly of the golden palace on the backs of pteratygers, but these were black-winged, black-furred, for they had come from Elloran's stables of mourning. And they were fewer now. Only Ton Elloran himself, and Siriss of the opal eyes, rode. Sajit lay on a hoverhearse drawn by thirteen of the pteratygers of night, and the two Inquestors had come to Shentrazjit to bury him.

Faintly now, under the breeze's breath, came the strains of Shentrazjit's music. Sirissheh urged her pteratyger on until she was side by side with dying Sajit; together they crossed three little clouds like furry fishes in the pearlbright sky. Sajit lay on a mattress stuffed with kyllap leaves. His eyes were closed; at first Siriss thought him already dead. "Sajit, Sajit," she called softly; and she leaned from her mount to touch his brow. It was warm still, and the old man opened his eyes and clutched feebly at the whisperlyre that lay beside him.

"Listen! Listen!" he whispered.

They had begun the long descent to the city; the crosswind grew stronger now, and on it she could hear the echoing of thousand-colored music: the high pure mountain voices soaring, the fugue of interwoven streets, the ostinato of the marketplaces. She watched Sajit's face for a while. It was a weathered face, but comfortingly beautiful. There was no sign of weakness. When he opened his eyes she saw that they were still unclouded, like a child's. They passed a herd of clouds, roiling and purple, to which some great cloud-sculptor had signed his name. And now they broke through a stratum

241

of fine mist, falling earthward in a shaft of silver light, and Siriss caught sight of Shentrazjit for the second time; and the music stormed over her senses all at once, intoxicating, exalting. For a long while she rode with her eyes closed, ensorcelled by the strange harmonies that Sajit had wrung from the very mountains. At last she said, "You mustn't die, Sajit. There's going to be a war, do you know that? And after, when we've all but destroyed ourselves, if I still live, I would come back to Varezhdur, Sajitteh, and hear a new song you have written. I don't think I will be able to bear this war without your music. They have ripped my heart in two, Kelver and Arryk. How will I heal without you? From the first day that I was made Inquestor and was brought into Elloran's palace, your music surrounded me. My whole childhood will die with you, Sajitteh. Will you kill that too? Am I not precious to you, *hokh'Shen*?"

In the windrush he put her smooth hand in his age-gnarled one. It was dry, like the giant leaves of a myriadendron in the autumn. She bent down to kiss the old hands, though he was merely of the short-lived and she was of the High Inquest. For she knew that an age was ending. And Sajit said, "Oh, Sirissheh, I must die. Do not cling to me as children cling, because you are not a child, and you must understand as all Inquestors must the nature of transience. Have you seen the dawnlight skimming the firesnow-clad slopes of northern Ont, when the marble dragons burst from their glacial subterranean lairs and shatter the crystal peaks with their plaintive song? It lasts only a few seconds, and comes to Ont but once in a thousand years; but to see it men will cross half the galaxy, as I once did, when I and Elloran quarreled over a woman. You see how transitory it is, and yet it does have a kind of immortality, living a millennium in song and in rumor, so that when it comes it draws as many visitors as before, though none alive can possibly have seen it, to tell of its glory. It is a self-renewing myth. And that is all the immortality we can ever hope for; to return incarnate in others' remembrances, and in remembrances of remembrances. This is a harder lesson for you than for me, girl, because you will live to forget even me, whom you think you cannot live without. Be comforted, Sirissheh."

She did not answer him. For the music had risen in a great roaring. The voices pealed from the peaks to mingle with the shifting of old echoes. But somehow the music did not possess her completely, as it had done before. For she remembered the war of illusions that had followed, and the wind keening through the ripped torso of Aoauei the srinjid. There was blood in the music, and she had helped shed it.

Now came Elloran riding the wind, his pteratyger pawing the air and scattering the cloudstuff with its wings. He drew close to Sajit's hearse; he summoned a nearby cloud to him, tethered his pteratyger, and walked to Sajit across the forcefloor buried in the cloud's heart. And he embraced Sajit, ceremonially, as kings embrace; from this Siriss knew that they had said their farewells already, and in private. And she knew that though Elloran's heart was breaking he still must mask his grief, must maintain the Inquestral dignity; that was the way he had always been.

Sajit said, "Oh, Elloran, you and I are already of the past. Don't you feel it?"

"Yes."

"The children have come to change things."

"Yes."

"They will bring back the homeworld of the heart."

"I hope for that."

"Will you remember me?"

Elloran was silent.

Then, beckoning, he called Siriss over to him. They stood together, their feet swathed in the artificial cloudstuff, which swirled and tendriled, but had no moisture in it.

Sajit closed his eyes.

"Is he dead?" said Siriss.

"Yes. Yes."

"Shall I give the order?"

"Yes."

"I . . . I can't."

"Well, then." He turned to the pteratygers that drew the hoverhearse. "Perform your office, children of the winds of death."

They cried out at once, in their voices at once thunderous and catlike: *"We obey—father of compassion—we are only animals—the wings of your words—we obey—we obey—"* And one by one they gnawed at the bindings of their reins, and they soared free, until the hoverhearse was loosed and began to tumble down to the singing city.

They watched together, the old man and the girl.

"It's just you and me," said Siriss, "when we should all be

together: Kelver and Arryk and even Davaryush and Darktouch and Lady Varuneh."

"And you, Sirissheh, will soon leave me."

"Yes." She could not deny it.

"Where have the others gone?"

"I gave Davaryush a tachyon bubble; he did not tell me where he wanted to go. I left Darktouch on Shtoma, in the arms of the sunlight. Kelver has gone south. I do not know where Arryk is; I think he is preparing for the war. And Varuneh has vanished."

"As she has often done," said Elloran, and a smile flickered for a moment across his face.

The hearse had shrunk now to a speck. It was falling still. And now—

Silence!

Siriss held her breath. The silence had fallen swiftly, suddenly; in midphrase the mountains had stopped their song. She waited. Every second was agony. And then there came sounds once more. A ferocious jangling stealing up the alleys of the city. The once clear mountain melody a cluster of dissonances. Rhythms gone mad, clattering, jarring, pounding uneasily. Cacophonous screechings from the towertops. It was chaos.

"It's not music!" Siriss cried. "It's a nightmare!"

Then, as abruptly as it had come, the chaos resolved into a single pure concord. Quiet at first, as though it were only the wind that had somehow found voice; then more vibrant. She waited for melody to arise from the chord, for change, for motion. But there was none. What has Sajit done now? she thought. But the chord went on, seeping into her senses, casting a quiet spell on her; she was entranced, hypnotized by it. Still there was no movement. It was warm, luminous. It did not have the searing joy of Udara; it transcended even joy itself. It was like touching a piece of eternity. She knew then what Sajit had done; in relinquishing movement itself, he had gone beyond music. He had resolved his personal chaos, his dissonance, for once and for all. So she made her mind blank, absorbing. She stood, steeping her soul in the unearthly stillness until she had been cleansed even of her pain at Sajit's death.

The chord sounded, arclike, over the mountains and the city.

Beside her, Elloran spoke: "Are you ready to take possession of Varezhdur, last of my children? Long ago I promised it to you; and I have been too long saying farewell. I must turn my back on all of it: on the splendor and the grandeur and the harrowing anguish."

"Yes, *hokh'Tón*." She did not cry out, as she yearned to, No, Elloran, no, I am not ready . . . and how can we survive this war without Inquestors like you? You are the last of the great Inquestors, whose hearts were still illuminated by the High Compassion, who did not fall prey to the corruption of the power beyond powers.

In the space between their words there rang out that great consonance, like a rainbow of sound that spanned the sky, an aural reflection of its million-starred radiance, a bridge from earth to heaven.

"Father," she said, she whose father had long ago perished in a cataclysm of Elloran's design. In calling him father, she absolved him of that, she banished the anger she had felt since seeing her homeworld in the Sepulcher of Worlds. He did not move toward her. They did not touch. He did not answer her, but their silence said everything.

They stood for a long time, illumined by the changeless chord. Presently Elloran closed his eyes and seemed to be communicating with the thinkhive of Uran s'Varek. At once the cloud rolled back to reveal a huge throne: the Throne of Black Rock Woven with Starlight. Upon it rested a double-yolked shimmeregg, and various crystals and scepters that represented the many principalities Varezhdur governed.

"Ascend, child. They are yours."

And slowly she climbed the starstrewn steps.

She knew what to do; she had been groomed for this moment since childhood. She lifted the crystalgleaming egg and broke it; then she smeared its oily fluid on her head, anointing herself. Soon she could feel the filmy strands work their way downward, weaving, bonding to her body. As soon as she knew the shimmerbond would take, she slipped her old cloak off and tossed it onto the steps. The chord resounded. Elloran stood at the foot of the throne, thinking his own thoughts.

A long time passed. Then, in the distance, she saw a pteratyger, black-furred, with gold-tipped wings, crossing the radiant sky. It came nearer; and presently Arryk leaped from the beast's back onto the cloud where they stood.

"What is this?" he cried. "Who has stilled the music? Who

has crowned Sirissheh?" Wildly he stared at Siriss and Elloran. Then he noticed against the horizon the freed black pteratygers, and Siriss saw that he divined what had happened. "Why did you not call me to Sajit's funeral?"

"No one was called, Rikeh." Elloran's voice was subdued.

"And the music? Has motion become stasis then? What heresy!" he said. "But . . . I have come to see you about another matter. You know there will be a war, and I need allies—wise, powerful allies who possess the High Compassion. You must help me—"

"To defeat Kelver?" said Elloran.

"But he has broken our most fundamental precepts! Surely he doesn't have your blessing. I am the one who has always striven to be like you, who has preserved your every word in my heart."

"Oh, Arryk, Arryk . . . I cannot side with you. I am going away. I have reached the end of my personal *makrúgh*. The Inquest falls. Even I cannot cling to the old beliefs."

"You've made me what I am," said Arryk slowly, "and you can't turn your back on what you taught me."

And Elloran said, with such gentleness that Siriss could hardly hear him through the web of shimmerfur that wove itself around her, "You have loved me, child, and like a child you've tried to copy what you admire . . . but you must copy the shadow as well as the light. I am not a god, Arryk, but a man. Don't you understand? Our glory will fade into violence; the violence of your all-too-human anger against Kelver and his all-too-human retaliation. When the Inquestors are only a memory, perhaps we will once more be deified. But we have not the right to deify ourselves. I've loved you like a father—isn't that enough?"

"You reject me?"

"Of course not, Rikeh," said Elloran. "I only reject my own past, my now useless philosophy. Let's not have a squalid argument about it. You are always welcome."

"But you *are* rejecting me!"

"Do you equate yourself with my philosophies? Are you an abstraction? Is the universe black and white, that we must take opposing sides?"

"No," Arryk said bitterly. "It's not light and shadow, but *all* shadow." And he gave a terrible cry, and Siriss saw that he was reaching out with his mind.

And suddenly fell darkness. It was a cloud of childsoldiers! They were descending to Shentrazjit!

"Poor Rikeh," she said from her throne. "Will nothing assuage your torment?"

He shot her a look of unmitigated hatred.

The shimmercloak wove a veil over her face; she could hardly see and hear now. But the childsoldiers had reached the city, and stifled Sajit's perfect chord, and she could make out through her gossamer mask a line of fire shooting up the main street of the city, dividing now, an asterisk of flame. In a second the city was dead.

But . . . what was this now? The chord . . . it sounded still . . . Arryk gasped as the childsoldier swarm ascended. "Is it not dead, the city?" she heard him cry out

And the sky resounded with a thousand childish voices, high-pitched, pitiless: "Dead, dead, *hokh'Tón! Ishá ha, ha, ha!*"

And she saw their pattern against the pearlglow, a swirl of metaldust, a whirlwind of silverdoves. . . .

And then the chord still. She saw that Elloran, still standing at the foot of the throne, was weeping openly. For a few moments the strands twisted over her face; now she was completely encased in a translucent cocoon of rubysapphire light.

And the chord.

She knew then what Sajit had done. He had predicted this moment, and he had built the essence of the chord into the mountains themselves, cunningly twisting the passageways and the tunnels so that the very wind would wake the sound from the dead rocks. And now she understood what he had meant by the different kinds of immortality.

And the chord.

The chord was good. Her soul could feed on it. Sajit had made it for her and Kelver and Elloran, so that they could always return there and be at peace, and be renewed. She would sit on the throne, sustained by the shimmercloak and the timeless music. Until Kelver came for her.

At last she smiled.

The people of the snakescale city kept little track of time. Their days were warm; they farmed the twining vegetation that clung to the sides of their boats; they fished; they were at peace. It might have been years later, or only a few sleeps, when in the great circle of their nomadic travels they arrived once more at Dragonstooth. One of their farsighted children had seen it first, a halo of light around the black promontory. At first it had shone with unbearable brilliance, and then it had subsided. They decided to bring the city there, to investigate.

As Hakra stepped ashore he found Lady Varuneh already waiting. She had dismissed the shuttlecraft. She was alone.

He was speechless. For she had not changed at all, but he himself was old, dying he thought.

She said, "I told you I would return."

"But it has been so many years. . . ."

"For me it was but a few sleeps. There was a mighty plan for the future of the human race, and I had to play a final role. But I am free now. I have stepped away from the cycle of history; as far as it is concerned, I am no more."

"So long . . ."

"I have sailed the overcosm."

"Yes."

"Perhaps the Inquest is already fallen."

"No matter." And Hakra turned to tell them that their Queen had come home; and an immense cheer rose up from the sea.

Varuneh said: "An age ago, there was a little girl who played in the reeds by a sandstone fortress, watching the sun grow red, kindled to explosion by a human war. The girl said to her nurse, 'Lulla, when I grow up I'll have my own world! And I'll be Queen of it, and rule forever, and be wise and compassionate . . . Vara's world. And I won't allow any fighting.' " And it seemed to Hakra that he remembered something so ancient it belonged to the time of myths, of living dreams.

He said, "It has come true."

And Varuneh said, "I have found the homeworld of the heart."

The shouts rang clear. Like mirrors the snakescale boats speckled the water. The wind stirred. The sea glittered.

NINETEEN: **WHISPERSHADOW**

This time it did not take months to traverse the three hundred or more hokh'klomets to the Throne of Madness. Kelver had only to call out; the Throne drew him in on a cord that threaded the tachyon universe, and he was there before he had completed his thought.

This time, though, the Throne did not stand in a wilderness, half-buried in sand. It had raised itself up onto the summit of a ziggurat; there were more than a thousand steep steps to climb. And the desert was gone; it had bloomed; lush meadows and forests spanned his vision, climbing the sky all the way up to the impossible horizon. And filling the vast plains were childsoldiers numberless as the stars. At first, like birdsong, their chattering had filled the air; but when those in the front ranks saw him they grew silent, and the hush moved slowly outward until it reached the edge of the plain.

"Where is Tya?" he said.

At once the girl was at his feet, prostrated.

"How is the war of shadow?" he asked.

Tya-without-a-clan said, "Your childsoldiers have swept over a hundred worlds, Lord, spreading the rumors of the fall. In those worlds they cry out your name as a benediction. Already we have prevented one planet from *falling beyond*, by ambushing the forces of the Inquest."

"You've changed." It was true; the hard little child was becoming a woman. "Would you like me to release you from childsoldiery, to gain a clan name? Once you told me you hoped to be clanned by the time you were thirteen. A terrible war is coming, Tya, and you've done enough for me. . . ."

She smiled. "Don't make me laugh, Inquestor," she said. "I would never desert you. Nor would a single one of those children out there. We've always obeyed the Inquest; how could we otherwise? It was obedience or death. We drilled ourselves into machines. You've taught us something new—to love you, to die for you. We'll never die in vain again, Ton Keverell."

And she turned to give a signal to the childsoldiers. At once came the topax lightning of a million eyes, burning ten-klomet-wide pennants in the air; Kelver saw the standards of Bellares and Katámavras, two of the great garrison worlds.

"Look!" Tya cried. "See how many have deserted to our side!"

But before Kelver could answer there came a roar over the plains, a million treble voices raised up in the anthem of the High Inquest:

I, a slave, a chattel, a nothing
throw before you all my heart,
my thoughts, the works of my hands . . .

No! thought Kelver. I didn't ask them to love me, to cast away their tiny lives for me—

O you who bask in the High Compassion
whose heart is illumined by its radiance.

He stood and listened to the ancient words, words of abject servitude composed by a tyranny he intended to crush utterly. The plains rang, rang with them; joy was in all their faces. They were the childsoldiers who had learned to smile. Their eyes were lit up with childish adoration. He stood, his eyes stinging from the words' irony. How could he stop this worship? What monster had he unfettered?

At the final hour
you will take me up into your arms
suddenly, as in a planet's destruction.

As the words thundered over the plains he felt no darkness in them. But they talk of death! he thought. Of their own deaths, and the deaths of whole planets! But still they sing with utter innocence.

And Kelver despaired of changing anything. But he knew that he must continue. That the war must be fought, and that he must be the link between the old cycle and the new; he must redeem the Dispersal of Man. . . .

> *O protector, skyfather:*
>   *have a compassion on me,*
>   *a slave, a chattel, a nothing.*

The hymn was over. Wild shouts now, assaulting his ears, and new pyrotechnics as the soldiers drew more standards in the sky with their laser-irises. . . .

And then came pain, clawing his skull, unbearable. It was as if an animal had been let loose in his head, and it was whispering, whispering, whispering, muddling his thoughts—

"No!" he screamed. "Let me alone!"

And he turned to begin the ascent to the Throne of Madness. But as he did so a tachyon bubble materialized on the steps above him; as it dissolved, he saw that it was Davaryush. They looked at each other. It seemed that Davaryush's face was contorted with an ancient sadness. Was it illusion?

Davaryush reached out his arm, preventing him from ascending. "Wait," he said. "Wait, Kevi, listen."

Kelver waited, perplexed.

"When I made you Inquestor," Davaryush said, "I didn't expect it to turn out this way."

Kelver said, "What do you mean, Father Davaryush?"

"Look around you! My plan did not include a vast and bloody war, Kevi! It didn't include setting you up as a god in the Inquest's place! It is my own fault. I was wrong, Kevi. I didn't have the right to abrogate my responsibility, to force the sins of the universe on the shoulders of a boy. Kevi, you don't have to go up to the Throne. It is I who must go—"

"You're too late!" Kelver said, feeling the intensity of the old man's pain, but still more fiercely the tug of the Throne of Madness and the soundsmear of the million childish voices—

"But you'll destroy it all . . . you won't just break the Inquest's stranglehold on man . . . you'll sweep away its beauty, its glory—"

"Oh, Daavye, Daavye," said Kelver, sighing. And once more came the whispering, chiseling at his skull. "You have given up your power, Father Davaryush. Do you suddenly crave it again, then?"

"I, not you, must possess this Throne of Madness. You have abandoned the vision I had, boy. I wanted to conserve what good there was left in the Inquest. You've succumbed, Kevi, to the curse of the Inquestors, to the corruption! You're wallowing in personal godhood! For love of you, every one of those children will willingly fling himself into the black hole at Uran s'Varek's heart!"

It was true. How could Kelver deny this? And yet . . . how could Davaryush ever understand that the old things were over, truly over? "You're old, Daavye. Your vision was only a beginning. In rejecting you I also fulfill what you saw. You told me that you needed a new kind of person, who had seen the light as a child, who could enter the Inquest with his eyes already opened, because anyone else would be freeing the Dispersal with tainted hands . . . I *am* the one you chose, Davaryush. You could not do it, because you are what you are; the Inquest made you, and now, when we stand on the brink of the ultimate revolution, we find you still clinging to the past. The Throne is not for you. Let go, Daavye, let go."

"No!" The old man clutched his arm, refusing to let him ascend, while the childsoldiers' praise-song crescendoed, drowning their thoughts. Kelver, who worshipped Davaryush, could not speak. For a moment he considered throwing it all away. What difference would it make? he thought. The Inquest will fall, one way or another, even without me as its scapegoat.

But tenderly, reluctantly, he pried Davaryush's fingers loose. In that moment, irrevocably, authority changed hands. For Davaryush had walked his personal *makrúgh* to its very end. In naming Kelver to the High Inquest, he had named him also the ineluctable agent of his own defeat. They both knew this. There were no more tears to shed.

"What will you do now, Daavye? You've freed yourself from your cursed destiny. But all I have is at your disposal. Be content now."

He called a tachyon bubble for his former master.

"I will not ask where you are going," he said.

And Davaryush stood tall, though his shimmercloak was frayed and lusterless. Kelver felt a surge of pride, that this great man had raised him from the dust of Zhnefftikak. There was pain, too, in this pride.

They embraced and parted. For Kelver it was like hugging a ghost, a shadow. For he knew now he was completely alone.

The summit of the ziggurat. Biting cold; the dust coiling in a frozen whirlwind at the foot of the Throne of Madness.

You return, dustchild. You want more power. Is that not so?

Kelver sat down.

"No! I don't want your power!"

Whispering, whispering—

Yet you're back, child of dust.

"What is this terrible whispering madness that torments me, that seems to grow stronger with every move I make? Why did Udara turn his back on me?"

I wish you did not want to know.

"I have to!"

It is always so; and so I will tell you. There are many stars like Udara, Kelver, stars that have awoken to sentience in this continuum; they are of all kinds, good, evil, and indifferent. And the black hole at my heart is their destroyer, their ultimate death. I am the soul of the Eater of Stars. Do you see why they hate me, dustchild? But there is more. When you first came here you were an innocent; when you left me you were no longer innocent. And you saw that a century from then there would be a great Lightfall at the southern pole; and you declared a grand and final makrúgh to be played out then. That time draws ever nearer, does it not? And from now until then you will have this galaxy-smashing war of yours.

"Yes."

And that star-death will be the Inquest's last Lightfall, its final celebration of glory . . . that is what you have seen. But your vision is but a splinter of the whole. I will tell you another thing. Stars do not see time as a single journey from one point to another. When they achieve sentience, they come to life already with a remembrance of their own death; and as their death approaches so the shadow grows darker, more palpable. This is what a whispershadow is, Kelver; it is not a bogey of the Inquest to frighten the childsoldiers with, but the ghost of a thing yet undead, its unsung deathsong, the shadow it has never cast. Know also, Kelver, that the galaxy is not a dead thing of rocks and dust and gaseous vapors, but throbs with a tenuous and death-haunted life; and all things in it are conjoined—stitched together through a thousand overcosms. And so, when you called upon the star's death, its whispershadow fastened itself to you. It is your shadow, too, now. How could Udara love you, knowing as he did that you come from me, the Eater of Stars? That your power comes only from the deaths of stars?

"It is not my shadow! I reject it."

You have no choices, Ton Keverell n'Davaren Tath. You are an Inquestor.

And Kelver knew that it was true; that in the final moment, at the star's death, he would be called upon to sacrifice his very soul, in some manner that he had no way of understanding. But how could he think of that now? Lightfall was ninety years away, and Kelver had barely reached his twentieth year.

Now was not the time to think of the price he would have to pay. Now was the time to be impetuous; to crush, never looking back at its multitudinous beauties, the brutal thing that had enslaved the human race for a thousand times longer than he had lived.

"But what shall I do now?" He already knew the answer to this question. He thought of Davaryush, who had raised him to glory only to be rejected by him. In the cold of his aloneness, he thought, he's still happier than me, freer than me. The liberator is the ultimate slave.

You ask me what to do! You, who sit upon me, who possess me. I am but an instrument of your will.

"My will! My will! It wasn't my will that the Inquest came to be, and it wasn't my will to destroy it! It's—it's—"

Destiny?

"Are you mocking me?"

That I, a machine, should mock you! Listen, then. I will tell you what you already know. You will descend the steps to the great plain where a million soldiers wait. There will be millions more, millions upon millions; and many will perish for love of you; yet in an eyeblink their number will be replenished. They were already prepared to sacrifice their tiny lives to you; for your whim of makrúgh, for your pleasure, for sheer vainglory even. But you have demanded of them their love, which no Inquestor has demanded before. And love is a fire that death cannot quench. Do not think, Ton Keverell, that they will understand the higher purpose of your war. Their embryo intellects will not encompass philosophy. Be content, Kelver, with love; it is a visible manifestation of that higher purpose, one that even the people of distant backworlds, their spirits broken, their minds stupefied, can comprehend, embrace, rejoice in. It is this love, dustchild, that will be the Inquest's downfall.

"I know." And in that moment he did know. He did not weep for his childhood, abandoned on Gallendys in the shadow of the Skywall mountain. He felt greater than himself, at one with history.

You do not speak?

"I'm afraid. Not of what I have to do next, but of the end. The whispershadow."

I shall be with you until the last few seconds of the epic. Until the moment of star-death itself. Only then will I forsake you; I will pull the final veils from your eyes, and you will understand Uran s'Varek for the first time.

"Paradoxes and enigmas!"

Be content. Go down now. Revel in the worship of worlds. Listen! Hear the joyroar, like the crashing of many oceans. Devour their love, Kelver! Consume it! You will need every morsel of it, child of dust, to fuel the grandest conflict this galaxy has ever seen. Go now, child, go down now, go.

And Kelver walked down the thousand steps, down to the child-packed plains that rang with exultant battlecries, to begin his war.

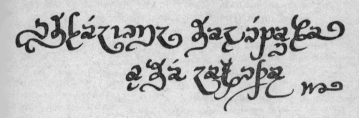

Ektásiens kasséranda arkhá savezhas.
"The breaking of joy is the beginning of wisdom."
—Inquestral Text

Alexandria, Rome, Athens, Mycenae, Paris: 1981–2

TOWARD AN INQUESTRAL CHRONOLOGY

by
PROFESSOR SHNAU-EN-JIP

With, at long last, the publication of this, the restored edition of the second volume of the Inquestor saga, it is now possible to consider the putative chronology of the events the saga describes. Having belabored the controversial "Inquestral Question" elsewhere, I will not tax my readers with another exposition of the many theories that have been advanced as to the identity of the author/authors of these sagas, which have tantalized academics for so many millennia. Nevertheless, having made it my life's work to study the four volumes of the so-called tetralogy, I have been able to compile a chart of what appear to be the main events of the Late Inquestral Age, insofar as such surmisings are possible from a work whose function must be considered literary rather than historiographic.

First, though, I should perhaps elucidate why I have referred to the Inquestral sagas as a "so-called" tetralogy. This thesis arises out of my conviction that the original author of the saga intended a five-volume saga. (See my notes to *Light on the Sound* for final proof of the single-author theory of the Inquestor sagas.) In the first place, the final "volume" is much vaster in scope than the other three; and in the second, it seems to be telling two wholly disparate stories, that of the Essondrish natives first introduced in *Utopia Hunters*, and that of the Inquestors continuing directly from *The Throne of Madness*, the volume presently under discussion. It would seem from this that *The Darkling Wind* is actually an editorial composite. While the tales are remarkably well blended, *The Darkling Wind* still appears to contain traces of a radically different structure. As to whether the work was actually compiled from two separate sources, as theorized by Halbjuling and Adarre, or the result of the putative bard's own second thoughts . . . this must still be considered a matter of some conjecture. Doubtless scholars will continue to exercise their thoughts over this literary conundrum until the end of time.

As for the Inquestral chronology:

It is sketchy. And yet I believe that what follows may be of some assistance in helping the first-time student of the Inquestor sagas to visualize, contextualize, and internalize the complex conflicts of this literary universe.

Please note that, for the purposes of this chronology, the Year 1 is taken as the year in which Davaryush was made Kingling of Gallendys, the opening event in the first of the four Inquestral sagas. Note also that lifespans are measured in realtime; time dilation must be taken into account in order to measure the biological ages of the protagonists.

YEAR	EVENT	LITERARY EPISODE
20,000 years	BEFORE DAVARYUSH Discovery of Uran s'Varek; unleashing of the power of the Throne of Madness for the first time	*Mother Vara*
15,000– 5,000 B.D.	Period of greatest Inquestral control; consolidation of Inquestral power; Power begins to wane	*The Web Dancer*
4,000 B.D.	Boyhood of Elloran; destruction of Elloran's homeworld	*The Rememberer's Story—Part I: The Rainbow King*

2,000 B.D.	Elloran on Ymvyrsh, aged 12; Death of Alkamathdes	*The Throne of Madness*
1,300 B.D.	Boyhood of Karakaël; Boyhood of Davaryush	*Light on the Sound*
922 B.D.	Elloran finds Kerrin	*The Rememberer's Story—Part II*
789 B.D.	Sajit leaves Varezhdur to find Zhendra	*The Dust-Sculptress*
237 B.D.	Meeting of Arryk and Sir iss on the planet Kailasa	*The Story of Young Arryk*
49 B.D.	Davaryush goes to Shtoma	*Light on the Sound*
1 DAVARINE ERA	Arrival of Davaryush on Gallendys; meeting of Kelver and Darktouch	*Light on the Sound*
2 D.E.	Kelver receives mission to defeat the Inquest	*Light on the Sound*
98 D.E.	Lady Varuneh, presumed executed, finds that she has been transported to the water world Idoresht	*The Throne of Madness*
112 D.E.	Kelver awakens on Uran s'Varek	*The Throne of Madness*
113 D.E.	Lady Varuneh rescued; Old Sajit visits Bellares	*The Throne of Madness* *The Comet's Story*
114 D.E.	Sajit dies; Kelver challenges the Inquest to a final game of *makrúgh*; the war begins	*The Throne of Madness*

147 D.E.	Young Jenjen meets Elloran	*Utopia Hunters*
172 D.E.	Essondras comes under discussion as a possible war site	*Utopia Hunters* *The Darkling Wind*
178 D.E.	Sajit's body is returned to Varezhdur	*The Book of the Darkweaver*
187 D.E.	Essondras destroyed	*The Darkling Wind*
189 D.E.	Zorn destroyed	*The Darkling Wind*
191 D.E.	Shtoma destroyed; the Dark Ages begin	*The Darkling Wind*
214 D.E.	Lightfall	*The Darkling Wind*
347 D.E.	Zalo and Darktouch found a new planet; the memory of the Inquest fades	*The Darkling Wind*
Approximately 10,000 D.E.	First known fragments of the Inquestral sagas; Inquestral question first raised by scholars	

SUPPLEMENTAL VOCABULARY

An exposition of the structure of *bhasháhokh*, the High Inquestral language, has been given in the new edition of *Light on the Sound*. Here is a brief list of some new words found in the current volume not included in the previous vocabulary. They appear in the order first encountered in the book, and are listed in the *dictionary form*.

kerávish, throne
várungs kerávish, Throne of Madness
lávorem, teardrop
dáss, god
gráv, solemn
greúrek, gray-eyed
shiklás, chocolate
mezhpéh, marzipan
perpálo, to juggle
varúng, insane
aívermath, overcosm
setálika, delphinoid shipmind
tekiánver, tachyon bubble
kós, universe
sarnáng, I (humble)
ashéver, Dispersal of Man
dhand-érud, dead earth
shéno, to yearn
áthera, sun
íris, rainbow
tembáraxas, dark mountains

261

kréshpo, to touch
púrr, impoverished
lúvo, to break
k'ykyl, circle
dhelyá, slave
tórak, chattel
níshis, nothing
verápo, to throw
zérver, thought
qéri, hand
díde, deed, work
hokhkéliass, High Compassion
lúktaar, to be illumined
luktárash, radiance
vidér, wing
yrshíltero, to shelter
kárakit, milk
essóndro, to sustain
amúdar, immutable
anáemat, unattainable
yverpréndo, to take up, assume
práx, arm
suvítek, suddenly
yrshítraor, protector
urázbedar, skyfather
ektásieh, joy
kasséro, to break
savézhe, wisdom

ABOUT THE AUTHOR

Somtow Papinian Sucharitkul was born in Bangkok in 1952. He grew up in several European countries and was educated at Eton and Cambridge. His first career was as an avant-garde composer; his compositions have been performed and broadcast throughout the world, and he has been named Thailand's representative to the International Music Council of UNESCO. In 1979 his first science fiction story, "The Thirteenth Utopia," appeared in *Analog* magazine. This was followed by a string of short stories, the 1981 John W. Campbell Award for Best New Writer, and a number of novels, beginning with the Locus Award–winning *Starship & Haiku*. He has twice been nominated for the Hugo Award. His books include the massive *Inquestor Tetralogy*, published by Bantam, and the satirical *Mallworld*. 1983 saw the appearance of his first mainstream novel, *Vampire Junction*, under the pseudonym S. P. Somtow. His first novel for young adults, *The Fallen Country*, was published in 1986, as was his Bronze Age historical novel, *The Shattered Horse*.